NO PRICE FOR FREEDOM

This new novel, one of the finest Philip Gibbs has yet written, does full justice to an inspiring theme. It is the story of Poland—of the young men and women who, the author writes, 'were first to make a stand against the armies of Hitler—a desperate challenge—and who went underground in a secret army until the amazing epic of the Rising in Warsaw'. It is the story of how Poland's drama affected the lives of one Polish family and their friends, a family typical of many, who, happy well-to-do people before war broke out, when it did come, were called upon to witness scenes of indescribable horror, to suffer bereavement, privation and persecution, and to realize the depths of degradation to which human beings could descend. The Mirskis, like many others, helped to keep up the gallant and unremitting struggle for freedom in the face of terrible odds, and their story is made all the more poignant by the fact that their unhappy country is still in chains. Although a novel—a vivid and imaginative re-construction of those times —the book is wholly authentic in the picture which it gives of Polish life at this terrible period in the country's history, and through its pages move some of the real heroes of the Polish Resistance, among them General Anders, Commander-in-Chief of the Polish Army which fought with the Allies on many fronts, and General Komorovski, who, under the pseudonym of 'Bor', raised a secret army of 40,000 men under the very noses of the Gestapo in Warsaw. Tragic though it is, it is also an exciting and deeply moving book which will bring alive for many readers an episode in recent history which none should forget.

PHILIP GIBBS

has also written

THE NEW ELIZABETHANS
EUROPEAN JOURNEY
THE PAGEANT OF THE YEARS (*An autobiography*)
THE WAYS OF ESCAPE
PEOPLE OF DESTINY
GEORGE VILLIERS, DUKE OF BUCKINGHAM
MEN AND WOMEN OF THE FRENCH REVOLUTION
ENGLAND SPEAKS
ORDEAL IN ENGLAND
ACROSS THE FRONTIERS
FOUNDERS OF THE EMPIRE
REALITIES OF WAR
THE SOUL OF THE WAR
THE DAY AFTER TOMORROW
THE ROMANCE OF EMPIRE
KNOWLEDGE IS POWER
TEN YEARS AFTER
FACTS AND IDEAS
KING'S FAVOURITE

Novels

THE WINGS OF ADVENTURE
THE HIDDEN CITY
THE AGE OF REASON
DARKENED ROOMS
UNCHANGING QUEST
THE MIDDLE OF THE ROAD
HEIRS APPARENT
THE STREET OF ADVENTURE
THE RECKLESS LADY
THE CUSTODY OF THE CHILD
VENETIAN LOVERS
INTELLECTUAL MANSIONS, S.W.
LITTLE NOVELS OF NOWADAYS
A MASTER OF LIFE
OLIVER'S KIND WOMEN
HELEN OF LANCASTER GATE
BACK TO LIFE
OUT OF THE RUINS
YOUNG ANARCHY
THE ANXIOUS DAYS

THE CROSS OF PEACE
PARADISE FOR SALE
CITIES OF REFUGE
BLOOD RELATIONS
GREAT ARGUMENT
THIS NETTLE, DANGER
BROKEN PLEDGES
SONS OF THE OTHERS
THE AMAZING SUMMER
THE LONG ALERT
THE INTERPRETER
THE BATTLE WITHIN
THROUGH THE STORM
THE HOPEFUL HEART
BEHIND THE CURTAIN
BOTH YOUR HOUSES
THINE ENEMY
THE SPOILS OF TIME
THE CLOUD ABOVE THE GREEN
CALLED BACK

LADY OF THE YELLOW RIVER

NO PRICE FOR FREEDOM

PHILIP GIBBS

THE BOOK CLUB
121 CHARING CROSS ROAD
LONDON W.C.2

Printed in Great Britain by
WILLIAM BRENDON AND SON LTD
THE MAYFLOWER PRESS
(late of Plymouth)
WATFORD

To

IRENA RYBOTYCKA

who went through the tragic years of War in
Poland, and now in her English exile is serene,
laughter-loving, and generous with the gifts of
the spirit. I am deeply in debt to her for information she has given me unstintingly about
her own experience and life in Poland.

Philip Gibbs.

[*The initials P.W. in the form of an anchor, as shown on the
wrapper of this book, stands for "Polska Walczy"—
Fighting Poland—and symbolized hope and the struggle
for freedom. During the Rising it was painted in huge
letters on the walls and pavements of Warsaw.*]

FOREWORD

THIS may be called an historical novel but, alas, the history as this book is written, is less than ten years old, and here in England, and all over the world, are Polish people in exile in whose minds is the recent and poignant remembrance of the tragic and heroic story I have written.

It is the heroism of those young Polish men and women who were first to make a stand against the armies of Hitler—a desperate challenge—and who went underground in a secret army until the amazing epic of the Rising in Warsaw, which has urged me to write this novel. One ought not to ignore supreme heroism even if it failed, nor the sacrifice of a nation in the cause of liberty, nor the suffering of a people still in chains.

I have had the privilege of meeting a number of the characters who appear in these pages, and they have told me of their own life during this period and of their own agonies, curiously without bitterness or self-pity, as though they had happened to someone else now that they are here in exile and peace.

I have met General Anders, Commander-in-Chief of the Polish Army which fought so splendidly in Italy and elsewhere, without much recognition from us; and Mrs. Anders, his charming wife, who has seen the war in Russia and Italy.

I have met that remarkable personality, General Komorowski (with his enchanting wife, the Countess Komorowska), who with great courage and self-sacrifice accepted the position of Commander-in-Chief of the Home Army, to which he was appointed by the Polish Government in Exile in July 1943. That was after the arrest, imprisonment and execution of General Rowecki who had been the chief organizer of the Resistance movement, under the pseudonym of 'Grot'. General Komorowski had been his assistant until the tragic and cruel death of this Polish hero. Then, under the pseudonym of 'Bor', he raised a secret army of 40,000 men in Warsaw under the very noses of the Gestapo, and led the Rising against fearful odds. He was also in command of the underground forces throughout Poland comprising about 300,000 men.

(In this novel I have spelt his name with a 'v' instead of a 'w' as it is pronounced in Polish.)

7

I have also met others who were in Russian prisons and concentration camps.

I have been favoured also by meeting and having long talks with Father Paul of Warsaw, one of the heroes of the underground war—a man whose blue eyes are filled with a spiritual light as well as sweetness and humour. He told me among other things of his dark and dreadful journey with a company of soldiers and young girls through the sewers of Warsaw.

My thanks are given to General Anders for his permission to use some of the facts in his impressive book *An Army in Exile*: and to General Komorowski for similar permission regarding his thrilling book *The Secret Army*.

Above all, my warm thanks are due, and given with gratitude, to Irena Rybotycka, who has written for me with immense generosity, copious notes of her own experiences during the war in Poland.

But I wish to emphasize that on the basis of much historical information given to me by my Polish friends I have used the novelist's privilege of creating imaginary characters and scenes fitting into the framework of authentic fact, and true I hope to Polish life, temperament and tradition.

It is farthest from my thoughts in writing this narrative to stoke up the fires of hate again. But it is a crime to falsify history, and I was bound to describe the terrible cruelties inflicted on Poland by the German police and army. They were without pity and without mercy. But the Poles themselves—or those I have met—do not condemn the whole German people, or hold guilty the young generation of Germans. For that they are generous and forgiving. For what the Germans did in Poland they paid a hundredfold, and among those who paid were many who had hated war—the civilized minds, and those too young to have had a hand in it.

In this novel I have tried to depict the amazing, the almost mad, heroism of the Polish people who fought alone, unaided by those who had pledged themselves to defend the independence of Poland—we went to war for that—and failed to fulfil this pledge which was beyond our reach.

'No Price for Freedom!' was the Polish rallying cry. But there is no freedom yet in Poland where the people suffer persecution for their faith, the subtle enslavement of the mind, and among their bishops and clergy, martyrdom.   P.G.

CHAPTER I

"A CHARMING scene!" said the owner of a house and garden overlooking the Vistula in a suburb of Warsaw on its right bank.

Having said those words with a smile on his thin lips he gave a deep, audible sigh and a grave look came into his eyes.

Certainly it was a charming scene, and there seemed outwardly no reason for a sigh. It was the summer of 1939, the last summer of happiness in Poland before terror came, and the crucifixion of a nation, and massacre and torture and atrocity and widespread ruin in which by some miracle there survived the unconquerable spirit of a people.

There was a party of young folk in the garden, with its lawns sloping down to the river. Most of them, seated on the grass with their hands clasped around their knees, were watching a tennis-match with a young man and a girl on each side of the net. A few others were seated at little tables under striped parasols, sipping cool drinks, eating ices, laughing and chattering. Beyond the tennis lawn was a rose garden in a glory of colour and the warm air was faintly perfumed. The sky was cloudlessly blue and the sun had turned the Vistula to molten gold.

The owner of this garden was Colonel Jerzy Lopalevski, a colonel of cavalry, tall, lean, straight-backed with a strong, clean-cut face and very vivid blue eyes—a man of thirty nine or so. He was talking to his brother-in-law, Dr. Mirski, who had come over from his own house on the left bank of the river.

Dr. Mirski was a different type of man, with a scholar's face, mild and thoughtful under greying hair. He lowered his voice and spoke anxiously.

"You look serious, Jerzy. You alarm me. What is happening across the frontier?"

The cavalry colonel shrugged his shoulders slightly.

"You ought to know more than I do, Antoni. You're a politician."

"We know nothing," answered Dr. Mirski. "Nothing more than appears in the papers. It's a war of nerves. Germany may be bluffing. With France and England on our side they won't risk an attack on us. That's our hope. That's my prayer."

"I am an ignorant soldier," said Lopalevski. "All I know is that the Germans are massing on the frontier with tanks, armoured cars, mobile guns and infantry divisions. It doesn't look like bluff to me. I hope to God. . . ."

He raised both hands for a second. Then he gave a short laugh, changing his tone.

"If it comes we shall put up a good fight, of course. The men are magnificent. By the way, your boy, Stanislav, will get his call-up in a few days, being on the reserve of officers."

Dr. Mirski, a well-known Member of Parliament, who had fought as a gunner in the Pilsudski campaign against Russia, suddenly lost the colour in his face and turned grey.

"That's bad news," he said in a low, tragic voice. "If anything happened to Stanislav. . . ."

His love for Stanislav was a secret passion, perhaps a secret weakness. He doted upon this handsome young man who was beginning to do well as a portrait painter and who had a charming, friendly, sympathetic nature even with his father. It was getting time for him to marry if he could make up his mind which girl he would choose among all those who flirted with him. There he was now on the tennis-court, playing with Irene Zamoyska, against his sister, Vanda, and her partner, the young fellow in the Italian Embassy, Francesco Ferrari. Stanislav was up at the net and smashed a ball from the young Italian.

Dr. Mirski gripped the arm of his brother-in-law, and spoke in a voice of anguish.

"Jerzy, we don't want any more war! It mustn't happen! Poland has been martyred too often."

Colonel Lopalevski glanced at him and there was a glint in his blue eyes, those vivid, steely-blue eyes.

"If it happens we shall fight as we always have done. But I hope it won't happen. Don't say anything about it to the young people. A pity to spoil their fun while they can get it. . . . By the way, your Vanda is becoming a beautiful girl. How old is she now?"

"Twenty," said Dr. Mirski. "That young Italian is making up to her."

He spoke in a strained voice and raised his hands in a gesture of despair.

"Christ spare us!" he said.

"Courage, my dear fellow!" said the Colonel, gently.

His wife Krysta came across the lawn to him.

"Hullo, you two gossips!" she exclaimed cheerfully. "What gloomy things are you talking about? Come and join the young people."

There was no shadow across her bright spirit. Her plump, good-natured face was smiling happily. She was having one of her good days. She adored young people and liked to crowd her garden with them.

Her husband looked at his wrist watch.

"I only have an hour or so longer," he said. "I have to get back to Lidzbark tonight, as well you know, my dear."

"Drat the man!" cried Aunt Krysta, as the young people called her. "Who would be the wife of a professional soldier? . . . Well, unless he were a very nice, professional soldier!"

She put her hand on her husband's shoulder and kissed his cheek and led him by the hand towards one of the little tables under the coloured parasols.

"Poof! I'm longing for a cup of tea. Isn't it warm? And isn't it glorious!"

A gust of laughter came from one of the tables. Stanislav was chaffing his sister Vanda about something which had happened in the tennis match. He was having a good time with the girls.

CHAPTER II

AT twenty Vanda found life wonderful. She was conscious of her womanhood after being a long-legged schoolgirl. At the University in Warsaw she had studied languages and hoped to take Honours. Her tutor, Professor Malinovski, had paid special attention to her and had given her some private coaching, much to the amusement of Stanislav who chaffed her with brotherly candour and asserted that the professor had been smitten by her charm and beauty. This had made her blush furiously and she threw a book at his head which missed him by a few inches. But how extraordinary it was, she thought, that young men should be inclined to flirt with her. She had never imagined that she was good-looking. She didn't believe that was possible even now, as once or twice she examined herself seriously in a mirror on her little dressing table.

'Just ordinary!' she thought, 'like dozens of other girls.'

But several of the University students had made up to her, asking her to go on the river with them or to join them in bathing parties. Now there was young Francesco Ferrari, a quite distinguished young man in the Italian Embassy, and terribly good-looking, with dark liquid eyes and the face of an Italian saint by Raphael or Giorgione, though certainly he was no saint, but a very amusing, light-hearted and flirtatious young man. She had met him through his sister, Beatrice, who gave her Italian lessons. Then Stanislav had become very friendly with Francesco, inviting him to the house and taking her to receptions at the Embassy. Francesco's look of adoration, his low musical voice saying pretty things to her, made her heart flutter, though she assured herself that this was the Italian way and was not to be taken seriously.

Anyhow it was amusing. Anyhow it was flattering to a girl who didn't think much of herself. Anyhow it added a little colour, a touch of secret drama to those summer days when everybody was in a holiday mood because of sunshine and beauty on the banks of the Vistula and its shining water.

A note came to her father's house in St. Theresa Street from Francesco Ferrari. It was written in Italian and begged for the great joy of her company, and that of her brother Stanislav, to a little party he was arranging for his sister's twenty-first birthday. He proposed that they should drive to the harbour at the Kierbedz Bridge and then go for a river trip on the steamer *Bajka* which in English means 'Fairyland'.

He put a P.S.

It would be pleasant if you would bring your young brother and sister. The more we have the merrier it will be. A riverderla, carissima Signorina.

Vanda read this letter in the morning-room of her father's house when they were all having breakfast. Her young sister Halina, still looking sleepy-eyed and with untidy hair—straw-coloured hair—and a cotton frock showing her bare legs was eating a melon rather noisily. Her brother Jozef, one year and a bit younger than herself, and a student at the Academy of Music, was tapping out some rhythm on the table-cloth with his finger-nails.

It was Halina who questioned Vanda about the letter.

"Is that from one of your numerous admirers, Vanda? Why does it make you blush so much?"

"It's an invitation to a party on the river," answered Vanda. "You and Jozef are included. A trip on the *Bajka*. Won't it be lovely? It's Beatrice Ferrari's birthday and her brother wants to give us all a treat."

"How nice of him!" exclaimed her mother who was behind the coffee-pot at the end of the table. "He's certainly a charming young man."

"A bit too charming, like all Italians," said Jozef, who was critical of his fellow mortals. "Don't let him play the Romeo to your Juliet, Vanda. Beware of his black eyes, my child."

Vanda blushed again but laughed good-humouredly.

"Don't be idiotic, Jozef! And you know you are sweet on his sister Beatrice."

"I'm not sweet on any girl," answered Jozef. "I have a mistress already. I'm in love with music till death do us part. I'm spending the day with Chopin."

"I'm for the *Bajka*!" cried Halina. "I shall eat strawberry ices on deck. I shall make myself look very beautiful."

"Well, you will have to brush your hair, my dear," said her mother, smiling at her indulgently. "You come down to breakfast looking disgraceful."

Dr. Mirski put down a newspaper which he had been reading with deep concentration. He looked round at his family anxiously and—could it be?—with pity in his eyes. He was a frightened man though once he had been a brave man. He was frightened for the sake of these young folk. The international situation was becoming more serious. Hitler was making alarming speeches. The German Press was heaping insults upon the Polish government and people. According to his brother-in-law the German army was massing on the frontier. It looked like war. It looked terribly like war, and yet there was no panic in Poland, no apparent apprehension. Everybody was enjoying these summer days. No shadow was on the minds of these young people.

"Have a good time, my dears," he said.

They had a good time. Everything went according to plan. Jozef had decided to abandon his beloved Chopin for the afternoon. Because the steamship landing-stage was quite a distance away they hired two *doroshkies* and drove along the Embankment. It was a hot day. The streets of Warsaw were quiet and empty—everybody seemed to be on the river. Stanislav was quiet but in a good mood. Halina, in her best summer frock, and her fair hair in plaits, sang little songs until told to shut up by Jozef.

Both river banks were crowded with girls in summer frocks and men in white shirts and flannels and children in swimming suits or in a state of nature, like little Cupids. From afar one could see innumerable yachts, rowing boats and motor boats going up and down the Vistula.

Francesco Ferrari and his sister Beatrice were already on the *Bajka* and greeted their friends and introduced them to others in the birthday party. Vanda could not resist blushing—how absurd that was—when Francesco raised her hand to his lips, and gave her a look of adoration in his dark, liquid eyes.

"How charming of you to come!" he said in Italian.

Vanda laughed lightly and avoided his gaze.

"How charming of you to ask us."

The *Bajka!*—the Fairyland—was the largest pleasure boat on the river and the most luxurious with a big saloon and dancing floor and a lounge and bar. Because of the hot sunshine most people stayed on deck. Francesco had assembled a number of deck chairs for his own party and his friends made a little group of their own from which came gusts of laughter and merry conversation. On the upper deck a band was playing light music and from the river banks came the tinkle of guitars and other music from tea-gardens. Because of a long heat-wave the river was low and the pleasure boat moved slowly and cautiously to avoid sand banks. It steamed northwards along the front of the Old City. The left bank of the Vistula is rather steep, but the right bank is low with a broad view over the suburbs of Warsaw and beyond to the open country, brown and baked under the burning sun, with dark woods in the distance, faintly blue.

Stanislav pointed out various places to Beatrice Ferrari, the beautiful Italian girl, who had not been this way before. Over there was the residence of the President—the old Zamek—the King's castle—with its gardens sloping down in terraces to the river. There was Stare Miasto—the Old City—with its narrow streets running steeply towards the Vistula, and high above it all, pencilled against the blue sky, the delicate Gothic glory of St. John's Cathedral.

Beyond green lawns with old trees heavy in summer foliage, there was a massive fortress called the Citadel.

Stanislav pointed it out to Beatrice Ferrari.

"A grim memorial of our tragic history," he said lightly. "That was built by the Russians after the Polish insurrection of 1831. It was a prison for political prisoners and many of our national heroes were executed behind those walls."

Beatrice Ferrari raised her beautifully shaped hands.

"Thank God all that is in the past," she exclaimed. "We have done with all those horrors."

Stanislav smiled at her and then looked serious for a moment. "I hope so!" he answered quietly.

On board the *Bajka* was Jan Raczynski who had been among the tennis players in Aunt Krysta's garden. Vanda raised her hand to him and he answered with a smile as he stood further forward on the deck. Vanda had been listening to Francesco's amusing stories about social life in Rome and Florence. Once or twice he had paid her a pretty compliment in a lowered voice as though there were a secret understanding between them.

"You must come out to Italy," he said. "My Italian friends will fall in love with you and I shall be jealous."

"Italians fall in love rather rapidly, don't they?" said Vanda, teasingly.

"Rapidly and passionately!" he told her. "We're made like that."

"It doesn't last, I'm afraid," said Vanda.

Francesco laughed.

"Long enough for the joy of life."

He was certainly not to be taken seriously, this handsome young man, she thought. Her eyes wandered towards Jan Raczynski. He was of a different type.

'If he loved one, he would be a faithful lover,' she thought.

He stood there looking at the passing scene on the river bank. His profile was finely cut, yet strong and beautiful, she thought. There was something noble and grave and spiritual in his look. Stanislav had painted his portrait, and had said it might stand for the portrait of an heroic type—high praise from her brother.

Presently Stanislav left his chair and went towards their friend and touched him on the arm.

"I want a word with you. Let's go to the bar and have a drink."

"All right," said Jan. "But I know what you want to say."

They moved towards the companion-way leading down to the saloon bar.

"Have you had it?" asked Stanislav in a low voice after ordering a vermouth for himself and his friend.

Jan nodded.

"This morning. It looks serious."

Stanislav shrugged his shoulders slightly.

"It may be only a precaution. Summer manœuvres. A sign to the Germans that we're ready on our side if they want to play the fool. I haven't told the family yet. No use scaring them."

"We have three days before we get back to the saddle," said Jan. "Three more days of playing about with everybody in a holiday mood. These crowds on the boat and the river bank seem utterly unaware of what may happen. They're not worrying!"

"I can't bring myself to believe it will happen," said Stanislav. "If it does I shall find it very interrupting to my portrait painting."

He gave a careless laugh and then raised his glass of vermouth.

"To hell with Hitler—that maniac!"

"A good toast!" answered Jan Raczynski, with a smile as he touched his friend's glass.

"We shall be meeting in camp," said Stanislav. "Then bugle calls, the jingle of spurs, and the stink of sweaty horses. Oh Lord!"

They went on deck again. The band was playing a selection from Offenbach. Some of the younger people were dancing on deck.

The boat stopped at Bielany, one of the Warsaw suburbs, with a big pine wood very popular for Sunday excursions. Some of the passengers disembarked there, but Francesco's party remained on board until they reached the landing stage of Mlociny which was journey's end. After landing they walked through the woods to a former palace like an old Polish manor house now turned into a kind of country club on the top of a little hill surrounded by a fine park.

They had tea on the terrace where groups of young people sat chattering at tea tables and admiring the view spread out below them. Halina and Jozef met some of their fellow students from the University and joined them in a walk through the woods.

Laughingly and with a little trepidation, Vanda accepted Francesco's invitation to stroll down to the river to watch some fishermen and the passing pleasure boats.

'I hope he won't make love to me,' she thought. 'I hope he won't be sentimental and romantic.'

But presently he spoke rather seriously for once.

"Stanislav tells me he has been called back to the cavalry brigade. I'm afraid it looks as though war is inevitable. If so, I shall have to go back to Italy and I shall hate to go. I've been very happy here in Poland."

Vanda answered with a laugh.

"Oh, don't let's talk about that kind of thing. It has been such a glorious afternoon."

That kind of thing! She had heard talk of war so many times. Day after day, month after month, there had been scare headings in the newspapers and gloomy stuff on the wireless—all that about Hitler and Mussolini and the international situation, and growing tension in Europe. Like others of her age she had not paid much attention to all that. 'We're living on the edge of a volcano,' her father had said a score of times and that had gone into one ear and out of the other because she was absorbed in her studies, and in the adventure of life and the emotional experience of young womanhood with its secret troubles and ecstasies because of the thrill of life itself. People who live on the edge of a volcano get used to it. She had just smiled at her father's pessimism and the dark forebodings of her elders. 'They're always worrying,' she thought. Now Francesco was talking like one of them.

"We're getting alarming reports in the Embassy," he told her. "It gave me a shock when Stanislav told me just now that he had been called up with Jan and all the others. It doesn't look good."

Vanda was thoughtful for a moment.

"Stanislav has said nothing to me about it. I don't think he takes it seriously."

Suddenly, standing there by this young Italian, she felt troubled. For a second she had a sense of something frightful creeping close like a shadow, like a menace, taking the glory out of this sunlight. Was it some horrible premonition? She laughed it away and raised a finger in rebuke.

"Are you trying to scare me?" she asked.

He smiled at her and answered after a moment's hesitation.

"It's because I love you that I'm talking to you like this. If war happens I shall have to leave you. That thought makes me very sad."

Vanda ignored that declaration of love. She was afraid that he was getting sentimental, but it was a funny way of making love, mixing it up with this war talk.

"You're very gloomy," she said reproachfully. "Do you honestly think that war is coming?"

He hesitated again and lowered his voice.

"Our Ambassador thinks so."

He gave a queer kind of laugh.

"It's all mad, isn't it? There are a lot of madmen in the world. Why should life be spoilt by a senseless war? The ordinary folk want only peace and the joy of life. So do I. That's why I admire you Polish people—these Warsaw crowds—because they insist on being happy until all hell breaks loose. That's the right philosophy of life."

For the moment he was no longer flirtatious and romantic. Some fear had taken hold of him at the end of this day of light-heartedness. Perhaps it was because of Stanislav being called back to the reserve of officers. The laughter had gone out of his eyes, those dark, liquid eyes which had been so amorous and gay.

'The Italians are like that,' thought Vanda. 'They're too emotional in all their moods. They go up and down.'

"I have another tragic thought," said Francesco. "If this war happens I shall be on the other side. I shall be your enemy—the

17

enemy of Poland which I have come to love. We Italians and Poles understand each other. In some ways we are alike. We both love beauty and intelligence and art and music. How horrible to think that we may be fighting each other!"

Vanda gave a little cry.

"Oh, that mustn't happen! It would be a crime. Why should it be like that?"

Francesco shrugged his shoulders.

"It's the fault of the English and French—your noble allies. They interfered in Abyssinia. They raised sanctions against us. Our Duce was deeply insulted. He's not a man to suffer insult."

"We had better be going back," said Vanda.

This conversation had struck her with a little chill in spite of the warm sunshine. An ugly spectre had touched her with a grisly finger.

They moved away from the river bank and walked towards the old palace.

Francesco's mood changed again. He spoke to her tenderly.

"Forgive me for having talked like this! It's because I want to tell you while there's still time, that I love you with all the passion of my heart."

Vanda laughed at him. It was her only defence against this emotional young man who certainly was adorably good-looking.

"First you try to frighten me and then you say you love me!" she exclaimed.

"*Carissima!*" He raised both hands slightly. "I'm very serious!"

"How many girls have you loved with that passion in your heart?" asked Vanda.

He laughed lightheartedly again.

"*Madre di Dio!* Those others meant nothing. It's you alone who will hold my heart for ever. Haven't you known for a long time? Hasn't Stanislav told you that I adore you?"

"I'm just a grown-up schoolgirl," said Vanda. "You can't adore a girl like me when Warsaw is crowded with pretty ladies."

"None so pretty as you, *carissima*. Like a spring flower on the banks of the Vistula. *Un fiore della vita.*"

Presently he became even more sentimental. It was very embarrassing.

"I want to hold you in my arms," he said. "I want to kiss you a thousand times. Look! Behind those trees. Come with me."

That romantic and dangerous idea of his was frustrated to the great relief of Vanda who would have resisted it anyhow.

Stanislav and Beatrice Ferrari had come to meet them. Stanislav shouted out from a little distance.

"Hullo, you two! We thought we had lost you. We must be getting back to the *Bajka*. She'll be starting in a few minutes. There's her siren calling."

Vanda went up to her brother and took his arm.

"Stanislav! Have you been called back to the Cavalry?"

Stanislav looked at her with raised eyebrows.

"How do you know? I was going to tell you. Summer manœuvres."

On board the *Bajka* there was no more talk of war. The band played light music again. Halina and Jozef with other young people were singing on the upper deck.

'This war talk is all a bad dream,' thought Vanda. 'I wish Francesco hadn't frightened me. Nobody in Warsaw is scared. Look at all these happy people on the banks. There's not a shadow over their minds.'

Her eyes were shy when they encountered those of Francesco. He had wanted to kiss her a thousand times. Italians were very charming—and very dangerous!

She talked mostly to Jan Raczynski, that noble-looking young man who sat next to her. They talked about books and the opera but now and then he became absent-minded and lapsed into silence.

The sun was sinking in the west and across the sky were bars of scarlet and gold. There was a red glow on the waters of the Vistula, as red as blood.

CHAPTER III

In those summer days of July and August the shadow of fear passed from Vanda's mind except as a faint disturbing thought as a dreadful possibility in the future. Francesco had frightened her for a few moments. Now she was reassured by the perfect calm in Warsaw, still enjoying fine days on the river. They weren't worrying.

She was reassured also by an invitation given her by Aunt Krysta who came in very cheerfully one morning to announce it.

"I want you to come with me to Poznan, my dear! It's our great day of August 15th—Our Lady's Day. A military parade, a grand ball, lots of handsome young officers to dance with you. You must bring your prettiest frocks."

"Oh, aunt, how splendid!" cried Vanda. "I shall love to come, especially with you."

"Oh well, I shall be one of the important ladies," laughed her aunt. "As the wife of a cavalry colonel. . . ."

There was unexpected opposition from Vanda's father.

"I don't like her going, Krysta. I beg of you not to take her. I forbid it."

"Oh, Father!" exclaimed Vanda. "It will be such a tremendous treat."

"It's too dangerous," answered her father. "Poznan is only fifty miles from the German frontier. If anything happened. . . ."

Aunt Krysta laughed at him.

"Bless the man! He's always expecting war round the corner. Vanda will be just as safe in Poznan as in Warsaw. It's stuffed with our army. Jerzy is already on the frontier with his cavalry. Don't spoil the child's pleasure. We shall give her a wonderfully good time."

"I don't like it," said her brother.

Vanda's mother was on her side.

"Oh, let her go, Antoni, my dear. Young people ought to have all the joy they can. And the military ball in Poznan is always delightful. I remember dancing the shoes off my feet with a young Roumanian officer. You were terribly jealous!"

She laughed at this remembrance and Aunt Krysta joined in her laughter and perhaps the sound of it, the merriment of these women, their absence of fear persuaded Dr. Mirski to give a grudging consent to Vanda's visit to Poznan.

A fine city with a strange and tragic history. It had been too near to Germany. There had been successive invasions of Germans and successive occupations by Germans when Poland was torn to pieces. Some of the Germans had become good Polish citizens with a loyalty to Poland, hostile to Bismarck's iron hand and endeavour to Germanize the province of Poznan (which the Germans called Posen) and his suppression of the Polish clergy in his Kulturkampf, and his suppression of the Polish language in the schools, enforced with great severity. Now lately there was a new German menace. Some of the younger folk of German blood had been converted to the Nazi creed, and were worshippers of Adolf Hitler, and drilled secretly, and were spies for their comrades on the other side of the frontier.

But none of all that came into Vanda's mind when she travelled with her Aunt Krysta to Poznan for the great day of

August 15th. It had a double significance, that day. First it was a great feast of the Blessed Virgin, always celebrated by Catholic Poland, as in other countries of the old faith. But in Poznan it celebrated 'the Miracle of the Vistula' that great battle under Pilsudski which had thrust back the Russian invasion when Warsaw was surrounded and seemed doomed. Several regiments which had their headquarters in Poznan had taken part in that battle and had fought with heroism—the 14th infantry division receiving from Pilsudski himself the highest order of merit in the Polish Army—the *Virtuti Militari*.

The day began with a Mass at a field altar and then there was a parade of infantry, tanks, armoured cars and battalions of Polish youth and workmen's unions. The crowds cheered wildly as the regiments passed and Vanda found herself cheering like the rest. But she was disappointed not to see her uncle with the cavalry. He was with General Anders who commanded the Novogrodek Cavalry Brigade.

"It's necessary as a precaution, no doubt," said her Aunt Krysta. "But a little bird whispered to me that Stanislav and his comrade Jan Raczynski will be able to stay at the ball till midnight. I can still pull a few strings!"

In her time as one of the prettiest girls in Poznan she had pulled a good many strings, and was not her own husband a colonel of cavalry?

"Oh, Aunt, how splendid!" cried Vanda.

There were several Roumanian officers present at the parade because there was a brotherhood in arms with the Polish army. One of the infantry regiments stationed at Poznan had the King of Roumania as its 'Chief of Honour'. The Roumanian Ambassador Franassovici, was there and brought two of his officers to be presented to Aunt Krysta and Vanda.

"A great day!" said the Ambassador with a charming smile. "There's nothing wrong with the spirit of the Polish army, nor indeed with the spirit of the Polish people. One feels it. It's like a white flame."

He bowed over Vanda's hand which he held for a moment, smiling at her.

"Will you spare an old fogey a dance at the ball tonight? If so I shall be the envy of many young officers!"

"I should be very greatly honoured," said Vanda, blushing very deeply.

"I am one of those who will be jealous," said one of the Roumanian officers, "unless I also get the promise of a dance. May I beg one for tonight?"

He was an elegant young man, very smart in his uniform.

"Let us take a cup of coffee somewhere," said the Ambassador. "I have learnt the Polish habit of the eleven o'clock rendezvous in the cafés where one is sure to meet many friends."

They went to Café Dobski which was a resort of the intellectuals of Poznan—writers, painters, singers, poets. On that day it was crowded with officers and civilians and pretty girls in summer frocks.

"A gay scene!" said the Ambassador, looking round with a smile.

Suddenly he gave a sigh and added some words in a lower voice.

"And only fifty miles from the German frontier!"

Two friends came to Vanda's table and she gave a little cry of surprise. They were Francesco Ferrari and his sister, Beatrice.

"I had no idea you were coming!" exclaimed Vanda. "Oh, Beatrice, how enchanting to see you!"

Beatrice Ferrari looked indeed enchanting. She was in a rose-coloured frock, cut low at the neck with bare arms. Her black hair was looped over the ears in the Italian style.

"When we heard you were going we could not resist coming," said Francesco.

"That's not quite true," laughed Beatrice. "Francesco is asked to represent the Italian Embassy."

"Quite an honour!" said Francesco. "I shall have the joy, I hope, of dancing with you tonight, Signorina."

It was all very exciting to Vanda. It was the first time she had been to a great ball like this apart from dances in Warsaw. Her first ball—and not then did she guess that it would be her last before the *danse macabre* which followed swiftly.

She dressed that night in the hotel where her Aunt had taken rooms. Aunt Krysta came presently to put the finishing touches to her frock and hair.

"Charming, my dear! I envy you your youth and beauty."

"Not much beauty!" laughed Vanda who had no conceit of herself. "Only youth, dear Aunt."

For some reason her aunt looked troubled.

"I shall be glad when it's over," she said. "I shall be glad to get back to Warsaw. People here in Poznan all seem worried to death. At least those I've been talking to."

"Oh, no!" exclaimed Vanda. "Think of the enthusiasm at the parade. It was wonderful. I was proud of being a Polish girl. I felt exalted. I felt ready to die for Poland, if need be."

Her aunt slapped her bare arm.

22

"For goodness' sake, child, don't talk about dying for Poland or anything else. I want you to live and be happy."

"I am happy," said Vanda. "This is a great day in my life, thanks to you, Aunt Krysta."

"Just a tiny touch of lipstick," said her aunt, more cheerfully. "Don't break too many hearts tonight!"

Stanislav and Jan Raczynski were waiting for them in the hotel lounge, and Stanislav embraced his sister and then held her at arms length with smiling eyes.

"Quite a beauty!" he exclaimed. "A credit to the family!"

He took a letter from the side pocket of his tunic and gave it to his aunt.

"From the Colonel," he said.

Aunt Krysta opened it and read its few lines.

You must take Vanda back to Warsaw tomorrow, without fail. This is an order, my dearest love. I am deeply anxious. Pray for me and all of us.

Aunt Krysta did not read out that message but her eyes looked troubled again.

Jan Raczynski shook hands with Vanda rather formally but there was a smile of admiration in his eyes.

"We owe this to Colonel Lopalevski," he said. "He gave us special leave on one condition which we shall find very hard to keep."

"What is that?" asked Vanda.

"Stanislav and I are like two Cinderellas. We have to leave the ball at midnight. But we mustn't leave our boots behind as Cinderella left her shoe!"

"That's rather hard, certainly," said Vanda. "The ball will be in full swing at midnight. You must dance with me before the witching hour."

"Thanks for the invitation," said Jan. "I am much favoured!"

He danced with her long before midnight but he seemed silent and absent-minded. She could hardly get a word out of him.

"You're not very conversational," she said, smiling up at him. For a moment he was startled by this remark.

"Oh, I'm sorry! The fact is it's rather like a dream—all this. It seems unreal, coming straight from the frontier. A mass of troopers, horses, guns, army rations, and sand in one's food. Bugle-calls. Soldiers' oaths. Now this—rather a contrast!"

He looked round the room with a grave smile at this scene in the big ballroom crowded with pretty girls in evening frocks and with young men in uniform like the Roumanian officers, and the notabilities of Poznan in evening dress, wearing their orders and stars. The band was playing dance music. The light of candelabra gleamed on the polished floor.

"How are things at the frontier?" asked Vanda.

Jan Raczynski glanced down at her and then spoke rather gravely.

"Not too pleasant! The Germans are raiding across the lines. We're not allowed to hit back by Government orders. It's all hushed up! No provocation on our side! That's to please the British and French who implore us not to act rashly."

Vanda heard a note of bitterness in his voice and in spite of the heat of the room she felt a sudden chill.

"Do you think war is going to happen?" she asked in a faint voice.

He hesitated for a moment before answering in a low tone.

"I'm certain of it. Very soon now."

Vanda withdrew slightly from his arms.

"That's frightful!" she said in a kind of whisper. "Are we strong enough?"

"We shall be vastly outnumbered," he told her. "The German war machine is formidable. But one ought not to talk like this in such a place. This dancing crowd is still living in a dream. They're not ready for what may come."

"Whatever comes we shan't show the white feather," said Vanda.

"No!" he answered. "We Poles know how to fight and suffer. Our people have done so a hundred times in history. They'll do so again for the sake of liberty. There's no price for freedom! One has to sacrifice everything for that. Don't you agree?"

"Of course!" said Vanda. "But what you tell me seems so horrible with this music playing and people dancing."

He smiled down at her.

"Yes, I feel like a skeleton at the feast!"

Later in the evening, just before midnight, he had another dance with her—the Mazurka—the traditional Polish dance, more lively and picturesque than the English foxtrots and the valses which had been danced earlier. They both laughed as they trod this measure and whirled around. He threw himself into the old dance—like all the others—as though there were no menace near at hand, no hostile army seventy-five kilometres away.

He took her back to her place and then held her hand and raised it to his lips.

"It's time for Cinderella to run away," he said. "The midnight hour!"

She looked into his eyes and spoke two words as he clasped her hand.

"Good luck!"

"Thanks!" he answered, and then slipped away through the crowd of dancers.

Stanislav hurried towards her.

"Good-bye, Vanda. I've had a wonderful evening. See you again soon, I hope."

"Take care of yourself," said Vanda.

As he was going away she called him back urgently.

"Stanislav!"

"What is it?" he asked, "I can't stay."

She tugged at a thin gold chain round her neck. At the end of it was a little golden medal of the Madonna. It had been given to her on her baptism.

"Stanislav," she said hurriedly. "Take this. Wear it under your uniform."

He did not jeer at her but took the little medal and nodded and put it into the side pocket of his tunic. Then he, like Jan Raczynski, disappeared through the groups of dancers.

She had the terrible thought that she might never see him again. The thought came to her like a premonition or like the dreadful moment of a bad dream. And yet all these people here were still laughing and chattering and the music was playing. Was it all false, this gaiety? Did some of them here know the imminence of appalling peril? Was their gaiety put on, or a deliberate act of faith with full knowledge that in a few days perhaps there would be no more joy but only agony and terror and blood? During the evening several of the men had grouped together and talked in whispers. She had noticed that. The Roumanian Ambassador had taken one of the Polish generals on one side and talked to him gravely. Several of Vanda's dancing partners, as well as Jan Raczynski, had become absent-minded as though their thoughts were elsewhere and troubled.

Francesco Ferrari came to her. He had been one of the absent-minded ones when he had danced with her.

"It's a wonderful night," he said. "Shall we take a stroll in the garden? The moonlight touches everything with loveliness and the air is quite warm."

She walked with him into the garden, very dream-like in the silvery light of the harvest moon. It cast long shadows across the lawns from the taller trees and shone white on the figure of a Mercury in stone, and upon the terrace of the house.

"You were in great demand tonight!" he said. "You only spared me three dances."

"I had to distribute my favours!" she answered, smiling at him.

He nodded as though accepting the inevitable.

They walked across the lawn silently until he spoke in a low, anxious and tragic voice.

"Vanda, *carissima mia,* this night, this dream-like garden, that dance music will be my last memories of Poland. I have to go to Italy tomorrow with Beatrice."

"Tomorrow!" she exclaimed, with a little gasp of surprise and apprehension.

"All our Italian families have been ordered to leave," he told her. "We have had urgent orders from Italy. The Embassy is packing up. The Ambassador wants me to leave tomorrow with Beatrice. I'm taking important papers."

"That sounds as though. . . ."

She did not finish the sentence but put both hands to her breast.

"Yes," said Francesco. "There's hardly a doubt now. The Italian Ambassador in Berlin. . . ."

He stood in front of her and spoke emotionally.

"I should like to stay here. I should like to be on your side. I doubt whether Italy can remain neutral. But how can I be an enemy of Poland? I shall never be that, and I hate war and the madmen who make it. Hasn't the world become civilized? Are we still in the cave-man stage? Aren't there enough intelligent people—lovers of art and beauty—to stop all this senseless slaughter? Why should I be called upon to fight against those I love? Don't the people of all nations want peace above all things?"

He flung his arms above his head and then let them fall.

"*Madre di Dio! È troppo horribile!*"

Then he looked at Vanda and his voice softened.

"I have to say good-bye to you. That makes me very sad. You have laughed at me sometimes. You thought I was only playing at love with you—one of the amorous Italians. I could see it in your smile. But now that I'm going to tell you again that I've loved you truthfully and with sincerity. I have tears in my heart because I leave you and because I may never see you again, your grace and sweetness. Do you believe that now, in these last moments I have with you?"

26

"Yes, I believe it," she told him. "And I thank you for it, Francesco, even though I am not ready yet for love. Forgive me if I tell you that."

"I know!" he said. "You are still a child at heart. That is partly why I love you. Dare I give you one kiss here in this moonlight?"

She did not refuse him and put her face up and let him kiss her lips.

He kissed her lightly and then turned away and spoke in a broken voice.

"The end of a dream! The end of all joy!"

A voice called him.

It was his sister Beatrice who came out to the terrace.

"Francesco! We must go."

Vanda ran towards her up the steps.

"Oh, Beatrice, my dear. Are you really leaving Poland?"

"Tomorrow," said Beatrice. "And I'm afraid for you, Vanda. and for all our Polish friends. I shudder at all you may have to suffer."

"We're not afraid," said Vanda. "We shall fight for freedom as we always have done."

"How brave you are!" cried Beatrice. "I have only fear in my heart."

That parting with Francesco and Beatrice was tragic and Vanda wept. From the dance hall came the music of a tango and the sound of dancing feet.

CHAPTER IV

VANDA was embraced by her father on her return home.

"Thank God you're back," he said. "Warsaw is safer than Poznan."

A few days before she would have laughed at him and called him an old pessimist but now she answered him gravely.

"Oh, Father! When is it coming?"

"I am told that the government has ordered General Mobilization for the end of August," he told her. "That looks serious. All our young men. Jozef will have to go."

"Jozef!" exclaimed Vanda. "How will he leave his music?"

Vanda's father raised his hands.

"They will all have to leave what they love best. That's war.

We shall have to sacrifice everything. Everything."

He gave a kind of shudder.

"I'm afraid for you and Halina and all our womenfolk. War is most terrible for them."

"Not more than for men," said Vanda.

Jozef came into the room and kissed Vanda lightly on the cheek and laughed.

"Funny, isn't it?" he said.

"What's funny?" asked Vanda. "I can't see anything funny."

"The idea of me being a soldier. I shall be no more use than any other piano-tuner."

He grinned and spread out his hands and looked at them.

"I don't suppose I shall be able to play Chopin again. My fingers will get all rough and horny, if I have any fingers or any hands."

"Oh, Jozef!" cried Vanda, and for a moment her eyes filled with tears.

He saw her distress and put an arm round her.

"It's all right! I'm not shirking it. I shall be in good company with all the others. I shall have to pretend to be brave. Who knows? I might be one of the little heroes."

He was almost gay and spoke with a kind of laughing irony but with a suppressed excitement and emotion.

Halina came in.

"Mother's crying," she said. "Personally I see no cause for tears. I wish I were a man, that's all, so that I could fight for Poland and kill a lot of Germans."

She stood there, a typical figure of Polish girlhood, slim, square-browed, frank-eyed.

"A pity you can't take my place," said Jozef jeeringly.

"The war hasn't happened yet," their father intervened. "We have still time to pray that it won't happen."

But the people of Warsaw had lost their gaiety. When the order came for General Mobilization it was a great shock to them. The holiday mood was over though they remained calm. Many still refused to believe that war was inevitable. With France and Great Britain as their allies—they had guaranteed Poland— the Germans would hesitate to attack unless they had gone mad. It might be just a scare, this mobilization.

It was more than that to mothers parting with their sons, and young wives from young husbands, and girls from their lovers. Vanda saw them weeping at the railway station where she and Halina said good-bye to Jozef. Their father had remained behind to comfort their mother who was in a nervous and depressed condition at this parting from both her sons and the terror of a coming war.

Jozef was late at the station.

"I'll meet you there," he told Vanda. "I must go round to Broadcasting House to tidy up a few things. I've left my music lying about."

He walked quickly to the big building where he had played the piano from time to time. He shouldered his way through the crowds gathered in the streets at a time when generally they were at work. Twice friends called out to him, to this tall young man with a lock of hair falling over his forehead, but he hurried on.

Inside the broadcasting station he sprang up two flights of stone stairs, strode down a corridor, and stopped at one of the doors. He thrust the lock of hair from his forehead and very quietly turned the handle of the door, opened it cautiously and went in silently. A girl was singing, accompanied on the piano by an elderly, bearded man. A little red light glowed above the door. They were on the air.

The girl, fair, blue-eyed, revealing the delicate curves of her young breasts within a thin white bodice, was singing an aria in Italian. She saw Jozef enter and her face flushed and she made a reproachful sign with one raised finger, though her eyes smiled. The song ended. The red light went out. The elderly pianist rose, gathered up some sheets of music and looked at Jozef severely.

"Strictly forbidden, young man!"

"I know!" said Jozef. "But I'm off to the war. If you would leave us alone I should be desperately obliged."

The elderly pianist looked at him less severely, with even a kind of compassion.

"Poor boy! . . . God be with you."

He left the room with his sheets of music.

"Marta!" said Jozef in a low voice. "I have to go—in five minutes. Before I do I want to tell you something."

"Tell me then," she said, avoiding his eyes.

"It's something you know. I love you. I'm sure you know that. I've told you so often with my eyes."

"Yes."

"I want you to love me. I want you to tell me that you love me—before I go. It would make things easier for me whatever happens. I should go with joy in my heart."

The girl—Marta—held out her hands.

"Of course I love you, Jozef. We both love music. That brought us together. I've loved you since we first met—when you played for me and made me laugh in the middle of a song. It was very wicked of you!"

"Marta," said Jozef, "you're saying a wonderful thing to me. If it weren't for this damned war. . . ."

He went towards her and held her in his arms and kissed her with passion.

He only had five minutes, and there was terribly much he had to say and to suffer—joy and agony, ecstasy and pain.

"I'm a coward," he told her. "I hate the idea of war. I don't want to be killed."

He had his arms tight about her and she raised her head to look into his eyes.

"You'll be brave for Poland's sake—and mine. We must all be brave, even if we're cowards. I'm terribly afraid, Jozef. You mustn't get killed."

"If I don't come back. . . ."

His voice broke for a moment.

"You'll come back. God will keep you safe. I shall be waiting for you."

"I bleed at the heart already. I feel half dead. How can I leave you? Your beauty, Marta—your loveliness——"

"Kiss me again, Jozef. Kiss my tears away—my silly wet eyes."

Five minutes. There was a clock on the wall. It went on ticking damnably fast. If only he could stop the clock, and stop Time itself!

He tore himself away and did not look at her again, not daring to because he would stay if he did. He ran down the stairs and went through the crowded streets again at a great pace.

At the station he found Vanda and Halina who were looking for him anxiously.

Vanda gave a cry of relief at the sight of him.

"Oh, Jozef! How late you are! I thought you might miss the train."

"Sorry!" he said. "I had to tidy up."

Halina pretended to be unemotional and matter of fact, though there was a glint of tears in her eyes when she kissed Jozef to say good-bye.

"See you soon," she said. "I don't suppose you'll have any fighting. Be brave anyhow."

Jozef grinned at her.

"Farewell, my child. Don't forget to say your prayers. You may need them."

To Vanda he whispered three words.

"Pray for me."

She embraced him and whispered back.

"God be with you."

He joined a long line of young men moving down the platform. Among them were some of his fellow students and three of his cousins—Jan, Stefan, and Antoni du Puget, the sons of Baron Louis de Puget.

From the crowd they raised their hands to her and she waved back.

"It's all very exciting, isn't it!" said Halina. "It will be an anti-climax if no war happens."

A friendly voice greeted her.

"Good morning, Vanda! Come and take a cup of coffee with me."

It was Jozef Birkenmajer, the poet, who had recently come back from the United States. He had been a friend of Vanda's father and had often come to their house.

"Can that be Halina?" he asked after shaking hands with Vanda. "She has grown a foot since I last saw her!"

"Only six inches," said Halina, "and now I must run like a hare to my next lecture."

The imminence of war did not stop her pursuit of knowledge and she hurried away.

In the streets little groups had gathered talking earnestly. From the bars came the sound of singing and cheering where young reservists were celebrating their farewells.

Vanda walked with the poet to the Café de l'Europe and after asking after her family he spoke of the gravity of the situation.

They entered the Café de l'Europe, threading their way through the chairs and tables on the terrace outside, and he led her to what was called 'the literary table', specially reserved for writers, actors, painters and intellectuals who generally made a group here. Some of them were at the table now.

They were mostly middle-aged men and Vanda felt shy among them though she had met some of them at her father's house. One of them rose and kissed her hand. It was Kornel Makuszinski, the famous novelist.

"How charming to have you with us!" he said. "Your presence, dear young lady, will restrain the speech of these pessimists who expect war to break out at any moment."

Vanda glanced at him, and looked surprised, and for a moment her heart gave a little leap with a kind of joy. Here was a very distinguished man who did not believe in the imminence of war.

"You're not of that opinion?" she asked, timidly. "You don'
think war will happen?"

"Good heavens, no! I refuse to believe in it—beyond a war o
nerves which is at least tolerable—if one has a sense of humour.'

"You're talking nonsense, my dear fellow," said a distin
guished-looking man whom Vanda knew by sight as the portrai
painter who had trained her brother Stanislav in his studio.

"I'm talking sense," said Kornel Makuszinski, "and I may be
rather lonely in doing so, because there is no sense in war. Who
wants it? Anything is better than war, as I know very well, having
been in two wars. Death, dirt, blood, agony, and the futile waste
of life. And at the end of it—what? Who wins?"

He looked over at Vanda's friend, the poet, and laughed
harshly.

"The presence of Birkenmajer here is a sign that war is not
going to happen," he said. "He is a sensible man and he wouldn't
have left the United States to come back here if he thought that
war was inevitable."

Jozef Birkenmajer smiled and shook his head.

"There you're wrong, my dear fellow. I came back because
I thought war was bound to happen. I came back to join in the
defence of Poland. I believe there are things worse than war.
Slavery. The destruction of the civilized mind. I believe in
Freedom. I believe that Poland is a bulwark of freedom in central
Europe."

"You disappoint me!" said the other man. "I believe in
passive resistance to oppression. War itself is madness—especially
for Poland, wedged in between two great powers. The Polish
soul, I agree, is unconquerable, but if it comes to war, if we
accept war, we shall be annihilated."

Several of his friends cried, "No!" and for a few moments
there was heated talk until Jozef Birkenmajer poured oil on the
troubled waters by his quiet, kindly voice and words.

"We're all agreed really. We all believe in Freedom. We shall
try to defend our dear Poland according to the best that is in us,
by whatever courage we have—spiritual, moral, intellectual,
even passive."

The Café de l'Europe was crowded with groups talking
quietly and seriously. Vanda saw some of her friends and raised
her hand to one of them. It was Eva Solska with her father and
mother. She had been at the great ball in Poznan, and Stanislav
had flirted with her.

Jozef Birkenmajer took Vanda home but would not go in.
He raised his hat to her and said, "Be of good heart!"

"I don't know what kind of heart I have," said Vanda. "I don't know if I have any courage."

He smiled as he answered.

"None of us know that yet. We shall all be tested if it comes. But I have faith in our history and tradition. All through the centuries we have had to fight for freedom, and learnt how to suffer—even to the last sacrifice. I don't think we've lost that spirit. I hope there's something of it in myself. But I'm not sure."

He walked away with a long stride and she watched him for a moment or two, tall and lean and straight-backed like a soldier, though he was a poet and a song writer.

'He will be brave if it comes,' she thought.

It came on the morning of September 1st, in that year 1939.

It was the first Friday of the month dedicated to the Sacred Heart, and according to custom in Catholic families many people went to early Mass on that day. Vanda went with Halina who had rushed into her clothes to be in time, after getting up late. It was a beautiful morning and very peaceful, sunny and warm, and not yet with any faint sign of the coming autumn.

The church was crowded more than usual, even more than on a Sunday. They were mostly women and girls, praying no doubt for the young men who had gone away, but here and there were elderly men deep in prayer also, as the priest moved about the altar.

Suddenly there was the sound of muffled explosions very far away, like distant thunder. Few people stirred. Only one or two men raised their heads and listened, perhaps recognizing a familiar sound, now very distant in the previous experience of their lives.

'It's another of our anti-aircraft exercises,' thought Vanda.

But a priest came into the pulpit and made an announcement while the Mass was in progress at the altar. He spoke in a quiet voice.

"It is an enemy air-raid. Everybody must remain in church until an all-clear signal."

There was no panic. Two girls near Vanda whispered to each other.

'How does he know?' thought Vanda, who had been praying for Stanislav and Jozef.

At the end of Mass the priest spoke again to the crowded congregation.

"War has come to us. We must pray for a just peace. As we are invaded we have to fight, but we must never be carried away by hatred or cruelty—we should always remember that charity and forgiveness are the most beautiful of virtues."

For a moment or two he was silent. Then he spoke again emotionally, with the fervour of his own patriotism calling to that in the hearts of these people below him.

"The days of trial have come, and as in bygone times the first Christians gave willingly their lives for their faith, we now have to sacrifice ours for our country. In the heart of every man there are two sacred ideals. Thy God and thy country—and now we have to prove it to fight in defence of these ideals. God bless you all. Go and say to all people of little faith: There is no price for Freedom."

It was strange that he had used those words. Jan Raczynski had spoken them to Vanda on the night of the ball at Poznan.

She was deeply moved by the priest's message. She accepted it without question and with a quickening of her heartbeat.

It was not then that she was able to say like Nurse Cavell in the hour of her death: "Patriotism is not enough."

'No price for Freedom.' She repeated those words to herself and wondered what price she might have to pay, and felt a little faintness at the thought. For Poland it might be a terrible price. It might mean martyrdom. For girls like herself it might mean unimaginable horror.

'Oh, Jesus, give us strength,' she prayed within herself. 'Oh, Jesus and Mary, don't let me be afraid.'

She was afraid.

CHAPTER V

"WHAT the hell is happening?" asked Stanislav leaning sideways in his saddle to talk to his brother officer, Jan.

"Only hell," answered Jan.

His head drooped and he slept for a few seconds in his saddle and then jerked himself awake again and stared with red-rimmed eyes at the road crowded with refugees from the border districts.

These refugees fleeing from the Germans had cluttered up all the roads, making it difficult, almost impossible for troops to move at more than a crawl with innumerable halts. Now the cavalry brigade was trying to get through them in the direction of Warsaw.

Stanislav stared at them. He hated them and pitied them.

How could the Polish army defend Warsaw—certainly they were going in the direction of Warsaw—with all the roads blocked like this? How could the Novogrodek cavalry brigade get a move on?

Most of these people were on foot pushing handcarts laden with bundles, pots and pans, babies and small children. Some of them were driving farm carts more heavily laden, dragged by tired horses. Farmers were driving herds of cattle before them. Most of them were peasants, but among them were well-dressed men and women, girls in smart frocks with high-heeled shoes, elderly men and women of middle-class. The white dust of the road and the yellow dust of the sandy soil was on their clothes and faces. They were unwashed and the women's hair was tousled after sleeping in the fields.

Stanislav looked down upon them from his tired horse and hated them and pitied them.

A halt was called at the cross-roads and he dismounted, feeling stiff in every limb, and drugged for lack of sleep.

A girl pushed her way through a group of people preparing a meal on the roadside and spoke to him.

"Aren't you Stanislav Mirski?"

He tried to moisten his lips with a dry tongue.

"I used to be. I believe I am!"

"I danced with you at the ball in Poznan," she said. "I'm Maria Kuszel. Can you tell me what's happening? How is the war going?"

Stanislav shrugged his shoulders slightly.

"We know nothing except that the enemy has thrust deep into Poland. They by-passed Poznan which could have held out for a long time."

"Can't you stop them?" asked the girl, with a kind of anger in her eyes as though Stanislav and his comrades were failing in their duty.

He managed to smile at her. Beautiful thought—to stop seventy German Divisions in the great pincers from the north and south which were driving deep into the heart of Poland with masses of tanks and mobile guns, and overhead a sky full of bombing aeroplanes smashing cities, railways, bridges, lines of communication. He had watched them pass like flocks of vultures. He and Jan had been with a cavalry outpost on the frontier. They had reported that the Germans had crossed the line at dawn on September 1st. They had brought the news to the cavalry brigade headquarters at Lidzbark, a few kilometres away from the frontier. They had watched with a kind of stupefaction the procession hours long, seemingly endless, of those black birds with the sun glinting on their wings. And no Polish planes had come to intercept or challenge them. No Polish planes had appeared anywhere within the gaze of the Novogrodek cavalry brigade falling back, getting contradictory orders, losing touch with other units. All they knew was that the 20th and 8th divisions were fighting rear-guard actions, and falling back, and being scattered and broken up by ceaseless bombing. He was going to answer this girl who had a look of anger when he was interrupted by his friend Jan, who gave a shout of "Swine!" He stood there by his horse and raised a clenched fist to the sky.

Overhead, swooping low, was a German aeroplane. The swastika was clearly visible on its wings. It skimmed over the heads of the refugees lying about on the grass or standing by their farm carts and other vehicles. There was a burst of machine-gun fire, the shrieks of women. Then it rose and became only a gnat in the blue sky. Little crumpled bodies of children were lying in the roadway. One of the mothers flung herself down with a scream of anguish, blood-curdling.

Maria Kuszel had slipped back to her group.

Jan Raczynski spoke bitterly to Stanislav.

"They'll have to pay for all this."

The Colonel, the uncle of Stanislav, Colonel Lopalevski came to have some words with his young officers.

"General Anders has taken over the command of the 8th and 20th divisions as well as our own brigade. I have great faith in him. A fine soldier."

"Isn't it too late?" asked Stanislav, blurting out his secret thought. The reports coming in were frightful.

The Colonel answered him sharply.

"Not too late to defend Warsaw. Not too late to save the honour of Poland."

Then he put his hand on his nephew's shoulder.

"We're all tired," he said in a kindly voice. "Lack of sleep gets on one's nerves. But our men are in good heart. I'm proud of the cavalry brigade. Grand fellows!"

He looked down the road at his leading troop of dismounted men. Some of them had flung themselves down on the sandy grass and were sleeping like drunken men. Others were standing by their horses. Stanislav noticed that his uncle looked tired and anxious and had dark smudges under his eyes. He too was suffering from lack of sleep. But he spoke calmly.

"It was inevitable that we should have a rough time at first. A withdrawal doesn't mean defeat. Unfortunately the enemy's armoured columns have broken through in many—places thrusting in like spear heads."

"It's time to stop them," said Jan Raczynski. "Even if we have to fight them with our hands."

There was a red hot fire smouldering in the mind of this young man as Stanislav knew by many talks with him. He was inspired by a patriotic passion which reached spiritual heights.

"This is not a war against the German people," he said once when they were held up in the tide of refugees. "It's a war against Evil. Hitler is possessed by the Devil."

"A homicidal maniac," said Stanislav.

He was not in a mood for philosophical argument. He was stiff and blistered from being so long in the saddle.

'That fellow is one of the idealists,' he thought. 'He's too noble for me. He's cut out to be a hero. I don't feel in the least heroic and I haven't shaved for three days, and we are certainly being defeated, curse it! We're in a hellish mess!'

He had snatches of conversation with other officers and men but once in the saddle again they rode silently except for a jingle of harness, and the clip-clop of hoofs on hard roads, and the creaking of axles of gun and transport wagons, and always the tumult of gun-fire in a narrowing circle around them.

One of the officers who talked with him now and then was Adam Socha, whom he had known at the University. He was a writer of short stories and sketches which he read now and then over the Warsaw wireless. He was a good-looking fellow from Vilno, with the face of a young eagle, with a sharply cut profile under dark brown hair. He was one of the world's humorists and found humour even in this war.

"We look like a bunch of brigands," he told Stanislav on one of their halts. "And you look like an awful scoundrel, Stanislav. I remember you as a fair-faced youth not more than a week ago."

He grinned at his comrade and felt his own stubble of beard.

That night he lay next to Stanislav under the stars and Stanislav heard him give a quiet laugh. It was cold, with a thin white mist creeping about them.

"What the devil are you laughing about?" asked Stanislav.

"An amusing thought," said Socha. "Three weeks ago I was trying to work out a short story—a dramatic little love affair. I was lying on a sofa in my room in a silk dressing gown. There was a shaded light on the table at my side. I had a red silk cushion under my head. Now here I am lying in a field of stubble staring at the stars, one ant in an army of ants who are

37

mostly going to be killed, in a few days or a few weeks. Quee
isn't it!"

"Shut up!" growled Stanislav.

"I'm not afraid of death," said Socha. "Are you?"

"Shut up!" said Stanislav again. "No good soldier thinks he
going to be killed. He always thinks the other fellow is going
get it."

Stanislav and Jan with a troop of horses were sent out a
scouts in advance of the cavalry brigade to keep in touch wit
units of the 8th infantry division. It wasn't easy to keep in touch
not easy to know the whereabouts of the enemy. Not far away—
a couple of kilometres—there was incessant gunfire. Field gu
by the sound of them. Their shells slashed through the surround
ing woods like the tearing of cloth. Nearer, half a kilometre awa
there was the sharp tattoo of machine-guns firing in short burs
and spasms. Heavier than all this were the dull thuds an
explosions, shaking the earth, as flocks of German bombe:
swooped low and circled round, and dropped their high expl
sives over living targets, scattered and broken up by this terro
from the sky against which there was no defence.

It was very close now. Stanislav felt his horse tremble beneat
him, terrified when a bomb fell a hundred yards away smashin
into a group of soldiers crossing a field. Four of them wer
carrying a wounded man on a stretcher until they staggered an
fell and did not rise again.

A young infantry officer was coming down a field track wit
about twenty men in straggling formation.

Stanislav rode towards him and leaned down over his saddl
"What's the situation?"

The young officer had a dead white face and his left arm hun
limp in a bloody sleeve.

"My battalion was rounded up by German tanks. Some of u
got away. We're ordered to scatter and get through if we car
The Colonel was killed."

"How far away are the tanks?" asked Stanislav.

"A quarter of a mile—or less. Look!"

He pointed to a farmhouse which had been heavily bombe
so that it was a huddle of ruin with naked rafters like ribs stickin
up above its broken walls. A brown monster like a great toad wa
moving towards it.

"Make for the trees," said Stanislav sharply.

As he spoke the young infantry officer gave a lurch and fe
before his men could hold him.

Stanislav rode back to his troop and spoke to Jan.

"We must get into that wood before they spot us."

He shouted an order to his men and they rode across the stubble field and took cover in the wood, leading their horses through the undergrowth.

The stragglers from the infantry battalion joined them. They were carrying their officer and put him down at the foot of a tall beech tree. They were all very young, and one looked frightened and was trembling with a kind of shell-shock.

"How is he?" asked Stanislav.

"Dead," said one of them. "That's what we'll all be soon." He gave a queer laugh and stared down at the dead officer. Another man spoke.

"Those devils are too strong for us. Human flesh can't stand up against a ton of metal belching out flame and fire."

But it could and did.

The German tank which had been nosing about the ruined farmhouse came lurching across the field towards the wood.

'We shall be caught like rats in a trap,' thought Stanislav. A little moisture came into the palms of his hands—the beginning of fear.

"What's the best thing to do?" he asked Jan.

"We must stop the swine," he answered.

He took hold of his horse and led it to the edge of the wood.

"Jan!" shouted Stanislav, thrusting his way through the tangled bushes. "Come back, man! Don't show yourself!"

He was mad of course, this Jan Raczynski. A damned lunatic.

The tank was about fifty yards from the edge of the wood. The sun shone on its gun barrels. It stopped. Doubtless the German tank officer inside was scrutinizing the wood itself for any sign of life there.

Jan Raczynski had mounted his horse.

"Jan!" shouted Stanislav again, in a strangled kind of voice. "Are you mad?"

Jan turned to look at him. Stanislav never forgot that look. There was a kind of mystical smile on his face. So might one of Arthur's knights have looked before attacking the devouring dragon.

He put his horse to the trot and rode straight for the tank. The German gunners held their fire. Perhaps they thought this Polish cavalry officer was coming to surrender. Within a stone's throw of them he flung two hand-grenades at the body of the tank. He waited for the explosion, then he drew his sword, rode forward and slashed at the caterpillar wheels.

His sword flashed in the sun, pouring down upon the stubble

field, and the dark woods, and the metal of the tank and the figure of that single horseman.

A machine-gun opened fire, slashing rider and horse with a scythe of bullets. On the field lay a crumpled mass of horse flesh and man flesh in a puddle of blood.

The German crew came out of the tank, staring at it, staring perhaps with wonderment, at this revelation of Quixotic courage.

For some reason they did not shell the wood. Perhaps they thought it might conceal Polish guns, or more madmen. It lurched back across the field.

Stanislav and his men waited until darkness and then rode back to rejoin their brigade and make their report. As they rode through the night they could see the flashes of gun-fire and the scarlet glow of flaming villages. Nothing good to report. Nothing certain except confusion and retreat.

A car with a pennon in front came slowly along the road threading its way through the long column of refugees and peasant carts and cattle. Inside was a tall man with a powerful, stern-looking face. He was wearing General's badges. There were two other officers with him and when they stopped they got out and stood talking to Colonel Lopalevski and a cavalry general.

"General Anders!" said Adam Socha, who was speaking to Stanislav as they stood near their Colonel. "I saw him in Warsaw."

They were close enough to hear something that the General was saying in a high clear voice.

"The cavalry brigade will hold the bridges over the Vistula. I have orders to hold the bridge at Plock at all costs. . . . It's a question of getting there in time. These refugees. . . ."

He gave a little groan at the sight of the road block ahead of him.

"Poor people!" he added with a note of pity in his voice which was not so stern as his face.

He stood talking there for some minutes. Once or twice he raised his arm and made a sweeping gesture as though describing the enemy's line of attack.

Stanislav heard only a few more words.

"It's serious, of course, but not yet desperate. . . ."

The cavalry brigade moved forward taking to the fields when the roads were impassable because of the slow moving tide of refugees.

A question of time to save the bridges across the Vistula at Warsaw and others up the river. The Novogrodek cavalry brigade could only go at a slow pace with their guns—too few of these guns—and baggage wagons and field kitchens, and signalling equipment. Some of the bridges had already been crossed by the enemy. General Anders received orders from the Commander-in-Chief, Smigly-Rydz, to blow up the bridge at Plock, though previously he had been told to hold it at all costs. It was a terrible decision. Inevitably some of the units on the right bank of the Vistula would be cut off. The Polish Army defending Warsaw was being out-flanked. They must pull out again or find themselves surrounded.

Stanislav and his squadron were at the bridge of Plock. Towards the south-east in the direction of Warsaw the night sky, still faintly blue, throbbed with the scarlet glare of fires.

Over there in Warsaw were Stanislav's people, his father and mother, Vanda and Halina, Aunt Krysta. Over there, beneath the bombardment were many of his friends and the girls with whom he had flirted, or who had flirted with him. A few weeks ago he had been bathing with them, playing tennis with them in Aunt Krysta's garden, listening to gay music on the pleasure boat down the Vistula.

The cavalry brigade was heavily bombed that night and many men and horses lay dead in pools of blood.

"Shall we get out of this?" asked his friend Adam Socha. "It looks like the end, doesn't it?"

"Only the beginning," said Stanislav. "Oh, Jesus!"

It was not blasphemy but prayer which made him cry out the sacred name. A bomb dropped by a low flying plane exploded among a group of his own comrades, blowing them to bits.

The bridge at Plock, by orders of General Anders, was blown up.

The main German Army had by-passed Warsaw in the Minsk Mazowiecki area, cutting off the road to Lublin. The Novogrodek and Volhynia brigades were ordered to attack Minsk Mazowiecki. On the right bank of the Vistula in the suburb of Praga Polish infantry units had been cut off

CHAPTER VI

BEFORE there was the tramp of German feet into Warsaw Vanda Mirska, as it seemed to her, had lived through such a storm of emotional experience that it had changed her into

41

someone else. She was no longer the Vanda who had danced at Poznan, who had laughed on the pleasure boat down the Vistula —who had been a student of languages at the University, conscious that young men were making love to her with their eyes and sometimes with their words—though she had been disdainful of them and yet liked it a little—coming back in the evenings to 'swot' at her books in her own little room after supper, studying so late sometimes that her father would knock at the door and call out: "Vanda, go to bed, my dear. You'll wear your eyes out, and that tired brain of yours!"

All that had gone. Everything was different and terrible. Beauty and gaiety had gone out of life after a few days of hope, a few gleams of hope. In their place were fear and grief, and for a time a desperate and overwhelming desire for death.

Warsaw was crowded with refugees from Poznan and the north and west of Poland. Many of them were dirty, dishevelled and exhausted, even women of her own class who had made the journey by train or by motor car, unlike the peasants who had been in wagons and hay carts or pushing prams laden with babies and bundles. Some of the trains were bombed and the passengers had flung themselves out at the first stop and crawled under the carriages. The refugees had been machine-gunned when they had fled from their carts and wagons and taken to the fields. Low-flying bombers had swooped through the blue sky and sprayed these people with machine-gun bullets, killing women and children as Stanislav had seen on his way to the Vistula bridges. The screams and wailing of mothers over their dead children seared the souls of their men.

It was a war without mercy—this German *Blitzkrieg*, and put a flame of hatred in their hearts. There was one gleam of hope. Over the wireless came the news that England had declared war. Vanda and Halina were in the crowds that gathered in front of the British Embassy, cheering wildly. Now Poland was not alone. England would come to her aid, with the whole British Empire and with France, their greatest friends in Europe.

Along Vjazdovska Avenue where most of the Embassies and Legations had their big houses national flags were flying above the white buildings. They were to let German airmen know that they were not to be bombed because of diplomatic immunity but with a cruel irony they looked as though they were banners flying for victory or triumph.

There was no victory. No good news came over the wireless, but appeals from Stefan Starzinski, the Mayor of Warsaw, for the citizens to remain calm and orderly, to remember with pride

42

the heroism of their forefathers and to remain loyal to this age-long tradition in the heroic soul of Poland. So he spoke. His voice sounded strong and resolute and even cheerful with a glorious kind of faith that Poland would be preserved. It was a call to courage, but Vanda, listening by the wireless set in her sitting-room, felt fear creeping upon her and tried to hide it from her family.

"That fellow is magnificent!" said her father. "His voice rings out like a trumpet call. I wish I were twenty years younger. I wish I were in Stanislav's place or Jozef's."

"Our poor boys!" cried Vanda's mother. "If only we could get a word from them."

"I agreed with father," said Halina. "I envy them. If only I hadn't been born a girl!"

She was only a tall, slim schoolgirl, with the beauty and innocence of her youth. She knew nothing of life—or death.

Vanda glanced at her and smiled, though inside herself she felt that creeping in of despair. What would happen to girls like Halina if the Germans came?

"Some girls have been heroic," she said. "There was Joan of Arc."

"Yes!" cried Halina, "I'd like to be a Polish Joan of Arc."

"She was burnt to death," said Vanda.

Halina shrugged her shoulders.

"A good death!" she said, carelessly. "Not worse than being buried under one's own house or blown to bits by a bomb. We're all risking that. Listen!"

There was a heavy crash not far away. Another German air-raid somewhere in the suburbs. The ornaments in the room shook and tinkled.

"I hope Aunt Krysta hasn't gone up in smoke and flames," said Halina.

"We had better telephone," said her father.

In those first few days it was still possible to telephone.

Aunt Krysta answered the call. She had not believed the war would come. Now that it had come she was astoundingly cheerful and courageous.

"Are you all right, Krysta?" asked her brother.

"Quite alive!" she answered cheerfully. "A bomb has just fallen in the garden—bang in the middle of the lawn. The house is cluttered up with refugees, poor dears. It's like a railway station. I can't refuse any of them. How I'm going to feed them, I don't know."

Presently it was the same in Vanda's house and in all the

other houses of Warsaw which opened their doors to these homeless people fleeing from the west—friends from Poznan, young soldiers who had been cut off from their units, and later on, when the air-raids over Warsaw had intensified, friends and neighbours who had been bombed out of their houses. They came round having lost everything, shaken, but—how extraordinary—still able to laugh at their own escapes. Vanda heard excited conversations and often a laugh among the younger men and women who were still undismayed because of their youth, because they were still alive, because this was an enormous adventure not yet unendurable.

Among those to arrive at the house late one night was Vanda's cousin Barbara, with her husband Stefan Ziemski, who was a well-known illustrator of children's books—afterwards very talented as a forger of false passports.

"Oh, Vanda!" cried Barbara. "Can your father and mother find room for us? Even if we have to sleep on the floor. We've had a nightmare journey."

She looked elegant in a fur coat. Many women among the well-to-do refugees wore fur coats, as the best way of carrying them on those tragic journeys.

"Barbara was desperate to come to Warsaw," said Stefan, after kissing Vanda's cheek. "But now we feel ashamed to ask you for shelter, even for a little while."

"We hate to refuse anyone," said Vanda, "least of all our blood relations."

She took them into the *salon*, a big room with a polished floor and a grand piano at one end and furniture of the French Empire style pushed back against the walls. A young man and his sister were sleeping under the piano. The girl was in a summer frock with short sleeves and had taken a silk cushion to use as her pillow. Her fair hair had become tousled and she had a wood-nymph look lying there with one arm outstretched, deep in sleep. And her brother had a faun-like look with a thin nose and pointed chin and untidy hair.

"Good heavens!" whispered Barbara. "There's Sophie and her brother. All one's friends are in flight. It's too frightful."

On the floor were other sleepers with their heads on bundles which they had brought with them, but wide awake and whispering with titters of laughter where four young people squatted on the floor, playing cards. On the chairs against the walls, nodding with their chins on their chests were a few old ladies and gentlemen, friends of Vanda's father and mother. They had fled from the west in the belief, the tragic belief, that they would find safety in Warsaw. The world—their world—had opened beneath their feet. They had nothing left but resignation, these old gentlefolk who had fled from cultured homes—resignation to the will of God.

Vanda took her newly arrived cousins into the kitchen where they could talk more freely and where she could give them some hot soup simmering on the stove. The two servants had gone to bed.

"This house is becoming like a slum tenement," she said. "But two of the slum-dwellers—we've put them in the bathroom —seem to find it like paradise! I expect you know them—Nunia and Tadek Mankovski. They've only been married a week and they're still love-making in a seventh heaven of their own."

"Poor babes in the wood!" cried Barbara. "Nunia is only eighteen, just a child in this dangerous world."

"There's a lot to be said for love," said Stefan. "There's also a lot to be said for hot soup. This is simply marvellous!"

"Stefan!" exclaimed Vanda presently, "you look so cheerful. You keep on making little jokes, and Barbara doesn't look frightened. I can't understand it. How can you be amusing when Poland is being defeated and the Germans are destroying us?"

Stefan looked at her with a smile and raised eyebrows. He was a delicate, fragile-looking young man. She had noticed his long thin hands when he was eating his soup. She remembered that he had been a sickly boy with asthma when they had been playmates as children.

"We're not defeated yet," he said. "The war has only just begun. Warsaw will hold out. That's why we're here."

"The news that comes over the wireless is simply frightful," said Vanda in a low voice. "And we don't get a word from Stanislav and Jozef. They may be dead already. We know nothing about anything."

Her voice broke for a moment and her eyes filled with tears.

"We must keep our nerve, my dear Vanda," said Stefan. "I believe in our heroic tradition, like Stefan Starzinski."

He gave a nervous laugh.

"Not that I'm one of the heroes!" he added.

He struck his chest and said, "My damnable asthma . . . I should have liked to be a soldier, like my father and grandfather, but I'm only an illustrator of fairy tales. Very unheroic!"

Later he became one of the heroes of an underground war, taking deadly risks.

Vanda had given up her own room in her father's over-crowded house. She slept on a mattress in the kitchen but she found room for one more refugee, impelled by pity and something in his person which appealed to her—a very handsome young man with finely chiselled features and dark, rather deep-set eyes, and a thin, humorous mouth.

She had gone out to a grocer's shop to buy some *kasha*, a kind of porridge, if there were still any to buy. There was a long queue outside the shop. Food was beginning to run out because of the rush of refugees into Warsaw.

Standing there she saw a young man with a bandage on his head. He crossed the road and then swayed a little and fell down on the sidewalk. Vanda ran over to him but he was already picking himself up.

"Are you ill?" she asked.

"Only a little faint," he answered. "Silly of me!"

"Are you wounded?"

"It's nothing. A cut which bled a bit. I was in the air-raid over Praga last night. I was playing the violin to some friends. There were four of us. One was playing the piano for me. Suddenly we heard a low-flying bomber. I went on playing but the fellow at the piano ducked. That's all I knew. It must have been a direct hit. I was knocked out and when I became conscious the room was like a shambles. I was the only one left alive. I crawled out and fell over a heap of rubble and lay there for a time. Then I walked to this side of the river to find some friends but they've gone off to Lublin. They had pinned a piece of paper on the door of their flat. 'Gone to Lublin'."

He gave a faint laugh.

"I'm talking too much. I suppose it's the shock, I feel—well—a bit shaky."

He shivered a little and rubbed his hands as though they were ice-cold.

"I lost my violin as well as my friends," he said. "It was smashed to bits. I'm sorry about that."

He looked at Vanda with that faint smile again.

"You'll think I'm callous in being sorry for my violin when three of my friends were killed. As a matter of fact it all seems like a bad dream. It doesn't seem real. I can't believe they're dead. Perhaps I shall do so tomorrow."

Vanda stared at him and seemed to remember him.

"Are you Jerzy Boberski?" she asked. "Didn't you give a recital in the Academy of Music?"

He nodded.

"Yes, that's right."

He raised his hands for a moment.

46

"All that's finished now. What's the use of fiddling when the enemy is at the gates? Anyhow, I haven't got a fiddle."

He seemed to be shivering and his face went white and he looked faint again and held on to a railing.

"Sorry!" he said, "it's silly of me. Please excuse me."

Vanda spoke to him almost sternly.

"It's ridiculous of you to be fainting in the street. I'll take you home."

"Oh, no! I'm quite all right. Really!"

He wasn't quite all right.

"Take my arm," said Vanda.

He took her arm and very slowly she walked with him towards her father's house. On the way he seemed to get a little better and talked again.

"It's frightfully kind of you. I assure you I can manage."

"I'm going to manage for you," said Vanda. "I'm taking you home."

"I'm sure to find some friends in Warsaw," he said presently. "I used to come here a lot from Lvov."

"You've found one," said Vanda. "I became your friend when I heard you play that day."

"It's good of you to say so," he told her. "I'm really a second-rate violinist. But that doesn't matter now. Why are you so kind to me? I mean, I'm deeply grateful for your kindness. May I know your name?"

"Vanda Mirska."

He stopped to look at her with surprise.

"Don't I know your brother Jozef? Doesn't he play the piano? I've heard him on the wireless."

"He's away with the Army," said Vanda. "He's not really fit to be a soldier. He lives for music."

"War spoils everything," said the young man.

She led him into her house. She found a place for him in her father's study with several others. That night he was delirious and she fetched a doctor to him. Dr. Joravski, an old friend of her family who had looked after them since childhood.

"He's suffering from delayed action after shock . . . what a handsome young man!"

"He's my special refugee," said Vanda. "I feel responsible for him in a way."

The doctor laughed.

"I hope he'll be grateful to you."

Then he gave a deep sigh.

"I'm afraid many of our best young men will be killed. It

47

will be a slaughter of our heroic youth. I've heard bad news today from one of our Generals. The enemy are smashing through our lines everywhere. There's no stopping their armoured columns. I fear the worst."

Vanda did not answer him but her eyes filled with tears and a sense of despair invaded her spirit. She too feared the worst.

CHAPTER VII

IT was when the Germans had almost surrounded Warsaw and had advanced to the outer suburbs that Vanda felt herself sinking into a black pit of despair. It sapped her strength and her courage. She felt that a dark and dreadful shadow was overhanging her. For the first time in her life she had a sense of horror. It was the thought of living in a defeated Poland, of hearing the tramp of German feet through the streets of Warsaw, of having to live with Germans and under the rule of Germans, arrogant and ruthless as conquerors. Standing in the kitchen, where she spent much of her time helping the servants cook for so many people in the house, she had a nightmare vision of what would happen, and her imagination was filled with such terrible forebodings that she shuddered violently and then began to weep convulsively until she heard footsteps coming down the stone passage outside the kitchen door.

She thought it was one of the servants who had been out waiting for food in the provision shops but it was Jerzy Boberski, her special refugee as she had called him.

"Can I lend you a hand?" he asked. "I should be glad to make myself useful."

She turned her face away from him so that he should not see her smudged eyes.

"No thanks. It's all done."

He had recovered in the past few days and was anxious to help in the house and especially in the kitchen. Two or three times she had let him do so and he hadn't been very useful really, preferring to talk while he held a damp cloth in his hand and looking too handsome—he was certainly very good-looking—to act as a kitchen drudge.

"I'd like to help in a humble way," he said.

"I don't want any help," she told him, almost crossly. She was anxious to get him out of the kitchen in case she should weep again.

He hesitated and looked hurt and then answered quietly, "Very well. I dare say I'm a bit of a nuisance really."

"Thanks all the same," said Vanda.

He hesitated again and said, "I could peel the potatoes."

"No potatoes," said Vanda. "Please go."

Of course she hurt him but she could not bear him to see her crying, and the tears were trying to rush out of her eyes again. He went away without another word and she sat at the kitchen table and put her face down in her arms. She had lost her courage. Something had broken inside her. Darkness had descended upon her soul.

That evening she slipped out of the house as dusk was creeping into the streets. She went round to a chemist's shop in a turning off Vjazdovska Avenue. She knew the chemist, an elderly man from whom she had often bought toothpaste and face creams and medicines for her mother. There were two or three customers in the shop and she waited until they had gone.

"Sorry to keep you waiting," said the chemist in a kindly way.

"It doesn't matter," said Vanda.

She spoke in a lower voice.

"I want you to do me a favour."

"A favour? I would like to do it!"

"I want you to give me something. Something useful in time of war. I mean something to put one to sleep."

"You are suffering from sleeplessness?"

"No, no! I'm too much awake! I want something which will put one to sleep for ever. Women ought to have it—girls like me. You must know what I mean."

The chemist looked at her gravely.

"Yes, I know what you mean," he said, "and I would not dream of giving it to you. Nothing like that, my dear young lady! You ought not to ask me. You ought not to have such a thought in your head."

"Isn't it the best way out?" asked Vanda. "Wouldn't it save one from all the horror that's coming, especially to women?"

"It's the coward's way out," said the chemist, harshly. "You belong to a good family. Your father fought for Poland under Pilsudski. I'm deeply shocked."

"I'm sorry," said Vanda. She slipped out of the shop hurriedly.

'The coward's way out' he had said. Yes she was a coward. Not that she was afraid of death. She wanted death.

That night Dr. Joravski came round to see one of the refugees

beauty. At least I think I have. It seemed utterly real. Forgive me for saying such things."

"I'm glad you've said them," she answered.

"You're too beautiful to kill yourself," said Jerzy. "It would be a crime against beauty—among other things."

"What other things?" asked Vanda, ignoring his remark about her beauty. She didn't think herself beautiful.

"A crime against Poland," he said. "You ought to live for the country's sake. Supposing we all killed ourselves? There wouldn't be any more Poland!"

He gave a laugh at this argument of his. It was a *reductio ad absurdum.*

Vanda smoothed back her hair and smiled faintly.

"I didn't know you were a philosopher!" she said.

He shook his head.

"Only a fiddler and a useless drone."

"Not a drone!" exclaimed Vanda. "Anyone who can play the violin like you gives a lot of joy to many people. We ought to take care of you."

"You took care of me when you found me in the street," he reminded her. "I'm very grateful, even though you took in a worthless fellow who can only make funny noises on four strings."

"Funny noises!"

She had heard him play enchantingly. That idea struck her as being comical. She gave a tiny laugh.

He remained with her until late that night. They talked together seriously and simply without any falsity or reticence. They talked of life and death. They both knew that they were very close to terrible danger. That reminder came all through the night when the kitchen floor shuddered beneath them and there was the crash of explosions not far away.

For some reason the dark cloud of despair was lifted from her. For some reason she did not want to die.

"Jerzy," she said, late in the night, "I think you have helped me very much. I feel quite different somehow, after this talk."

"Different? I should hate to think that!" he exclaimed. "I like you to keep the same—as far as I know you."

They exchanged a smile. There seemed to be a sympathy between them. They were both young and had the secret understanding of youth not often shared with older people.

CHAPTER VIII

THOUSANDS of refugees who had struggled into Warsaw from the west now began another flight further eastwards when they became fearful that the Germans could not be held back long from the capital. The news that the Government, under General Smigly-Rydz, had gone into exile after declaring that Warsaw was to be an 'open city', undefended, spread like wildfire. That was very ominous, they thought. Surely it meant that Warsaw was doomed. The peasants who had arrived with their farm carts, the well-to-do people who had motored from Poznan and Gdynia, those who had crowded into trains and lorries to be bombed on their way, and those who had found temporary refuge in strangers' houses, were now desperate to leave the city. The streets became noisy with the rumbling of this fugitive traffic, the creaking of wheels, the screeching of unoiled axles, the tramp of tired feet.

Vanda's home in St. Theresa Street lost some of its temporary inhabitants. Among them were that young husband and wife, Nunia and Tadek, who had occupied the bathroom and found it Seventh Heaven. They too had heard the bad news and one morning Tadek, looking troubled, told Vanda that for Nunia's sake he thought it best to go to Lvov where she had many relatives.

"I feel a bit ashamed of myself in leaving Warsaw," he said, "but I have to think of Nunia."

"Of course," said Vanda.

"Are you going to stay?" he asked. "Won't you come with us?"

"I shall have to stay," said Vanda. But the idea of going to Lvov and her mother's city so old and historic, so far away from Warsaw, tempted her. It would be safer there. She would not hear the tramping of German boots in Warsaw. It would be further from that horror.

Nunia flung herself into Vanda's arms at parting and wept a little.

"I've been so happy here!" she cried. "I forgot the war. Now I've woken up and I'm getting frightened."

"I'm glad you've been happy," said Vanda. "Remember it always, darling. Remember the fairy-tale of love when things become worse."

"Oh, Vanda!" said Nunia, "why don't you have the same fairy-tale? Or have you found it?"

Vanda smiled at this young girl who had dared to marry only a few days before the war began.

"Not yet," she answered. "Perhaps I never will now. War isn't favourable to fairy-tales."

"You're so brave!" exclaimed Nunia. "How are you so brave when even with Tadek I'm feeling terrified?"

She did not know that Vanda had wanted to kill herself.

Several of the old people left and the group of young people who had played cards on the floor one evening departed also.

The next morning her father announced his sudden decision to go to Lvov, like so many others. To Vanda it was startling and abrupt but he had been talking to his wife for hours on the previous night and together they had prayed for guidance.

"I'd like to stay," he said, "but I have to think of your mother and you two girls. Besides I've had a letter from your grandmother. She implores us to go."

"It's our duty to go," said Vanda's mother. "In any case it's foolish to stay here in Warsaw. The Germans will be here very soon now."

She gave a little shudder and raised her hands with a gesture of despair.

"But, Father," cried Vanda. "how can we leave the house? Who will look after the refugees?"

"I have asked your Aunt Krysta to come. She insists upon staying in Warsaw although her own house is in the danger zone. The Germans are always bombing Praga."

"It means abandoning everything," cried Vanda. "Our home —all our treasures—all that home means to us."

"Not for ever," answered her father. "We shall have to watch things. Everything is uncertain. If the situation improves we shall come back. It depends on your dear grandmother's health."

Halina had something to say and it was not cheerful.

"I would rather stay and be killed. I hate the idea of going."

"It's because we don't want you to be killed that we're going," said her father. "I haven't said anything before, but I have been deeply anxious, my dears. This decision hasn't been easy. We may be doing the wrong thing. We are in the hands of God."

Halina spoke bitterly again.

"It's running away. It's surrendering in face of the enemy. It's a hateful idea. Why don't we stay and fight the Germans?"

Then she burst into tears, grabbed at a handkerchief in her waist-belt, put it to her eyes and left the room.

Her father gave a laugh and a sigh.

"Poor darling! She's at the romantic stage of life. How little she knows of war and its abominations! I admire her spirit all the same."

Vanda was silent. Halina's words had startled her. The child had said something which was in her own mind. It was a kind of surrender—this flight from Warsaw. She felt that. And she would be sorry to abandon her refugees. Others would come. Jerzy was still there. They wouldn't be able to talk together late into the night. She would miss that. But Lvov would be quiet and safe for a while. Her grandmother's garden was like a paradise with the old manor house rising beyond its trees. There would be a sense of peace—however false.

"When must we go, Father?" she asked.

"Today. This afternoon. It may be our only chance. The enemy is bombing all the stations. There's a mad rush for the trains going east."

He was wonderfully calm now that he had made up his mind.

"We must start packing," he said, "but we mustn't take too much. A few clothes. We may be back again soon."

Did he really think that? Afterwards Vanda wondered if he had this hope, or was only saying such a thing to comfort her, and perhaps to deceive himself.

Before she left she had a few words with Jerzy who had been meeting friends in Warsaw.

"We're going to Lvov," she said.

He looked distressed.

"Oh? That's a blow. I'm sorry. I shall miss our talks—our friendship."

"Yes," said Vanda. "Why don't you come with us. Come with us, Jerzy. Lvov is your own home."

He shook his head.

"I have to stay. Have you heard the news on the wireless?"

"No! What news? Something terrible?"

"Warsaw is going to be defended. The mayor has called upon every able man—even the women—to dig trenches and help in the defence. It's a call to arms."

Vanda stared at him almost incredulously.

"Then I ought to stay!" she cried.

He smiled at her.

"All the more reason why you should go. It won't be amusing. It will be very—frightening. But I'm going to be one of the trench diggers. I shall wear an armlet and try to look brave. My future comrades may be deceived for a day or two."

He laughed but his eyes were fixed on Vanda's with a shy look of devotion.

"It's hateful to say good-bye," he said. "But I suppose I must say it. All my thanks again for your kindness to me."

"I did nothing," said Vanda. "It was you who dragged me out of a dark pit."

"Shall we meet again?" he asked.

"Of course! Why not?"

He gave his little shy laugh again.

"War is apt to be dangerous. Men are killed sometimes."

"Oh, Jerzy," she said in a low voice. "Try not to be killed. I shall pray for you."

"I'm not really afraid," he told her. "I believe in the other side. Do you remember?"

She remembered their talk about life and death.

"I have to go for that armlet," he said. "I have to say good-bye. . . . Good-bye, Vanda."

He took both her hands and raised them to his lips.

Then he turned and did not look at her again and went out of the room, and out of the house—and, perhaps, out of her life. She was sorry she had to leave him. It might have been her fairy-tale.

That evening after feverish packing of bags they hired a *doroshka* to take them to the station. The car would have to be left behind as the young chauffeur had been called up. The Central Station had been bombed out so they had to go to the big junction of Praga on the east bank of the Vistula. Halina was silent and in tears. This would mean the abandonment of her studies at the University. It was a flight from all she had loved best in life—her books, her small treasures, her student life, her home, which had seemed so happy and secure.

Their father sat staring out of the *doroshka* at the crowds of refugees making also for the junction of Praga, an interminable tide of homeless humanity with push-carts and prams laden with their household goods, trudging along wearily with tragic faces and dragging feet. Many of them had already a long journey behind them and looked haggard and exhausted, limping on sticks or holding on to the carts. Women were carrying their babies. All of them were urged forward by the desperate desire to get further east, further away from the approaching enemy.

Crawling along behind cabs, carriages, cars and carts the *doroshka* took three hours to reach Praga station across the Vistula by the Ponalovski Bridge. The waiting rooms had been bombed and they had to spend the night in the tunnel below the platforms. It was crowded with would-be passengers and others coming down to take shelter from air-raids which happened twice during the night hours. Among them were friends of Vanda's father and mother who greeted them emotionally and remained talking quietly and gravely.

Halina went to sleep for a little while with her head on one of the bundles. Vanda sat next to her but kept awake. Strange things were happening in her mind. Those words by Halina were like a refrain.

"It's like deserting in face of the enemy."

How wonderful that Halina should have thought that too—a young girl, so childish, so gay before these things happened.

Before day-break Halina woke up and looked about her.

"Halina," said Vanda in a low voice, "I've changed my mind."

"What about?" asked Halina.

"I shan't go to Lvov. I'm going to stay in Warsaw."

Halina stared at her in astonishment. She sat up straighter and there was an excited look in her eyes.

"Oh, Vanda, if you stay I shall stay!"

"No, no, you must go with Mother and Father."

"I shan't go. I shall stay with you."

"We shall have to tell Father."

"There'll be an awful row!" said Halina.

But there wasn't an awful row.

Astonishingly their father acquiesced after some hesitation.

"I don't want to coerce you, my dear. You're old enough to make your own decisions. Your mother will be glad to have Halina with her. That's one comfort."

"I shall stay with Vanda," said Halina, firmly. "You must tell Mother."

Her father was staggered and stared at her incredulously.

"No, no! That's impossible. I can't allow it. You must come with us."

"Father!" cried Halina. "You know how I love you. But I want to stay with Vanda. I implore you to let me stay."

They were in the tunnel below the station. Many people were sleeping. One of them stirred and half raised himself and said, "Do be quiet there." Vanda's mother had fallen asleep further down the tunnel where she had been talking to some friends.

"I daren't tell your mother," said Vanda's father in a low

57

voice. "What am I to do? You're no longer children. God have mercy on me. What can I do about it?"

He was deeply distressed about Halina, though he had accepted Vanda's decision without much argument. Presently he became calm again.

"At least Aunt Krysta will be with you," he said. "And perhaps we're exaggerating the danger. I think the Germans will respect our women."

Vanda did not tell him that Warsaw was going to be defended. It was not a deliberate concealment. She took it for granted that he had heard the news, forgetting that he had spent all the morning packing up and tidying his papers. They were speaking in whispers now because of the sleepers around them.

"We must tell Mother," said Vanda. "She is happy in going back to Lvov. Give our love to Grandmother."

It was perhaps lucky that a loudspeaker in the tunnel ordered all the people on to the platform for the train going east. There was a general movement. Everybody was awakened.

Vanda went over to her mother who spoke to her nervously.

"Are you sure we have all the bags?"

"Mother," said Vanda, "Halina and I are staying with Aunt Krysta. Come back soon, dearest Mother. I hope you'll find Grandmother all right."

"I don't understand," said her mother. "What are you telling me?"

When she understood she looked stricken and bewildered.

"Have we all gone mad?" she asked.

"It's all right, my dearest," said her husband nervously. "They'll be all right with Aunt Krysta. I dare say we shall be back in a few days, when the situation improves. Then we shall all be together again, thank God. But we must go, or we shall miss the train."

The two girls embraced their father and mother hastily and helped them up with the bags.

"God bless you, my dears," said their father. "God keep you safe."

There was a wild tumult on the station platform, a rush forward to the carriages. The two girls had lost their father and mother. They were both weeping.

"Why are we staying?" asked Vanda when they had gone. "Why didn't we go with them? It was some sudden impulse. I felt I had to stay. It came to me suddenly. I had to stay."

"Of course," said Halina. "It's the right thing to do. I'm going to dig trenches."

The citizens of Warsaw—men and women and young girls—dug trenches but in the end it was hopeless. The Germans closed in. Polish troops fighting in the outskirts were overwhelmed. Regiments marching to the relief of the city from garrisons in the east were stopped by another army who came proclaiming they were allies and friends and brothers. Warsaw was bombed ruthlessly. At night the sky was red with the light of flaming fires, and each day's dawn revealed new ruins and the unburied dead.

CHAPTER IX

THREE weeks later young Jozef Mirski was on the left bank of the Vistula in the outskirts of Warsaw with a battalion of infantry. That is to say he was in the cellar of a bombed house with two dead men and two living. It had been their machine-gun post until a direct hit on the house had brought it down on top of them and buried them with their machine-gun under an avalanche of rubble. Jozef had been stunned and cut about the head. When he returned to consciousness he was surprised to find himself alive—if he was alive. He was not quite sure of that until he moved his right arm and felt his head. His fingers were wet after that experiment and he looked at them by a glimmer of light which came through a hole in the cellar roof as afterwards he was aware. His fingers were wet and red. He was still bleeding. There was a man lying next to him, and presently he spoke to him.

"What happened? Where are the others?"

No answer.

Jozef raised himself into a sitting position, painfully, because his head seemed to be split in half.

"What happened?" he asked again.

He could see the face of the man lying next to him. He recognized it. It was the good-looking face of young Antoni, his cousin. Antoni du Puget. He had been a gay fellow, one of the brave sort, not caring a jot about danger, always making a jest of things. They had marched together day after day, until they were put in a troop train going back to Warsaw.

"That's a bit of a joke," he had said. "We say tearful farewells to our families and best girls and now we're going back again. I'll stand you a drink at the Café de l'Europe—with kind permission of the Germans."

Now he was dead. He was certainly dead. Jozef stared at him. His face was a grey white and although his eyes were open they didn't move. His body didn't move. He was dead. His face looked like one of the stone angels above the doorway of Warsaw Cathedral.

Someone was groaning, long agonizing shuddering groans.

"Who's that?" asked Jozef.

The groaning went on, but another man answered.

"He's wounded in the stomach. Is that you, Mirski?"

"Yes, who are you?"

There was only the glimmer of grey light coming through the hole in the roof.

"I'm Sergeant Savitski. I think I'm bleeding to death."

Jozef stood up and staggered against a wall and then clutched at a wooden post supporting the roof of this cellar and within his reach.

He could see better now. A film seemed to have passed from his eyes, or the grey light became stronger. He could see the sergeant lying on a heap of coal. Next to him on the grimy floor was the dead body of another man.

He felt the strength of his legs. He could walk in a drunken sort of way. He stumbled over some fallen masonry and reached the sergeant and the dead man. It was the son of a chemist in Warsaw. A pile of stones lay on his body.

"I'm losing blood," said the sergeant. "An awful lot." Jozef knelt down beside him and saw that his trouser leg was soppy with blood.

He took out a clasp knife which he had used for his Army rations and cut away part of the cloth. The man Savitski had a jagged wound in his thigh.

Jozef stared at it silently. Then he took off his tunic and his shirt. He tore the shirt into rags and used them to bind round the wound very tightly to stop the flow of blood. The fingers which had played Liszt and Mendelssohn, and Chopin and Ravel, were delicate and deft. He had told Vanda that he was no more use as a soldier than any other 'piano tuner'. He had told Marta that he was a coward. He did not think of that now. He was not thinking but was only acting by some instinct, like an animal helping one of its mates.

The sergeant winced and groaned slightly as the rags were tied. "Oh God!" he cried through clenched teeth.

Jozef put on his tunic again on to his bare body. He was in a kind of nightmare. This dark cellar, getting a little lighter, those dead bodies of his friends, his aching head, his bloody fingers— it was like a horrible dream.

The sergeant spoke to him.

"The Germans are all round us. The swine are still bombing."

"Yes," said Jozef.

He heard heavy explosions not far away.

"I'm getting out," he said to the sergeant after listening to those crashes. "I'll try and get an ambulance for you."

He couldn't stay in this cellar with its dead. He could do nothing more for the wounded. He had an animal instinct to escape into the open. He wanted to breathe the fresh air, to see the sky. He must get out of this hole somehow. It was filled with horror.

He stumbled back across the floor and went on his knees by the body of Antoni his cousin who had been so gay. He kissed his cold forehead and then stood up again with a strangled sob.

There was a door to the cellar. He tried to push it open but it resisted his strength. It was blocked up by a fall of rubble. He flung himself against the door and it yielded a few inches letting in a shaft of sunlight. He squeezed himself through the narrow opening, ripping up his tunic on a rusty nail. He was out. He felt the breath of air on his face and forehead. He felt the warmth of the sun. Presently he felt less dead. He could think. He put his hand to his head. It had stopped bleeding but the lock of hair which fell over his forehead was matted with blood.

He could think. He was in the back garden of what had once been a red brick villa until it had been hit by a bomb. That must have been last night. There was a big crater in the lawn and the garden fence was smashed and the flower beds were strewn with bits of brick and twisted iron.

'I must go and see Marta,' he thought. 'I must find out if she's alive. Perhaps everybody is dead. My father and mother. . . .'

He walked down a long, straight street in which several houses had been smashed into ruin. Nobody seemed alive in this suburb of Warsaw. He walked very slowly, stopping now and then with a kind of faintness. At the far end of the street a dead horse lay in the roadway. He knew his direction now. Through a gap between the houses—a newly made gap—he could see the tower of the Town Hall and the tall spire of St. Anthony's Church.

He heard the sound of a car coming towards him. It was an armoured car with a long barrelled gun. In a trailer at the back were soldiers in steel helmets with a machine-gun; but not Polish soldiers. They were Germans.

Jozef stared at them and staggered into the doorway of a grocer's shop, a shop without windows and a splintered door. They may have seen him but did not bother about one miserable-looking wretch, a straggler from the Polish Army. They passed. They would deal with him later and with all such as he.

He walked on again and saw no more Germans. He knew his way now, even narrow side-streets through which he went in the direction of the Town Hall. There were people about, though not many. They stood whispering to each other, mostly women. Some of them glanced at him with pity in their eyes. They had seen others like him during the past few days. Near the Town Hall a well-dressed girl spoke to him.

"You must hide yourself. You must take off that uniform. We're waiting for the Germans to come in. My father and mother will shelter you. Have you any friends in Warsaw?"

"My family," he told her. "I don't know. . . ."

"Do you know Marta Ostrovska?" he asked.

The girl shook her head, but seemed to remember the name. "The one who sings? I don't know her. I wish I did."

Jozef saw a Red Cross ambulance on one side of the Opera Square. He hurried over to it and spoke to one of the men.

"There are two of my comrades lying wounded in a cellar."

"Whereabouts?" asked the man.

Jozef told him and the man nodded and said, "We'll try to get through."

There was a crowd in the Opera Square and he stood among them. They were looking at what had been the Town Hall. Now it was gashed and broken, with the sky showing through its skeleton of stone. Piles of masonry lay about the ground.

The people were quiet. Some were even whispering to one another as though they might be overheard by spies and enemies. Only one close to where Jozef stood was weeping. It was a girl standing next to a man who looked like her father. Jozef knew him by sight. He was one of the professors at the University."

"We must accept it all," he said. "We must steel ourselves to whatever happens."

He put his arm round the girl's shoulder and drew her closer.

Jozef walked on. He was outside the broadcasting station where often he had been 'on the air', as they called it. It was here, in another kind of life—how long ago—days or years?—that he had held Marta in his arms for five minutes, five minutes of passion and agony.

She might be there now. By some miracle she might be there.

He walked into the building. No one was in the main hall. This place was empty and deserted where generally many people were hurrying about or greeting each other with chit-chat and laughter—singers, musicians, actors, talkers over the wireless, directors of plays and music, girls in the orchestra with their violins and 'cellos.

He walked up the stone stairs leading to the first floor and heard voices in a room with an open door. The stairs had exhausted him, strangely. Once he had run up them lightly, as easily as running down. Now he had to stop to take breath. His head had a dull, thudding ache.

He pushed open the door and went in. Two men were talking.

"It's the end of Warsaw," said one of them.

The other shouted out a denial, almost fiercely.

"No! We shall fight on. We must go underground. Poland will never give in. Never!"

"They'll be here in a quarter of an hour," said the other man. "I've had a message from my son. It was brought by a small boy who dodged them. They're moving towards us with their tanks and armoured cars. It's time we got away—if life is any good to us."

They were sitting in chairs facing the windows and did not see Jozef standing there until he spoke to them. Then they swung round to stare at him.

"Is Marta here?" he asked. "Is she in the building?"

They stared at him in astonishment.

"Mother of God!" exclaimed one of them. "What are you doing here? Aren't you Jozef Mirski?"

Jozef nodded.

"I've come back. I'm trying to find Marta Ostrovska."

The man gave a harsh laugh.

"You won't! Everybody has gone, except a few of the engineering staff to keep the wireless going—and us two. Don't you know the Germans are on their way here? We've just time to get away—if we have the luck to get away."

The one who spoke was the man who had said that Poland would never give in. He was the director of the musical programmes. He seemed quite calm except for nervous fingers which kept touching his short beard. The other man had fear in his eyes.

"I'm going," he said in a low voice. "I have to think of my family." He went out of the room and they heard his footsteps down the stone stairs and after a minute other steps coming up heavily.

A big middle-aged man, clean-shaven, square-jowled, flung the door wider open and strode in breathing noisily.

Jozef knew him. It was Stefan Starzynski, the Mayor of Warsaw whom he had seen many times on public platforms.

"Good heavens!" cried the Director. "Why have you come, Starzynski?"

"My Town Hall is in ruins," said the Mayor.

Tears were falling from his eyes and running down his face. "Our Glorious Town Hall!"

"It isn't safe here," said his friend. "The Germans will be here in less than fifteen minutes. They're on their way."

"Fifteen minutes!" exclaimed Stefan Starzynski.

He raised one arm and stretched it out as though addressing a public meeting—an immense crowd. His voice rang out loudly and defiantly.

"Then there are fifteen more minutes in which to tell the world that Poland still lives—that the spirit of Warsaw is as high as the stars, that the soul of Poland is undefeated!"

He turned to the other man and said a strange thing.

"Is there anyone here who can play Chopin?"

The Director looked at Jozef.

"Here is one—by some miracle. Jozef Mirski."

"You play Chopin?" asked the Mayor, staring at Jozef incredulously, this young soldier, dirty tattered, wounded.

"I used to," said Jozef.

He looked at his hands, filthy and blood-stained.

"Yes! I remember," said the Mayor. "I have heard you play. . . . Play now! Play Chopin. Play it as you have never played it before. Shame our enemies by the music of Chopin. Tell them that we are a civilized people, that Polish genius has been a gift to the world. And tell the Polish people themselves that by this music, by the loveliness of Chopin's melody, we still hold our faith. We do not surrender in our souls. Play Chopin until those barbarians are at the gates!"

He spoke with intense emotion in that loud strident voice, as though the enemy might hear him and all the people waiting indoors and listening for news over the microphone, as indeed many were.

"I'll turn on the juice," said the Director. "I'll signal down."

He crossed the room and touched some buttons. In a few seconds over the door a little red light gleamed on one of the walls. Down below were brave men. The Warsaw radio was still functioning.

"We're on the air," said the Director, in a low voice. "For the last time."

Those words *for the last time* spoken in a whisper, were heard by thousands of Polish men and women listening for the latest news of defeat and disaster and approaching terror.

Jozef had stumbled to the piano and opened it and sat on the stool and loosened his fingers above the notes. Then he played. It was perhaps an extraordinary thing to play, his choice of Chopin. It was one of his *mazurkas*, based on an old Polish dance tune but transmuted by Chopin's genius. It was lively, gay, joyous. There were dancing feet in it.

He played it as though his spirit were laughing—this young, wounded soldier who had lain with death in a dark cellar a little while ago. He was possessed, it seemed, by the soul of Chopin in that fateful hour when the Germans were entering Warsaw and by now were in the heart of it, near this building itself.

He stopped and his hands dropped to his knees.

"Go on!" said the Mayor, in a harsh whisper. "For God's sake go on! Don't stop!"

Jozef put his fingers over the notes again. This time he played one of Chopin's *nocturnes*, lyrical, exquisite, beyond the gross earth and the wickedness of men and all things of evil, reaching out to the higher spheres, disembodied, poignant in its limpid beauty.

People who heard it, and there were many, never forgot that last recital before the Germans came and seized the broadcasting station and took it over for their propaganda and false news, and grim threats to the population.

They came now. There were shouts of command in the street below. Orders in German rang out. There was the tramp of heavy feet on the stone floor of the entrance hall.

"They've come! . . . Time to go," said the Director, quietly.

He walked over to the Mayor and put his hand on his shoulder.

"We might get away by the back stairs," he said, calmly. "I know the underground way. Come, my dear Starzynski, old friend, I'll lead the way."

"I stay," said the Mayor. "I'm not afraid of them. I defy them."

"Then I shall stay too," said the Director. "I can't leave you here alone."

"I too," said Jozef.

The Mayor stared at this boy and his voice softened.

"No! You're too young. And your fingers are too precious. You played like an angel. Poland needs you. I beg of you to go, my dear lad. I order you to go."

Jozef hesitated. In that moment he thought of Marta and of his father and mother, and Vanda.

"Very well," he said, "I know the underground way. Goodbye, gentlemen."

He slouched out of the room with only two minutes to spare. Two minutes later a German officer and three men entered the room. There were others in the corridor outside.

"Who are you?" asked the German officer, grimly.

"I am the Mayor of Warsaw," said Starzynski, proudly.

"And this other?"

"I'm the Director of Musical Programmes."

They were both arrested, without violence by the young officer who was cold but polite. Not so polite was the treatment of Stefan Starzynski in the concentration camp of Dachau. A year later, on the anniversary of the German invasion, he was taken out of his cell and shot.

CHAPTER X

THEY were grim days and nights in Warsaw before the guns were silent. A fifth of the city was destroyed by terrifying airraids and the fire of German batteries. Every house in St. Theresa Street was gutted, except by some extraordinary chance, the house of Vanda's parents at the far end of it. A heavy bomb had missed it by a few yards, opening an enormous crater outside the front door so that there was only access to the house by the back garden.

A respite of twenty-four hours was granted by the enemy for the burial of the dead. Vanda saw the horror of it when for the first time she and Halina left the underground rooms of their father's house and walked to the open square beyond where several shallow graves were being dug. One of them was for a friend and neighbour to whose house they had often been for dances and parties when this lady had been a beautiful hostess. Now, wrapped in a blanket, she was being lowered into the grave. Vanda wept during the funeral service and others were weeping round other graves, while they were being newly dug by volunteer grave-diggers—the relatives of the dead. Women brought flowers from the gardens to lay upon them and the loveliness of these bouquets was pitiful amidst the wreckage around them.

The streets of Warsaw were heaped with rubble and twisted iron and broken glass, and the blue sky was visible through the rags and tatters of ruined houses. In the roads lay the carcasses of horses with broken carts and lorries and in one street a young soldier lay dead with his arms outstretched, until his body was removed and buried in one of the squares. A few soldiers passed, walking singly, the stragglers from a defeated army but greeted warmly by the citizens of Warsaw who were proud of them still. They had fought for freedom. They were not to blame. They were the victims of this tragic war.

Vanda looked at these young men with a kind of eager hope.

"Halina," she said, in a low voice, "if only we could meet Stanislav or Jozef! If only we knew they were alive!"

She wondered also if one of them might be her special refugee as she had called him, but she did not recognize one of these passing soldiers.

They returned to the underground rooms—a servants' hall, kitchen, a wash-house, a coal cellar, where they now lived and slept while the battle was on.

Aunt Krysta was there, her own house having been wrecked, with shell craters in her lovely garden over at Praga, now in possession of the enemy. And they had been joined for a few days by Dr. Joravski with his wife and two children after their house had been destroyed and before they found rooms elsewhere. There were three other refugees who had been their neighbours, a mother with two daughters about as old as Halina.

Aunt Krysta was wonderful and Vanda was thankful for her company. Never once did she show a sign of fear. Never once did she moan or wail. She was cheerful, helpful and devoted. She remained calm even when the very earth trembled beneath them and when they heard the heavy explosions of bombs in houses close to them.

"That was a nasty one!" she would say. "The Germans seem to have a grudge against our street. Well, they can destroy our houses but they can't kill our spirit. . . . Now then, you young people, don't look so frightened. You can only die once, and death is the gateway to a better world than this, which is not really a nice kind of world! . . . Besides this is a well-built house. We're reasonably safe down here. Cheer up and don't forget to say your prayers."

Every evening she read out the Litany and the others, joining in, were comforted.

Once or twice she expressed to Vanda anxiety about her husband.

"I should like to get a message from him. I'm not worrying unduly because I'm sure he's alive somewhere, but of course I can't help being a little anxious, being a faithful wife—though a great trial to him now and then, poor dear!"

She smiled at Vanda, making a joke of it.

"Wives can be trying sometimes, you know—or perhaps you don't know!"

Vanda was shy of seeing Dr. Joravski again. She had once asked him to give her 'something' and he had refused rather severely and preached a little sermon. Not by the flicker of an eyelid did he remind her of that. On the contrary he put her to the test of courage one evening.

"Would you like to help me in the hospital? The wounded come pouring in and we need volunteers to look after bandages and lint and do a bit of simple nursing now and then. Bed-making, sweeping floors, and all that. Drudgery, but in a good cause. Are you willing?"

"Of course!" cried Vanda. "A thousand times willing."

"What about me?" asked Halina. "Why do you leave me out?"

The doctor smiled at her.

"You're so young! There are unpleasant sights and sounds in the wards. A tragic ordeal, my dear."

"I'm not a child," Halina answered, almost angrily. "I'm ready for anything. Do you think I'm afraid?"

"No!" said the doctor after a quick glance at her—this slim beautiful girl with the face of a young novice, with the flame of the spirit in her eyes. "I think you're ready for anything, as you say. I don't doubt that."

"When do we start?" asked Halina eagerly.

With the doctor they started very early the following morning after a night of air-raids. Guns were firing from Polish batteries in parks and gardens. It was a long walk to the hospital and they had to cross the broad street. Some of the side streets were blocked by fallen masonry and the doctor and the two girls had to climb over piles of rubble. Now and again men came up to give them a hand, surprised to find them walking about when most inhabitants of Warsaw were underground.

A queer thing happened on the way. Over some of the rubble heaps darted a great number of red squirrels. They were making their way to the deserted gardens of wrecked houses. They had come out of the parks, terrified by the gun-fire of the Polish batteries. Afterwards Vanda found one under the big maple tree in her own garden where it stayed all the winter. Then something else happened. Even the birds and beasts were not indifferent to this siege of Warsaw.

"Look!" cried Halina. "Flocks of crows! Why are they coming?"

There had been no crows in Warsaw, but they were flying in from the countryside with a chorus of harsh cawing.

Vanda shuddered. They had smelt blood. Dead horses and dead bodies in the streets of Warsaw had called them from afar.

"Horrible!" said the doctor staring up at them.

He too had guessed the reason for that flight of crows.

In the hospital there was the smell of iodoform and disinfectants. Wounded soldiers were being carried in on stretchers. The surgeons were busy in the operating theatre. In the wards the nurses were looking after a new batch of wounded. Vanda and Halina were put to dirty work, cleaning out bed-pans, burning blood-soaked bandages, preparing lint.

"Halina," said Vanda, "can you stand this? Isn't it all too frightful for you?"

"Some of the wounded boys are in agony," said Halina. "This is nothing to what *they* have done."

There were times when Vanda felt very sick, and only prevented herself from vomiting by will-power and an urgent prayer.

At home one night in the underground rooms Aunt Krysta told them the news of the Russian advance into Poland. They had moved down the wireless set and could still keep in touch with the outer world.

Vanda gave a cry of distress.

"But Aunt, it can't be true! It's unbelievable. It's a great betrayal."

For a few moments even Aunt Krysta could find no cheery word.

"Yes, it's terrible news. It means that our poor country is doomed."

"Aunt Krysta!" cried Halina. "What will happen to Father and Mother? They will fall into the hands of the Russians."

Vanda was stricken by the same thought.

Aunt Krysta was silent for a moment. What could she say to these two girls?

"We must hope for the best. Your father and mother are elderly folk. The Russians will respect them. I dare say they will be safe in Lvov. At least we have the comfort of knowing that it's less dangerous than in Warsaw."

"I feel conscious-stricken about them," said Vanda. "We abandoned them. We were selfish because of pride."

"We didn't run away," said Halina. "We're helping in the defence of Warsaw, even if it's only in a hospital wash-house."

"It's good work," said Aunt Krysta. "I envy you, my dears. I should like to be with you."

They were listening to the wireless when the last hour of the siege had come. Their heroic mayor, Stefan Starzynski, speaking with tragic emotion, announced the capitulation of the city. He called upon the people of Warsaw to remain calm, to preserve their pride.

"In our souls there is no surrender. The Polish people will always struggle for freedom. . . . Our glorious army have fought like heroes against overwhelming odds. . . . We have taught the world that Polish boys know how to fight and how to die for their beloved country. . . . We are not ashamed. We have won new glory, even in defeat. . . . Now we must endure all things with the courage of martyrs and with our Christian faith as our light and consolation."

Such things he spoke and Vanda listening to them burst into tears. But suddenly she dropped her hands from her face and listened intently. The wireless had gone silent until presently the Mayor's voice sounded again, but as though he were speaking to someone in the wireless room.

"Play Chopin. . . . Play it as you have never played before!"

Into this underground room of the house in St. Theresa Street came the music of one of Chopin's melodies.

"Halina!" cried Vanda, "Aunt Krysta! . . . That must be Jozef. . . . I'm sure it's Jozef. . . ."

They all listened intently as though to heavenly music in this hell of Warsaw.

"If it's Jozef it's a miracle," said Aunt Krysta. "It's a sign from God."

Presently there was silence. The guns were quiet. There was no bombing raid. After days and nights of ceaseless gun-fire, and the drone of low-flying bombers, and the roar of explosives, and the noise of houses shattering into ruin, this silence was intense, profound and startling. Warsaw had capitulated. The Germans were marching in.

CHAPTER XI

JOZEF escaped easily enough through the cellars of the wireless station which led him into a small square near the ruins of the Town Hall. He walked slowly, by way of side streets to St. Theresa

Street, stumbling over the débris of gutted houses. He was aghast at the ruins around him and at the silence and emptiness of the city. The inhabitants were still underground or in the houses which had escaped destruction, hating to see the first arrival of the enemy. The Germans themselves, with their tanks and armoured cars, had not yet entered the back streets unless they led to the main thoroughfares.

Jozef was alone. He had an idea that everybody was dead except himself. It was a horrible feeling in this loneliness and desolation. It frightened him. He was more frightened when he came into St. Theresa Street and saw the broken walls, the empty windows, the smashed roofs of house after house.

'My people are dead,' he thought. 'They're all killed. My father and mother, Vanda, Halina. . . .'

This thought, this fear, made him tremble and took the strength out of his legs. He walked on like a drunkard, or like a blind man groping his way.

He cried out, "Oh God!" and then started to run in a kind of panic, until he came to his father's house at the far end of the street. It was untouched except for a big shell crater outside the front door, and broken windows upstairs. It seemed like a miracle. Perhaps it was a miracle. He made his way to the back garden. An ugly looking thing lay on the garden path—an unexploded bomb. The leaves of the maple tree were turning scarlet. Sunflowers had grown tall. There was a scent of sweet briar. A red squirrel scuttled up the trunk of the maple tree at the scrunching of his footsteps on a gravel path.

He went to the garden door and turned the handle. It was open and he went into the sitting-room. It was where the refugees had been sleeping and there were mattresses and blankets on the floor.

He called out in a queer, husky voice.

"Father! . . . Mother! . . . Vanda! . . ."

It was Vanda who came to him. For a moment she stared at him, as though he might be an apparition. Then she gave a cry of "Jozef!" and held out her arms to him with a look of joy.

"Oh, Jozef! . . . Thank God! We heard you play. I was certain. . . ."

Jozef stumbled towards her, put his face down on her breast and began to cry like a small boy who had been hurt.

"My dear," she cried, comforting him. "My dearest brother! Our darling Jozef!"

Aunt Krysta and Halina came rushing into the room and

flung their arms about the boy, with tears running from their eyes. It was as though he had returned from the dead.

He knew nothing about what had happened, not even about the advance of the Russians into Poland. He was stunned by the news that his father and mother had gone to Lvov, now in the hands of the Russians.

"Do you know anything about Marta?" he asked presently.

They knew nothing about Marta.

The coming back of Jozef was the first happening to relieve the sense of despair which had overwhelmed them at the news of the capitulation. There was another which rejoiced the heart of Aunt Krysta. Half-way in the afternoon of the next day there was a timid knock at the garden door. It was Vanda who went to open it. Outside stood a young girl of thirteen or so. She was untidy and unwashed, but had shy, smiling eyes.

"Excuse me," she said timidly, "I carry a letter from Colonel Lopalevski."

Vanda looked at her with astonishment.

"Where do you come from? How did you get the letter?"

"From Javorov," answered the girl.

"From Javorov! That's impossible. The Germans are there—they hold all the country round Warsaw."

"I came through their lines," said the girl. "I hid under the hay in a farm cart. Then I walked a long way, creeping past German outposts at night. I had other lifts from farm folk in the columns of refugees. They gave me shelter and food. They were very kind. The Colonel is a prisoner of war in a private house. He gave the letter to my father who is the gardener there. I volunteered to bring it."

Vanda called out excitedly.

"Aunt Krysta. . . . Wonderful news! . . . Brought by an angel or a little heroine."

"That was nothing," said the young girl, who did not look at all like an angel but—one never can tell—more like a heroine because of her keen, vivid, smiling eyes.

Aunt Krysta read some scribbled words on a dirty scrap of paper which then she kissed.

"Praise be to God!" she cried. "My soldier man is alive and well! I was sure of it. Didn't I say so? I should have known otherwise."

She embraced the young girl and looked at the little creature with astonishment as Vanda had done.

"You brought this all the way from Javorov? It's incredible, my child!"

"It was nothing. I wanted to make myself useful, for Poland's sake."

She was the first of those girls, thousands of them, who in the years that followed joined the underground army, carrying messages, acting as secret agents, distributing illicit papers and risking their lives in dangerous ways.

That morning Vanda saw Germans in Warsaw for the first time—only two of them.

"Halina!" she called, "come and look. Don't show yourself."

They looked through a slit in the window blind of Vanda's bedroom. Down in the street were two young Germans. They were taking photographs of the ruined street. One of them laughed as though these ruins amused him.

"Beasts!" said Halina.

"They find it amusing," said Vanda. "Our ruins! Our agony! It's the victors' point of view."

"Aunt Krysta says there are good Germans," said Halina, incredulously.

Vanda smiled.

"Aunt Krysta studied art in Munich and she thinks the best of everybody. I think she has a little pity for the Devil."

CHAPTER XII

THE Germans were now all over Warsaw with headquarters in the Ujazdowska Avenue and other administrative offices in the big buildings which had escaped bombing. There were tanks and armoured cars in the parks and squares. Sentries in steel helmets were posted outside these houses, and the streets resounded with the tramp of feet at the changing of the guard. Intelligence officers, S.S. men, officials, journalists, officers of transport, artillery, aviation and propaganda established themselves in comfortable quarters. They took possession of the wireless station. In due course a civil government for central Poland was proclaimed under the governorship of a man named Hans Frank, ruthless, arrogant, brutal, who delighted in issuing proclamations to the Poles full of menace and dire threats against any citizens who dared to thwart his orders. It took some little time before his cruel policy was revealed, before the firing squads got busy, before the seizure of able-bodied men for deportation to Labour Camps.

Before the fighting ended there was a wild confusion and bewilderment among the tides of refugees on the roads. Those who had been fleeing eastwards heard suddenly that the Russians were advancing from the east, occupying Polish cities, while those who had been trying to reach Warsaw turned at the news of its siege and danger zone. Troops had been ordered from eastern depots to assist in the defence of Warsaw. They found themselves cut off by Russian divisions who took them prisoner. Three hundred thousand men who tried to break away through Hungary when they were caught between the two armies of invasion found their way barred, as General Anders had done with the remnants of his army.

News of all this came to Warsaw by different ways and means —by stragglers from Polish units who had flung away their uniforms and had joined the columns of refugees, by refugees themselves who had talked with Polish officers and men before they were captured, by messages scrawled on the roadside and sent to relatives, in the hope that one day they would arrive. After weeks, and sometimes months, some of them arrived. It was like throwing bottles into the sea after shipwreck to be washed up by the tide, a sea of misery and a tide of uprooted humanity.

Vanda heard of such messages and news but no word came from her father and mother and nothing was known about them. Lvov was behind a wall of silence.

She saw nothing much of Germans in Warsaw. Several times she passed some of them on her way to the hospital but did not look at them, turning her face away.

In one of the wards of the Ujazdovski Hospital Vanda was fetching some bed linen when she heard her name spoken. The ward was filled with sick and wounded men and for a moment she was uncertain from which bed the call came. Then she saw one of the patients raise a hand. She went over and saw that it was Jerzy Boberski, the violinist whom she had brought to her house during the siege.

His eyes had lighted up at the sight of her and he held out his left hand to take hers.

"I'm still alive!" he said, with a smile. "It's good to see you."

"And you!" she answered. "Are you badly wounded?"

He shook his head.

"Not too bad really. My right arm is smashed. So you didn't go to Lvov?"

"I changed my mind," she told him. "I wanted to stay. My father and mother are there. The Russians have taken it."

He nodded.

"Poland is torn in half. We're all prisoners now."

She lingered by his bedside. He looked very handsome with his dark hair against the pillows and there was a smile about his lips when he looked at her.

"I didn't think I should see you again," he said. "That night I said good-bye I had a very strong idea that I was going to be killed!"

"Thank God you weren't!" she said in a low voice.

He put out his left hand and held hers for a moment.

"We must have some more talk. Do you remember how we sat up all night and talked about almost everything?"

"I'm not likely to forget," she said, with a shy laugh.

They had revealed themselves to each other. They had talked without masks on their faces, simply and honestly, and she had liked the things he had said. She had liked his mind. In those hours they had become friends.

"No chance of talking here," she said, "I'm only a serving maid. I only pass through the wards."

"Perhaps afterwards when I get out. I shall look forward to that."

"Is your arm bad?"

"Not very good. My hand is smashed up."

Vanda gave a little cry but not loud enough to disturb the other men in the ward.

"Oh, Jerzy! Your violin. . . ."

For a moment he was silent. Then he gave a faint laugh.

"I know. I shall never play the violin again."

"Oh, I'm sorry." Vanda looked at him and her eyes filled with tears. "My heart bleeds for you. That's terrible."

He answered bravely.

"It doesn't matter much. I should never have been a Kreisler. I was only second-class. I shall have to find other things to do."

"I must go," said Vanda.

She picked up a pile of dirty linen from the floor.

"Come back soon!" he pleaded.

She did not answer but went out of the ward. Her eyes were wet. It was terrible about Jerzy's hand. Never to play the violin again! God ought to have spared him that, if God had pity. Perhaps he had been saved for something else. Perhaps he was needed for something else. Supposing Jozef had lost his hands! Her tears fell on to the dirty linen she was carrying in her arms. She dried them quickly as she went down to the wash-house. Nurses and helpers were not supposed to weep. That would be bad for the patients, bad for discipline, bad for one's own pride.

'Perhaps,' she thought, 'I've been saved from death for some special purpose. Could it be for this work I'm doing? Someone has to do it. It's all a mystery. God takes one and leaves another. God is the great mystery. I wish I could understand. We none of us understand why humanity is tortured, and life is full of agony, and what seems unjust. We just have to cling on to faith and grope our way through darkness. One has to pretend to be brave and cheerful. Perhaps by pretending one becomes brave."

One of the nurses spoke to her.

"I say, can you lend me a hand with these water bottles?"

"Yes, of course."

"I'm dying for a cup of tea," said the nurse. "Funny, isn't it, how one wants what one can't have."

She laughed at this absurd thought.

Vanda laughed back. Was it a pretence, that laugh?

"What you want you can have this time. I'll make you one."

"Angel!" said the nurse with another laugh.

Poland was defeated. Up in the wards were dying men. Jerzy had had his hand smashed. He would never play the violin again. But it was still possible to laugh. It was necessary to laugh even if there were tears in one's heart. So Vanda thought.

CHAPTER XIII

STANISLAV MIRSKI of the Novogrodek cavalry brigade staggered up from the sun-burnt grass where he had been sleeping for half an hour and with the toe of his right boot prodded the rib of his fellow officer, Adam Socha, who still lay asleep, sleeping like a drugged man. Then he stooped down and shook him roughly.

"Wake up! We're moving on."

His friend stirred slightly, opened his eyes for a second—blank, un-seeing eyes—shut them again and slept again.

All around them were sleeping cavalrymen. Their horses, lean-ribbed, and miserable, were trying to find some moisture in the burnt grass or had lain down with their heads drooping. Along the road beyond the grass was a battery of field guns with their metal gleaming in the hot sunshine. The gunners lay beside them like dead men, like the dead that Stanislav had seen during the past few weeks—or was it years—in many battlefields, in burnt-out villages and deserted towns like Garvolin where lay the corpses of men and horses under clouds of flies.

Stanislav had changed in those few weeks. He was no longer the handsome young man with whom the girls had liked to flirt, laughing and debonair. His eyes were deeply sunken. He was unshaven and haggard and dirty with dust from the roads.

"Damn that man!" he said aloud.

He bent down again and shook his brother officer again.

"Wake up, can't you?"

Adam Socha groaned heavily and sat up with dazed eyes.

"Hell! Can't you let a fellow sleep?"

Stanislav laughed harshly.

"You've been sleeping like a hog. The General has just given orders. We must get a move on."

Adam Socha rose to his feet by some kind of miracle, or some spirit inside him which made his body work.

"A ruthless fellow, that General!" he said. "Always on the move. Always sending us into the jaws of death. One of those terrible heroes!"

A faint smile touched his lips which he tried to moisten with his tongue. The cavalrymen were being roused by other officers. Some of them were mounting their horses.

"Where do we go now?" asked Adam presently. "If only we could find a pub at journey's end. I mean a pub with real beer in it instead of dead bodies. I could drink ten bottles of beer without blinking."

"Shut up!" growled Stanislav. "You make me feel as thirsty as a lime-kiln."

"I'm afraid," said Adam thoughtfully, "that this time we're in the bag."

He stared across to a line of dark woods. They were being shelled by German field-guns, invisible behind rising ground.

"I guess that closes our last way out," he said gloomily. Then he laughed.

"Our heroic General will certainly order us to cut our way through—not for the first time. Never say die is his motto, but we die all the same—except you and me, Stanislav. We have charmed lives, old boy."

"The Tenth has been cut to pieces," said Stanislav. "It's the bombing that does us down. There they come—those devils of hell."

High up in the blue streaked a flight of German bombers. Suddenly they swooped low and the swastikas on their wings were plainly visible. Then the crash of exploding bombs shocked

77

through the silence of the woods and fields. Half a mile away the remnants of the heroic Tenth Division—groups of men, marching slowly and painfully—scattered and flung themselves to the ground while the bombers circled round and came back to them and bombed them again, raising fountains of earth and smoke on the low hillside.

A car, in which there was a general and two staff officers, came slowly down the road and stopped by the cavalry column now mounting their tired horses.

The General came out of the car and stood on the roadside and spoke to the senior cavalry officer.

"You must take cover in the woods over there. How are the horses?"

"Dead beat, sir. Can we get through this time?"

General Anders, tall, lean, haggard, limping slightly from a recent wound, answered calmly.

"They're closing in on us. We must try to get through somehow. I'm making for Chelm. We must keep moving south towards Hungary."

"Then it's the end!" said the cavalry officer with a gesture of despair.

"Only the beginning," answered the General. "We shall never give up the struggle—if not in Poland then with our Allies. Don't lose heart, my dear fellow!"

Stanislav heard this and had the favour of a few words from the General himself, who recognized him with a friendly smile.

"Glad to see you again, Mirski. Have you had any sleep?"

"Not enough, sir!" answered Stanislav, standing to attention.

The General laughed.

"I could sleep for a week. But we have to keep awake with our eyes skinned."

He gave another order. The men were all mounted now. They stumbled across a ploughed field. Then the men dismounted again and led their poor beasts into the dark wood.

So it had happened many times during these terrific weeks. For days and nights they had been fighting, riding across country, always harried by enemy aircraft. They had made a feint attack against the Germans along the Lublin road, giving the others time to cross the river Wieprz by one bridge, getting their armoured cars across, and by enormous luck, their supplies and ammunition. But as every day passed the situation worsened, the German army closed in from all sides, their tanks and armoured cars smashing through any line held by the Polish infantry, who had fought with grim heroism—those untrained boys—against overwhelming odds and the irresistible terror of the *Blitzkrieg*.

Stanislav and his friend Adam and other young officers were with General Anders one day at a place called Kozlovka when they were retiring in a south-easterly direction. Stanislav and his comrade had managed to get a shave and bath and felt refreshed after a snatch of sleep.

They were in a farm yard, stinking of pigs and manure. The weather was still glorious with golden sunshine lying on the stubbled fields.

"If only we could stay here for a week!" said Adam.

Stanislav grinned at him.

"I give it half an hour more—with luck. Unless we keep moving we shan't slip through the noose. You said yourself that we're in the bag."

"What's the end of it going to be?" asked Adam. "I hate the idea of being a prisoner. After all death is a long sleep. I prefer a long sleep."

"There's a waking up," said Stanislav. "The soul goes on."

"I'd rather shoot myself than fall into the hands of those swine," said Adam.

"You're getting morbid," said Stanislav, "and you're showing the white feather. Also you seem to forget that we have to keep alive if possible. There's always a chance of escape."

"Stanislav," said Adam presently, in a low voice, "if I go under and you get through will you take a message from me to a girl I know? As a matter of fact I've written her a letter. Will you put it in your wallet for future delivery? I should be deeply grateful."

"Nothing doing," said Stanislav. "You've just as much chance of getting through as I have. I'm a very unsafe postman. Who's the girl anyhow? Do I know her?"

"It's Sophia Solska. You know—the ballet dancer, the most beautiful thing on earth, one of the flowers of life. I'm passionately in love with her."

Stanislav raised his hands in protest.

"Don't talk about girls, or I shall burst into tears! I've put all that side of life out of mind. It's very weakening to the morale."

He grinned again at his brother officer.

"We can't afford to be sentimental," he added. "At the moment we're in a pretty grim situation and our job is to fight our way out by the skin of our teeth with blood-shot eyes."

"You're a heartless devil!" said Adam. "You're one of those terrible fellows who are filled with blood lust and the heroic spirit. I admire you as a soldier, but I detest you as a man."

"You saved my life the other day when my horse was shot under me. You dragged me from under the poor beast, when we were being bombed to hell. Don't you call that heroism, you silly blighter?"

"Good heavens, no!" exclaimed Adam. "I was in a blue funk, but I thought, 'Poor old Stanislav! He's not a bad fellow apart from being a detestable character'."

"Give me a bit more of your blue funk," said Stanislav.

They were of course the closest comrades. They abused each other with the utmost good feeling. But Adam Socha—a sensitive plant—was inclined to be morbid and sentimental until, after a snatch of sleep he became argumentative, ironical and amusing.

It was on that evening at Kozlovka that astounding news came to them. Terrible news. Ghastly news.

It was the General who asked for the wireless to get going. "Let's comb the ether for some scraps of news." he said.

They were cut off from most means of communication. Telephones were no longer functioning. All lines were down. There was no longer any liaison between the retreating divisions. It was an officer named Kuczihski who fell back from the wireless set as if it had shot him.

"General!" he exclaimed in a tragic, stupefied voice, "the unbelievable has happened. It can't be true!"

"I can believe anything," said the General. "What's the worst?"

The worst had happened.

Soviet armies had crossed the Polish frontier and were marching westwards.

Adam Socha gave an audible gasp and his face whitened under its tanned skin. The other officers looked stunned. All eyes were turned upon the General. His face had gone pale but he spoke calmly.

"We all know of the Molotov-Ribbentrop pact. This is the poisoned fruit of it. They're going to carve up Poland between them. Our poor Poland will be torn in half. It will be the crucifixion of our people."

There was excited conversation in low voices. Would the Russians impede the passage of Polish troops? Would they be actively hostile or would they encourage the Poles in their fight against the Germans? They were incalculable, those Russians.

"I have no illusions," said the General. "It's a stab in the back by men without shame. Poland is betrayed. It puts us into a desperate situation. At all costs we must break away south."

At all costs. They were heavy and terrible when they fought

their way across the Lublin-Chelm highway. The remnants of the Tenth Division fighting a rearguard action suffered the heaviest casualties. Then it was the turn of the Novogrodek cavalry brigade ordered to make a breach in the enemy lines for the rest of the army to pass through. Stanislav and Adam were in that attack which surprised the enemy and forced them back, making a gap in their lines. Stanislav's blood-shot eyes were inflamed by dust and smoke. He was incapable of any thought, of any reasonable thought. He was like a drugged man, acting as an automaton. He had no sense of fear, none of grief when men and horses fell dead or writhing in their last agony. He did not feel brave or cowardly, or exalted, or inflamed by hatred and the lust to kill. The hot sunshine parched his lips and his tongue was swollen. Silly ideas, not thoughts, came into his brain—images as in a dream. Once he thought he saw his sister Vanda riding ahead of him. He had sense enough to know that it couldn't be Vanda. For a second or two he was asleep on his horse—dreaming perhaps. His horse stumbled and nearly fell.

Another silly idea came into his head. 'Perhaps I'm dead! Perhaps this is my dead body riding on.' The ribs of a lean horse and a man's riding boot lurched against him. The horses were sweating and gasping. Something struck him on the arm. It was like a blow from an iron bar. He lurched and fell from his saddle. Someone was bending over him. Someone was speaking to him.

"A bullet through the arm. Bad luck!"

It was Adam who had dismounted and was on his knees beside him thrusting something between his teeth, pouring precious liquid down his throat, the elixir of life—water.

"What's happening?" asked Stanislav. "Have we broken through?"

It was the first time he had begun to think.

"We've made a breach," said Adam. "The enemy didn't like the look of us, and I don't blame them, if they took a look at you."

Stanislav's arm felt wet and sharp pains were shooting through it.

Adam was hurting his arm, he was hurting it deliberately like a torturer.

"O Christ!" cried Stanislav with a prayer to God.

"Steady!" said Adam, "I dare say it hurts a bit. But I didn't learn first aid for nothing. I can't let you bleed to death."

"Help me up," said Stanislav. "Why are we waiting here? We must ride on with the others."

He gripped Adam's arm and staggered up. His left arm hung limp and felt on fire.

"Help me on to my horse," he said.

"Take it easy," said Adam. "Our job is done for the time being. We've made the gap. The infantry is coming through. Look at 'em, poor devils. Heroes all, by God!"

The remnants of battalions were on the move in disorderly formation. Men were being carried back on stretchers. Guns were passing with transport wagons, ambulances, field kitchens, the slow crawling tide of retreat. The men—mostly young fellows —looked as though they could hardly walk. Some had their arms round the necks of their comrades. Yet others in better shape were singing some old Polish marching song and came along with their heads up, proudly.

For some reason Stanislav had tears in his eyes. It was the sight of those boys keeping their spirit high in desperate hours.

"And I make a fuss about a wound in my arm!" he muttered to himself.

With Adam's help he climbed on to his horse. Then he turned in his saddle and spoke to his comrade.

"Damn it!" he said. "You've saved my life again. You're making a habit of it."

"Yes," answered Adam. "You're more trouble than you're worth."

They exchanged a grin—a painful grin to Stanislav who had to clench his teeth because of that shooting pain in his arm. That night he had a bullet removed by an army surgeon. He lay in the open on the grass. No chance of getting into a nice comfortable hospital with a beautiful nurse to tend him, or even an ugly one. The breach made in the German line did not remain open for long. Enemy reinforcements closed the gap and the retreating units were heavily shelled. Many units were cut off and taken prisoner under heavy shelling and bombing which caused frightful casualties.

"We must push south towards Hungary," said the General. "Our only chance is speed."

Speed! What speed with horses that could hardly stumble along, with cavalrymen so lacking sleep that they slept in the saddle and had to be awakened by officers riding along the lines. Presently it was impossible to call a halt because the men would have fallen asleep, unable to be roused again. It was open country with few woods until further south. The ground was hard and sunbaked. There was no moisture for the horses, dying of thirst. In the last battle most of the motor transport had been lost. The field guns had to be drawn by four pairs of weary horses who stumbled on, lathered in sweat with glazing eyes. Infantry units marched on with swollen feet. Several times Polish peasants ran out with warning words.

"The Germans are over there! They're holding those villages beyond the cross-roads."

The cavalry took to the fields avoiding the roads.

News came from the peasants that the advance guards of another army were in the neighbourhood.

"The Russians! . . . Swarms of Russians! . . . They're billeted in the farmhouses. . . . Masses of Russians are coming up."

The cavalry brigade was making for a village called Dernaki when they learnt that it was already occupied by Soviet troops.

What about it? How would they behave? Would they bar the way to the retreating troops?

General Anders sent the officer named Kuczinski to the Russian headquarters of this advanced force with a request to pass towards Hungary without fighting. He was robbed of everything he had—wristwatch, field glasses, revolver, pocket book, and he was roughly handled. The request was refused. Suddenly they opened fire on the Polish troops.

Stanislav, standing among a group of officers, gave a shout of rage and raised his unwounded arm to high heaven.

"Bandits! . . . Fiends of hell! . . ."

General Anders himself was filled with a cold passion of rage for this dastardly action. No need to ask now whether the Russians had come as enemies. Their tanks came nosing out of the villages firing their guns. The 9th Battery of the Horse Artillery unlimbered and with a cool nerve knocked out several of these monsters.

On September 27th the artillery fired their last rounds and the rifles their last shots as their General has recorded in tragic words.

"We can do nothing more, gentlemen," he said. "We must split up into small units and find what way we can between the German and Soviet lines. I give no more orders. It is every man for himself, every group must use its own initiative."

His voice broke for a moment.

"Good luck to you all! We may meet again on other fronts. . . . Long live Poland!"

Stanislav and Adam were with the General's group of officers and men who were led by guides through the wooded country approaching the Hungarian frontier, hiding in the dense, trackless forests by day and advancing slowly under cover of darkness.

Now and then there was time for sleep—deep, prolonged, exhausted sleep—and time for talk during those hours in hiding.

Once Adam Socha with his back to a tree looked down at

Stanislav who was stretched out and staring up at the sky through the intertwined branches.

"What's going to happen to us?" he asked. "To what place and what adventure is Destiny leading us?"

Stanislav sat up with his hands clasped round his knees.

"I don't believe much in Destiny. We have free choice, haven't we? It depends on what's inside ourselves—plus a little luck."

"That's Destiny," said Adam. "Luck is another name for it. It will be lucky if we escape from the Germans on one side and the Russians on the other. It will be luck if we don't find ourselves in a Russian concentration camp. In other words we are, to some extent anyhow, the helpless victims of Destiny or Fate."

"Have it your own way," said Stanislav carelessly. "I've mapped out my own course."

"Tell me!" said Adam, curiously.

"If I can get across the mountains to Hungary I shall head for Italy. Having eaten a considerable amount of spaghetti—wonderful thought!—I shall make my way to France. There I shall eat *tripes à la mode de Caen* and enlist in the French army or air force. Then with our Allies—England and France—I shall return to Poland for the final defeat of Hitler and the downfall of Stalin and his gentlemen in the Kremlin."

Adam's eyes lighted up.

"Magnificent!" he exclaimed. "I should like to go the same way."

Another time he spoke gravely.

"If I remain alive, when so many of our friends have been killed, I shall feel that my life must be dedicated to the purpose for which they died—the freedom of Poland."

"Of course!" said Stanislav. "That goes without saying."

And at another time Adam spoke to him in an emotional voice.

"Stanislav, we've been good comrades during these frightful weeks. If we get separated I shall feel lost without you. Thanks for your friendship, my dear fellow!"

Stanislav struck him a light blow on the shoulder.

"That's nonsense! Haven't you saved my life twice? Don't I owe you that and something more. Isn't our friendship sealed in blood and sweat?"

"That's true!" said Adam. "I mean the blood and sweat part of it."

General Anders was with them. He had had to abandon his car for lack of petrol. He remained calm, steady-nerved, resolute, with a refusal to despair, though Poland had been utterly defeated, though the Russians were advancing with masses of men, masses of tanks, masses of guns, though in those dark woods the remnants of his army were hunted men.

They were with him when he was grievously wounded. It was after dark when they were passing the village of Zastovka. They were suddenly attacked by Russians. A group of partisans— Polish irregulars who were still holding out—rushed out of the darkness. Shots rang out. There was hand to hand fighting, fierce and bloody. Suddenly the General gave a cry and fell back bleeding from two wounds into the arms of his officers.

"Leave me," he said, faintly. "Look after yourselves."

They would not leave him, but carried him out of the village until they laid him down. He was bleeding in a fearful way.

"Gentlemen," he said. "I give you an order—an order, you understand. You must press on to Hungary. . . . It's your only chance. . . . For Poland's sake. . . ."

He raised one hand feebly, gave a smile, and said, "Good-bye and good luck."

He was taken prisoner by the Russians and was treated courteously for a time, having his wounds dressed in hospital. Then he was flown to Moscow, questioned courteously again, by high ranking officers until one day he was led into the Lubianka prison and was in the hands of the N.K.V.D., the secret police of dreadful fame. In this house of whispers and enforced silence and beatings, torture and questioning under bright lights— always being questioned—questioned in the middle of the night or for hours by day—this soldier, this hero of Poland, this leader of a future army fighting on many fronts, endured all things with an unbroken spirit, as he has told.

Stanislav and Adam and other comrades plunged into the dense forests of the Carpathian mountains on the other side of which lay the plains of Hungary. No word came back from them.

CHAPTER XIV

STANISLAV and his friend Adam had to be cunning and wary in escaping through the Russian net, but they found good friends among the Polish peasants who gave them food and lodging at the risk of their own lives. Several times they came at night into villages occupied by Russian troops. The urge of hunger made them take this risk after hiding in woods without food for as long as two days. They were unshaven and dirty and had changed into the clothes of a peasant who had given them his old trousers and jackets with touching generosity.

"You have fought for Poland," he said. "These old rags are a poor reward but all I can give to two of our soldiers."

Those peasants were simple and primitive but had a kind of traditional chivalry. Anyone harbouring Polish soldiers and helping them to escape was liable to be shot, but never once did they refuse to open their doors when Stanislav and Adam sought shelter with them.

"It's dangerous here," said one of them who kept a small inn. "This place is crawling with Russians. You had better go before you get caught."

"We're famished," said Stanislav. "We're frozen to the bone."

The man hesitated and then shrugged his shoulders.

"It's your risk as well as mine. There's a barn at the back. Hide yourselves under the straw. Don't show a light. My daughter will bring you some food. If they find you we shall all be shot."

The two friends found their way to the barn by the light of the moon. Snow had fallen and was now hard frozen. The branches of the bare trees blackly etched against the moonlit sky were touched by the snow. Each twig glistened as though with tiny diamonds.

"I'm frozen stiff," said Adam. "I can hardly walk. My very brain is frozen. I can't think or feel."

"Get under the hay," said Stanislav.

They buried themselves under the hay, frozen like the ground around them, but in a little while it gave them bodily warmth.

They spoke in whispers now and then.

"I shall have to eat my boots if they don't bring us food," said Adam.

"I'm past hunger," said Stanislav. "I only have a dull ache in my belly."

A light gleamed upon them in a flickering way.

Two women came into the barn with a lantern, one a middle-aged woman with greying hair and a leathery face, the other a young girl. Both wore shawls over their heads. They were carrying tins from which there came a hot fragrance of steaming soup.

"Here you are, dearies," said the elder woman. "Don't make too much noise when you're eating it. There are six Russians in the inn, getting drunk."

"Drunk already," said the girl.

"Certainly you are two angels," said Stanislav. "I think you come from heaven!"

The girl spluttered with laughter.

"I don't think I look like an angel," she said, in a low voice.

Adam roused himself in the straw and grabbed at the tin of soup.

"You're the most beautiful creatures I've seen for years," he exclaimed. "If I weren't under this hay I would kiss your feet."

The old woman gave a cackling laugh.

"You must be gentlefolks," she said. "They always like a bit of fun."

"Oh, wonderful!" said Adam, after drinking some of the soup. "The nectar of the gods! The elixir of life!"

"Keep quiet!" said the woman. "Those Russians have long ears, drunk or sober."

The two women crept out of the barn extinguishing the light.

An hour later the two friends heard footsteps and buried themselves under the hay.

A man's voice spoke to them quietly.

"You'd best be moving on. You mustn't stay here till morning. My daughter will guide you on the way by footpaths and tracks, avoiding the road. I expect you're bound for Hungary like the others. They keep coming. It's getting more risky. The Russians have stiffened up their frontier guard."

He thrust two loaves into their hands when they had roused themselves.

"These will keep you going," he said.

Stanislav shook hands with him.

"How can I thank you?"

"No thanks are needed," said the man, embarrassed by any thanks.

"God bless you," said Adam. "That's all I can say and I say it with all my heart."

Outside the barn the man's daughter was waiting. She was a girl of sixteen or so with a sturdy peasant look and bright eyes peeping out through the shawl which was pulled tightly about her face and shoulders.

"I'm your guide," she said. "Through that gate is a track which leads to a field path. Go along the stream which is frozen hard."

They followed her and presently she walked between them talking in a childish way, but talking terrible things.

"The Russians have captured thousands of Polish prisoners. They don't give them food for a long time. Some of them die on the roads."

"The Russians ill-treat our women. I have to hide when they

come to the inn. You can hear the screams of the women in the village."

"Sometimes they're good-natured. In one cottage they nursed the baby and sang songs to the other brats. One of them played the accordion.

"There was a fight in the inn. The Russians shot my brother who tried to defend the woman who was serving them."

"Shot him dead?" asked Adam.

"No, only through the arm. Then they were sorry, and bandaged him up and gave him vodka. They're very funny, the Russians—cruel one time and kind the next."

After walking two miles she pointed to the south.

"Take that path. It goes up and up to the mountains. You'll have to get a guide across them to Hungary. You'll come to an inn called the White Eagle. It belongs to my uncle. He takes Polish soldiers across the frontier. They haven't caught him yet but one day they'll find out and then they'll shoot him."

They found the inn called the White Eagle, a remote and poor-looking little shack up the mountain path. They were afraid to approach it in daylight and hid behind an outhouse until the night came. They talked in low voices.

"It looks as though we might be free men," said Adam.

He made the sign of the cross over himself and then laughed.

"It would be horrible if we were caught on the last stage!"

Stanislav spoke of his family.

"I hope to God they're still alive. I haven't heard a word since the war began. They may be dead. Or if they're alive they may think I'm dead. I hope young Jozef came through. He wasn't made to be a soldier. He was a musician to his finger-tips. He lived for music."

"Poland is crucified," said Adam presently. "Russia has played the part of Judas."

"It was a stab in the back," said Stanislav fiercely. "It is one of the foulest acts in history."

"Stanislav," said Adam after a while, "you and I must have been saved for some special purpose. I find it rather frightening. What can I do to make my life worth while? We're dedicated men, you and I, my friend."

"We can fight for Poland," said Stanislav. "What else?"

"It's more than a fight for Poland," said Adam. "It's a fight for the freedom of the soul everywhere, among all men. It's a battle against the powers of darkness."

"I'm a Pole," said Stanislav. "I think only of Poland."

"I should be glad to think that I am a soldier for humanity," said Adam, "and for civilization, debased and debauched by Hitler and Stalin."

Strange conversation between two men, dirty, unshaven, looking like scarecrows, numb with the bitter cold on this mountain height.

"Time to try our luck," said Stanislav, when the sky darkened.

They went to the inn on the side of a mountain track. There was a light inside the front room. A dog barked fiercely. Stanislav pushed the door open and saw a family seated at table. The heat of the room came in a hot waft to his face. An elderly man rose from the table, stared at them and then gave a gruff laugh.

"What, more of you? Can't I get any peace?"

He hushed down his dog which was hostile to the strangers.

"We're two Polish officers," said Stanislav. "We want you to be our guide across the Carpathian mountains into Hungary."

The man gave his gruff laugh again.

"They all say that! And being a good Pole and a patriot I show them the way at the risk of my own life, you understand? I'm already under suspicion. The police have been here three times, snooping around, asking me questions, forcing me to tell lies for which I ask God to pardon me."

A woman's voice broke in.

"This must be the last time. What's going to happen to me and the children if my man is shot? You soldiers don't seem to think of that. You think only of yourselves. You're a shameless lot."

"Hold your tongue, wife," said the man, sternly. "We must think only of Poland. I was a soldier under Pilsudski. I can't turn traitor now."

"Poland! . . . Poland!" cried the woman. "There's no more Poland. We must accept the fact, with the Germans on one side and the Russians on the other. There's no hope for us. We must look after our own lives and save the children. In this district we should make friends with the Russians who are now our masters. If we're wise we shall do that."

"Never!" shouted her husband. "And I'm ashamed of you for talking like that in front of Polish officers."

He turned to Stanislav and spoke in a tone of apology.

"You must excuse her. It's fear that has got hold of her. Fear for me. Fear for the children. You understand?"

"Perfectly," said Stanislav. "In her place I should be frightened too. If I had children. . . ."

"Sit at our table," said the man. "We have but simple fare but your hunger will spice it. . . . Wife, serve the gentlemen with this potato soup and get the bread out of the oven."

Round the table four children stared at the two strangers with big solemn eyes.

"We must make the journey by night," said the man presently. "We'd better start as soon as you've eaten."

Adam gave a groan.

"I should like to sleep in a bed," he cried. "I should like to stay in the warmth of this house. It will be as cold as death on the mountains."

"It will be as cold as death if you stay," said the man. "No fun to be taken out and shot. That's likely to happen if you stay. More than likely. And I should be shot with you."

An hour later he led them up a mountain track.

"How far?" asked Adam.

"Five hours, climbing."

"God help us," cried Adam.

At the end of four hours he collapsed in the snow.

"Leave me!" he said to Stanislav, "I can't climb any farther. I'm done. Leave me here in the snow. I implore you."

"Get up," said Stanislav, sternly. "If you lie down you'll die."

"I don't mind dying," said Adam. "Leave me, my dear friend."

"He's in bad shape," said their guide. "We must keep him walking. Hi! up there! Up!"

Together Stanislav and the guide hauled up Adam and put his arms round their necks and dragged him along between them. Three times they fell with him and staggered up again.

"In half an hour," said the guide, "we shall come to the last cottage in Poland. With luck your friend can rest there. But we must keep our eyes open for the frontier guards. There must be no talking when we get near."

There was a friend of his in the cottage where Adam collapsed on the floor.

"He can't stay here," said the other man. "The frontier guards are sure to come at dawn."

"He's near dead with cold," said his friend.

They dragged Adam upstairs into an attic room. It stank of onions which lay there in heaps. There was no heat in the room but it was a shelter from the outside air.

"I'll cover you over with sacks," said the man. "They're not likely to search up here. I'll bring some brandy."

Brandy! A few drops of it went down the throats of Adam and Stanislav like some ethereal fire, life restoring. Adam thawed out and lost the numbness in his limbs and didn't want to die.

Some baked potatoes were brought up to them by their host who was gruff, abrupt, but good-natured.

Before dawn their guide aroused them from heavy sleep.

"Time to go. Only five hundred yards or so."

"I want to go on sleeping," said Adam. "I want to sleep for weeks and weeks. I want to keep warm."

Stanislav hauled him out of bed.

"Your body gets in the way of your intelligence," he said.

It was still dark when they left the cottage.

"No talking!" the guide reminded them in a whisper.

It was still snowing. That perhaps was lucky. It obliterated the track of their footsteps. No frontier guards could see them through the heavy flakes, blinding them as they walked.

The guide led them along a track through the edge of a forest. The ground was falling away from them. It was going downhill. The guide halted and spoke above a whisper.

"Down there is Hungary. You're safe."

Down there were the Hungarian plains. Down there was the way to Italy, to France, to England, to a Polish army in exile, to future battles on many fronts in which Polish soldiers fought with heroism, unrecognized, unrewarded, except by their brothers-in-arms, and betrayed by the leaders of those for whom they had fought and died.

Stanislav raised his hands high.

"Freedom!" he cried.

"Good luck to you," said the guide.

He returned down the path to the cottage. A year later he was shot in his own backyard.

CHAPTER XV

FOUR German officers were billeted in the house of the Mirski's in St. Theresa Street. They demanded the use of the big *salon* and two bedrooms. It was Aunt Krysta who received them on an afternoon when Vanda and Halina were at the hospital.

They were all officers of the Intelligence Corps, as Aunt Krysta knew by their badges. The senior of them was a tall, spectacled man who in civilian clothes might have been a schoolmaster or scientist. He introduced himself as Lieutenant Holzapfel, with a slight bow and a click of the heels. The others were younger men who might have been undergraduates in uniform, smart, well-fed, and with a touch of Nazi swagger. They behaved correctly, and Lieutenant Holzapfel was conciliatory in a cold formal way.

"We regret having to disturb you. We shall endeavour to give you as little trouble as possible in the occupation of your rooms."

Aunt Krysta answered him in German which she spoke fluently.

"It is, of course, useless for me to object to your presence here, but you will understand that as a Polish family we don't welcome it. You have come as enemies and we shall behave accordingly."

Lieutenant Holzapfel blinked his eyes behind his horn-rimmed glasses and said, "*Natürlich.*"

Aunt Krysta caught the glance of one of the younger men, a good-looking boy, she thought, with very fair hair, cut short, and grey-blue eyes in which there was a faint smile. He had been looking round the room, studying the pictures and some eighteenth-century miniatures above the fireplace.

One of the others, a stout, broad-shouldered fellow, with big hands and feet, opened the piano with a grin, touched the notes without striking them, and then shut it again.

'No doubt he plays the piano,' thought Aunt Krysta. 'Jozef will want to murder him if he plays badly.'

Lieutenant Holzapfel spoke to her again.

"We shall require a list of all the members of your family and staff, and of any friends who may reside here. The names will also be taken of any visitors who may come to see you. You will doubtless understand that this is a necessary formality for security reasons."

"It seems to me quite unnecessary," said Aunt Krysta, "but I know that Germans like that kind of thing, especially when they invade other people's countries."

Lieutenant Holzapfel blinked his eyes again and for the first time his mouth hardened into a sulky look.

"We wish to behave with courtesy but that depends upon the way in which we are received. I think it necessary to remind you that this part of Poland is under our military occupation and that the inhabitants have to obey our orders and regulations."

"If I know anything of my countrymen," said Aunt Krysta, calmly, "you will find it very difficult to enforce your authority. We are a very high-spirited people."

Lieutenant Holzapfel made a slight gesture as though to dismiss this subject.

"We shall be absent during the daytime. Our breakfast and

dinner will be provided by our own orderlies. They will need the use of your kitchen."

"That will lead to a lot of trouble," said Aunt Krysta, dryly.

Lieutenant Holzapfel shrugged his shoulders slightly.

"That will be unfortunate."

"May I ask how long you intend to remain here?" asked Aunt Krysta.

Lieutenant Holzapfel raised his hands in a vague way and gave a wintry smile.

"That is very uncertain. The Army of Occupation is likely to remain in Poland for some years. Western Poland is now a province of the German Reich."

"Well, we shall see," said Aunt Krysta. "There are no certainties in this world—not even for the Germans."

Again she caught the glance of the fair-haired young man and saw that look of amusement in his eyes. He was not a bad-looking boy, she thought. Once as a young girl she had danced with German boys like this and had even fallen in love with one who was afterwards killed in the First World War. She had liked the Germans in those young days. They had been gay and good-humoured. How was it possible that they should have changed so much, making war on other peoples, ruthlessly and brutally, without pity, and without chivalry, under their madman Hitler?

That evening she told the news about these four German officers to Vanda and Halina.

They heard it with consternation.

"How horrible!" cried Halina. "How frightful!"

"They will spy on us," said Vanda. "We shall have no privacy. There will always be an abominable feeling of their presence in the house."

"They're not bad types," said Aunt Krysta. "One of them seems to have a sense of humour. They behaved correctly, I must say, though I was very rude to them. They're not fighting soldiers and I expect they do the dirty work for that dreadful creature Goebbels."

Halina looked at her accusingly.

"Aunt, if you ever talk to them, if you ever get friendly with them, I will never speak to you again."

"Bless the child!" exclaimed Aunt Krysta. "Do you think I'm going to embrace them? They're the enemies of Poland. I'm not likely to forget that."

"It's very dangerous for Jozef," said Vanda, anxiously. "What are we going to do about that?"

"I think he'll be safe for a little while," said Aunt Krysta.

"He can pass as a refugee, of whom there are thousands in Warsaw."

A few nights later Jozef came home from some mysterious work he was doing which kept him away from home all day. He suddenly turned pale and gripped the arms of the chair in which he was sitting. Someone was playing the piano—his piano. Someone was rattling out Strauss waltzes in a loud, noisy way, but not badly played.

Jozef was sitting with his aunt and two sisters in one of the bedrooms which they turned into a sitting-room. Vanda and Halina were wearing their fur coats because the room was without a fire, for lack of fuel.

"Hell and damnation!" said Jozef in a low, fierce voice.

"It's an outrage!" cried Halina. "It's an insult! How dare they make such a row in this house? They have no decency, these Germans."

"I used to like those waltzes," said Aunt Krysta, mildly. "I used to dance to them. The *Beautiful Blue Danube!*"

She looked across at Jozef whose face was contorted with rage.

"I'm sorry, my dear. It's hard on you that one of our enemies should be playing your piano."

"I can't bear it!" answered Jozef, in a voice of anguish. "If he doesn't stop I'll strangle him."

He put both hands to his ears to prevent himself from hearing this accursed music. Then suddenly he strode out of the room and they heard his footsteps going down the back stairs.

They now used the back stairs leading down to the garden door. Previously Vanda had used the main staircase several times, and twice had met one of the young Germans coming down. It was the young fair-haired one with grey-blue eyes. He had waited on the landing to let her pass and had said, *"Guten Morgen"*. She had felt herself get pale and cold and had passed him silently like a white ghost. Every evening she could hear them, talking and laughing in a boisterous way and every night to the disgust and rage of Jozef one of them played the piano while another sang, *Lili Marlene* and German student songs, very cheerful and rowdy, or sentimental ballads which were even more disgusting to the two girls.

"How can they be sentimental—wallowing in sentiment—when they're deporting thousands of our young men for forced labour or starving them in concentration camps?"

So Halina said.

One afternoon when the Germans were out Jozef came home in a black mood. Instead of going upstairs into his own room he stood at the door of the *salon* for a moment and then went in. There were signs of German occupation. On the mantelshelf were photographs of German girls. A silver cigarette case lay on one of the tables. Some long-necked bottles of German wine were on another table. A pile of newspapers—the *Volkische Beobachter*—was on the sofa.

Jozef drew a deep breath and there was a smouldering fire of rage behind his eyes. He went over to the piano and opened it up so that he could see the strings. For several moments he stared at them. He had played on this piano since his boyhood. He had loved it. It was his most precious treasure, opening up the world of music in which his soul had been enchanted. He thrust his hand into a pocket and pulled out a clasp-knife which he opened. He looked like a man about to commit a murder. He was about to commit a murder. He slashed at the strings and cut half a dozen of them so that they snapped with a loud twanging. His face was dead white and his hand shook when he shut the piano again and crept out of the room.

He went upstairs to the bedroom which had been turned into a sitting-room. Aunt Krysta was there doing some needlework. She looked up and was startled by the sight of Jozef's face, white, with a look of anguish.

"Jozef!" she cried. "What's the matter? What has happened? Are you ill?"

"Yes, I'm ill," he answered. "I'm mad. I've killed something. I've killed something that belonged to my own soul."

Suddenly he burst into tears.

The next day Lieutenant Holzapfel spoke to Aunt Krysta on the landing outside the *salon*. He had a grim look and spoke harshly.

"The piano has been broken. Someone has cut the strings. It is abominable. It will have to be punished if we find the culprit."

"It must have been an accident," said Aunt Krysta. "Or perhaps the cold weather snapped the strings. It happens sometimes."

"I can hardly accept that explanation," he answered, less fiercely. "My friend, Lieutenant Hevel, is deeply distressed."

Nothing more was heard of that incident. No more noisy music was heard upstairs until some months later the piano was mended.

CHAPTER XVI

JOZEF heard that Marta was to be found in the Actresses' Café where she was acting as a waitress. It had recently been opened in a big house in the Ujadovska Avenue by many well-known actresses of the Warsaw theatres who waited on their guests and customers, and consisted of a large drawing-room, a lounge, a terrace and garden. There was no sign-post outside and it looked a private residence with the atmosphere of a country manor house.

Jozef had heard of Marta's whereabouts from Halina who had met her in the street and gave her the news that Jozef was alive. She blushed very deeply and for a moment her eyes were filled with tears.

"I'm glad!" she said simply. "My father and brother were both killed in the battles round Warsaw."

Jozef lost no time in going to see her but in a workman's clothes felt shy and awkward as he entered the café where there was a little crowd of well-dressed people and those pretty actresses serving at the tables. He saw Marta at the far end of the room and went over to her and spoke in a low voice.

"Marta! I've come back. It's a bit of a miracle. Did you pray for me?"

She looked even more shy than he was.

"Of course! But I prayed also for my father and brother who were killed. My prayers were no good."

"I want to kiss you," said Jozef, ignoring this theological mystery. "Where can I kiss you?"

"You can't," she told him firmly, but with a smile at the corners of her lips. "If I were you I wouldn't stay here. This place has been visited already several times by the German police. They suspect it as being a rendezvous for the Secret Army."

Jozef looked startled for a moment.

"What do you know about the Secret Army?"

She glanced over her shoulder nervously and put her fingers to her lips.

"Aren't we all in it?" she asked. "Women as well as men?"

"One doesn't talk about it," said Jozef. He changed the subject abruptly.

"How beautiful you look, Marta? When you move it's like music."

"Go!" she said urgently. "It's dangerous here. The Gestapo is arresting young men—thousands of them in Poznan."

"I'm perfectly safe," he told her. "My papers defy suspicion. I'm a packer in the German newspaper office and I'm one of the Volksdeutsche."

She stared at him and went a little pale.

"You a traitor? Working for the enemy?"

He smiled at her and said, "They think so!"

His next words were spoken pleadingly.

"Do you think I could have a cup of coffee? I want to sit and watch you."

"Please go!" she urged, but he took an empty chair at one of the little tables and one of the pretty actresses brought him his coffee.

He had taken a chair next to a priest, who had been talking to two or three people who had now left the café. He was a handsome man of middle age, with something mystical in his eyes though he had a friendly smile for Jozef, whom he had known as a boy making his first Communion. It was Father Paul of Warsaw.

"How's your beautiful sister Vanda?" he asked.

"Is she beautiful?" asked Jozef.

The priest laughed.

"That's just like a brother!"

He lowered his voice.

"When do you take the oath?"

"This evening," said Jozef. "How are things going, Father?"

The priest glanced over his shoulder, as Marta had done. There was no danger among these people seated at the little tables. He knew most of them. But he kept his voice low.

"It's quite marvellous! Everybody is getting into the Underground movement. They come to me asking how they can help, how they can join. The nation refuses to be defeated—young men and girls, old men and women, intellectuals and artisans. They are ready to die, if need be, for their country and for their faith."

"What about the Volksdeutsche?" asked Jozef. "There are many dirty dogs."

Poles of German ancestry, or those who might claim to have German ancestry, were permitted to apply for German nationality and were treated as 'second-class German citizens' with promises of immunity from being transported to concentration camps. Many people driven by fear, and others sympathetic to the

Germans because of their own origin, were taking advantage of this offer.

Father Paul smiled and raised his hands slightly.

"Poor people! Some yield to terror. I don't blame them but there are many Volksdeutsche who are working for us and we're providing them with papers—and the identities which they take over from dead persons. We're already getting very expert as forgers of passports. By this means we're helping to get many refugees across the frontiers into Roumania and Hungary—lots of ex-soldiers. Dangerous work!"

He laughed again and then a moment later that mystical look came into his eyes.

"There has been a renaissance of faith in Poland. The churches are overcrowded. We priests—thank God—have the confidence of our people and we shan't let them down. We too are prepared for martyrdom. We shall wear that crown gladly whatever the agony."

Jozef looked at him with a smile.

"You're one of the heroes! I'm only a raw recruit in the Secret Army. In fact I haven't yet taken the oath. I'm not enrolled."

A middle-aged man with a thin, haggard face and very piercing eyes in which there was a look of extreme will-power and intensity of purpose came over to the table where Jozef was sitting with Father Paul of Warsaw.

Jozef rose to his feet like a soldier in the presence of a high-ranking officer.

"Sit down!" said the newcomer sharply.

He spoke a few words to the priest.

"I want to have a talk with you. But not here of course. Where can we meet?"

"The Journalists' Café," said Father Paul. "It's fairly safe at the moment and they're all our friends there."

The priest's friend smiled grimly.

"No place is safe for me! I'm a hunted man. I never sleep twice in the same house. Well, I'll see you at eleven tomorrow. I daren't stay here more than a few minutes. It's liable to be searched, I'm told."

He shook hands with Father Paul and said, "You're doing fine work, like all our priests."

"God bless you!" said Father Paul, holding out his hand.

As the mysterious man was leaving the table Jozef rose to his feet again smartly, and again the man said, "Sit down!"

As though to soften this command he put his hand on Jozef's

shoulder and said, "One can't be too careful, my young friend, you must learn to be discreet and fail to recognize those who don't want to be known."

He raised his hand and went out of the café.

"You know him?" asked Father Paul.

Jozef nodded.

"A friend of my uncle, Colonel. . . ."

"Hush!" said the priest. "No names, please!"

It was Colonel Komorovski, who was at that time assistant of General 'Grot'-Rovecki, the Commander-in-Chief of the Polish Home Army. With untiring energy Colonel Komorovski collaborated with his commander in the organization and direction of the Resistance movement. After the death of 'Grot', who was captured by the Gestapo and executed in the Moabit prison in Berlin, General 'Bor'-Komorovski was appointed the Commander-in-Chief, and with unflinching courage and passionate hatred of the Germans, who had invaded his country, he carried on this dangerous and responsible task. It was a fight against a reign of terror inflicted by the orders of Hans Frank who had declared that Poland was to be 'an intellectual desert'.

Jozef was able to speak again to Marta—a few words only. He had watched her waiting at the tables. She moved with the poise of a dancer. In his eyes she was the most beautiful girl on earth with her delicate features cut like a Greek cameo, and her slim grace of body.

"Where can I see you?"

"It's very difficult. In the Park one evening before the curfew."

"Tomorrow?"

She nodded.

"I'll try."

He would have said, 'this evening' but for an oath he had to take.

It was in a cellar below a bombed house not far from his own in St. Theresa Street.

There were five men there among whom was Father Paul of Warsaw. The leader of this company was a middle-aged man who had been a professor at the University. He welcomed Jozef with a friendly grip of the hand.

"You know what you're letting yourself in for?" he asked with a smile. "It's no child's game. It may mean death. You are ready for that?"

"I'm no hero," said Jozef, "but I'll take the risk."

"We act in groups of five," said the professor. "Each member of a group knows only his four fellow members, each in turn forming a new group of five. No one must be known by his real name. We all must use pseudonyms."

"I know," said Jozef. "I'm already working in the Underground under cover of being in the office of the German newspaper."

"Good!" exclaimed the professor. "Excellent! You will be a useful recruit in the headquarters of enemy propaganda. Now I will ask you to take the oath."

He took a silver crucifix from Father Paul and held it before Jozef.

It was a solemn and formidable oath. Jozef found himself with a quickened heart-beat as he recited the words. It was no child's play—no play-acting. It was the dedication of his life to the cause of Poland. Would he have the courage to go through with it? He was a pianist. He had devoted himself to music. He had found life's beauty in that vocation. He was not like his brother Stanislav, athletic, hearty, devil-may-care, a born soldier. He was one of the sensitive plants—one of the romantics perhaps. He loved Marta as Romeo loved Juliet. But this was a grim set of words he was asked to repeat. These words might mean a concentration camp or a firing squad. The Germans were already shooting hostages chosen at random for acts of sabotage by the Underground.

He saw Father Paul's eyes fixed on him with an encouraging smile. These other men had already taken the oath. He couldn't funk it. It was necessary to sacrifice everything for freedom's sake. His voice faltered for a moment as he repeated the words, then he felt a kind of exaltation. He was joining a secret army, he was being received into a noble company, an order of chivalry, the defenders of the very soul of Poland.

He repeated the words:

"Before God the Almighty, before the Holy Virgin Mary, Queen of the Crown of Poland, I put my hand on this holy cross, the symbol of martyrdom and salvation, and I swear that I will defend the honour of Poland with all my might, that I will fight to liberate her from slavery, notwithstanding the sacrifice of my own life, that I will be absolutely obedient to my superiors, that I will keep the secret whatever the cost may be."

The professor who was swearing in this new recruit spoke a few words in a solemn voice.

"I receive thee among the soldiers of Freedom. Victory will be thy reward. Treason will be punished by death."

The professor handed the crucifix to Father Paul who came over and put his hand on Jozef's shoulder.

"Well done, Jozef! We're proud to have you. We know you will do good work. You've already done it! It was when you played Chopin in the last broadcast before the Germans took it over. It was like the spirit of Poland asserting to the world the loveliness of her genius and her civilized ideals still uncrushed. I wept at the sound of it."

"I shall never play the piano again," said Jozef. "Beauty has gone out of the world."

"No, no!" cried the priest. "We must cling to that. We need it more now than ever. You must keep on playing. Perhaps that is your work for our poor Poland."

"I've smashed my piano," said Jozef. "But it doesn't matter now."

His new name in the Underground was to be 'Róg'.

CHAPTER XVII

VANDA's father and mother had an exhausting and perilous journey to the beautiful old city of Lvov. German aircraft flying low machine-gunned the train when it halted at a junction and all passengers had to get out. There seemed to be no chance of another train and Dr. Mirski hired a cart and horses from a peasant who agreed to drive them to Lvov. But it was necessary to make a long détour as there was fighting near Lvov at Grodek, which they had to avoid by taking to the country roads. When they arrived in a suburb of Lvov groups of people were in the streets looking frightened and talking in whispers.

Dr. Mirski spoke to a man when the farm-cart stopped.

"What is happening?"

The man shrugged his shoulders.

"The Germans have cleared out. The Russians are coming in. One legion of devils depart for another to arrive."

"The Russians? What do you mean, my dear fellow?"

"They're marching this way," said the man. "That is to say they're on the way with their tanks and armoured cars. They're deep into Poland already according to the wireless news."

Dr. Mirski turned pale.

"I refuse to believe it," he said harshly. "Have you all gone mad in Lvov?"

"The whole world is mad," said the man. "The Devil is loose."

Mirski's wife clutched his arm.

"If it's true, we're lost," she cried. "I wish we had stayed with the girls. God have mercy on us!"

"It's a wild rumour," said her husband. "It's unbelievable. Nothing was said to us on our journey."

They had travelled in a carriage with other refugees from Warsaw, two professors of the University of Lvov, with their wives and children, an old lady and gentleman who had abandoned their home in Poznan, a young girl going to join her grandparents after her father and mother had been killed in the air-raids. Not one of these people knew that Russia was advancing into Poland. It just couldn't be true.

Polish soldiers who looked like stragglers from a beaten army were talking to the civilians. A battery of field guns drawn by lean-ribbed horses came to a halt in one of the squares. They had just arrived. Refugees were encamped outside the station and in one of the squares.

There was a tide of them both ways now, as Antoni Mirski soon came to know.

He spoke to his wife on the way to her mother's house and estate on the outskirts of the city.

"It was our duty to come because of your dear mother. Whatever happens we shall know that we acted for the best. I still cannot believe this story about the Russians."

His wife clasped his hand and said, "I'm terrified."

"We must pray for courage," said her husband. "You have never lacked that, my dear. As a young wife when I was fighting under Pilsudski. . . ."

"Then I was young," she cried. "I have no courage left. I feel very ill. It's the horror of it all. We go from one horror to another."

He had had trouble with her in the train. She had been very angry about Vanda and Halina. She would never forgive them, she said. But this was worse than anger. She was a frightened and despairing woman. She looked very ill indeed, sitting there in the farm-cart white-faced, with fear in her eyes. He had never known her like this until the war began and her two sons had left her. She had been a cheerful, bustling woman, a wonderful mother and loyal wife. All this was too hard for her. Terror had taken hold of her.

They drove past the lodge gate of the park belonging to her mother, the Countess Volska. As a young man, Dr. Mirski had first met his future wife there and had fallen in love with her at first sight. They had gone out riding in this park. They had danced in the big ballroom of this house with a crowd of young people—students from the University of Lvov, young officers from the garrison, artists, poets, painters. All that seemed like a dream now. Three weeks of war had blotted out all that for ever.

"Marietta," said her husband. "We mustn't frighten your mother. She is very old."

His wife nodded and he saw her dab her face with a little colour from her handbag. It was a sign of returning will-power perhaps of returning courage.

The house was old, with a classical portico of the eighteenth century and tall windows and a flight of stone steps to the terrace. Nothing had changed outwardly and here in the park was quietude and a look of peace, except for the tracks of gun wheels on the lawn in front and some trampled bushes.

An old manservant opened the door and his eyes lighted up at the sight of them, having known them both as boy and girl.

"Thank God you have come!" he said in a tremulous voice. "Madam has been anxious about you. We have had many refugees from Warsaw."

"How is my mother?" asked Marietta.

The old manservant raised his hands.

"She's wonderful. She shows no sign of fear."

The Countess Volska came into the hall at the sound of these voices. She was white-haired, tall, thin, erect, still with a trace of the beauty which had made her famous in Lvov as a young woman, but now wrinkled and faded.

"My dears!" she cried. "So you have come through safely, thank heaven! but where are the two girls?"

"We will tell you later," said Dr. Mirski.

"Mother!" cried Marietta, kissing the old lady on both cheeks and clasping her in her arms, and trying not to weep.

"Now, my dear," said the old Countess, "don't shed tears or anything like that. We must set a good example to the others."

She patted her daughter as though comforting a young girl in distress.

"Things are very unpleasant," she said, "but we're not going to show the white feather. Polish women aren't like that, nor Polish men either—except old Jan here who trembles like an aspen leaf."

"Mother, you're wonderful!" cried her daughter.

"Not a bit of it," said the Countess Volska. "Just an ordinary old woman trying to be brave."

She led them into her big drawing-room—the room in which Dr. Mirski had first danced with his future wife. There were several people in it. Two of them were asleep, though it was not yet night. There were bags and bundles dumped on the Persian rugs and polished boards. Others were talking together in low voices. Two men rose from their chairs as the old Countess came in holding her daughter by the hand.

"Marietta!" cried one of the ladies, rushing forward to embrace her.

It was one of the elderly women who had joined the exodus from Warsaw a few days previously. Her husband, who was an old friend of Dr. Mirski's, clasped his hand and spoke emotionally.

"The situation is terrible. We're between the devil and the deep sea. The Russians are only a few miles from Lvov. They'll be here very soon. I regret having left Warsaw."

"It is true about the Russians?" asked Dr. Mirski. "I find it unbelievable."

"Would to God it were untrue! Poland is doomed."

His hand trembled as he fumbled for a cigarette out of a gold case. He had been the owner of a steamship line on the Vistula.

The terror of the Russians was worse than that of the Germans. Some of those who had taken refuge with the Countess Volska left her in the hope of getting to Hungary or Roumania—in most cases a vain hope after tragic and desperate journeys on the road. For many of them journey's end were Russian concentration camps, where they starved and died.

It was on the third day after the arrival of Dr. Mirski and his wife that the house of the Countess Volska was entered by Russian soldiers.

The old manservant, Jan, came into the *salon* where his mistress was sitting with her daughter and son-in-law.

"They have come," he said in a tremulous voice.

For two nights now there had been sounds of shooting in Lvov and one of the servants who had been there to visit her mother had come back in a state of terror. The Russians, she said, were looting the houses and shops. They were outraging women of all ages. She had heard their screams and shrieks. She had hidden herself in a barn under a heap of hay and had walked back when darkness came, running with panic-stricken terror when two Russian soldiers belonging to a tank on the roadside had tried to grab her.

"Where are the maids?" asked the old Countess.

"They have hidden themselves. They are terrified. If it had not been for my duty to you my lady. . . ."

"That is very good," said the Countess. "You are after all a brave man."

"Mother!" cried her daughter. "What shall we do?"

"Go into one of the barns," said the Countess. "Antoni and I will deal with these ruffians."

Her daughter's face had gone dead white under its rouge but she refused to desert the old lady, and her husband was glad of that, though he too felt the cold sweat of fear in the palms of his hands, not for his own sake but for these two women whom he loved.

Outside in the drive there was the sound of grinding wheels and hoarse shouts in Russian, and a banging at the door above the flight of steps.

The old manservant looked appealingly at his mistress.

"Shall I open to them?" he asked.

"That will be best," she told him.

She rose from her chair and spoke to her daughter.

"Let us show dignity. Let us remember our pride, my dear."

They heard the stamp of heavy feet in the hall and the door of the *salon* was thrust open roughly and six Russian soldiers with one officer marched in.

"Good day, gentlemen," said the Countess in Russian.

They looked a tough lot as they entered, with a grim and menacing appearance, but at the sight of the long *salon* with its polished floors and gilt-backed chairs, and in the presence of the old countess who had spoken to them in Russian they began to look ill-at-ease. One of them shuffled his feet on a hearth-rug as though ashamed of his big, clumsy, dust-covered boots.

The officer saluted and gave a gruff laugh.

"You speak Russian, old mother?"

"I speak Russian. I am the Countess Volska. Most people are polite to me."

He grinned at her.

"We have no countesses in Russia. They all went with the rest of their crowd in the bad old days."

He stared round the room and laughed again.

"So did their big houses like this. Now they belong to the people, with all their land. Their down-trodden serfs have been liberated."

"And are now slaves on so-called collective farms," said the old lady.

The Russian officer stopped grinning.

"You had better be careful, old woman. This part of Poland belongs now to Soviet Russia. You and your like will be turned out of your palaces and parks. It's the end of your exploitation of the proletariat. Generalissimo Stalin will see to that."

"We will not discuss politics," said the Countess Volska, "and I shall be much obliged if you will tell your men to keep their hands off my belongings."

One of the men had taken a little ormulu clock off the mantelshelf and was holding it to his ear with a childish grin. Another had put an eighteenth-century snuff box into one of the pockets of his tunic. Another had grabbed two silver candlesticks.

The Russian officer shrugged his shoulders.

"Everything belongs to us now."

But he gave a sharp order to his men and they refrained from further loot at that moment.

There were noises in the passages outside and up the staircase and in the rooms above. There was a tramping of heavy boots with loud laughter and rough horse-play.

"This house will be taken over for headquarters," said the officer. "You will have to clear out as soon as I've made my report. It's big enough for an infantry battalion. Why the devil should it belong to one old dame like you?"

"I share it with many friends," said the Countess, "but they do not steal my clocks or my candlesticks."

He stared at the Countess and his eyes softened.

"I have an old grandmother in Russia. You remind me of her. She doesn't fear man or devil."

"I am glad to know that," said the old lady. "Doubtless there are many devils in Russia."

The officer gave a good-humoured laugh.

"That's good! I dare say you're right. In any case you're a brave old woman, and I must say I admire you. We're not all savages you know, we Russians. We have a soft spot in our hearts for old people and children. Well, I'll have a look at the other rooms."

He spoke sharply to his men and left the room with them. They heard him tramping upstairs and along the corridors above.

Dr. Mirski had not uttered a word during this scene. Twice the Russian officer had glanced at him but did not take any further notice of him. He had gone hot and cold at his mother-in-law's answers lest they should arouse the fury of the man. Now he breathed a deep sigh of relief and spoke to her in a low voice.

"You were very brave, my dear lady, but you made me very frightened. One doesn't poke sticks at a tiger."

The old Countess was trembling now. He saw her thin, veined hands clutching at her dress. But she spoke calmly.

"He is a peasant, that officer. He had no manners, but a certain amount of good nature. I have known other Russians like that—rough but good-natured. When I went to Moscow with my father who was, as you know, in the Diplomatic Service, to the Imperial Court. . . ."

Upstairs the din grew worse. They could hear the clumping of feet on the floors above. Something crashed—a table with china on it.

"They're wrecking the house," said Dr. Mirski. "I must go and stop it."

"Antoni!" cried his wife. "They'll kill you! Stay here!"

But he went out of the room and stood at the foot of the stairs. Russian soldiers were coming down laden with things that they had looted—a servant's clock from one of the bedrooms, china ornaments, a chamber pot, silver-backed hairbrushes from the old Countess's room, a scent bottle and spray, silk eiderdowns, a jewel case half opened with a string of pearls hanging out of it, a silver Buddha brought back from India by one of the family, precious things and rubbish. They were laughing, and two of the men were struggling with each other for possession of the servant's clock.

"Bandits and robbers!" shouted Dr. Mirski.

One of the men struck him a blow in the chest, knocking him back against the wall, But the officer who had come into the *salon* rebuked him sternly.

"Keep your hands quiet, comrade. He's an old bird and I have a respect for men of my father's age."

The man answered sulkily.

"He's only a Polish louse."

Presently they all slouched out of the house with their loot, bursting into hoarse laughter, arguing, grabbing at another man's booty. There was something childish about them in spite of their size and strength. They were like a lot of children who had been treasure-hunting and now were quarrelling over their share.

For some time after that the house of the Countess Volska was left alone. Every day the family expected another raid or orders to leave. But for some reason, perhaps because the house and park were some distance from the city, that did not happen. The Russians in Lvov were organizing their hold on the city, quietly and methodically, carrying out the Soviet methods of interrogating the inhabitants, collecting evidence against those they suspected of being 'enemies of the people' as they called them. A number of priests were arrested and taken off. Well-to-do landowners were expelled from their estates and their houses were looted or requisitioned. Criminals from the prisons were released and enlisted in what was called the 'militia', armed with rifles and wearing red armbands.

They were joined by men who had been in sympathy with Russian Communism—unemployed and tavern politicians. Others were induced by fear, or class-hatred, or bribery, to accuse well-known people of oppressing the poor and exploiting the proletariat. News of these things came to Dr. Mirski from the gardener and maids whose parents were working in Lvov.

'It's our turn next,' he thought. 'I can't understand why they don't come.'

He was certain that the Countess Volska would be on the black list. She was one of the great ladies of Lvov. Her husband had been a distinguished diplomat who had been received by the Czar and Czarina in the old days of Imperial Russia.

'I am myself *persona non grata* to Russian Communists,' he thought. 'My political record will be unpleasing to them. Why don't they come for me?'

Many times during sleepless nights he wondered if it were possible to get away with his wife and mother-in-law. The siege of Warsaw was over. By some miracle he had received a letter from Vanda saying they were safe, and begging for news of their parents. That was a load off his mind and was of comfort to his wife who had been deeply anxious about the two girls. There was one other piece of good news in Vanda's letter—wonderful news.

Jozef has come back. We do not hear from Stanislav.

'We must get back to Warsaw,' he thought. But how to get back? Russian police had taken charge of the railways. Suspect people would not be allowed to travel. There were guards along the frontier of what was now Russian-controlled Poland. It would be madness to take to the roads with the old lady and his delicate wife—madness, though perhaps it was equally mad to stay. He was racked by anxiety and apprehension.

CHAPTER XVIII

EVERY morning at five o'clock Dr. Antoni Mirski went to the outskirts of Lvov to buy food for his family, the two maids, and various friends who had been turned out of their flats in the city because they were requisitioned for the wives and families of Russian officials. Food was getting scarce and presently some of the shops were closed. But there was a baker's shop still open in the outer suburbs and one or two others who received supplies from farmers and peasants within reach of Lvov.

From the baker—a sturdy, middle-aged man of good type and character—Dr. Mirski heard news of what was going on in the city. More arrests were being made by the N.K.V.D.—priests, schoolmasters, doctors, professors, lawyers, and the entire police force, whose places were filled by militiamen and avowed Communists. There was a kind of haphazard choice of those arrested in flats and private houses. The Russians would arrive late at night, turn people out of their beds—even mothers with their children— and give them varying times—ten minutes or half an hour—to dress, collect a few things, but no jewellery or gold, before they were forced into police vans and taken to the railway station, where they were crowded into cattle trucks on their way to Russia.

"My daughter, Janka, escaped by the skin of her teeth," said the baker one morning. "Those Russian devils came to the house where she is a nursery maid. You know them perhaps—the family of Plisowski. Nice people with two children of six and eight, a boy and girl, to whom Janka was devoted. What harm have they done? Why should they be seized? Mr. Plisowski was a dealer in antiques. You may know his shop full of fine furniture, not far from Castle Hill. His lady wife was educated at St. Bridget's Convent and is as near a saint as any woman may be. So my Janka tells me. The little girl began to scream but the boy rebuked her and said, 'We don't cry in front of the Russians. We must be too proud to cry.' That's what he said to his little sister. They were all carted away, and of course we shall never see them again. They're sure to die in Russia. Janka hid herself and then fled here weeping her eyes out. She's upstairs now with my poor wife who is bedridden."

Almost every day the baker had some tale like this—another

family taken off, even a company of Boy Scouts, because the Russians said they were enemies of the proletariat.

In the streets of Lvov Russian soldiers slouched about staring at the shop windows as though fascinated by the wares, and going in to buy things which were quite useless to them, just for the sake of buying, as a pleasure denied them in Russia. Their women were utterly ignorant of civilized life and customs and were amazed by what they saw in Lvov. Two of them appeared at the opera in pink and blue nightgowns in the simple belief that they were evening dresses.

Enormous portraits of Stalin were pasted upon the walls and shopkeepers were forced to hang them up. Every day new posters and placards were put up with orders to the civilian population, and one morning Dr. Mirski stood in front of one and read it with consternation.

It was an announcement that the *zloty* and all Polish money was no longer valid. Savings in Polish currency would be worthless. It would be replaced by Russian roubles.

Dr. Mirski was with his wife who was carrying a shopping basket. She did not read the poster as she was watching, very nervously, a squad of Russian soldiers marching along with a batch of civilian prisoners. She heard her husband give a queer-sounding laugh.

"What's the matter?" she asked. "Why do you laugh like that?"

He pointed to the poster and said, "Read that! It means that we're ruined. It means that the money I brought from Warsaw is utterly useless. It means that your dear mother is as poor as any beggar whom she used to feed."

"Why do you laugh?" asked Mrs. Mirska, her face getting pale.

"I don't know why I laughed," he answered simply. "I once heard a man laugh when he was sentenced to death. I'm afraid this also is a sentence of death."

They broke the news to the Countess. She heard it calmly.

"We shall have to tighten our belts. If money is worthless we shall have to take to barter. In any case I have good friends among the peasants. They will come to our rescue. They won't let us starve."

She was right and several times a week peasants came to the house secretly with gifts of cheese, butter, bread, vegetables, and eggs, for which they asked no payment and would accept no gift. For the time being these peasant folk were left alone on their farmsteads and small holdings by the Russian officials and police.

Among those turned out of their flats who sought shelter with the Countess Volska were a young husband and wife named Jankovski. Helena, the wife, was a delicate young woman whose nerves were already at breaking point. Tadeusz, her husband, had been a lieutenant of cavalry under General Anders and had been very good friends with Dr. Mirski's son, Stanislav.

In the evening he sat alone with Dr. Mirski when the Countess and the other women had gone to bed.

"I feel like a rat in a trap," he said one evening. "I'm sure to be discovered as an ex-officer. That means a concentration camp —or worse. If it weren't for my wife I would blow my brains out."

Dr. Mirski shook his head.

"That's the worst way of escape, my dear fellow! While there's life there's hope, and anyhow our religion forbids that kind of thing."

"I've lost my religion," said Tadeusz, "and I've no hope at all."

Dr. Mirski tried to comfort him but he was deep in despair. One word of warning was necessary.

"If I were you I wouldn't stay here too long, my dear boy. This house is not a good hiding place. They're sure to come for us. It would be better for you to take refuge in the countryside in some peasant's hut, dressed as a farm labourer, working on the land."

Tadeusz nodded.

"I've thought of it, but Helena couldn't stand such a life. She's in a delicate state of health. She's going to have a child."

"For her sake," said Dr. Mirski, "wouldn't it be better to separate? She would at least have the hope that you were safe somewhere."

"I can't leave her," said Tadeusz. "If I did I should feel a coward and utterly disloyal."

It was no use arguing with him, though Dr. Mirski argued in his gentle way.

One day Tadeusz and his wife went into Lvov to call on some friends. Helena wanted some warmer clothes. When she had been turned out of the flat to make way for the wife of a Russian official there had been no time to pack them and in her terror she had left everything behind.

Tadeusz and his wife walked into the heart of Lvov. They both felt nervous and Russian soldiers, looking slovenly and unshaven were in one of the streets through which they passed. A Russian officer walking with a woman stared at Tadeusz suspiciously but let him pass without a challenge. A Russian police car drew up alongside the kerbstone just behind them and Tadeusz felt his heart give a lurch. A group of Russian women dowdily dressed, with short hair and flat chests, were queuing up outside the opera house where a ballet was being performed.

At last the young husband and wife stood on the steps of the house where their friends lived and knocked at the door. It was opened after some delay by a young girl who gave a cry at the sight of them.

"Helena! Tadeusz! I thought it might be the Russian police." She gave a half-frightened laugh.

"We get scared too easily! Any knock at the door gives us the creeps. Come in and I'll try and get you a cup of tea."

In the hall she embraced Helena, and then put a finger to her lips.

"This house is like a slum tenement. Half a dozen families, and all as frightened as mice, poor dears! But my mother pretends not to be frightened and my father is as brave as a mediaeval hero, and my two young sisters play cards and laugh and quarrel as though life were as happy as a fairy-tale."

They went with her into a small room where her family were crowded. Her mother and father greeted them warmly and the two young girls, who were sitting on the floor playing cards stood up politely for a few moments until they had shaken hands.

"It's brave of you to come, my dear," said the mother. "The streets of Lvov are not really pleasant for an afternoon stroll."

"I had to come," said Helena. "I want you to lend me some clothes."

Mr. Poziomski turned to Tadeusz.

"You look ill, my dear fellow. Are you being starved?"

Tadeusz shrugged his shoulders.

"Not starved yet. It's the mind rather than the body that suffers."

Mr. Poziomski smiled at him.

"That's the worst disease! One has to adopt a kind of fatalism. I would rather call it faith and fortitude."

"I've neither," said Tadeusz. "I'm deeply apprehensive of what may happen to Helena and the unborn child."

The two men spoke in subdued voices while the others in the room were talking and the two young girls on the floor were laughing and chattering.

Somehow it was reassuring to be in this family scene. Even Helena brightened up and Tadeusz lost his immediate sense of fear. After all Lvov was a big city. It was unlikely, he thought, that the Russian police would raid this house crowded with inoffensive people.

It was unlikely—but it happened.

It was April 13th, 1940—the blackest day of tragedy in the history of Lvov.

It was Irena who first raised an alarm.

She had gone to the window to pull the curtain when she turned and spoke in a frightened voice.

"Father! There are military cars parked on each side of the street."

"Come away from the window," said her father. "Pull the curtains. Don't be frightened, my dear."

"I *am* frightened," said Irena, in a low voice.

Helena was talking with Mrs. Poziomska. She seemed more cheerful. Tadeusz was smoking a cigarette and sitting on the carpet with the two young girls, joining in the game of Snap.

Suddenly there was a heavy knocking at the front door, and then a sharp shattering blow as though it had been struck by the butt-end of a rifle.

In the room everyone stood up listening.

Helena's face was dead white and she put both hands to her breast and there was a look of terror in her eyes. Tadeusz sprang to her and held her in his arms.

They heard a tramp of feet. Upstairs people were running about, as though in panic. A woman screamed.

The door burst open and two Russian policemen came in.

One of them spoke in Polish with a heavy Russian accent.

"Everyone in this room is arrested. Everyone in this house is a prisoner. Your identity cards if you please."

Mr. Poziomski spoke to him emotionally.

"In this house there are none but innocent and inoffensive people. There is no reason why they should be arrested. I protest in the name of justice and humanity."

"Your protest is dismissed," said the Russian. "Your identity card, please."

Terrible noises came from other rooms in the house. Women were wailing and children crying. Floorboards creaked under heavy footsteps.

One of the two Russians came to Tadeusz and examined his identity card.

"You were an officer in the Polish Army?"

"I was."

"Stand on one side."

Helena clung to him and gave a cry when he was thrust away from her violently and thrown against one of the walls.

"This lady is going to have a child," said Mr. Poziomski. "I beg of you to treat her gently."

For a moment the Russian showed some embarrassment.

"We have to carry out our orders. The lady may sit down."

Helena fell down across the sofa and Mrs. Poziomska bent over her.

"You have time to pack a few things," said the policemen.

"How long?" asked Mr. Poziomski.

"Twenty minutes or so. We are very busy tonight."

Tadeusz was allowed to embrace his wife before he was taken away.

It was late in the evening when the cars and vans in the street were packed with the inhabitants of Mr. Poziomski's house and others in the street. Then they were driven away.

It was happening all over Lvov. It was a mass deportation. There was no method in it, no plan, no order. It all seemed to be done at random without reason and in an arbitrary way. When the N.K.V.D. came to a house, because perhaps they had someone there on their black list, they took not only the whole family but everybody under its roof, relations, friends, strangers. That night thousands were taken away.

The next day Lvov seemed to be a dead city. Only the churches were filled with men and women who had not been taken. All their faces were like tragic masks. Many were weeping. It was as though they were mourning for the dead. As history has now recorded, they were mourning for many who would soon be dead, in cattle trucks on long journeys, in forests where they were forced to cut down timber, in Eastern Russia which some of them reached with their women and children.

Few Russians were seen on the streets next day. Were they ashamed? Did they have some pity or some twinge of conscience? No one will ever know what passed in the strange minds of those Russian soldiers and officials who had obeyed orders of some higher authority, perhaps as high and remote as the Kremlin itself, where Stalin, with his inscrutable smile, raised his glass to visitors of high rank from other lands who found him friendly and even jovial over a glass of vodka. In England at that time they called him 'Good old Joe'.

Dr. Antoni Mirski and his wife with the old Countess waited anxiously for the return of the young husband and wife.

"They won't be back now," said Dr. Mirski at last. "It's dark outside and too dangerous to walk through Lvov. They must be staying with their friends."

"I'm afraid something has happened to them," said Mrs. Mirska.

"My dear Marietta," said the Countess Volska, "you're always afraid. That's a great mistake. Don't meet trouble half way."

She was playing a game of Patience as though peace reigned in Poland, and in her own mind. Once or twice she became peeved and said, "Drat the cards! Where's that Queen of Spades —the old wretch?"

The next day they heard what had happened in Lvov—the mass arrests, the mass deportation of civilians, the disappearance, perhaps for ever, of many families.

Dr. Mirski was stunned. It seemed incredible that such things should happen in a world which once he had believed to be civilized. This went far beyond the inevitable cruelties of war. It was a devilish policy of extermination—the crucifixion of a people who had done no evil, who had wanted only peace and a chance of happiness. These people of Lvov, more even than other Poles, had been merry, happy-go-lucky, full of jests and laughter, always ready for a joke. The educated classes had reached a high state of culture with many poets and painters and scholars. The University of Lvov had produced many distinguished men and women. They had loved music. Their home life had been gay and charming. Why had this martyrdom come upon them—this wholesale torture?

"O God!" cried Dr. Mirski. "Why hast thou abandoned us?"

He was stricken with pity for that girl Helena who was going to have a child.

'Poor creature!' he said to himself many times. 'Poor creature! That beautiful girl! That young wife!'

It was by accident that he found out her whereabouts. For some reason—could it have been a touch of pity in some Russian mind?—she had not been put into one of those cattle-trucks going eastwards. They had put her in the Brigidki prison, once a convent of St. Bridget.

This news came to him some weeks later from a priest to whom he spoke after hearing Mass. In the church were those women whose faces bore the stamp of pain, and Dr. Mirski kneeling at the back of them was astounded to see two Russian soldiers. Had they come as spies or to gloat over the victims of their cruelty? He watched them come in, sheepishly, even stealthily, as though afraid of being seen there. They were at the end of the church by the door close to where Dr. Mirski had taken his place. They were staring towards the altar with its lighted candles, as though seeing a vision beyond this earth. One of them bowed his head and crossed himself three times in the Russian way. Was it possible that there were men in Russia, soldiers of Stalin, citizens of the Godless state, who still believed in God, or who yearned for some faith in some God whom they were denied? Dr. Mirski watched them with a kind of stupefaction until they nudged each other and went out quietly, trying to silence the clump of their heavy boots on the stone floor.

It was after Mass that Dr. Mirski spoke to a young priest who stood in the doorway of the church. Dr. Mirski knew him. He was a nephew of the Countess Volska and a cousin of Marietta. He stood there after his congregation had left with his head bowed and his hands clasped until he gave a start when Dr. Mirski spoke to him. His face was haggard and drawn but he looked like a mediaeval saint waiting for martyrdom. He greeted Dr. Mirski with affection, clasping his hand and holding it. It was he who knew that Helena was in the Brigidki prison. He knew because his own sister had been taken there on the night of the mass arrests and a prison doctor had seen her and told him of the others

"They are allowed to receive gifts of food," he said. "Without that they would starve."

Suddenly he put his hands to his face and began to weep.

"All this is too terrible," he said after a struggle within himself. "My heart bleeds for all these poor people."

Every day small groups stood outside the door of the Brigidki prison with parcels containing food and clothes. A prison official checked up the name and number of each prisoner. Some of the parcels were refused. "Not allowed." "No longer here." Dead, executed, or deported to the east? No information was given. Dr. Mirski stood among these people with parcels for Helena prepared by Marietta and the Countess Volska until one day they were refused by the official at the door.

"No longer need."

"Why not?"

"No longer needed," repeated the man gruffly.

Helena had died with her unborn child, as afterwards they heard.

"Death is best," said his wife when this news came to them. Dr. Mirski wondered within himself.

How long were they going to be left? By what accident or mystery was the Countess Volska's house forgotten by the Russian police?

CHAPTER XIX

THEY did not wait long. One day a truck-load of Russian soldiers arrived with two officers of the N.K.V.D.—the secret police, as afterwards he knew. With them was a Polish militiaman with his red arm-band.

It was the old butler who warned them that they were coming up the drive.

Dr. Mirski and his wife and the old lady were taking a little wine with biscuits at eleven o'clock that morning. They indulged from time to time in having this little pleasure as long as there were still any bottles of wine left. The Countess was in a tapestried armchair with a high back. She had put a white shawl over her shoulders because of the cold weather. Marietta had raised the glass of wine to her lips when the old manservant came into the room with a look of anguish and announced that the Russians were arriving.

So they had come at last.

"Let us be calm," said the old lady. "Let us avoid panic."

But as once before her hands trembled and her thin fingers fumbled at her dress.

"Antoni!" cried Marietta. "What will they do to us? Is it the end? May our Blessed Lady protect us."

"Perhaps it is nothing," said Dr. Mirski. "They came before. Then they went away."

The truck full of soldiers drew up below the terrace.

They could see them through the windows of the *salon*. The militiaman with his red arm-band climbed out of the truck with the others. Presently, after what seemed like a long time, the door of the *salon* opened and two Russians with the militiaman entered the room. A sentry was posted at the door with his bayonet fixed.

One of the Russian officers came forward.

"You are the Countess Volska?" he asked in a cold, quiet voice.

"I am," answered the old lady in Russian. "This is my house. What is it you want?"

"The Soviet High Command has requisitioned this house. You will have to leave within half an hour. You are permitted to take what you can carry in two handbags. The same order applies to your staff. How many servants have you?"

"My faithful butler and two maids," answered the Countess.

"Send for them, please. They must all assemble in this room."

"Marietta," said the Countess, "touch the bell, please."

"Yes, Mamma."

Her daughter crossed the room in an unsteady way, as though feeling faint, and touched the electric bell.

The old manservant appeared again.

"At your service, madam."

"Tell the two maids to come here and return with them, please."

She turned to the Russian police officer who had spoken to her.

"I am an old woman. I have a right to respect. I protest against being expelled from my house with my family and staff. It is an outrage."

The militiaman spoke in a harsh peasant voice, after an ugly laugh.

"You have no right to respect. You are one of those who have wallowed in luxury at the expense of the poor. You have treated your servants like slaves. You have been an enemy of the proletariat. All that is changed. The people are free, their chains have been broken. You and your accursed aristocrats will now be punished for the crimes of centuries. It is you who will go hungry. It is your turn to suffer and die."

The Countess Volska looked at him with a kind of pity.

"My poor man!" she said. "You are a Pole and you are also a traitor. One day you will be punished by your own conscience or by your fellow Poles who are loyal and patriotic."

"Shut your mouth, you old witch!" shouted the man, furiously. "We are all Communists now. You and your kind will be wiped out, and none too soon."

The Russian police officer had listened to this with an expressionless face—a face with the eyes of a dead fish.

"That's enough!" he said. He made a gesture to the militiaman to stand back and after a quick, furtive glance at him, the man obeyed.

The Russian police officer turned to Dr. Mirski.

"You are Antoni Mirski?"

"That is correct."

"I have a dossier about you. You fought under Pilsudski in the war against Russia?"

"I did. I am proud of it."

"You were a member of Parliament?"

"I was."

"You are an enemy of Communism, according to reports of your speeches."

"I am, and always shall be. I am a Catholic and a Pole."

The police officer with the eyes of a dead fish, utterly expressionless, was silent for a moment.

"I have that information already," he said after that moment's pause. "What you have just said will be reported. It is my duty to arrest you. You will come with me at once, please. If you resist, you will be shot."

"I have been expecting this," said Dr. Mirski.

His face had greyed to the colour of death but his voice was steady.

His wife gave a cry of anguish.

"Antoni! My beloved!"

She tried to rush over to him but the police officer made a sign and one of the soldiers thrust her back.

The old Countess had risen from her chair and spoke to her son-in-law.

"We shall pray for you, Antoni. May God give you courage!"

Dr. Mirski turned to her and then to his wife, speaking in French.

"I'm not afraid, my dears—not for myself. When you leave this house. . . ."

"Speak Polish or Russian," said the police officer, sternly.

The old manservant came into the room with the two maids —young girls who were white and trembling.

The officer glanced at them and spoke to the old man.

"You are to leave the house in half an hour, you understand? Anyone found here after that will be arrested. Is that clear?"

"I have been in this house for sixty years, man and boy," said the old man. "I have had the honour of serving this family. . . ."

The militiaman gave a jeering laugh.

"You've been a slave and a lickspittle. Now you're free, if you're not too old and stupid to know what freedom is."

"That's enough," said the police officer, sharply. "Be silent."

He turned his head slightly towards Dr. Mirski and said, "Come, please."

Two of the soldiers stepped forward at a sign from him.

Marietta gave a piercing scream as they led him away. At the door he turned and looked back at them with a smile, a smile in which there was love, and pity, and courage, and resignation, as when a man goes bravely to his death.

The two maids were weeping bitterly. Tears were falling down the wrinkled cheeks of the old manservant. Suddenly Dr. Mirski's wife swayed and fell on to the polished floor.

The old Countess looked down at her and then spoke quietly to one of the maids.

"Fetch some brandy, my dear. My poor daughter needs your help, not your tears."

"Madam," said the old manservant, "I will go on serving you until my strength fails."

"Of course!" she said. "I know that. We will all go together."

Two Russian soldiers stood at the door of the *salon* after the officers had gone with their prisoner. One of them helped to carry two handbags down the steps of the terrace in a good-natured way.

"War is hard on old people," he said in Russian. "It's not amusing for anyone."

Marietta Mirska had recovered from her faintness but was still weak and the agony of grief had made her face like a tragic mask.

"Take my arm, Mother," she said in a low voice.

"No, no," said the old Countess. "You need help, my dear. I can walk alone."

Very slowly she walked down the steps of her big house leading the way out of the park. Behind her, supported by the old manservant came her daughter. The two maids followed behind, carrying the handbags. They were fugitives taking to the roads.

A truck filled with Russian soldiers swung through the gates towards the big empty house of the Countess Volska who was walking slowly away from her home, a thin, straight-backed old woman who did not weep but held her head high, proudly, with tightened lips.

CHAPTER XX

THE winter after the capitulation of the Polish Army was bitterly cold and the lack of fuel in Warsaw caused much suffering. Aunt

Krysta, Vanda and Halina sat always in fur coats during the long dark evenings and were angered by the knowledge that the Germans billeted on them were sitting round a warm stove in the *salon* well supplied with fuel by their German orderlies.

With those unwelcome guests they had no social contact. Only Aunt Krysta had a few words with them from time to time when the orderlies made use of the kitchen or when Lieutenant Holzapfel desired to see her with complaints or demands.

It was inevitable that Vanda should meet them on the landing or in the hall when they were coming in or out, and always she passed them silently as though she were a ghost or they were ghosts.

Once she was forced to have conversation—painful and embarrassing conversation—with one of them. It was the quiet young man, Lieutenant Naumann, whom Aunt Krysta had described as a good-looking boy, to the annoyance of Halina who would not admit that any German could be good-looking.

It was on the landing outside the *salon*. He stopped and smiled at her and stood in her way.

"Could I have a few words with you?" he asked very politely.

"I prefer not," said Vanda. "Please let me pass."

"My friends and I would be enchanted if you and your sister would spend the evening with us now and then. It would be a great favour to us. We are very lonely without any social contacts with the Polish people, for whom personally we have no hatred or dislike."

Vanda glanced at him disdainfully and angrily.

"How dare you say that?" she asked. "Your cruelties to our people are infamous. You are behaving like savages without pity or humanity."

"Personally," said the young man, "I regret all that very deeply. It is our Gestapo who are responsible for these police methods in reprisal for the acts of sabotage by your Resistance movement, which I admit is heroic, though ill-advised."

"I refuse to talk to you," said Vanda, who had turned pale. She tried to pass him but he stood in her way again.

"It is very sad for us—very sad for me—that you dislike us so much. There are some of us who hate this war. I am one of them. I love books and the beauty of life. I have been brought up with civilized ideals. If you would allow me to talk to you now and then—perhaps to render you a little service now and then. . . ."

"I am a Polish girl," said Vanda. "You are my enemy and I am yours. Stand out of my way, please."

"Forgive me!" he said. "I hoped that this dreadful silence between us might be broken. We live in the same house. We are human beings. I would give much to have the favour of your company now and then."

"Never!" said Vanda.

She passed him with a dead white face and a burning fire in her eyes.

"We are human beings," he had said. She had seen a pleading in his look when he said that. But they were not human beings, these Germans, she said to herself. They were deporting thousands of young Poles for forced labour. They were shooting and torturing young men and women caught in the Underground movement. They were shooting innocent hostages as reprisals for the blowing-up of German trains and ammunition dumps, or for the killing of German soldiers in drunken brawls. The German Gestapo trained in the technique of torture, were sadistic monsters. Did he think that she could put all that on one side and make friends with him because he felt the need of women's company and no doubt would like to make love to her? He loved books and the beauty of life! He declared that he hated this war. But he wore the German uniform. He was a hound of Hitler. She felt deeply disgraced by having this conversation forced on her. She felt humiliated and outraged. In her own room she burst into tears. It was almost like treason—communication with the enemy—abominable and disgusting. Had she not taken a vow as a member of the Underground? Was she not committed heart and soul to service of any kind—even at the risk of death and torture—to the Polish resistance against the enemy occupation?

In the summer of that year after the beginning of the war the news came to Warsaw of the German *Blitzkrieg* in France and then of the retreat of the British to Dunkirk and the collapse of France. It was tragic and terrible news and yet with one tiny solace to Polish pride. The French and British armies had not been able to withstand the German onslaught any more than the Poles, who had been first to resist the enemy by desperate battles. They had blamed the Government for being unprepared. They had been humiliated by the rapid *débâcle*. Now they knew at least that the Polish army had fought with hopeless heroism against a monstrous and irresistible power. It was only a solace to pride, and an evil portent for Poland and all Europe. The struggle would last longer. The period of servitude would have to be endured for more years. Yet, by some miracle of faith, there was no belief in the Polish mind that it would endure for ever.

England would come back. One day, without the slightest doubt, Germany would be defeated. Poland would be freed. The Underground movement would be ready for that day of glory.

The night when France capitulated was celebrated by the Germans in Warsaw and by those four young officers in Dr. Mirski's *salon*. Vanda could hear them laughing and clinking glasses. What about that young German with his love of books and beauty and his hatred of war? They were merry that night in the *salon*.

The next morning Lieutenant Holzapfel came to Aunt Krysta with some trivial request but really with the wish to express his exultation.

"You have heard that France has surrendered and that the British Army has been annihilated?"

"It's a long way to Tipperary," said Aunt Krysta, who remembered the First World War. "In the end we shall get there and Germany will be destroyed."

Lieutenant Holzapfel laughed behind his horn-rimmed glasses.

"We are masters of Europe! Our German destiny has been fulfilled. The supreme genius of our Führer is all conquering."

"What about Russia?" asked Aunt Krysta, calmly.

Lieutenant Holzapfel looked startled.

"Russia?" he asked. "We have a pact of friendship with Russia."

"Not worth two marks!" said Aunt Krysta. "Not worth twenty pfennigs."

She had given Lieutenant Holzapfel something to think about. He went away without another word, looking troubled. But that evening he drank too much wine with his comrades who had a party of friends. Several of them certainly became drunk and rowdy. The next morning Lieutenant Holzapfel looked pale and unwell. But the young officer named Naumann passed Vanda on the landing again. This time he did not say more than "Good morning!" and for a moment their eyes met. He gave her a queer look. What did he mean by that look? Was it pity? What right had he to pity her—if it was pity?

She was dejected. This news of the French capitulation was terrible. Most of the British Army had escaped from Dunkirk in the little ships and England was now alone to carry on the struggle. Perhaps England would be invaded next. What hope then?

There was a visitor at the house that evening and Vanda was

left alone with him as Aunt Krysta and Halina had gone to see some friends. It was Father Paul of Warsaw, the young priest who had spoken to Jozef in the Actresses' Café. He had been a friend of the family. He was, she knew, an ardent member of the Underground.

"You are looking well," he said, "in spite of all this terror and tragedy."

"I'm not well," she told him. "I'm losing my faith in God."

Father Paul raised his eyebrows and smiled.

"Are you feeling like that? Tell me. Why are you losing faith in God? We have nothing but God to cling to now. We need divine protection as our only hope."

"Father," said Vanda, "how can we believe in God and God's mercy when He allows such frightful things to happen? How can we reconcile our faith with what is happening in Poland? Poland has been a religious country. We're civilized and without cruelty. The churches are crowded with mothers praying for their sons, and girls for their lovers, and children for their parents, and it's all in vain! One can't see any justice or mercy. God has abandoned us, if ever He cared for us."

The priest raised his hands with a gesture of pleading to some invisible spirit above him or about him.

"I understand all you say," he answered. "I don't pretend to explain it. It's all a profound mystery and one doesn't know why all this evil is permitted and why the powers of evil seem to prevail at times. God works in mysterious ways, and sometimes to human creatures like ourselves they seem unjust and unfair. That's because we don't see the whole picture nor the end of the story, and only think of our own individual agony and suffering. But perhaps suffering and agony are necessary. Perhaps they are cleansing. Sacrifice and the will to sacrifice, may be necessary to redeem the world—this evil world of ours—as our Lord sacrificed himself on the Cross. I have an idea that Poland may be called upon for this sacrifice as an example to the rest of the world—as a victim for other nations' crimes. The heroism of our people— no one can deny that—and our resistance to evil forces and a cruel creed may be wanted as a reminder to the civilized world— the so-called civilized world—that there must be no surrender to the powers of darkness which work for the destruction of the human soul. That is why I am in this Resistance movement. It's a resistance not only against German oppression but against Satanic powers which threaten Christianity itself and all civilized ideals. We can't yield to such powers. We mustn't yield. This Poland of ours refuses to yield. Perhaps God calls upon us to fight this battle even if we lose it, even if we die, even if it ends in defeat for the time being and not in victory or triumph. But if we struggle on, our defeat will be a victory and the enemy's victory will be a defeat, for we shall have proved, as the saints proved, that we are defenders of the faith as martyrs and crusaders. Saints and martyrs who died on the gallows after torture were not defeated. Their deaths gave life and liberty to others. The gallows tree bore noble fruit. Their agony wasn't wasted."

Vanda watched his face and saw the look of mysticism in his blue, luminous eyes and saw, or thought she saw, the white flame of this man's spirit. He had dedicated himself to martyrdom. He looked like one of the mediaeval saints who risked the rack and the thumbscrew before death and cried out to God joyfully in the consuming fire.

"One must be very holy and heroic to go that way," she said. "My faith weakens. I'm not holy or heroic. I'm filled with hatred and despair."

He laughed at her good-humouredly. He was a great laugher in spite of his touch of mysticism, or maybe because of it.

"Most un-Christian!" he exclaimed. "Our Lord had no hatred in his heart for anyone and preached against it. Despair is the corrosion of the soul."

Vanda spoke passionately.

"Don't you hate the Germans? Am I to love them for their acts of brutality and cruelty? Am I to love my neighbour in my mother's *salon*?"

Father Paul shook his head and smiled.

"I admit that's a poser! But not if you think it out. One isn't expected to love those who do dreadful things. One has a right to hate the things they do anyhow. But better than hate I think is pity. I pity a murderer, though in the interests of justice he has to be hanged. I pity all sinners because they create their own hells. I hate the cruelties of the Germans and I am fighting to prevent them as much as I can, but I love the souls of the Germans and I am fighting to save them also, as much as I can. I pity them too because many must be conscience-stricken and they will suffer a terrible retribution. I am certain of that. Their punishment will be no light one. They will be destroyed as a nation. They too will be homeless, with tides of refugees on the roads, like ours. Their cities will be annihilated as ours have been. And as usual the innocent will suffer for the guilty."

He spoke as though seeing the writing on the wall.

"Are there any innocent?" asked Vanda in a hard, cold voice.

Father Paul gave a quiet laugh.

"I can't bring a verdict of guilty against decent civilized Germans for the abominations of Hitler and his ruffians. Many have gone to concentration camps, because they have dared to criticize the Nazi régime. Children yet unborn will not be guilty of Hitler's lust for dominion though they will pay the price for it in hunger and disease."

"You talk like a saint and a prophet," said Vanda, with a laugh. "You are willing to pardon many things which I find unpardonable."

He looked at her with a tenderness in his blue eyes.

"You're young!" he told her. "You're shocked and horrified by the terror around us. That's all right. So am I. But I know that you are with us in the fight against evil. One day you will see things with the pity of which I've been speaking, with a touch of the divine pity for the very worst of human beings. 'Father, forgive them, for they know not what they do'."

"I shall never get as far as that," said Vanda. "I am a living flame of hatred. I burn with it."

"Don't hate too much," he said gently. "Or if you must hate for the time being, intensify your love for God and men and those who suffer, and for the children of life and the beauty of life. Kill this despair in your heart, my dear. Cling to your faith. Try to laugh again. I believe in laughter as a cleansing thing for the mind and heart. We Poles like a joke. We like laughing. It is part of our courage. We couldn't be brave without it."

They talked much more than this and at the end when Father Paul rose to go she raised his hand to her lips and said, "Thanks Father Paul. I don't feel so desperate. I'll try to believe in God. 'Lord I believe. Help Thou mine unbelief'."

He raised one finger with a whimsical smile.

"Don't forget that the Devil can quote scripture!"

The idea of Vanda looking like the Devil struck him comically and he burst out laughing and in spite of herself she laughed with him.

"That's better!" he said. "Thank God for a good laugh! And now I must go. God bless you, my dear. Say a prayer for me. I'm much in need of it."

"Not you!" cried Vanda. "You're too frightfully good!"

That made him laugh again and he went away laughing.

That night Vanda went down on her knees with her forehead pressed against her bed and prayed for faith in God and for some sign of pity over Poland.

CHAPTER XXI

THE Countess Volska with her daughter and Jan the old butler, and the two maids, Janina and Sophia walked as far as the Kilinski park, the most beautiful park in Lvov which has more parks than any city in Poland. It descends two of Lvov's seven hills and covers the broad valley between them with large lawns, ancient trees, and decorative shrubs laid out in the style of an 'English garden' as it is called on the Continent.

"I'm afraid I'm a little tired, my dears," said the old Countess, "I think we must take a rest on one of these seats."

"Mother!" cried Mrs. Mirska. "You must be exhausted. My own poor feet are hurting terribly."

"Tired but not exhausted," said the old lady. "I belong to the older generation. I'm what the young people call a tough old bird."

She gave a little cackling laugh as she sat down on one of the park seats and spread out her dress with her thin, wrinkled hands.

"My lady," said the old butler, "I am very anxious. In an hour or two it will be bitterly cold. How are we going to spend the night? In what direction are we going?"

"In what direction?" said the Countess. "Why, bless the man, haven't I told him that we're going to Warsaw?"

The old man cried out in astonishment.

"Warsaw! How are we going to get to Warsaw?"

"With the help of some peasants, of course," said the Countess. "By easy stages. They will give us lifts in their farm carts. They're very friendly folk. I've always found them so."

The old butler turned to Mrs. Mirska and whispered to her with a look of consternation.

"It's incredible! It's impossible! Her ladyship would die on the roads. We should all die."

Mrs. Mirska raised her hands with a sign of despair.

"What's that you're whispering?" asked the old lady, suspiciously. "No secrets behind my back, please!"

One of the maids—little Janina—spoke timidly.

"My father has a cottage not far from here at Persenkovka. He is a shoemaker, and my mother does washing. It would be a great honour if her ladyship would take shelter with us."

"My parents would also be honoured," said Sophia, quickly. "My father makes coffins, but I am sure he would stop hammering if you would stay under his roof."

"Janina's cottage is nearest," said Mrs. Mirska. "We had better go there. Tomorrow I will find friends in Lvov who will put us up. All our friends in Lvov will be eager to help us."

"Of course!" said the Countess. "But it might be dangerous for them. My name is not pleasing to Russian ears, it seems. Also, my dear Marietta, I think it would be unwise of you to stay in Lvov, now that our dear Antoni has been taken prisoner. The wives of political prisoners are often sent to concentration camps, I'm told. It has happened already to poor Countess Tarnovska and her dear little daughter."

"Oh God!" cried Mrs. Mirska. "It makes me terrified."

"No use being terrified, my dear," said the old lady. "Terror is a bad bed-fellow. Remember that you're a Polish woman."

"My lady," said the butler, "Janina has a Thermos flask with hot tea. It will refresh you and keep you warm."

"Serve me last," said the old lady. "There was an English knight—I have forgotten his name—who said, 'Thy need is greater than mine'. That was when he was dying, and I'm not dying yet."

They all drank tea out of one tin mug and it seemed to give new strength and vitality to the old lady. She became very cheerful and reminiscent.

"Do you know, Janina, why this park is called the Kilinski Park?"

"No, my lady," said the little maid.

"Tut tut!" said the Countess. "You ought to know that, child! It's called after a shoemaker. He led a rising of partisans in Warsaw against the Russians. It was a fight for independence all over Poland after the partition. It was started in Cracow by General Kosciuszko with whom my grandmother once had the pleasure of dancing as a young girl."

"Mother," said Mrs. Mirska, "drink some more tea. It's getting cold."

"You're always interrupting me," said the old lady. 'When ever I am saying something interesting you interrupt me."

"My lady," said the butler, "Sophia wishes you to put on her shawl. Now that the sun is going down. . . ."

"Sophia must wear her own shawl," said the Countess. "If I

get pneumonia it doesn't matter. I'm old enough to die. But Sophia is young and has a right to live."

"Do take it, my lady," cried Sophia. "I beg of you!"

"Do what I tell you," said the Countess. "Put it round your head and shoulders. It will make you look like our Blessed Lady. Why, child, you look like the Madonna by Guido Reni."

A farm-cart drawn by an old horse came down the road outside the park and Janina cried out excitedly.

"There's old Peter! He will give us a lift to my father's cottage."

She ran out into the roadway and hailed the old man who pulled up his horse and cart.

"That's providential!" said Mrs. Mirska, "I couldn't walk another step."

"Permit me, my lady," said the butler, when the Countess had walked across the grass to the waiting cart. He helped up his mistress, guiding her foot to one of the axles as if he were handing her into one of the carriages which had belonged to her in the old days. The others climbed up and sat on the floor of the cart which then jogged off.

That night the Countess was delirious, singing nursery songs which she had learnt in her childhood. Mrs. Mirska sat up with her mother all night, and for some days she was too weak to be moved. The news of her presence in Janina's cottage became known to the neighbourhood and not a day passed without a peasant woman bringing small gifts of food and vegetables. So far from being hostile to one of the great ladies of Lvov, like the militiaman who had shouted abuse at her, they were filled with pity and affection for this old Countess who had been kind to them in the past, opening her park to their families, giving Christmas parties to the children, coming to sit with them in their cottages when anyone was ill.

Her daughter sat with the old butler and the two maids in the kitchen which was also the sitting-room with low beams covered with cobwebs and a brick floor on which they slept at night, having sacks of straw for their bedding put down by the shoemaker who could not do enough for them.

The old butler, who had been used to a great household, muttered lamentations from time to time in conversations with Mrs. Mirska.

"It's the end of Poland. Those Russians are terrible people. They will make serfs of us all. It's better to be dead."

"We must try to live for the younger people," said Mrs.

Mirska. "You remember my dear Vanda and Halina, and my sons Jozef and Stanislav?"

"Indeed, yes! Many a time they stayed with my lady, and I confess they were up to every kind of mischief. Master Stanislav was always getting into trouble. I trust he is safe and well."

"I don't know whether he's alive or dead," said Mrs. Mirska. She began to weep, to the distress of the old man.

"We must get back to Warsaw at all cost," said Mrs. Mirska, one evening. "We shall have to take to the road."

"It will be terrible for all of us," said the old butler, raising his wrinkled hands. "To be on the roads—to sleep in a covered wagon day after day, and night after night, is a terrible ordeal. My dear mistress will never survive it. It's better to remain in Lvov."

"No," said Mrs. Mirska. If I stay in Lvov I shall be sent to a concentration camp or taken to Siberia. My husband is a political prisoner. The wives of political prisoners can expect no mercy. And my dear mother is in danger."

That danger was removed one night.

Janina, the little maid, was sitting by her bedside while Mrs. Mirska and the others were having an evening meal with the shoemaker and his wife—frugal fare of potato soup served in little earthenware bowls. Suddenly they heard Janina give a cry.

"Come! Oh, come quickly!"

Mrs. Mirska rushed up the narrow stairs, followed by the old butler and Sophia and the shoemaker and his wife.

"She's dying," cried Janina, bursting into tears.

The old Countess was dying, but regained consciousness for a few moments. Her thin, veined hands plucked at the blanket which had been spread over her.

"I'm very tired, my dears," she whispered. "I'm not so strong as I used to be. I suppose it's old age."

She spoke three more words before she died.

She tried to raise herself and held up one hand, transparent against the candlelight, and smiled and cried out as though seeing some public show or military parade which so often she had attended as one of the great ladies of Lvov.

"Long live Poland!"

They fell down on their knees by her bedside. The old butler, who was sobbing, kissed her dead hand. The shoemaker's wife went downstairs and brought up more candles and lit them and placed them at the head and foot of the truckle bed.

The next day many peasants came with a priest for her burial.

Mrs. Mirska tried to find out a possible way to get through to Warsaw. It seemed to be extremely difficult. But by a stroke of luck she got in touch with Tadeusz and Nunia Mankovski who had similar plans. They went together. Old Jan decided to stay behind in his native town, feeling too old to take to the roads. Warsaw seemed a world away.

CHAPTER XXII

In the spring of 1940 before the downfall of France, Stanislav and his friend Adam were in retreat from the Maginot Line with a battalion of the 1st Polish Grenadiers. They had reached France by way of Hungary and Italy and had joined this Polish unit commanded by General Duch.

The Maginot line had seemed impregnable. The entire French nation had relied upon it as a kind of Chinese wall behind which they would be safe.

"If the Germans attack our Maginot line," said a French colonel to Stanislav, "they'll get a pain in the stomach."

A cheery fellow that French colonel, with a noble moustache under a hawk nose. The 'phoney' war was still continuing when he showed Stanislav and Adam over one section of this famous Maginot line.

"*Les sales Boches sont demoralisés,*" he said with a laugh. "*Ils n'osent pas nous attaquer.*"

He was of the opinion that the madman Hitler would never dare to attack France and this impregnable line.

"*Voyez donc!*"

He conducted the Polish officers through that underground fortress with its long galleries lit by electricity, its gun-turrets fed with ammunition by electric lifts, its kitchens, hospital, mess rooms, sleeping quarters, and observation posts in communication with the gunners by an elaborate system of signalling. Little buttons were touched, the lights flashed. Little bells rang. In rooms deep below earth with concrete walls, French officers who were also scientists—Stanislav noticed the pallor of their faces in this warm, moist atmosphere which made him feel a little faint— sat at tables studying maps divided into squares, each one numbered. Each square represented a small section of the ground beyond the Maginot line across which the enemy would have to pass. At the first sign of attack a light would gleam, a bell would ring and every inch of that ground would be swept by fire.

"Not a little mouse could live," said the colonel. "It would be a massacre of the Boches, even before they reached the tank trap which is a pretty box of tricks with big guns at each end to blow them sky high."

"Magnificent!" exclaimed Stanislav. "The Maginot line extends to the coast, of course?"

A slight shadow crept into the smiling eyes of the French colonel.

"Not as far as the coast," he said. "Politics interfered with its completion. Those damn fellows in Paris! But we are not worrying about that. If the Boches attack us here they'll come up against a *bec de gaz*."

He twirled his magnificent moustache and his eyes lighted up *À bas les Boches!*"

It was later that Stanislav in conversation with a French lieutenant—a pessimistic young man—learnt that on each side of the Maginot line there was an open gap far extended and very weakly defended.

"If the Germans attack," he said, "they will ignore our beautiful Maginot line and outflank it through the gaps. A child could see that—a schoolboy with his ears sticking out. It is a gigantic bluff, this Maginot line."

The Germans attacked and broke through at Sedan where there was no Maginot line. They attacked with every infernal weapon of destruction which they had been preparing during the 'phoney' war and for years before that—stupendous gun-power, swarms of bombing aeroplanes which dived low over the French troops, and their lines of communication, and their gun positions, and flame-throwers burning everything with scarlet tongues of fire; and armoured columns with heavy tanks which broke through the French lines and thrust deep into the heart of France. *Blitzkrieg*—overwhelming, irresistible, terrifying, annihilating.

Stanislav and his comrade Adam had seen this on a smaller scale in Poland. History was repeating itself. They were in retreat again, outflanked, in danger of encirclement, stupefied and stunned by the fury of this onslaught. They saw the helplessness of the French army under this storm of steel with their lines pierced and the German Panzer divisions cruising behind them, cutting them to pieces, however far they fell back.

There were bodies of gallant men who held out and hit back. The Polish grenadiers fought an heroic action under General Duch on the Marne-Rhine canal. They had been in retreat with the French 20th Army. On their left was the 52nd French division who fought with valour against great odds. Two German divisions attacked the Polish troops but in spite of their superior numbers and gun-power were forced back over the canal.

Stanislav was with a battery of field guns—the French *Soixante-quinzes*. He was separated from Adam who was with another battery. He was unshaven and had sunken eyes. It was a repetition of his war in Poland. War is always like that. The individual soldier knows nothing of what is happening on his left or right, nothing of the broad picture along a line of front. He is concerned with his own small group and his own experience of killing or being killed. Shells were falling close. The Germans were trying to knock out the guns. Two of the gunners were killed and their bodies blown to bits. Stanislav did not look at them. He had no time for pity nor any emotion. His tongue was dry and he couldn't moisten his lips. He had no sense of fear and no excitement of which he was aware. He could see the German shells bursting among bunches of the Polish infantry. They were making short rushes and then lying down and then advancing a few yards. On the left and right the German guns were busy with the French divisions. Clouds of smoke and dust drifted over them. Several times Stanislav heard the sound of Polish cheering.

'We're shoving them back,' he thought. 'They're pulling back their guns.'

He became light-headed for a time though he could still keep his guns firing until there was no more ammunition. He had an idea that the Vistula was over there instead of the Marne-Rhine canal. He had a boat on the Vistula but something was barring the way to it. Once he found himself singing a nursery rhyme which he had learnt as a small boy. It didn't matter. Nobody could hear him in this infernal racket. A shell burst within a few yards of him, throwing up the earth and leaving a deep crater. A bit of steel tore the air past his right ear with a sharp twang.

Fine fellows, his Polish gunners. They were good boys. He had known one of them in Warsaw. He used to write poetry. He had been rather soft about Halina. . . . Vanda. . . . Halina. . . . The pretty girls of Warsaw. . . . Another dream in another life.

He had orders to retreat with his field guns. The enemy had outflanked them. German tanks were threatening to cut them off.

Retreat. Always retreating, along roads crammed with French soldiers and guns and wagons and ambulances.

Stanislav had occasional words with French soldiers.

"*Nous sommes foutus. . . . Nous sommes dans le panier.*"

So spoke the pessimists and exhausted men.

Others still had hope.

The German armoured columns had turned west towards Boulogne. They were stretching out their neck, those *sales Boches*. General Weygand would cut it off. General Weygand was just waiting for the counter-stroke. Hadn't he done it in the First World War?

Stanislav encountered Adam again a week later.

"Not dead yet?" asked Stanislav, grinning at him.

"They can't kill me," said Adam. "Nor you, my comrade. We have charmed lives. But you ought to shave. You're a dirty looking ruffian."

Hadn't he said the same thing on the retreat in Poland? Wasn't it all happening again?

"Speak for yourself," said Stanislav. "You have the appearance of the ape-like Tarzan. You ought to be shot at sight."

After that comradely abuse they talked seriously, sitting on a French roadside with its long lines of poplars, eating French army rations, washed down by coarse throat-biting wine, which seemed to be a life-restoring fluid of liquid fire.

"It looks like the end of France," said Adam gloomily. "I've been talking with French officers. They're cursing old Pétain. They say Weygand has betrayed them. They say the end is near. Pétain will surrender if he hasn't done so already."

Stanislav groaned.

"That means a longer ordeal in Poland. The Liberation will be postponed—perhaps for a few more years. Horrible thought!"

Adam spilt a little wine into the dust of the road as though he were making a libation to the gods.

"There's only England now," he said presently. "Will England carry on?"

"The English lose every battle except the last," said Stanislav. "Of course they'll carry on. The English don't know when they're beaten and in the end they win. Didn't you read that in your history books? I hope to be with them."

"How are we going to get to England?" asked Adam. "The Germans may put us in the bag before we reach the sea. Then we have to cross that dirty ditch with dive bombers overhead and submarines under our boat—if we get a boat!"

Stanislav laughed loudly.

"You're getting morbid, my lad! Drink some more of that *pinard*. Pass the bottle and cheer up."

The other Poles about them remained very cheerful. A lorry

load of them passed down the road and the men were all singing as though they had won a victory.

General Sikorski had been in touch with London. Sitting in a bunker by the Admiralty Arch was a heavily built man smoking a cigar. Messages were coming to him over which he pored. Marshal Pétain had surrendered to the German Army. England was alone.

"Take a signal to the Admiralty," said the man with a cigar.

It was an order that the Polish Army was to be evacuated from all ports available in France.

It was on a boat from St. Jean de Luz, near Biarritz, crowded with Polish officers and men from other units, that Stanislav and Adam crossed the Channel.

The Polish Grenadiers retreating from the Maginot line had been encircled and only a few of them were lucky to slip between the German armies and reach the western coast of France. The remainder of the Grenadiers escaped later from Marseilles and through North Africa.

"The white cliffs of England!" said Stanislav, staring across the smooth sunlit sea, over which numerous British aircraft were flying in circles. A destroyer cut across the bows of the old cargo boat on which the Polish soldiers were packed.

"We shall be a long way from Poland," said Adam, with a long-drawn sigh—a gay fellow as a rule, but stricken by the fall of France.

"The nearest way home!" said Stanislav, who refused to be despondent.

CHAPTER XXIII

THE Journalists' Café in Warsaw was one of the rendezvous of the Underground in which many people were secretly engaged. The waiters were journalists whose papers had been taken over by the Germans. During the first raid on the café by the Gestapo, one of the policemen spoke suspiciously to one of the waiters.

"You're a journalist by profession. Why are you employed here as a waiter?"

"Because," answered the young man, "times have changed and now waiters are writing in our journals, so journalists have to be waiters."

Everyone in the café knew that its frequenters were doing secret work, but no inquiry as to what kind of work it was. A young man would come in, sit at a table with a friend, and then suddenly leave. What was he up to, that young man? Was he a forger of passports, identity cards, labour certificates, movement orders? There was now a perfect factory of forgers split up into sections and employing artists, photographers, priests with a gift for penmanship, girls with quick eyes and delicate fingers. They were fighting a secret and constant battle with the Gestapo. It was a battle of wits. The Germans altered their passes frequently and they had to be procured and copied so that agents of the Underground could move from one part of Poland to another with their papers in order and new identities, often of dead men, which would deceive the watchful police.

A young girl would come into the café and slip a piece of paper into the hand of a man reading the *Novy Kurier* produced by the Germans with their latest orders and regulations. What message was that innocent-looking young girl delivering? Information which would be sent by courier to France or England? A warning that the Gestapo were on this man's trail? Or was she one of the liaison girls collecting letters for the leaders of the Underground, never staying more than a night or two at one address, never getting together in one group, always in danger of arrest because one of their agents may have given them away under torture.

What was inside the handbag or vanity bag of that charming lady talking and laughing with a group of friends? What was concealed in the little mirror which she took out to glance at her pretty face?

An old gentleman with silvery hair had bought some toys for his grandchild's birthday, and was showing them to an old lady who found them delightful. What secret document was hidden in the Jack-in-the-box? What message in cipher lay inside the roof of that Noah's ark?

These hiding places were always being changed. The leg of a kitchen table was a secret *cache*, the inside of a mandoline, the cover of a book—nothing too often lest the Gestapo would spot it.

In many rooms of Warsaw, in many cellars, but always changing, there were wireless sets and transmitting sets worked by very expert and daring young men. From time to time one of them was seized and shot, but others carried on. At first they were able to operate as long as ten hours without much fear. But the Gestapo had a special corps for wireless detection and searched the city with mobile units and sensitive machines which would locate any wireless instrument sending out messages or receiving them. The time limit was reduced to an hour or two and later to a few minutes. They had to be very quick and nimble to find new hiding places, those expert young men who risked their lives every hour of the day and night.

Into the Journalists' Café came two of them to take a cup of coffee and chat with a friend, and glance at a newspaper and smoke half a cigarette before a girl passed them and made a sign. The way out through the kitchen was best for a quick escape.

"Excuse me. . . ."

Other frequenters of the café glanced up, or resisted glancing up. Two agents of the Gestapo came through the door with searching eyes. Why come to the Journalists' Café? A most innocent place! Just the ordinary groups of Warsaw folk dropping in to meet their friends.

Halina had enrolled as one of the 'Rush' liaison girls. She had not been accepted without preliminary tests. One of them was to be shadowed until she could throw off her pursuer. She came to know that shadow. He was a young man with a thin, delicate face and fair hair which needed the attention of a barber, and tiny side whiskers rather fluffy. He might have been an actor or a singer. She came to know him as 'Danek' a member of her own unit of five.

She failed in her first test. She was aware of being followed and led him a pretty dance—at first through the market square where ladies were selling their trinkets and little useless things. They were refugees who had abandoned their homes and were now destitute. Halina stopped to talk with one and bought a pair of baby's shoes which certainly she did not need.

"Are you from Poznan?" she asked.

"No, Lvov. I fled from the Russians."

Halina nodded. She would have liked to ask whether by any chance this lady had met her father and mother in the house of the Countess Volska. But she was aware of the fair-haired young man standing close to her. She walked at a quick pace through the market place, shot down a narrow alley, and rushed into a butcher's shop. The butcher was sharpening his knife.

"May I go through your back way?" she asked. "I'm being followed."

The butcher stared at her and then nodded.

"The Gestapo? That way. Be quick, my dear."

She ran through a back yard and into another narrow street. It was a *cul de sac*. At the end of it stood the fair-haired young man.

"It's no good!" he said. "You can't shake me off. You'd be useless as a 'Rush' girl."

Halina had tears in her eyes.

"I intend to be a 'Rush' liaison girl. Give me another chance."

"Tomorrow," he said. "Starting at the Journalists' Café. And now let's have a rest there. I'm quite exhausted."

They went into the café. Jozef was there at one of the tables. 'Jozef has changed his job,' thought Halina. He was hardly ever at home. When he came home he was apt to dart off suddenly and say, "Sorry, I must go."

He was sitting in the café with Father Paul of Warsaw and two other young men. They were talking in low voices and laughing. There were still people who could laugh in Warsaw—lots of them. Perhaps this life of danger and secret work exhilarated them. Or perhaps they laughed and made jokes because there would not be much time ahead for laughter.

Jozef raised his hand when he saw Halina and spoke to her as she passed with the fair-haired young man.

"Making yourself useful?" he asked with a grin.

"Trying to!" she told him.

At the table the fair-haired young man asked a question.

"What shall I call you? I'm Danek."

"Call me Cinderella," said Halina.

He glanced at her and laughed.

"You don't look like that girl. Too smart. And I can't play the part of the fairy prince. Not in these trousers!"

He was shabbily dressed, and his trousers were patched.

"You belong to my unit," he told her. "We shall be seeing each other if you pass the test. . . ."

She wouldn't object to seeing him. He was a nice-looking boy though perhaps slightly effeminate, or at least made on delicate lines. She noticed his hands, almost like a girl's hands with long fingers beautifully shaped.

"You led me a dance!" he said. "You must be one of those athletic girls—hockey, ski-ing, and all that."

"You were pretty quick after me," she admitted.

She passed the test the next day. She threw him off the scent by going into St. Jozef's Church, saying one *Hail Mary,* and slipping out by a side door.

"Pretty good," he said, when they met by arrangement at the Journalists' Café again. "I lost you in the crowd of people hearing Mass. I didn't see you go out. I'll report that you are quite the right type to be a 'Rush' girl."

"Thanks," said Halina. "I know I am! I was born for the job."

The young man gave a slight groan.

"It's a mad world when girls like you have to risk their lives at this kind of game. You're too young and you're too pretty to be scragged by the Gestapo."

"We're all in the same game," said Halina, carelessly. "It's no worse for me than for you."

"I can't say I find it amusing," he admitted. "Those fellows in the Gestapo are very unpleasant."

"Funking it?" she asked, raising her eyebrows.

"Now and then. I get a cold sweat at the thought of being caught."

"Then you must be very brave," said Halina. "The true hero is one who is afraid but risks everything all the same."

He coloured up slightly and laughed.

"That's very generous. Anyhow, what I've said is between ourselves."

"I shan't blab," said Halina. "How old are you, Danek?"

"Twenty-one," he told her. "And you?"

"Eighteen."

"The right age for Cinderella."

She was beginning to like him. Later on she came to like him a good deal, partly because she was sorry for him. He was nervous. She could see that. He had a horror of being caught by the Gestapo. He hadn't the stamina for their ways of interrogation. But that was later when things were very hot indeed. It was after Germany had attacked Russia, after June 22nd, 1941, when the work of the Polish Underground became more urgent and more dangerous.

CHAPTER XXIV

Dr. Antoni Mirski was imprisoned at first in a small cellar in a suburban villa of Lvov. There were four other men in the cellar which was lighted only by a narrow window heavily barred and half underground. Outside was a Mongol Russian guard with a rifle and long bayonet. The guard was changed twice during the day and once at night. The prisoners could hear the tramp of heavy boots outside the cellar, up and down and the noise of coughing and spitting. Now and again, but not often, one of these men would abandon his post for ten minutes or so, probably warming himself at a kitchen stove.

Dr. Mirski knew one of his fellow prisoners named Orzelski, a professor of Lvov University, with one of his professional comrades, a younger man. The two others had been members of the City Council of Lvov.

"My dear Mirski," exclaimed Orzelski, when the new prisoner was pushed in by the police who had arrested him. "What are you doing here? You belong to Warsaw."

Dr. Mirski explained briefly.

"Welcome to our palatial residence," said the younger professor whose name was Konopka. "We wallow in luxury. We are fed once a day. Everything is free!"

He had laughing eyes and looked like a shipwrecked pirate instead of a professor of philology. They were all unshaven with newly grown beards and their hands were grimed by the coal dust in this cellar.

"What is our fate going to be?" asked Dr. Mirski. "How long can we live in a place like this?"

One of the City Councillors answered him.

"It's a toss up whether it's a firing squad, a concentration camp, or Siberia. Not agreeable alternatives!"

"Why are we here?" asked Dr. Mirski. "What is our crime?"

His friend Orzelski enlightened him.

"We're guilty of the abominable crime of being so-called intellectuals. The Russians will, no doubt, liquidate our class as they did in their own country after the Revolution, and as they are doing in Estonia, Latvia, and Lithuania. They regard us as very dangerous fellows and a menace to Soviet philosophy and faith. So of course we are!"

"Worse still, some of us have been politicians," said one of the City Councillors. "I've been questioned at all hours of the day and night. God knows why! I suppose they want me to incriminate my colleagues."

"I've been promised my release if I denounce them," said one of the men.

"And are you going to?" asked the young professor with the laughing eyes. "It's an easy way out of this damned cellar."

The others laughed. They knew their own loyalty. But they feared physical torture as Orzelski confided to Dr. Mirski one night.

"Under physical torture a man may confess anything and give away the names of his best friends. It's happening in Warsaw under the technique of the Gestapo."

Dr. Mirski turned pale at the thought and gave a slight shudder.

It was as cold as death in this cellar. A draught like a sharp sword came under the bottom of the door. At night they lay huddled together for human warmth. There was no sanitary convenience and Orzelski had an attack of diarrhoea. The cellar had the stench of a latrine.

"We must get out of this," said Konopka, the young professor. "It ought to be easy to escape through that window."

He tried the bars with strong hands but they stood firm.

But one morning he gave a shout.

"Eureka! God be praised!"

"What have you found?" asked Orzelski. "Diamonds? Or something to eat?"

Konopka had been grubbing about in a heap of coal. He had discovered two three-inch nails.

"The instruments for escape!" he said. With the heel of his boot he hammered each nail through a bit of board. Another discovery rejoiced him—a bit of old iron bent at the top.

"A wonderful find!" he exclaimed. "We won't trouble about the bars. We'll take out the whole window by scraping round it. It's only plaster."

One of the City Councillors looked at the window with scepticism.

"I'm too stout to get through a hole like that—bars or no bars."

"Nonsense, my dear fellow!" said the young professor. "Where the head goes the body will go. I learnt that as a schoolboy."

"The sentry will hear us if we make a noise by scraping," said Dr. Mirski, warningly.

"We must make other noises," said Konopka. "You must all sing while I'm doing the dirty work. Or you can talk loudly as though you were quarrelling. It's going to take some time, of course. We must go carefully and quietly."

On the third day of his imprisonment the door of the cellar was opened and Dr. Mirski heard his name called. Outside was a young Russian officer who said, "Come this way, please."

Dr. Mirski was led into the yard outside the cellar and then into the house, and to the right of the hall, into a well-furnished room with an upright piano against one of the walls, and comfortable looking chairs. A typical room in a suburban house of Lvov.

With his back to the stove which gave out a pleasing warmth stood a Russian colonel of the new pattern—young for his rank—

in a smart uniform. He was clean-shaven and had steel-blue eyes and the square face of a Slav.

"You are Antoni Mirski?" he asked.

"I am."

"Sit down please. A cigarette?"

He held out a paper packet of cigarettes.

"I don't smoke," said Dr. Mirski.

"I have to ask you some questions," said the colonel. "My colleagues and I have to ask you a lot of questions. I advise you to answer them."

They were tedious questions, going back into Dr. Mirski's political life and opinions. The Colonel had a dossier in front of him which he consulted from time to time. It was probably the same dossier which had been in the hands of the officer of the N.K.V.D.

Dr. Mirski admitted everything—his denunciations of Communism, his own political faith, his work for one of the parties in Warsaw.

"And your political colleagues? I shall be glad to have their names."

Antoni Mirski shook his head.

"I cannot give you any names. That would be treason to my friends."

The young Colonel smiled grimly.

"There are ways of making you tell them. It is not my branch of duty but doubtless you have heard of the N.K.V.D.

"I have!" answered Dr. Mirski. He could not refrain from giving a slight shudder.

"They're experts in extracting information," said the Colonel. "Especially from witnesses who do not wish to answer."

Dr. Mirski remained silent. He felt very cold in the stomach. The Colonel turned over some papers.

"I'm interested in your speech on May 21st, 1939."

"I've forgotten it," said Dr. Mirski.

"It's a criticism of the agricultural situation in Soviet Russia."

"Very likely."

"On the platform you were supported by many of your party members. You will oblige by giving me their names."

"I give no names."

The Colonel suddenly banged his fist on the table at which he was sitting.

"Give me their names!" he shouted.

"I have no recollection of them," said Dr. Mirski.

The Colonel's politeness had departed from him. His mouth assumed a brutal expression.

"You are an obstinate fellow. You forget that we know how to punish those who resist us."

So it went on, this questioning, until the Colonel gave a faint sigh, lit another cigarette, and said, "Enough for this time. My colleagues will deal with you later. You'll be questioned again tonight."

But he was not questioned again that night. He escaped with his four friends. The young professor had been working hard. He had disintegrated the plaster all round the barred window.

"We just have to lug at the frame and out it will come," he told them. "We must wait until our gorilla goes to warm his backside."

They waited hour after hour. The sentry strode up and down, stamping his feet. Suddenly silence. It was eleven o'clock at night.

"Now!" said Konopka.

He seized the bars and tugged at them with all his strength. The whole window frame came out and fell with a frightful clatter of iron bars.

They waited with beating hearts. No one seemed to have heard that terrible noise.

"Come along!" whispered Konopka. "You first, Mirski."

"No. You first. You did the work."

One by one they scrambled up and wriggled themselves through the empty space where the barred window had been. The stout Councillor stuck half-way and Konopka could hardly resist laughing aloud. With great effort the stout man was liberated and pulled through by his comrades, falling to the ground heavily. They were free men.

They had already decided to go separate ways. They clasped hands and wished each other good luck before creeping away down the dark street, and then taking different directions.

Dr. Mirski found the house of a friend in Lvov. He hid in the back garden until dawn and then ventured to ring the bell of the big house with a green door under the portico, above a flight of steps.

After ringing several times a chain was pulled and the door was slightly opened and a man in his dressing-gown looked out.

"Who are you?" he asked. "Why do you come at this hour?"

"It's Antoni Mirski. Forgive me my dear friend. I have just escaped from the Russians."

The door was opened wide. The man in the dressing-gown caught Dr. Mirski in his arms.

"My dear old friend! For God's sake come in. You look like a coal heaver. I hardly recognize you."

It was Stefan Bobinski, famous as a portrait painter.

"I should be glad of a bath and a shave," said Dr. Mirski, after their embrace and half an hour's talk.

He had a bath and a shave and felt a different man. But he was conscience-stricken.

"I'm putting you in danger," he said. "I ought not to be here."

Bobinski shrugged his shoulders and laughed.

"One can't escape from danger anywhere in Poland. With the Germans on one side and the Russians on the other. . . ."

He led Dr. Mirski into his morning-room. On the table was a steaming jug of coffee and some stale bread.

"My wife will join us in a few minutes," said Stefan. "She'll be surprised to see you—except that nothing surprises us now. We won't wait for her. You must be devilish hungry, my poor fellow!"

Dr. Mirski was so hungry that he swayed and had to clutch a chair to keep himself from falling. Or perhaps it was the emotion of being a free man again, in this civilized room, with that hot coffee fragrant in his nostrils.

"Steady!" said his friend, clutching him.

Dr. Mirski found other friends in Lvov who sheltered him at great risk to themselves. Then he trudged out to the countryside and was taken in by a farmer and his wife whom he had known in the old days. His abiding thought was to get back to Warsaw, and some months later disguised as a peasant he found a place in a covered wagon and took to the road like so many other refugees.

CHAPTER XXV

SOME new disposition of the occupying troops caused the departure of the four German officers from the house in St. Theresa Street, to the great relief of Vanda and Halina.

They had behaved reasonably well, apart from parties when some of them had been drunk and disorderly, judging from the rowdiness which went on in the *salon*. They were ordered to leave Poland for some other destination and came to make their formal farewell to Aunt Krysta, who had been the only person in the household to have communication with them.

"We regret having to leave," said Lieutenant Holzapfel, with a slight bow and a click of the heels.

"We are glad for you to go," said Aunt Krysta, in her blunt, uncompromising way.

The two Nazi-looking young men laughed loudly.

"You may get less agreeable fellows," said one of them.

The quiet young man—Lieutenant Naumann—who had once told Vanda that he loved books and beauty, came later than the others to pay his respects to Aunt Krysta before he left, and he too expressed his regret at going.

After that he hesitated for a moment and then spoke a few astonishing words—astonishing from a German officer.

"I should like you to believe that I deplore the ruthlessness of our occupation of Warsaw. There are some of us who do not approve of this and many of us are filled with admiration for the heroism of your people, with whom we should like to be friends instead of enemies."

Aunt Krysta stared at him with surprise. He was like one of those boys with whom, when a girl, she had danced. He was certainly a boy of good family and upbringing. Perhaps he was a survival from the days when the German people were civilized and, she had thought, charming.

She answered him less sharply than she had spoken to the others, but with emotion which suddenly shook her.

"I used to love the Germans. I had a love affair with a German boy like you. How is it possible that you do these things in Poland? Why have you become cruel and brutal, shooting our young men in batches, dragging them off the tramcars for deportation—which means death—using torture to make them reveal their secrets, killing our young girls if they are caught carrying messages in the Underground? You stand there in German uniform. You are one of those who obey the orders of that monster Hans Frank and his master Hitler. You all obey those orders. You share the guilt of these terrible crimes against humanity. How do you explain that? How do you excuse yourself? It is a mystery I cannot understand. Why have the German people become devils and torturers? Tell me!"

The young officer's face flushed slightly and he raised his hands as though in protest.

"Not the German people! Not those who are innocent and ignorant of these things. There are many German officers like myself who are filled with shame for what is happening and pity for your suffering."

"Filled with pity?" cried Aunt Krysta. "I have seen no pity in Poland."

"We have to obey orders, however merciless," he said. "As soldiers we have to obey."

"It's obedience to the Devil," said Aunt Krysta.

Lieutenant Naumann was silent. He crossed the room and stared out of the window and then came back.

"I'm outside all this," he said. "I'm not a fighting soldier. I used to be a poet and writer of songs. I hate the Gestapo and all its methods. I hate war and all its cruelties. It's all senseless and degrading. But there is one cause of cruelty which perhaps you do not understand."

"What is that?" asked Aunt Krysta sharply. "What cause can there be for barbarism and savagery?"

"There is Fear," he said.

"Fear?"

"We are frightened men. The Germans in Warsaw—in Poland—walk with fear and sleep with fear. They know that every man, woman and child hates them with a deadly hatred. In the streets the girls turn their heads when they pass. No German soldier dare walk alone in Warsaw. They know that everyone is a member of the Underground, vowed to resistance and to the killing of Germans when the time comes. We know that you have a secret army preparing to rise against us. The German army of occupation is like an army of ghosts. No one speaks to them. No one has a friendly word. They see the hatred in all Polish eyes. It makes them afraid. It makes them cruel. Fear is the father of cruelty."

"You are talking dreadful nonsense," said Aunt Krysta. "Why should you Germans be afraid of unarmed Poles, of young girls and old women? Are the hounds afraid of the hare, or the hawk of its prey? Is the Gestapo afraid when they beat up our boys?"

The young officer raised his hands again.

"The Gestapo is in a separate class. They are educated in cruelty. The German officer class loathes the Gestapo. They are our enemies as well as yours."

Aunt Krysta laughed scornfully.

"The German officer class does not protest against them. It does not rise against them and wipe them out. The German officer class have been enslaved by Hitler and they're agents of his homicidal mania."

"As a German officer . . ." said the young man.

He hesitated and then checked himself.

"I have been talking in confidence. I have revealed my secret thoughts to you not as a soldier who has sworn allegiance to the Führer, but as a fellow who once wrote songs and love lyrics—a sentimentalist and hater of war."

He laughed nervously and then ckicked heels and bowed.

"I must say good-bye, madam. Kindly give my respects to your nieces whom I should have been glad to know if I had not seen the hatred in their eyes."

"Good-bye," said Aunt Krysta. "I have to hate you, too, but I'm sorry for you because you have a conscience and a sensitive mind, and even, I think, a good heart—unlike the rest."

"You are hard on us," he said. "You have a right to be hard on us."

He saluted and turned to leave the room but then stopped and said something which startled Aunt Krysta.

"Your nephew Jozef is in great danger. He ought not to come here any more. He's being watched by the Gestapo. I give you this warning as a gesture of goodwill."

He saluted again and left the room.

CHAPTER XXVI

A HANDSOME middle-aged man, shabbily dressed, came out of the station at Praga—its lines had been repaired after their destruction in the first weeks of the war—and walked across Paderevski Park towards a house whose big garden went down to the Vistula. It had been his own house. Now it was a ruin. He stared up at its gaunt, empty shell and for a few minutes he poked about the piles of rubble underneath, as though trying to find something. He was trying to find some small piece of his former life here—a bit of pottery, a broken mirror, anything. But there was only rubble and twisted iron and jagged pieces of wood.

Then he went into the garden, thrusting his way through overgrown bushes, treading down high weeds on what had been smooth gravelled paths, rolled every day by an old gardener. An immense shell hole had cratered the middle of the lawn, now like a pasture field. But there were still flowers—a mass of marigolds at the end of the grass, hollyhocks tall as grenadiers, by a broken bit of wall which had been one of the outhouses. Little blue lobelias twinkled among the weeds. There were even a few roses in a jungle which had been the rose-garden. He picked one and put it to his lips, and breathed in its scent. For a moment tears came into his eyes. It was the scent, this fragrance, which brought back memories of his former life here. He had been very happy with Krysta. She had always filled this garden with young folk. He remembered a tennis party just before the war. His pretty niece Vanda had been playing with her brother Stanislav. There had been a lot of chatter and laughter without a thought of war except in his own mind, because he knew it was coming.

All that seemed a long time ago—a lifetime ago—or was it the day before yesterday? He had been a prisoner since then, until he had escaped from hospital being wounded and captured during the retreat of the cavalry. For some time he had been living in disguise with peasants who had sheltered him, and he had been afraid to come to Warsaw lest he should endanger his wife Krysta. If he had not escaped he would have heard from her as all prisoners of war were given postcards to send to their families. He had tried to send Krysta a letter but it must have failed to get through, and he had not had a word from her. He felt like a ghost now in this desolate garden outside the ruins of a house in which he had had his study and billiard-room and where he had entertained his friends, many of whom were dead—killed in the first weeks of the war. Where was his wife Krysta? What had happened to young Vanda and Halina?

He left the garden and walked over the bridge into the centre of Warsaw. After a long walk he felt tired and dejected. There were many ruins in Warsaw. He wondered if the Mirski's house had been destroyed and when he strode down St. Theresa Street he abandoned hope about the survival of his brother-in-law's house, the last in the street. Every other one had been bombed into rags and tatters of broken masonry. Then to his amazement he saw that the Mirski's house was standing. He stood in front of it and gave a queer laugh. Too good to be true—Marvellous! The shell crater outside the front door had been filled up and the steps were clear.

He went up them and stood with his hand on the bell-pull hesitating. Two German soldiers passed and he had a momentary alarm. He was without papers. He was an escaped prisoner of war. If they questioned him. . . . But they passed without a glance at this shabbily dressed man standing on the steps.

The door opened without his ringing the bell. A woman came out, carrying a shopping basket.

"Krysta!" he said. "My darling wife!"

She dropped the basket which rolled down the steps. She was staring at him as though she saw a ghost. Then she flung her arms round his neck, laughing a little and weeping a little.

"I knew you'd come back!" she cried. "My dear soldier man! I knew you weren't dead. . . . You're not dead, are you? I told Vanda, 'I know he's alive'. I told everyone. I told God. Oh, my dear! Thanks be to God!"

He had his arms round her and she put her head on his shoulder and he kissed her hungrily like a lover, until suddenly she cried out.

"We mustn't make this public exhibition! It might arouse the suspicion of any Germans coming this way—two elderly people kissing and hugging!"

She dragged him inside, laughing rather wildly.

Presently she was able to ask him a few questions.

"How did you escape? How very clever of you to get away!"

"I just walked out of hospital," he told her. "One of the nurses smuggled in some civilian clothes. The German guards thought I was a visiting doctor and saluted me. It was laughable."

He laughed then at the memory of this escape.

"I don't believe a word of it," said his wife. "But I'm glad to know you can still make up a fairy-tale."

The door opened and Vanda came in. They were in the *salon* which had been occupied by the German officers. She had been there already that morning, throwing open the windows, getting rid of every trace of its previous inhabitants—empty cigarette packets, old envelopes, torn newspapers, empty tins, and one photograph of a German dancing girl, half naked, which she tore into small bits before flinging it into the waste-paper basket.

Now she saw her uncle and gave a cry of joy.

He rose and kissed her.

"All this is like a dream," he said. "I can't quite believe it yet."

There was a lot of family news to be told and a lot of terrible news about what had happened in Warsaw during the fighting, and what was happening now.

Vanda's father and mother were missing. No news came from Stanislav. Jozef had survived the war.

"But he's still in danger," said Aunt Krysta. "I had a warning. The Gestapo are after him."

She lowered her voice.

"Of course he's in the Underground."

"Of course," said the Colonel. "That's where I'm going to be. That's where all of us ought to be."

"That's where we all are," said Vanda, with a little secret smile.

She added a few words.

"We must get you some papers, Uncle, unless you have them already."

"I've nothing," he told her. "I bluffed my way through as a refugee."

Vanda was horrified.

"You must get a proper identity card. Jozef will arrange that for you. You must have a labour certificate. What would you like to be? A plumber, a carpenter, a road mender?"

"You'll never be able to disguise yourself," said his wife. "You're too handsome, my dear. You look exactly what you are —a colonel of cavalry."

"I shall have to grow a beard," said the Colonel. "I shall have to develop a stoop. I shall have to bleach my hair and look like an octogenarian."

He laughed and stared round the room as though it might be the last time he should see it.

"It's a dream! Three days ago I was in a peasant's cottage pretending to be an old rustic half-witted. I believe this is heaven. I feel extraordinarily joyful. I'm in danger of losing my normal poise as a professional soldier never to be thrown off his balance, don't you know?"

He was thrown off his balance that evening at supper when there was a sudden sound of firing in St. Theresa Street.

"What's that?" he asked, listening intently.

"Only some more boys being shot," said Vanda, turning pale. "One of our Underground run to earth and caught."

She cried out in anguish.

"How long can we go on like this? How long can we endure these things?"

"Until Poland is free again," said her uncle. "We must never give in, my dear. Never!"

With papers nicely forged by his niece and her fellow conspirators the Colonel adopted the identity of a bookseller's assistant. With newly grown beard and a pince-nez he looked an old man of no account, badly paid, shabbily dressed. But his hands were clasped one day by a man who called himself 'Bor' —a hunted man, always in hiding, but always getting messages from the liaison girls and sending out messages as far as England by special couriers who were brave men. He was the Commander-in-Chief of the Home Army—the Secret Army of Poland, preparing for the day of Liberation.

The Colonel became an important officer in that organization, though by day he worked, or pretended to work, in a book seller's shop in a back street of Warsaw.

CHAPTER XXVII

AFTER the departure of the four German officers no others were billeted for some time in the one remaining house in St. Theresa Street and there was joy in it when the mother of the family came back. She had survived the perils of the roads in a covered wagon, but was hardly recognizable, even by her daughters when she embraced them weeping. She was like a peasant woman escaped from a concentration camp, except that she had not been starved. Her hands and clothes were begrimed by mud and dust. She seemed to have grown older by ten years until gradually those years dropped away one by one because of this home life.

One day there was another home-coming. It was Dr. Mirski who came back after his escape from the Russians. He too had changed and grown older. For a time his clothes hung upon him like those of a scarecrow, the skin of his face was tight over its bones giving him a skull-like look, except for his eyes which shone with his old ardent spirit. It was amazing to Vanda and Halina that he talked of this time as though it had been a valuable experience and very educative.

"I learnt a lot," he told them. "I believe it taught me something fine—the nobility of the human soul in adversity—especially among men of high culture who were able to suffer these things better than the uneducated, perhaps because of tradition, and intellectual pride, and reserves of mental and spiritual strength. *Noblesse oblige!* Those fellow prisoners of mine who helped me to escape by removing the bars of the cellar showed great courage and did not even lose their sense of humour. Then afterwards my friends in Lvov risked their lives on my behalf. How wonderful and how generous."

"Father, you're a saint!" cried Vanda.

"No, no, my dear! For goodness' sake don't say such a thing. It's most untrue and most embarrassing."

In Poland at that time friends and relatives who had disappeared suddenly appeared as though from the dead. But also thousands, and scores of thousands, still believed to be alive by those who refused to give up hope, were lost for ever and had no home-coming, and are still lost, and are now accounted dead.

How can one give a true picture of life in Warsaw at this time? It would be false to say that it was all grim and gloomy. It would be false to the character of the Poles who are fond of laughter, and amusing conversation, and music and social life. They lived dangerously, but perhaps because of that they made the most of any time or place in which they could find good company and even—incredible as it may seem—good fun. Like the characters in *Boccaccio*, who told merry tales in time of plague, these people of Warsaw, up to their eyebrows in Underground activities, had light-hearted moments, even light-hearted hours, when they put all thought of that on one side. It was still possible to make love, and in the love of young people there was forgetfulness of tragic things. There was much love-making in Warsaw because Poles are Poles. There was enchanting romance as well as grim reality. There was laughter as well as weeping.

After the return of Dr. Mirski the house in St. Theresa Street became a rendezvous of intelligent people who had once been professional men and women, or studying for the professions and arts. They were mostly young, being friends of Vanda and Halina, but there were elderly visitors who had remained in Warsaw during the fighting and so far had been left in peace by the Germans.

Among the younger folk came that violinist Jerzy who could no longer play the violin because of the damage to his hands. That did not seem to deject him—he wore a glove on one hand to hide its wounds—and he was gay and amusing, but Vanda was shy of him now, especially when friends were there, because he did not hide his devotion to her. His eyes followed her about the room. He came to sit next to her whenever there was a chance. He lamented his bad luck if other friends held her in conversation.

"I want to talk to you desperately," he told her one evening, "but you don't give me a chance."

"Is there anything special you want to say?" she asked, smiling at him.

"Good heavens, yes! I have a thousand special things to say."

"Tell me one—before Jozef plays again."

The piano had been mended again since Jozef had slashed its strings with a clasp-knife, and now and again, but not often, he played for them. He was mostly upstairs on secret business, very secret in this household because he could not subdue the thump thump of a small printing press upon which he was working.

"I would like to tell you one thing which is very important to me," he said in answer to her challenge, "but it's impossible here with all your friends in this room."

"I'm curious to know," said Vanda.

She knew perfectly well. But she was not quite ready to hear it. He wanted to tell her that he loved her. He told her so a score of times with his eyes. Other people had noticed it—Halina, who chaffed her about it, Jozef, who said, "That fellow Jerzy is frightfully gone on you." It was good, this comradeship, but she did not want to get deeply involved. She was not quite sure of her own emotional response to his devotion. She liked talking to him. Every time she looked at that gloved hand she had a sense of pity for him. He was an idealist, very serious underneath his amusing conversation. He had an intense sensitiveness to beauty and the lovely things of the mind. Perhaps she was a little afraid of being loved. Many young men had tried to make love to her—she remembered Ferrari, that amorous Italian—but she was still reluctant to be swept off her feet or consumed in the fire of a great passion.

'I'm too cold,' she thought. 'I'm incapable of love as other girls are. I suppose it's because of this war and all its horrors. It has made me rather dead inside. How can one indulge in romantic love when one is surrounded by fear and agony?'

Something of the sort she hinted to Jerzy himself when one evening he spoke to her under cover of other people's conversation and when Jozef was playing the piano again.

"Vanda, I'm off on a rather—well adventurous—journey. Before I go I want to tell you what you already know. Can you bear it?"

Vanda spoke in a very small voice because of the others in the room. One of them was that mysterious man called 'Bor'. He was talking vivaciously to her father and Aunt Krysta, nothing about Underground work, nothing about being a hunted man. It was something about his friends in Cracow.

"Jerzy," she said, "I know what you want to say. I love you very much also, but in a different way."

"You can't love in a different way," he told her. "There's only one kind of love."

"There are different ways," said Vanda. "The word itself is abused by some men and women to whom it's just a romantic episode, half sentimental and half physical. A kind of animal love."

"The love I mean," said Jerzy, "is when the body and spirit become one, when everything in life—all its loveliness of sound, colour, touch, are intensified, and made more radiant."

153

"I don't feel like that," said Vanda. "No such fire has touched me like that. I think I freeze the fire. I feel a bit dead inside."

He laughed aloud to the annoyance of Jozef who looked over his shoulder and scowled.

"Hush!" whispered Vanda.

"You're so very wrong," he said, lowering his voice. "You're almost terribly alive! You're always in a hurry to serve other people, to sacrifice yourself to their happiness, or comfort, or safety. You were quick to come to my rescue in the street that day! And now I know that you have volunteered for dangerous work."

"Hush!" said Vanda again. "We shall get into hot water with Jozef."

They got into hot water. Jozef slurred the keys of the piano.

"What's the good of playing," he asked savagely, "if people go on chattering?"

"Sorry, Jozef!" said Vanda.

She left Jerzy while she handed round some little cakes to the company. They were all laughing and talking again. A young artist friend of Halina was telling a funny story about a practical joke he had played on some fellow students to whom he pretended to be an Indian Rajah.

Suddenly the story and the laughter were frozen into silence by the howl of a siren on a police car in the street below. A few moments later there were rifle shots, and a man's scream. Then the car sounded the siren again and they heard it roaring down the street, until presently there was silence again.

Mrs. Mirska crossed herself. Her husband gave an audible sigh.

The man named 'Bor' rose from his chair and said, "I'd better be going."

He shook hands with Dr. and Mrs. Mirski and Aunt Krysta and disappeared from the room.

"They never spotted me," said the young artist, going on with his story. He told that story very well, acting his part as the Indian Rajah.

Jerzy had a chance of a few more words with Vanda.

"I shan't see you for some time. It's a question of luck whether I shall see you again. I want to carry your love with me—to give me courage."

"You have it," she told him. "A loving friendship. Not more than that yet, my dear."

"That 'yet' gives me hope!" he answered. He raised her hand to his lips.

"Come back safely!" she whispered.

He laughed and said, "I'll try! Wish me luck."

He shook hands with Dr. and Mrs. Mirski and with Halina and Jozef.

"You chatterer!" said Jozef. "Always flirting with Vanda!"

He was in a good humour again before going upstairs to work the printing press with its betraying noise of thump, thump. Everyone in the house would be shot if that were found by the Gestapo.

"Flirting is an atrocious word," said Jerzy, hitting him on the shoulder and laughing again. "Your sister and I talk seriously."

"Oh yes, I know," said Jozef. "Soul stuff! Very dangerous. The most subtle form of flirtation."

Jerzy turned to smile at Vanda. She stood there watching him. He was going on a dangerous mission, perhaps as a courier for 'Bor' who had been with them that evening, without a glance at this young man who was serving him. So she guessed.

Their eyes met. Her lips moved. He read her message quite easily.

"Good luck!"

He was away a long time, so long that she believed he must be dead. If so, she had lost a great lover and a good friend. She liked his friendship best because she wasn't ready for complete and absolute love, annihilating all other interests, demanding surrender of her heart and spirit. She was very busy otherwise. She was a dedicated woman and getting very expert in forgery.

CHAPTER XXVIII

AFTER their arrival in England when France had capitulated Stanislav Mirski and his friend Adam Socha walked across the bridge in St. James's Park and then past St. James's Palace to Pall Mall. If they had been walking in Paradise they could hardly have been more astonished or more blissful.

This was their second day in London and they had been invited to lunch at a place called the R.A.C., which, being interpreted to them, meant the Royal Automobile Club. Here was a Polish friend who had been in England for some time. As an airman he fought later with English pilots in the Battle of Britain which saved England from invasion and saved the world, perhaps, for civilization, or a chance of that.

In St. James's Park Stanislav had leaned over the bridge and looked at the ducks, and then on the other side at the flower beds gay with autumn colours.

"Charming!" he exclaimed, "but not so good as the Kilinski Park in Lvov."

He stared at Buckingham Palace in the far vista.

"What's that building?" he asked Adam.

Adam shook his head.

"I'm not yet qualified as a London guide."

"I expect it's a prison for captured Germans," said Stanislav. "I hope it's crowded."

He laughed heartily at his own joke, so ringing a laugh that two girls turned round to smile at him.

"London, as far as I have seen it," said Stanislav, "is a fine city. Not quite so good as Warsaw, of course."

"Warsaw must be a heap of ruins," said Adam, with a groan.

Stanislav made another remark which amused his friend and himself.

"I say, Adam, I haven't seen a pretty girl yet. . . . Oh yes, I have! She's coming this way. I would like to kiss her."

"Behave yourself," said Adam. "We're in a civilized country."

"Is it uncivilized to kiss a pretty girl?" asked Stanislav, who felt very happy with himself and life. He was in England. It was unbelievable. He was in Paradise, walking on air.

The pretty girl caught his admiring glance and the corner of her lips twitched for a moment as she passed without a hat, in a low-necked frock, with a swinging stride.

"I expect she's a goddess," said Stanislav. "She walks like a goddess."

"I expect she types letters in an office," said Adam.

They both laughed. Anything made them laugh. They had escaped from the Germans and the Russians. Tonight they would not sleep in a barn or a trench. They were on the way to have a good lunch in a place called the R.A.C.

In the hall of that club they asked for their friend and his name was called out loudly by a small page boy with a big voice.

"Mr. Kaminski . . . Mr. Kaminski."

They followed the boy up a little flight of stairs and stood in a circular lounge with an enormous spread of carpet. On one side was a bookstall and a post office, and a place where one could buy cigarettes. Rounds the walls were busts of the Roman emperors on pedestals.

Stanislav glanced at them.

"I expect they're members of the R.A.C.," he remarked. "They look typical Englishmen of the 'John Bull' type."

This remark made Adam laugh in a suppressed way. They were both laughing when their friend came to greet them. He was in the uniform of a flight lieutenant and had a nice-looking girl with him. He flung his arms round Stanislav regardless of three or four Englishmen who were coming up the stairs.

"Stanislav! My dear fellow! What a joy to see you! And there's Adam Socha. What adventures you must have had! I'm longing to hear."

Having embraced Adam and patted him on the back he turned to the girl with him who was smiling at this effusive greeting and the flow of words in Polish.

"This is my wife. She's teaching me to speak English, and I'm not a bad pupil."

Stanislav raised her hand to his lips in the Polish way. He felt abashed at meeting an English lady for the first time. He noticed that she resisted him slightly when he raised her hand and then gave a tiny laugh and blushed.

"In England," said Kaminski, speaking in Polish again, "we don't kiss ladies' hands, unless we're engaged to them, or married to them. You must remember that, Stanislav!"

"I must get engaged," said Stanislav. "I must certainly get engaged, and possibly married, to an English lady."

Kaminski interpreted this to his wife whom he called Audrey. She glanced at Stanislav with a shy smile.

"We must do something about it," she said.

CHAPTER XXIX

IT had seemed so peaceful to Stanislav and Adam crossing the bridge in St. James's Park, looking up the vista of the lake to Buckingham Palace. So far from Poland! So far from the Maginot line, so far from the muck and blood of war. But both of them were aware that all this was deceptive—a beautiful illusion. Tomorrow or the next day England might be invaded. In the eyes of those girls whom they had passed in the Park there was a new gravity which they had failed to notice then, having no comparison as yet. The men who passed were talking together quietly and earnestly. At the luncheon tables in the big room of the R.A.C., not very crowded, quiet words were spoken and there was no laughter or light chatter.

'These English people,' thought Stanislav, 'know what I know. Their army in France must have lost its guns. They must have blown up the ammunition dumps. They must have left their tanks behind.'

He ventured to ask his friend a question in Polish.

"How will England defend herself in case of invasion? Have they strong reserves of men and weapons?"

His friend shrugged his shoulders slightly.

"They've nothing! They've lost everything on the other side."

"Will they carry on?" asked Stanislav, "or shall I be a prisoner of war in England? This club would make a nice head-quarters for the Gestapo."

His friend looked at him warningly.

"Better not say things like that. Nobody here asks, 'Shall we carry on?' I haven't heard it once. They take it for granted. If need be they'll fight with their hands or with bricks and stones. They have an age-long tradition of courage. Their history is heroic. They haven't lost anything of that. Look at the faces round you. Look at the people in the streets. You will see no panic."

"They must be rather like ourselves," said Stanislav, "if your wife will allow me to say so."

His friend's wife had been talking in French to Adam but she turned and spoke to her husband.

"What are you two saying? Tell me."

He smiled at her and hedged a little.

"It was in praise of England. We were speaking about the courage of the English people."

She looked at Stanislav gravely.

"We shall need it," she said in French. "Now that France has surrendered we're terribly alone and terribly weak."

So she knew, this English lady. In her eyes was awareness of dangers to come. England would be fighting for survival and her old liberties. 'She has no illusions,' thought Stanislav. But she said no more about that, and turned to Adam again and asked him about Poland, and the fighting in France. Stanislav watched her curiously and with admiration. When coffee came she asked for a cigarette from her husband and her hand did not tremble when she lit it. She wasn't losing her nerve.

He watched other people at the tables. The greatest disaster had befallen them. There was a deadly menace on the other side of the Channel. If Germany invaded them by sea or air—perhaps in swarms of aircraft dropping men and machines—the streets of London would run red with blood and the English countryside, its peaceful villages, its hamlets below the little hills and rolling downs, which he had seen from the train, would know the horrors of war and hear the screams of women and the rifle shots of firing squads. All that had happened in Poland. All that was happening now.

Stanislav was attached for a time to the headquarter's staff of General Sikorski in London, while Adam, his best comrade, left him to train as an anti-aircraft gunner with an English unit somewhere near Greenwich, not too far away for them to meet now and then in Soho restaurants where other Polish friends came from time to time.

Some of them were young airmen attached to the R.A.F. Some of them had fought in France, in the retreat from the Maginot line. Others—a few mysterious young men, reticent about their activities—seemed to come and go between Warsaw and London as though it were a safe and easy journey in time of peace. They were bringing reports to General Sikorski from General 'Bor' and carrying back orders and dispatches with the utmost secrecy.

One of these lads, taking fearful risks, was Jerzy Boberski who gave Stanislav news of his family and of all the horrors that were happening in Warsaw. After their first meeting Stanislav took him to lunch in one of those little Soho restaurants—the Pôt-au-Feu—in Old Compton Street.

At the table were a few other officers on the staff of General Sikorski and some French officers on the staff of General de Gaulle. They were talking and laughing and smoking cigarettes between the courses, and drinking cheap French wine. Gay fellows, in spite of the tragedy of Poland and the downfall of France and the deadly menace to England.

A man named Churchill had become Prime Minister at this time. His words had been translated into Polish which Stanislav had read, with a kind of wonderment and then a sense of something heroic, and traditional, and stark in courage. When he took office he said, "I have nothing to offer but blood, toil, tears and sweat." Not a cheering message, but it seemed to raise their hearts, the hearts of these queer people among whom Stanislav had come. When invasion was threatened he said, "We shall go on to the end. . . . We shall defend our island, whatever the cost may be.

We shall fight on the beaches. We shall fight on the landing grounds. We shall fight in the fields and in the streets. . . . We shall never surrender."

'Our spirit is like that,' thought Stanislav. 'Our people are like that. We share this honour with England. But our agony is greater.'

That second meeting with Jerzy was after the Battle of Britain in which young Polish airmen had fought with the same heroic spirit as the boys of the R.A.F.—those 'few' who had saved this Britain from invasion and the liberties of a shrinking civilization.

He liked this young man Jerzy, a quiet fellow with steady eyes and a lurking humour. It was a joy to get news of the family from him. He spoke of Vanda and said very simply—"We love one another. If peace comes, or if I'm not killed. . . ."

"I hope to come to your wedding in Warsaw," said Stanislav.

They both gave a laugh. The hope was a long way off—inevitable years away.

Other Polish officers in the little restaurant were laughing at some joke they had made. It was getting dark outside and black curtains were being drawn by one of the French waiters, careful not to let out a chink of light.

It was perhaps an hour later when there was a heavy droning noise above the London roofs.

"Another air-raid," said Stanislav. "German bombers—blast them!"

The head-waiter—an old Frenchman—called out sharply.

"*Attention! . . . A la cave, messieurs!*"

Two or three officers stood up uncertainly. One of them lit a cigarette. Two seconds later one of de Gaulle's men made a dive under a table. There was a tremendous crash. Stanislav heard it and then heard nothing more until a voice spoke to him—was it a second later, or an hour, or in a dream? In his head there was a stabbing, throbbing pain.

"He's coming round."

Coming round where?

It was Jerzy's voice speaking in Polish. Jerzy was stooping over him, putting an arm beneath him. Somebody was pouring liquid fire down his throat. There was fire in the street. He was lying on a heap of rubble and broken glass. There were houses burning along the street. Flames were licking up above the chimney pots and the night sky was red above them. The Pôt-au-Feu where they had been having a pleasant little dinner did not seem to be there any more. Something had smudged it out. Men in black helmets were playing water on to the flames from fire engines a few yards away. A girl in a nurse's uniform bent over Stanislav and he felt a prick in the arm and then nothing else until he was aware of an aching head and something queer about his right leg, something extremely painful with sharp shooting pains, agonizing.

He called out to God in Polish.

A nurse—he could see she was a nurse—held his wrist and spoke to him in English which he didn't understand. It was not until the next morning that he was able to ask a question. He had been rehearsing it in English.

"Where am I, please, kindly very much?"

The nurse gave a little laugh.

"Charing Cross Hospital," she told him, but the words conveyed no meaning. English was a terribly difficult language. All the words seemed to run together.

Stanislav Mirski was a patient in Charing Cross Hospital for the greater part of the London Blitz.

Every night there was an air-raid. He heard the howling of the sirens followed by the heavy drone of German bombers and then the shock and roar of high explosives, and the tremendous thunder of the London barrage with one gun quite close, firing with an ear-splitting noise. The windows of the ward in which he lay after an operation on his right leg—it was in plaster now—glowed red through the black-our curtains. They rattled, those windows, as though shaken by a great gale. The floor of the ward trembled and creaked. Buildings were crashing very close. Lying there he could hear the avalanches of masonry and rubble and breaking glass. Very close, that one! One night a length of kerb-stone outside was hurled up and hit one wing of the hospital. Every night new patients were carried in, smashed up, or cut by glass, or stunned by falling masonry.

'It's ridiculous, patching up my leg,' thought Stanislav. 'It's certain that we shall all be bombed to death in this damned hospital. . . . The nurses are wonderful. That pretty one keeps as cool as a cucumber.'

He spoke to the pretty one.

"You have very much courage."

She smiled at him and said, "Think so? I wish I did!"

"You are very much beautiful," he told her in his best English.

She laughed softly and said, "And you're a Pole, aren't you? They all talk like that. Can't help it, poor dears. It's their glands."

"I should be very honoured and pleased if you would give me a kiss," said Stanislav. "It would be very much joy to me."

"Nothing doing!" she told him with laughter in her eyes.

"Now take these two pills. They'll make you sleep. . . . Good night, Mr. Pole. Happy dreams."

When Stanislav left Charing Cross Hospital he did not return to General Sikorski's headquarters. He hadn't come to England to do clerical work. He was a fighting soldier. He was determined to fight for Poland on any front. He went to a training camp in Scotland. It was training men for future fighting with the Allied Armies.

CHAPTER XXX

On September 14th, 1941, General Anders stood in a forest clearing at a place called Totskoie in Russia, reviewing the first contingents of a new Polish army of which he was to be Commander-in-Chief by request of General Sikorski, head of the Government in exile now in London, and with the consent of Stalin and his subordinates in the Kremlin.

Here in Totskoie where they had set up tents were 17,000 men newly liberated from Russian prisons and concentration camps, the first to be disgorged after Germany's attack on Russia. They were without boots and paraded bare-foot. Many of them had no shirts and all were in rags. They were emaciated, like living skeletons, and many had ulcers on their bodies, caused by starvation and bad food. But they were all shaved and pulled themselves up with a soldierly bearing at the arrival of their Commander-in-Chief, to the astonishment of General Zhukov who accompanied him.

General Anders walked down their lines looking into the eyes of these officers and men. It was only with difficulty that he could restrain tears coming into his own eyes. These men had come out of hells on earth. They had seen many of their comrades die. They had lived with filth and hunger and disease and lice. They knew nothing of the fate of their families. They had been unbelieving when they had been told that they could go free. What then had happened? What miracle?

General Anders had been released from his cell in Lubianka prison in Moscow where he had been knocked about, tripped up, on his way to be interrogated by the N.K.V.D. at all hours of the day and night. There had been strange bedfellows in his prison cell—a fanatical Communist, a German convinced that the German armies would march through Russia as a knife cuts through butter. That was when General Anders, with quick and expert ears had heard German bombers over Moscow, and even in his cell, knew that there was war between Germany and Russia.

One morning his cell door was opened and he was told to come. He was led down long corridors and this time was not tripped up or knocked about. He was led down soft-carpeted passages into a luxuriously furnished room. Two high officers of the N.K.V.D. received him politely, even deferentially. One was Beria, chief of the Secret Police.

"Sit down, won't you? Have a cigarette."

There was a Russian-Polish agreement, he was informed. They were in touch with General Sikorski in London. Polish prisoners would be liberated. They would form a new army to fight with the Russians against Germany.

"Brothers-in-arms, you understand?"

"I am a free man?"

"Perfectly free, General! All good wishes."

There were further interviews with Russian generals and diplomats. All very polite! All very deferential to this Polish soldier whom they had kept like a wild beast in a prison cell—where he had not been allowed to shave for twenty months and where he was under observation by day and night.

General Anders set up his headquarters at Buzuluk, like 10,000 other small-sized Russian towns, deep in mud during the autumn months and with one brick building over which the Polish flag was flying. That emblem of freedom lit up the eyes of liberated prisoners who were coming from all parts of Russia to form this new army, presently thousands of them. They were all in bad shape—an army of the starved—bags of bones, hollow-eyed, weak-chested. Could he ever make a fighting army out of them? He knew he could, given time. A spirit looked out of their eyes, proud, unconquered, stronger than their bodies.

General Anders talked to them and listened to them. They told terrible tales of their sufferings. The Russian concentration camps had been hellish. Worse still had been long journeys in cattle trucks without food or water, with dead and dying comrades among them, and the long marches where many had dropped on the way, never to rise again in spite of blows and kicks from their guards.

"But where are the others?" asked General Anders presently. Thousands had come by slow degrees. But all the other thousands, the greater part of a million men who had been sent to Russia. Were they all dead, or still kept in captivity?

Where were the Polish prisoners sent to Kolyma near the Arctic Circle beyond the Sea of Okhotsk? Ten thousand Poles had been sent there to dig for gold in the mines.

"Kolyma means death," said a few who came back. Prisoners were frozen to death after losing their toes and fingers and their legs and arms. Out of those 10,000 only 583 returned.

And where were the 15,000 officers and non-commissioned officers who failed to report for duty? Only 400 had been released after the Polish-Russian agreement.

Where were the 4,500 officers sent to Kozielsk, and the 3,900 sent to Starobielsk, and the 380 officers sent to Ostashkov with over 6,000 non-commissioned officers, priests, frontier guards and officials of the Polish Courts of Justice?

General Anders was haunted by these questions. He asked them in Moscow of Stalin himself, who gave one of his sly, inscrutable smiles and professed ignorance of the missing men. He asked them of Russian generals, who made evasive answers. He asked them of liberated prisoners who had been in other camps.

It was the Germans who gave one answer. In the forest of Katyn they found the bodies of 4,500 Polish officers. Each one of them had been shot through the head. "By the Germans themselves," said the Russians, but they refused an inquiry by the International Red Cross, and evidence, beyond question now, tracked down these dead officers to a Russian camp from which they were sent to an unknown destination, never being seen again until their bodies were found in Katyn forest.

The name Katyn causes a silence and a shudder whenever it is named in Polish company. In that name is indescribable horror and tragedy, and a crime beyond imagining.

CHAPTER XXXI

JOZEF who had been an impassioned pianist had become an impassioned printer. That small printing press in his own room did not satisfy his ambitions nor those of the friends with whom he was working. It was also very dangerous for the family in St. Theresa Street. Propaganda against the Germans—an activity on which the mysterious 'Bor' was especially keen—required full-sized printing presses, and presently there were seven concealed in Warsaw.

The most important was an underground hall or crypt under a modest looking villa in a side street. A gang of young Poles, of whom Jozef was one, scooped out the earth from the ground floor of the villa, taking care that all trace of excavation should be removed and capable of being hidden under a clean and dust-free floor at a moment's notice. How to remove the earth without attracting the attention of the German police was one of the greatest difficulties. It was solved by enrolling schoolboys and girls sworn to secrecy. At intervals, and never more than two at a time, they carried it away in baskets, and in satchels, spilling it elsewhere in different places—rubble heaps, back gardens, gutted houses. Then the printing machinery had to be taken in bit by bit in small sections followed by the stores of paper and ink. It was one of the marvels of this Underground movement that all this should have been done under the very noses of the Germans without attracting their suspicion.

Aunt Krysta was in secret collaboration with her nephew Jozef. To the astonishment of the family and her own husband, who came now and then from his bookseller's shop to spend an hour or two, she announced one afternoon that she was going to change her name and address.

There was general consternation.

"Aunt! What are you up to now?"

"For God's sake, my dear Krysta!" exclaimed Mrs. Mirski, staring at her as though she had taken leave of her senses.

Dr. Mirski smiled at her.

"I'm quite sure you're up to mischief," he said. "Probably you've been made Commander-in-Chief of some battalion of death."

"Not quite so distinguished as that," she answered with a cheery laugh. "I'm only going to be a housekeeper in that very modest villa where poor Mrs. Salinska used to live with her husband before they were arrested. It has been empty since then. The Germans haven't commandeered it. By the way, my name will be Mrs. Ranska. I have perfectly good papers and I shall be glad to see any of you to tea now and then."

Vanda looked at her with a smile.

"Aunt, you're incurable! You have the spirit of a lioness. I'm sure Jozef is at the bottom of this. You've been putting your heads together for hours lately. Don't get into too much danger. Don't take too many risks. Those ought to be left to girls like me."

"Stuff and nonsense!" cried Aunt Krysta, cheerfully. "I'm

not going into any danger. I merely want to give you more elbow-room in this house."

There was a general laugh. Nobody believed her, but they were trained not to ask indiscreet questions.

She went with Jozef for a little walk to her new house.

He took her into the sitting-room.

"This is where you keep guard," he told her. "Look! Do you see that little button by the wainscotting?"

"Not easy to see!" she remarked.

"It's just shoulder high. You have only to lean against it and it changes a green light down below into a red light. That means danger. All printing presses to stop. No one to go in or out, even if the signal lasts for days."

"Charming!" said Aunt Krysta. "I'd like to see what's underneath. What's that faint whirring noise?"

She touched one of the walls which had a slight vibration.

"Come and see," said Jozef. He was excited and gave a little laugh as he went into the small hall, stooped down and brushed away some dust. He touched a wire which made a signal to those below that someone was coming down. With a rusty nail he opened a trap door revealing a narrow ladder.

"Don't break your neck," he said to his aunt. "This has to be closed again when we're on the ladder. Go backwards."

Aunt Krysta went backwards down the ladder as though in a ship. From below two hands held and guided her. Jozef jumped down after her.

"Well, I must say . . ." exclaimed Aunt Krysta, staring about her with astonishment, "this is a nice box of tricks!"

It was something more than a cellar. It was a crypt large enough to hold four printing presses which were running with a smooth purring noise under the guidance of four men stripped to the waist. In a little outer room sat two soldiers of the Underground armed with revolvers and grenades. On one of the walls was a shield with a white eagle—the emblem of Poland.

"This is my printing shop," said Jozef proudly. "I'm in charge here. Twelve hours a day on duty."

"You lads will suffocate!" said Aunt Krysta. "Poof! I'm in a bath of perspiration already. But there's one thing I want to know before I get up to fresh air."

"You know too much already," said Jozef, grinning at her.

"What happens if the Gestapo get news of this and come through that trap door after stepping over my dead body?"

Jozef shrugged his shoulders and one of the young men stripped to the waist who had overheard the question laughed.

"We shall have to fight for it . . . that's all."

He guided Aunt Krysta up the ladder again, closed the trap door with the greatest care, smoothing the dust back to hide it. Then he went with her into the little sitting-room.

"You can't stay here alone," he said. "That would be rather unconvincing. You want some lodgers. I'm going to provide them."

Aunt Krysta saw a dancing light in his eyes.

"Very kind of you," she said dryly. "Agreeable people, I hope."

"A charming couple," he told her. "I'm going to marry Marta. We'll come and live with you. It'll be safer for all of us. We both have our labour certificates of course. Father Paul will join us in holy matrimony."

"Have you fixed it up with Marta?" asked Aunt Krysta. "That seems rather necessary, doesn't it?"

"I'll go and ask her now," said Jozef. "No time like the present. Come with me, Aunt. Another little walk won't do you any harm."

They walked to the Actresses' Café where Marta was still acting as waitress. She saw him come in and fluttered her eyelids at him. There were a few people at the tables at one of which Aunt Krysta took a chair.

"Shan't be long!" said Jozef. "I'll bring you a cup of coffee."

He went over to Marta who was arranging little cakes on a tray.

"Marta," he said, "I'm taking you away from this place. You've had enough of it, haven't you?"

Marta looked amused but not astonished.

"Where do you want to take me? To a beautiful concentration camp, or a still more beautiful prison?"

"A nice little house in Rozâna Street," he told her. "Modestly furnished with all conveniences. My Aunt Krysta will be our housekeeper. A wonderful woman and a wonderful cook. Dancing angels in attendance. Seventh Heaven up one flight of stairs."

"I don't believe in fairy-tales," said Marta. "Not in Warsaw. When does all this happen?"

"Next Sunday at six o'clock in the morning. It will be an Underground wedding. Father Paul will marry us at the Church of the Holy Cross. There'll be a choir and an organ for us."

Marta laughed quietly after a glance round the café.

"Aren't you talking nonsense?" she asked.

Some other customers came in and she moved towards them. He held her bare arm for a moment.

"Will you be there?"

"Go away, Jozef! People are looking at us."

"Will you be there?"

"Possibly, if I can get up as early as that."

She moved to one of the tables with her tray full of cakes. Never once did she look at him again while he sat with Aunt Krysta.

"It's all right," he told his aunt. "I knew it would be. We've talked it over many times—getting married, I mean."

He laughed excitedly.

"I'm going to have a good time. Marta! The printing presses! And you, my dear Aunt! What a wonderful combination of delight!"

"For goodness' sake don't look so joyful!" said Aunt Krysta. "They'll think you've killed the German governor of Warsaw."

They were both laughing as two S.S. men in uniform came in and sat down pretending not to be interested in the company of the Actresses' Café which they knew to be a hot-bed of the Underground.

Marta was only five minutes late at church where she was married to Jozef on the following Sunday. Marta had married the printing machines with which Jozef shared his love. It was like living over a volcano, or over a cave for which savage men were searching. Would Jozef be caught that day or the next? It was a dangerous marriage, but not without laughter after working hours. Jozef was a laughter-maker as well as a pianist and a printer. His happiness with Marta seemed to kill the sense of danger. But Aunt Krysta kept a wary eye on the little button which turned a green light red downstairs.

CHAPTER XXXII

THAT mysterious man who went by the name of 'Bor'—and many other names, always changing, always with labour certificates and identity cards for these different personalities—became the Commander-in-Chief of the Secret Army and the head and centre of all Underground activities.

He adopted many disguises, sometimes having a beard, sometimes being clean-shaven, sometimes hiding his watchful, vivid and humorous eyes behind dark glasses. He had as many addresses as he had disguises and seldom slept in the same bed twice. The Gestapo, after having captured and executed General 'Grot', the chief organizer of the Polish Resistance movement, were always searching for his successor, the man who continued the battle of wits against them and had organized a military force all over Poland. Who was he? Where was this master mind? Who were his chief associates? Young prisoners caught with wireless sets or with secret messages were questioned, bludgeoned, knocked about, starved, to make them tell the secret of this man, and to give away the names of their other leaders or their own confederates. Often they did not know. The system of working in small groups unknown to each other was a safeguard, but there were others who knew and were heroic in their silence. Their greatest fear was that under torture they might blab. They carried little capsules of poison in case this happened. It would not be a selfish suicide but a noble death to save the lives of their friends. One man, a courier named Jan Karski cut his wrists in hospital anxious for death but he was prevented from bleeding to death and escaped from the hospital with the help of friends, and went on working underground with the same risk ahead of him.

Not all were so heroic. Every now and then a man under torture gave away important secrets. Then it was necessary to change papers, identity cards, secret addresses, with the greatest possible haste, and with the uncanny skill which had been attained by the team of expert forgers.

'Bor' was a man of humour. He had a headquarters staff— never assembling in a group, but always in touch with him—who were equally humorous at times. Nothing pleased them more than to answer German propaganda by counter-propaganda so ingeniously devised, so perfect in its knowledge of German psychology that their enemies were bewildered, confused and completely hoaxed.

One such hoax was the issue of the German-sponsored *Warsaw Courier*, perfectly counterfeited in type and form but with contents highly embarrassing to the German authorities, giving accurate news of the military situation abroad and a speech by Winston Churchill.

Another glorious trick was when they tapped the wires of the megaphones used by the Germans for broadcasting their own orders and propaganda, replaced by a patriotic Polish speech and the playing of the Polish national anthem. Poles passing down the chief thoroughfare stopped, stared, took off their hats, and were deeply moved, until the arrival of police cars and agents of the Gestapo.

False proclamations were issued in the name of Governor Frank, that tyrant, and in the name of Chief of Police, Koppe, hated for his brutality and cruelty. In many cases leaflets coming from the Underground presses, like that of Jozef's were so subtle and ingenious that the Germans themselves were deceived and believed them to emanate from anti-Hitlerite organizations in Germany.

Thousands and hundreds of thousands of leaflets, brochures, and news bulletins were printed and distributed among the Polish population to keep up their morale and to tell them the truth of what was happening in the war—the plight of the German Armies in Russia during a terrible winter when German soldiers were ill-clad and frozen—the surrender of the Afrika Corps, the retreat from Stalingrad, the heroic fighting of Polish troops—their sons and brothers—on many fronts, as the moving picture of Fate was unwound after the first years of German victories.

All this propaganda directed by 'Bor', a little man with charming manners, and gaiety of heart, and steel nerves, was devised to embarrass and demoralize the enemy. For other reasons many of the Germans were becoming demoralized in Warsaw. The Gestapo was up to its neck in black market racketeering. They were open to bribery from Poles in the Underground. Many of them were living with Polish women of the lowest class who even in their degradation still retained a sense of patriotism and acted as spies or confederates of Underground groups, giving warning of coming arrests or betraying the men who bought them.

They were not all angels in Warsaw, nor all heroes and heroines. There was a riff-raff of gunmen and gangsters in the underworld, quick on the trigger in low haunts. They black-mailed women, and especially the Jews in the Warsaw ghetto, by threatening them with the concentration camps and the gas-ovens unless they paid large sums to their 'protectors'. They were outlaws and ruffians, reckless of their own lives and regardless of other people's lives, if they were in a killing mood.

In Warsaw also there were many Communists whose sympathy was with Russia, in spite of all the misery inflicted on Polish prisoners in Russian concentration camps, and whose political allegiance was not to General Sikorski and his government in exile but to Stalin and his associates in the Kremlin. They shot up the Germans and the Gestapo. They derailed trains carrying German supplies and ammunition. They had an Underground movement of their own independently of that directed by 'Bor' until later they agreed to join forces with his Secret Army.

Warsaw was a city of divided loyalties and of bloody incidents, not all to be put down to the German occupation. There were Polish criminals in the underworld and in the forests where they lived as outlaws and bandits and gunmen.

But they were in a minority. They were just the scum which surges up in times of violence and warfare, or *la bête humaine* to be found in the slums of great cities even in times of peace. They had nothing in common with the great majority of Polish inhabitants, like those known to Vanda and her friends—intellectuals and idealists—or like the peasants, simple, honest, generous, and heroic, in every part of Poland, risking their lives for liberty and the freedom of the soul, and the love of country.

CHAPTER XXXIII

STANISLAV learnt to speak English rather quickly and rather well. It was English with a Scottish accent.

He was in a Polish training camp not far from Aberdeen. He liked his comrades. They were good fellows, on the whole, though too apt to chase the girls, some of whom were not very respectable —they hung round the camp—and not very virtuous.

Stanislav was fond of girls, but he was fastidious, and owing perhaps to his family life and upbringing, liked them of good class and good morals.

He spoke to his friend Adam about this.

"I want to meet a nice English family."

"You can't," said Adam. "We're in Scotland."

Stanislav laughed.

"Anyhow they all speak the English language, and anyhow I want to get to know them. What's the good of being in a foreign country if you never meet the natives? I want to find out what's going on in their minds—if anything. I want to find out what they think of the Germans and the Russians, and why they don't come to the rescue of Poland."

"My dear fellow," said Adam, "you'll never find out. The English, and no doubt the Scottish, are very reserved people and don't give themselves away. I've read that in a book. They're a very mysterious slow-thinking people and act by intuition and tradition rather than by deliberate thought or philosophy; and they think that everything they do is right and that what other people do is mostly wrong. I read that in a book also."

"Some people who write books are liars," said Stanislav. "They lead one astray. I want to find out for myself. In any case I want to escape from this camp now and then where our brother Poles are always lamenting the fate of Poland and are disgusted with the bread of exile, and unduly impatient to rejoin their families."

"You're a humbug," said Adam, hitting him on the shoulder. "No one is more impatient than you to fight for our liberation."

Stanislav groaned.

"True! Perhaps that's why I want to get away from this camp now and then. I find myself brooding. I'm getting melancholy. Sometimes despair sits on my bed and gibbers at me. To be quite honest I feel in need of love."

Adam laughed loudly.

"Now we're getting at the truth of things. Our little Stanislav feels the need of love in a climate which rains every day and in a country where the natives have frozen knees and frozen hearts."

Stanislav came to know a family in Aberdeen. One of his fellow officers introduced him to a certain Mr. Bulloch, who was, he said, professor of anthropology, or some such subject, in the University of Aberdeen. They took tea with him one day and found him hospitable, friendly and intelligent. He had been to Poland in the 'thirties in the time of Pilsudski, and admired the cities of Warsaw, Vilno and Cracow. He had travelled extensively in Europe and had made a study of its peoples and languages and historical origins. He spoke three languages—French, German and Spanish—with a strong Scottish accent. It was, indeed, in French with an Aberdonian intonation that the two Polish officers were able to exchange ideas with him.

He had strong convictions about the outcome of the war.

"The Germans will lose themselves in Russia," he said, "just as the *Grande Armée* of Napoleon did. They'll freeze to death—poor devils. They'll die of typhus like Napoleon's men. And Russian manpower, enormous and inexhaustible, will overwhelm them in the end by sheer weight of numbers."

"And then?" asked Stanislav. "What happens then to Poland?"

Mr. Bulloch looked at him with steel-blue eyes under shaggy red eyebrows.

"That's a difficult question," he said slowly after intensive thought. "Shall we ever get the Russian back to his own frontiers? I'm sorry for Poland, crushed between two aggressive powers."

"Poland must be liberated," said Stanislav's fellow officer. "The honour of England is pledged to that. It's for that purpose alone that we are here fighting, or ready to fight on any front."

Mr. Bulloch agreed, still speaking in French.

"*Vous avez raison*. But neither England nor Scotland can do the impossible or quarrel with those who are fighting Hitler and his legions. At the moment Generalissimo Stalin is much in favour with us. General Zhukov is one of our heroes, as long as he defeats the German *Wehrmacht*. There are very few in this country whose minds have moved as far as asking the same question as yourself —What happens then?"

"What do you think, sir?" asked Stanislav in French.

Professor Bulloch of Aberdeen University answered cautiously after many puffs from an old pipe.

"I've studied the history of Russia," he said. "I've read the writings of Karl Marx and Lenin, and some of the speeches of Stalin himself. All that is not very encouraging."

"The Russians," said Stanislav, "are like the hordes of Ghengis Khan. They say they are the friends of Poland but they rounded up our retreating army. They put them into concentration camps where many starved to death. I was lucky to escape from them."

Professor Bulloch looked at him again with those steel-blue eyes with a deliberate gaze which seemed to look right through him.

"Most of you Poles have had a terrible time," he said. "If the Russians smash Germany with our help from the west, it may be very unpleasant for all of us. How shall we thrust them back? How shall we establish a *cordon sanitaire* against the creed of Communism, which is very infectious? Besides Communism there is the old Russian Imperialism which will be encouraged by victory. Generalissimo Stalin will become a new Czar of All the Russias, in all but name. I foresee that, but the idea is unpopular over here just now—even in Aberdeen University."

The door opened and the professor laid down his pipe.

"Tea, I expect, gentlemen. Here are my wife and my daughter, Janet. Let me introduce you if I can remember your names."

Stanislav sprang to his feet and spoke his own name and bowed to a middle-aged woman with a cheerful smiling face, and to a girl with red hair and a little freckled nose and blue eyes like her father's, but not so steel-blue, nor so penetrating. There was a smile in them as she shook hands with the two Polish officers, as though amused by their visit.

"Come into the next room," said Mrs. Bulloch. "Tea is on the table. Janet, my dear, open the window. This room reeks with smoke!"

It was a well-spread tea-table with cakes and hot scones.

"Have one of these," said the girl called Janet, holding out a plate of scones to Stanislav. "Just out of the oven. Home-made—by me!"

Stanislav thanked her in English and then spoke in French.

"*Vous parlez français, mademoiselle?*"

The girl laughed and shook her head.

"After ye manner of Stratford-atte-Bow!"

That was beyond the understanding of Stanislav who then attempted a little English.

"I am very happy to be here. It is *très charmant*—for me to be in an English home."

"Scottish," said Janet, smiling at him.

"I beg your pardon," said Stanislav. "To me Scottish and English are—how shall I say?—*la même chose.*"

Janet gave a ripple of laughter.

"That's a terrible thing to say! We're very Scotch in Aberdeen."

"Scotch—Scottish?" said Stanislav. "That is very difficult. I wish very much to know the English language, or—how do I say it?—the Scotch or Scottish language?"

"You know quite a lot," said Janet. "But I wouldn't advise you to learn the English of Aberdeen."

"You speak that?"

"I'm bi-lingual. I went to school in England. I acquired the accent of the B.B.C."

This was again beyond the range of Stanislav's knowledge and the girl's mother reproved her laughingly.

"Janet, you're talking nonsense!"

"I like talking nonsense now and then," said Janet.

She had a merry glint in her eyes which met those of Stanislav.

He liked the look of her. He liked the little freckles on her nose and her red hair caught on fire when it was touched by the watery sunshine coming through the window of this little room, and the humour which lurked about her mouth—a pretty, kiss-able mouth, he thought.

'She's charming,' he thought. 'And it's very pleasant to be in this Scottish—or Scotch—home. It reminds me of my own home in Warsaw. It's better than being in an army canteen.'

"What's happening in Poland?" asked Janet presently, perhaps for the sake of making conversation and being polite to a foreign visitor.

Stanislav would have been glad to answer that question at some length. There were a thousand things he would like to tell her about Poland, but his English was severely limited.

"It is hell in Poland," he said. "It is very bad. It is terrible. The Germans are very bad. The Russians are very bad. They kill many people. For us it is *une tragédie déplorable*."

He gave a laughing groan, at his ignorance of the girl's language.

"I cannot speak English. I cannot express myself. It is very unhappy for me."

"Speak in French," said Professor Bulloch. "My daughter understands more than she pretends. In any case I'll act as interpreter."

Stanislav became eloquent in French. He talked too much and too fast. He described the war in Poland when he had been with the Novogrodek cavalry brigade. He told them of the heroism of the civilian population and the sufferings of the refugees, and the treachery of the Russians who had pretended to come as friends and had disarmed Polish soldiers in retreat and had occupied half the country. He became excited and impassioned.

"We Poles in exile have only one thought and one hope. It is to liberate our country. For that we are willing to fight and die. The Polish people love liberty. They think life worthless without it. One day they will rise against their enemies. It will be the day of liberation."

Professor Bulloch shook his head almost imperceptibly.

"They must bide their time," he said. "A premature rising would lead to massacre."

Janet had listened to Stanislav intently, struggling to understand his rapid French. He saw the pity in her eyes and a look of warm sympathy.

"The Poles are very heroic," she said. "Everybody admits that. I've no doubt they're having a terrible time, though we don't hear much about it. It doesn't come into the newspapers."

Stanislav's brother officer had been talking mostly to Mrs. Bulloch. He spoke very good English and grinned now and then at Stanislav's struggle with that language. Presently he rose to take his leave.

"We must go, old boy," he said to Stanislav in Polish. "We mustn't outstay our welcome."

When Stanislav took Janet's hand and bowed over it she said, "Come again. Learn some more English."

"That would be a great pleasure," he told her gratefully. "You will teach me a little more English?"

She laughed and said, "If you like. Now and then."

"Pleased to see you again," said Professor Bulloch cordially. "There are many things I want to know about Poland. I have agreeable recollections of it."

"Yes," said Mrs. Bulloch in her motherly way. "Do come again. I dare say it's a change for you."

He went again. Presently he made a habit of going again, always received with kindness, and meeting many of their friends. His English improved quite rapidly. It was a boon to him to have these glimpses of home life. It was of course inevitable that he should fall in love with Janet. He fell in love with her—with the little freckles on her nose, with the red fire of her hair, with the merry glint in her eyes, with the honesty of her Scottish character —straight-thinking and straight-speaking. He told her about Vanda and Halina and his Polish relatives and friends. He made her laugh quite often, but he did not flirt with her in a frivolous way. She wouldn't have stood for that, he knew instinctively. She gave him her friendship and for a time he was patient and did not ask for more. One day he would ask for more.

CHAPTER XXXIV

JOZEF had to leave his printing presses from time to time to buy food for Marta and Aunt Krysta. Marta was going to have a baby to his great joy, and was in no state for standing about in queues. In any case it was good for Jozef to get some fresh air above ground after working for long hours in the heated atmosphere of the printing hall. But there was always a risk now that he might be caught by a *lapanka* and one day he was nearly caught.

The *lapanka* or hide-and-seek, was the slang name given by the Poles to a round-up by the S.S. and Gestapo, now becoming more frequent.

It always happened suddenly. Some empty military trucks would be drawn up in a side street. Then the green cars of the S.S. and two lorries crowded with police arrived from opposite sides of the main street when they would stop, jump out, cutting off all side streets and closing both ends of the main street. There would be shouts of *Halt!* Everyone and everything had to stop. No one was allowed to enter a house or leave the street. All buses, tramcars, and other vehicles were brought to a standstill and people had to get out, hands up. Then many of them were put into the empty trucks and driven off to the Paviak prison where their identity cards were checked. Some of them with good labour certificates were allowed to go, perhaps after two weeks in prison, but many of the able-bodied young men, whatever their credentials, true or false, were herded into trains for forced labour in Germany.

Jozef was walking along a street leading out of the Ujazdowska Avenue. He was in a happy mood and whistling an aria from *Cosi Fan Tutte*. Marta was going to have a baby. He would soon be a father. That would be extremely amusing, he thought. It would make Marta very happy and perhaps make her less nervous than she had been lately. She was nervous and frightened if he came back fifteen minutes late, or if there were a knock at the door by some stranger.

A boy selling newspapers at the corner of the street spoke one word to him. "*Lapanka!*" It was often these newspaper boys who gave the first alarm.

"Where?" asked Jozef.

He had stopped whistling. He felt a little moisture break out in the palms of his hands and on his forehead—the first sign of fear. If he were caught Marta would be in a terrible state. If he were put into the Paviak prison they might track him down and discover the printing presses. They might do a bit of torture with him and force out a confession, before they shot him against a wall. That would lead to many other deaths—his comrades, his fellow workers. These grim thoughts rushed into his mind, and for a moment or two he felt faint.

"We're in the net already," said the boy. "They've shut off every street round us. Look out!"

There were shouts of *Halt!* at the end of the street in which he stood. A police car sounding its siren was coming his way. A few people in the street stood still, frozen by terror.

Jozef was standing by a private house with a green door. There was no time to ring the bell. In three seconds that police car would be on him. There was no way of escape. He was caught like a rat in a trap.

Suddenly the green door opened and a voice said, "Quick!" A woman's hand clutched him, dragged him in, and shut the door swiftly and noiselessly.

"Only just in time!" said a girl's voice. She gave a little laugh and Jozef could hear her panting breath.

Then she recognized him and spoke in a whisper.

"Good heavens! It's Jozef Mirski. What luck!"

It was a girl named Tereska whom he had known when he was broadcasting as a pianist before the war. She had been a friend of Marta as a fellow singer.

For a few moments he could not speak to her. His heart was pounding. There was a singing in his ears. He had been terribly frightened.

Then he pulled himself together, stifling that fear.

"Thanks a thousand times. I thought I was for it that time."

"Come upstairs," said the girl. "You'll have to stay here for quite a while. How's Marta?"

She was still speaking in whispers as though those police in the street might hear.

"She's going to have a baby," said Jozef. "She'll be alarmed if I don't come home."

"Poor darling!" said Tereska. "Isn't it a mistake to have a baby in times like this?"

He didn't answer that. The idea had not occurred to him that it was a mistake to have a baby. On the contrary the thought of it had given him great joy, as though Peace reigned in Poland and life would be kind to a new arrival.

He went upstairs with Tereska and found himself in a room overlooking the street. Tereska's mother and two sisters were there, looking out of the window by concealing themselves behind the curtains.

"Another frightful *lapanka*!" said Tereska's mother. "But who are you young man? I seem to know your face."

"It's Marta's husband," said Tereska. "Jozef Mirski. I dragged him in only just in time."

Jozef looked out of the window. A lorry passed down the street with civilians who had been rounded up. They looked terror-stricken and despairing as they sat huddled together. But for the grace of God and Tereska's quick rescue Jozef would have been among them.

"Marta will be waiting for me." he said in a low voice. "She'll be frightened."

He had to stay there two hours. They could hear the police cars sounding their sirens. Once they heard a piercing scream, of some woman whose husband or son had been taken away. Then everything was quiet again.

"I must go," said Jozef. "Marta will be waiting for me. She'll be frightened," He repeated that dominant thought which distressed him miserably.

"Get back before the curfew," said Tereska.

She took him down to the front door and he kissed her hand before going.

"I owe my freedom to you. Perhaps my life."

"We were lucky," said Tereska. "Give my love to Marta."

He walked home through deserted streets. Aunt Krysta opened the door to him.

"Thank God you're back!" she exclaimed. "I was getting anxious. Marta has been terrified."

He rushed upstairs and held his wife in his arms.

"I couldn't help being late," he told her. "I was almost caught."

"I nearly died," said Marta. "Every minute seemed like an hour."

Her face was dead white until presently a little colour came back when Jozef kissed her lips and her closed eyes.

An hour or two later when he went down to the printing hall he was startled to find only three of his comrades instead of four.

"Tadeusz is missing," said one of them. "He went out to buy some tobacco. It was two hours ago. I'm afraid they've caught him in that *lapanka*."

Jozef turned pale and he felt his heart give a lurch.

"Supposing he has to give us away?"

His comrade shook his head.

"Not Tadeusz! He'll keep his mouth shut. Besides he has a little capsule in case of accident. He'll swallow that rather than blab on his pals."

Tadeusz never came back, but he didn't blab.

CHAPTER XXXV

HALINA was looking out of the window of the *salon* one morning when she saw a German car draw up outside the house. It had a military driver and inside was a German officer and she had a glimpse of a young woman whom she could not clearly see.

It was not agreeable when a German car stopped outside a Polish house. She called out to her sister who was coming downstairs.

"Vanda! Something's happening. A German car has drawn up outside."

Vanda was alarmed. On her table upstairs she had left a number of forged papers at which she had been working since six o'clock that morning. She rushed out of the room to put them in a hiding place, inside a picture-frame with a portrait of her grandmother as a young girl.

Halina stared out of the window again. She saw the German officer get out. He helped out the girl with him. She was carrying a young child of about two. The officer spoke to her, smiled, saluted, and drove away in the car. Presently there was a knock on the front door.

'How very extraordinary!' thought Halina.

She rushed downstairs and opened the door. On the step was the young woman carrying the child.

"Oh, Vanda!" she cried. "I had to come here to save my little boy. Perhaps your mother can find room for us."

Halina stared at her.

"I'm not Vanda. I'm Halina. Who are you?"

"I'm Gena. I'm one of your cousins. I come from Zamosc which the Germans call Himmlerstadt. Terrible things are happening there."

"What were you doing with that German officer?" asked Halina, suspiciously.

"He drove me here all the way. A friend of his—another officer—gave me the warning."

She was incoherent and began to weep, clutching the child.

"You had better come in," said Halina.

She led this unknown cousin into the *salon* where the girl sank into a chair still weeping. The child crawled away from her and began to play with the tassel of one of the curtains.

Vanda came down and gave a cry of astonishment.

"Gena! . . . I seem to remember. . . . Weren't you living in Zamosc? We've heard terrible rumours. . . ."

Terrible rumours from Zamosc called Himmlerstadt. They were impossible to believe. In the old town with its Italian-looking arcades there was a big German garrison, mostly of S.S. men under the orders of Himmler. The inhabitants were being turned out of their houses and villas to make way for the families of the S.S. men and were put into a transient camp, as it was called. Here they were segregated, the young men and women being sent in batches to forced labour in Germany. The conditions in the transient camp were bad and many of the older people died. But rumours had come to Warsaw of something more atrocious, something unbelievable. The S.S. men, it was said, were taking young, healthy, fair-headed babies and young children from their mothers and sending them into Germany to be brought up as Germans. God alone could know why that should be. Were the Germans short of fair-haired babies of their own? Why should they want any more?

This girl Gena told an extraordinary story when she was able to speak about it. There was a German officer billeted in her house. She had hardly spoken to him but one day he tapped at the door and asked to see Gena's father with whom she was living.

"Excuse me," he said, "but I have a friend going this afternoon by car to Warsaw. He is willing to take your daughter and the baby. If you know anybody in Warsaw with whom they could stay I think you ought to take this opportunity. Needless to say this has to be kept a secret. No one is allowed to leave the district, as of course, you know."

Gena's father was astounded at this offer from a German officer with whom he had hardly been in contact, maintaining the coldest possible reserve.

"A thousand thanks," he said, deeply moved by this amazing kindness from a man he had hated as an enemy.

"*Nichts zu danken!*" said the officer. "We cannot interfere with police orders but as a German officer I consider it my duty to act in this way. I'm glad I have the opportunity to do so, and I deeply deplore the things that are being done by the S.S. in Himmlerstadt."

So now there were two more members of the Mirski household. That night Gena was delirious with a high temperature, the baby was crying, the electric current was cut off for all Poles by 9 p.m. Vanda had to work by candlelight on her secret tasks.

So it went on, with increasing difficulties and dangers as the months passed and one year followed another. It was hard to get food and most shops were closing down. It was only by smuggling and the black market that food could be obtained. There was an elaborate system of smuggling by peasants who came by train from the countryside with their bundles of produce, jumping out at stations the other side of Warsaw and making the rest of the journey on foot. The German police turned a blind eye to much of this, very willing to be bribed, or in some cases sympathizing with the population. The peasants sold their goods in return for silver cigarette cases, boots, clothes and other useful articles or charged high prices, always increasing as the zloty was devalued.

The Mirski family had their own private smuggler—a sturdy courageous and good-natured fellow—who came once a week with butter, cheese, eggs and other farm produce. Even then there were hungry days and periods of undernourishment, worse during the cold days of winter without fuel to heat the rooms.

Vanda sat many times in her room numb with cold, hardly able to do the fine work of copying German movement orders and identity cards as one of the team of expert forgers dispersed all over Warsaw. But this girl who had once told the man who loved her that she was a 'dedicated woman' had a fire inside her, a fire of the spirit, which urged her to go to work for long hours, to ignore the coldness of her body. Each forged paper, or part of a forged paper, because others did the printing and provided photographs, might save a man's life, might cheat the Gestapo, might enable one of 'Bor's' young men to move about freely with secret messages.

She worked with a passionate intensity of concentration. One slip of penmanship, one wrongly coloured ink, one poor copy of the signature of the German police chief—Koppe—she made a speciality of that—might lead to arrest and a firing squad. Lives depended upon her accuracy and observation of the most minute detail. There was a thrill in the work. It was in a way a spiritual adventure. It obsessed her mind and soul. Perhaps it was the reason why she had been so unresponsive to Jerzy, pushing him off from ardent love-making, resisting the temptation in her own heart. She was too busy for that kind of thing! She was too deeply involved in this secret adventure.

She was always busy, morning, noon and night, for she had to make time to go down to the black market, even to stand in the market-place with small treasures from her father's cabinets, to keep the family pot boiling. She would have found that a humiliation except for other girls and women of her class standing there beside her. Often she had to come into the *salon* for some part of the evening to entertain her parents' guests and Halina's young friends. She had to talk with them, smile with them, laugh with them, while she thought: 'How can I get away without being rude? How can I get back to my work?'

Some of these visitors brought danger with them. They were wanted men—men in hiding. There were no less than eight officers from her uncle's cavalry brigade who had escaped as prisoners of war. They did not come altogether, of course, but one by one, or two by two, and often had to sleep the night because they stayed after curfew hour. They slept in armchairs or on the sofa, and had to be fed, being as hungry as hunters.

None of them knew the whereabouts of Stanislav. She could tell by their guarded words that they believed him to be dead—either killed in war or starved to death in a Russian concentration camp.

"I think he's still alive," she told them firmly.

One of them looked away to avoid her eyes.

"I hope so!" he answered evasively. "There's always a chance."

Then one day she heard news of Stanislav. Jerzy came back from his mysterious journey. Several people were in the *salon* that evening. Someone was playing the piano—not Jozef who was with his printing machines. Halina was talking and laughing with two young men who were telling her how they had dodged a *lapanka*, escaping by sheer bluff and pretending to be Germans to a stupid policeman who did not detect their Polish accent, speaking a frightful dialect of his own. A visitor from Mars, arriving in this room would have thought it a rendezvous of gay, care-free people, a little sanctuary of civilization.

Then Jerzy arrived, coming into the room quietly because of the music which was being played again.

He raised his hand to Vanda and came to sit by her side on a low stool with his hands clasped about his knees, one hand gloved as usual.

"Welcome back!" said Vanda, giving him her hand to kiss. "You've been a long time away. I was getting afraid."

"That was kind of you," he answered gratefully. "I'm glad you thought of me."

"Often!" she told him. "While I was working."

He looked round the room with a smile.

"It's wonderful to be in a room like this! On the way back I've been sleeping in barns and forests, and turnip fields and ditches. This is like heaven especially with you sitting here and looking like an angel."

"I don't look much like an angel," said Vanda, laughing at him. "I don't feel like one. But I feel very happy at seeing you again."

"It's good to hear you say that," he said in a low voice. "On the way back it was the thought of you, the vision of you, which kept me going when I was very nearly done. 'I must see Vanda again,' I thought. 'I must tell her the good news. I've something to tell which will light up her eyes.' So I kept plodding on over the mountains and through the forests when I was pretty weak with hunger and very near exhaustion. You see, I'm not one of the world's athletes. I used to be a poor devil of a violinist—one of the long-haired brigade."

"Good news?" asked Vanda. "Is there any good news nowadays? Tell me, quickly!"

"I've seen your brother, Stanislav," he said, watching her

face for that lighting up. "He sends his love to you. He's in fine shape."

Vanda's eyes lit up as he had hoped they would. A look of joy and wonderment rushed into them. As brother and sister she and Stanislav had been devoted to each other in spite of hair-tuggings as boy and girl and Stanislav's gift of satire as a young man. They had understood each other, with a secret code between them, laughing at the same jokes, talking nonsense, revealing now and then a deep affection.

"Oh, Jerzy, how wonderful! Where did you meet him? Dare I ask that?"

Jerzy did not keep that secret.

"I've asked 'Bor's' permission to tell you and your family. I met him in London—on his way to Scotland. It was when I was reporting to General Sikorski. He was in the ante-room and we started talking. He told me that he came from Warsaw and that his name was Mirski. 'Stanislav?' I asked, and he laughed and said, 'How do you know that?'"

"Oh, Jerzy!" cried Vanda again. "How marvellous! You have been to England and back? You've actually met Stanislav? I must tell Mother and Father and Halina and Aunt Krysta. We have all been praying for him."

"Don't tell anybody else," said Jerzy, warningly. "It mustn't get about that I'm one of 'Bor's' Mercury boys."

Vanda waited until the guests were gone. During that wait Jerzy asked a question, half humorously, but a little shyly.

"Can I claim a reward for this good news?"

Vanda avoided his eyes.

"If you don't ask too much! Don't hold me up to ransom."

When the last guest had gone she rushed over to her father and mother and cried out to them.

"Jerzy has seen Stanislav! He's alive, and well. He's in England. He sends us all his love."

It was as though she had announced a miracle.

When Jerzy had to go she went down into the hall with him.

"Did you say something about a reward?" she asked.

She was aware that her heart was fluttering. She was filled with a sudden tenderness and gratitude. Jerzy had risked his life to bring her this news. He had gone beyond his strength to bring it through those dark forests and on night-walks through enemy country.

"I withdraw the claim," he told her. "Whatever you give me must be of your own free will. Without obligation!"

She moved towards him and let him take her in his arms and kiss her lips. Presently—how long was it?—she put her hands against his shoulders and pushed him away a little, but very gently and with a kind of reluctance.

He looked at her and dropped his arms and said something with a grave simplicity.

"Thank you! That fulfills a dream I've had—a recurrent dream."

"Oh, Jerzy," said Vanda in a low voice. "Don't ask too much. Don't take me away from my work."

"No!" he promised. "That wouldn't be fair. And I have my own work. I'm starting off again quite soon."

He held her in his arms again unable to resist one more embrace.

"When the war is over, when Poland is liberated. . . ."

"Yes," said Vanda. "Then, there'll be time for love. Oh, my dear—let's pray for that."

So he went away, releasing her with infinite tenderness.

CHAPTER XXXVI

When Hitler had ordered his armies to invade Russia the Polish people had felt their hearts uplifted by a new hope and by a kind of unholy glee which was inevitable even to good Christians. Those two nations who had torn Poland in half and treated them with such cruelty would destroy each other.

In Warsaw the house in St. Theresa Street was only one of many in which groups of friends had come to discuss the new situation excitedly.

Halina had made everyone laugh when she raised her right hand and said, "May the two dragons swallow each other and leave nothing behind but their tails!"

Yet as time went on, with the Germans deep in Russia, and afterwards when their retreat from Stalingrad began and the Russian armies—fighting bloody battles, reckless of life—came westwards in a slow-moving but irresistible tide, there was a kind of confusion and bewilderment in Polish minds. Orders had come from the government in exile that General 'Bor's' Secret Army in Poland should give all aid to Russia, and these orders were carried out by the sabotage of German supply lines, by raids on their ammunition depots, by espionage of all their troop movements—such information being sent over to England by wireless or courier service.

All aid to Russia? All aid to those who had committed the mass murders of Polish officers in Katyn forest? They had deported a million and a half Polish citizens into the unknown vastnesses of Russia when their armies were in retreat. They had made a pact with Sikorski pledging themselves to friendly co-operation—and it had not happened. They had promised the release of all Polish prisoners but had not liberated thousands of them. They had obstructed the formation of a Polish Army under General Anders and he was forced to apply to Stalin himself for the transference of his 40,000 men with their wives and families from Russian territory to the Middle East. Even then he was balked and tricked. But they were ordered to give all aid to Russia so that Germany might be defeated.

'Bor' carried out those orders loyally, as he did all orders from the government in exile—but with no love for the Russians. They had martyred his friends and fellow citizens in Eastern Poland. But they were helping to defeat Germany. Hitler must be destroyed. One devil must be cast out by the Devil himself, if need be. Then what? Who would chain up that other devil and keep him within bounds, and—possibly!—convert him to angelic sweetness? A question for the future, not to be asked or answered in the present, even by men like Winston Churchill and President Roosevelt and General 'Bor' himself. He was in touch with his saboteurs, his wireless agents, his spies behind the German lines, his couriers to Europe, his armed bands in the forests, his volunteers in Warsaw who had sworn the oath of allegiance to his Secret Army, his men with the secret printing presses, and with hundreds of women and girls carrying his messages and orders, and old women—cultured old ladies— hiding hunted men like himself, giving shelter to escaped prisoners, wrapping up parcels for those in the Paviak prison. They were all in it, these people of Warsaw, and many other Polish cities. Even the Communists were co-operating now on behalf of Russia. Even the riff-raff and the scum of the earth in the city's underworld. One day—not too soon—not too soon— all this emotion of a people, strained beyond bearing, all this hatred of cruelty and oppression, would reach boiling point and explosion point. Nothing could stop it then—no orders from London, no cautionary words, no pleadings for restraint and prudence. There would be a surging up of passion—passion for liberty, passion for revenge, passion for freedom of the soul. The old ladies would be in it, the young girls, the priests. It would be an army of saints and heroes, and here and there a few cut-throats, and here and there a few cowards and traitors, but overwhelmingly a rising of those who loved Poland beyond their own lives, and freedom at any price.

Not too soon. . . . Not too soon.

The time came when 'Bor' had to say such words to his young men, impatient for action "Not yet!" The explosion point had not been reached. Much had to be done before then. Much had to happen.

Much had to happen—awful things—in Warsaw.

The German police, under orders from men as high as Himmler, were becoming more cruel because of this work of the Underground, tricking them, harassing them, thwarting them, and interfering seriously with the lines of communication of the German armies in Russia. In his headquarters behind the German lines, Hitler himself had reports about all this. An angry message came from him to the German governor in Warsaw. "Why don't you keep those Poles in order?"

What happened in Warsaw during all that time touched the lives of every family, and, not least, of the Mirski family in St. Theresa Street.

Vanda's mother had died not many months after her return from Lvov—that journey in a covered wagon. The hardships of being a refugee on the roads had been too much for her and to the great grief of them all she was taken very ill one night, frightening them. Vanda had rushed round to Father Paul who came in time to give her the last sacrament before she died, while on their knees they wept at her bedside. They heard her last words spoken in a whisper.

"Give my blessing to Stanislav."

She was buried in the cemetery of Povaski, and sometimes with her father and Halina but sometimes alone, Vanda went there to put flowers on her mother's grave. It was peaceful and beautiful there. It was like a park with many old trees and flowering shrubs and wide stretches of greensward across which long shadows fell on sunny afternoons. Vanda liked being alone here. She had time to think and to be aware of her own mind and self, and to renew her vows of dedication and service. Once she had wanted to kill herself. Once she had told Father Paul that she had lost her faith. Now in this quiet cemetery she seemed to be conscious of a divine spirit and to have a glimpse of eternal peace beyond the cruelties and struggle of life. This beauty around her, this peace, those dead, had some meaning beyond the short life allotted to man. Several times she had an extraordinary sense that her mother was close to her, even touching her with a loving hand. Once she looked up startled and cried out, "Mother!" as though she saw her—this mother who had been so gay and playful when they were children, before she was stricken by the war.

Here, in this quietude she thought of Jerzy who had gone away on one of his dangerous journeys. She said a prayer for his safety and found herself smiling in this loneliness of the cemetery and in this sorrow of remembrance when she thought of Jerzy's love for her and hers for him. She had let him take her in his arms. His kisses had been warm on her lips. It was, after all, good to be loved by Jerzy who was so brave and humorous and kind. She thanked God for his love, and then found herself weeping because of the tragedy of this war and all its cruelties which spoilt the happiness of life for so many lovers, for so many husbands and wives, for everyone.

She prayed for strength to go on with her job. Not with deliberate words nor with any set prayer, but with a kind of spiritual awareness she prayed for courage if ever she should be caught by the Gestapo copying their passports, forging signatures —even of the police chief Koppe.

Somehow she seemed to get strength from these quiet half-hours in the cemetery of Povaski. But she had to pay a painful price to get there, painful and distressing. The cemetery lay the other side of the Ghetto and she had to go in the tramcar through that quarter.

The Germans had established the Ghetto in 1940 and most of the Jews in Warsaw were forced into it, whatever their class or standing—intellectuals and professors, painters and musicians among the mass of uncultured and poverty-stricken Jews. A big wall was built all round this district near Povaski with its gates guarded by police. No Jew was allowed to leave it for any length of time without special permit, rarely given, unless the police were heavily bribed.

The tramcar emptied before it came to the Ghetto. Only a few people stayed in it on their way to the cemetery. Then it entered through one of the gates after it had been boarded by police who kept a sharp eye on all passengers. Vanda stared out of the tramcar windows. The streets were crowded by Jews of every type. It was curiously oriental as though the Jews had reverted to their ancient life and customs. On each side of the streets were little booths and stalls at which young and old Jews were offering their wares, with shouts and gesticulation to little groups who gathered about them and fingered the goods on sale. From the window Vanda saw with surprise piles of white bread and many kinds of food which it was impossible to buy in Warsaw even at terrific cost, but these Jewish people—many of them having been rich shopkeepers in Warsaw—were willing to pay high prices in gold to the Germans outside who controlled the traffic of merchandise and were open to any way of bribery. For a time, which ended abruptly later on, there was no lack of food in the Ghetto, and for those who were still well-to-do many luxuries could be had while others starved.

Restaurants were open and young Jews and Jewesses, smartly dressed, came in and out talking and laughing—laughing in the Ghetto of Warsaw over which, invisible, stretched the hand of a man named Himmler. Cafés were open and crowded. Gay dance music blared out of them. People were queueing up outside a music hall or cinema, and pushing through the crowds were thin and hungry-looking women carrying babies in their arms and begging for food from the passers-by. On the side-walks against the walls were old people sitting motionless, like living skeletons, starving to death in the midst of plenty. And here and there a well-dressed man with a fine intellectual face and tragic eyes came through the crowds as though unaware of them, as though alone in a forest, as though walking in a dream world, as a ghost.

Vanda found this painful. Like many other Poles she had once disliked the Jews. She had been brought up with prejudice against them because of their religion and their different race and their sharp ways in business and trade. Now her heart was filled with a deep pity for them, and she found the sight of them all herded into the Ghetto of Warsaw so unbearable that soon on her visits to the cemetery she went a long way round to avoid it.

It was later that the awful news came of thousands of Jews being driven out of the Ghetto and taken away in trucks to concentration camps in Germany where they were put to death in the gas ovens. At first many of them had gone willingly, beguiled by false promises that they were being taken to places where they would find good conditions and kind treatment. Then the frightful truth was revealed to them, filling them with terror and despair. A group of younger men decided that they must prevent further deportations and defend their lives by armed resistance. They set up a Jewish Military Organization in touch with 'Bor's' Secret Army which provided them with arms and ammunition smuggled into the Ghetto at night, and taught them how to make hand-grenades—the home-made *filipinki*.

Pity for the Jews touched many Polish hearts. Polish mothers adopted Jewish babies to save them from the Ghetto at the risk of their lives if discovered. Jews escaping through holes in the Ghetto wall, as many did, were hidden by Polish families and friends. But often the bodies of young Jews lay in the streets of Warsaw shot at sight by the Gestapo.

It was impossible to avoid tragic sights in Warsaw itself. They took people unawares. They shocked their vision and tore their hearts at street corners while they were chatting to friends, or taking a casual glimpse out of a window. That was in the dreadful year 1943. So it was when Vanda was going one day to the Church of the Holy Cross with that Cousin Gena who had come from Zamosc with her small child. They were feeling very sad because of terrible things happening during those autumn days. The Gestapo had been rounding up young men as hostages to be shot in batches as reprisals for the killing of a German soldier, whoever was guilty or whoever innocent. The Paviak prison held these boys among the other prisoners. Several of them were Vanda's friends—fellow students with Jozef and herself before the war. One of them had been round to her house quite recently, an attractive young man who had talked to her about books. He was studying English in the evenings after working in a German-controlled factory by permission of his unit in the Underground.

Gena was saying something about her small child.

"I hope he will grow up in a happier world. He knows nothing of all this. I hope he never may."

Vanda put her hand on Gena's arm and said: "What's happening?" Her face had gone pale and she had a startled look. They had arrived at the Krakovski Broadway and had to cross the wide street just opposite the church when suddenly several police cars pulled up and barred the way.

"It's a *lapanka*!" said Gena in a frightened voice. "What shall we do, Vanda?"

"It's something worse," said Vanda, feeling terror clutch at her heart.

A police van had arrived. Inside it were two rows of young men. Vanda had guessed the awful truth. It was to be a public execution of hostages.

She stared about her wildly. How could she escape this scene? She would not be able to bear the horrible sight of it. Gena must not see it. It would be a torture for both of them, too dreadful, too heart-rending, unendurable in its horror.

They were already cut off from any side-street by armed

police who were driving the people closer to the place of execution. Vanda realized that this would be against the wall close to the church into which some people were running as their only chance of escape from what they knew was going to happen.

Vanda seized Gena's hand which was ice-cold. She felt her own heart beating faster. She could hardly draw breath. She felt suffocated and faint and cold. She would have fallen if she had not clutched Gena's arm to steady herself.

The boys were slowly getting out of the van. Their hands were tied behind their backs and they stumbled as they went towards the wall. Their mouths were covered with plaster like the boys whom Father Paul of Warsaw had seen. They were not allowed to die with the cry of 'Long Live Poland!' on their lips.

Vanda turned her eyes downward. She would not look at the atrocity which was going to happen. She would rather die herself than see those boys shot against the wall.

Suddenly a change happened in her whole being, or in her soul. She looked up and saw the faces of the crowd about her, grave, pitiful, ennobled by compassion and tenderness for those boys about to die. A great silence was in this crowd. No one shed tears. No one stirred. In these people's eyes there was an intensity of suffering and love sent out from the depths of every heart and soul towards those boys who faced a firing squad.

Vanda seemed to be struck by a blinding revelation.

"I will look," she said within herself. "It's a privilege and honour to be here at this moment. It's a moment of martyrdom and we must send out a message of love and sympathy for those heroic boys who are innocent of any crime. We must send it out to them from our hearts so that they may feel the warmth of it and the love of it. These people around me feel a unity of spirit with those boys and with one another. We are all one. At this moment everything base in us, everything selfish, falls away. I'm standing here among people spiritualized by pain and pity."

Those thoughts went through the mind of Vanda, transfiguring her.

Out of the church on to the steps came a young priest. He had the face of a saint. The compassion of Christ looked out of his dark eyes. He was in the white albe and stole which he had worn in the church. He raised his outstretched hand, turning towards the boys against the wall and made above their heads the sign of the cross in absolution and blessing.

At that moment the squad fired and the boys fell and the wall was splashed by their blood. Afterwards the young priest was seized by the police and sent to the Paviak prison in which he died. . . . The bodies of the dead boys were thrown on to an empty lorry. A dustman was ordered to cover with sand the marks of blood on the pavement. The crowd was allowed to move on, and they left, silently.

Gena wept on her way back but Vanda walked on with a grave face.

'Those boys died for their country's sake,' she thought. 'They are the young martyrs of Poland. They leave us a testament of courage. We who survive must carry on their spirit. We must be ready for the same sacrifice.'

She was a Polish girl, this Vanda. To her the liberation of Poland and her love for it was a kind of religion, bound up with her religion, spiritualized and exalted beyond the common touch of patriotic sentiment.

When she came home that day in a mood of deep emotion she felt that she could never face these streets again, and never go near that blood-stained wall by the Church of the Holy Cross; but that very afternoon she was impelled by a mysterious sub-conscious urge to go that way. She went there alone but other people had come and, leaving the pavement, passed the spot now sacred to them, in single file. A bunch of white chrysanthemums was lying on the damp and rusty-coloured sand. And always before every spot where an execution had taken place—Novy Sviat, Jerozolimska Avenue—however crowded the street, and however hurried the people might be, they stepped off the side-walk and passed slowly in reverence before the blood-stained wall where fresh flowers were lying on the pavement beneath. Fresh flowers always, though it made the German police furious so that they forbade such demonstrations, vainly. A large white cross was painted on the wall—washed out many times by the police but every time newly painted, in spite of their patrols, by boys of the Underground. Anyone seen laying down flowers was arrested, but always a little bunch was dropped there.

These tragedies burnt deep into Polish minds. That Governor of Warsaw, and his police chief, and the Gestapo, were the greatest enemies of the German people. Did they think these things would be forgotten and unavenged? Did they ever stop to think what would happen in Warsaw and other cities of Poland when the German armies in Russia were being flung back and hard pressed and hopeless in retreat? Were they not stoking up fires of hatred which one day would break into flame and fury?

Wherever Polish people met in secret, whenever they exchanged some whispered words, one sentence was sure to be spoken.

"The Day will come. . . . We are waiting for the Day. . . ."

They were becoming eager for that day of reckoning when they would rise and their Secret Army would come into the open and they would throw off this tyranny and win their way to freedom. It would be the Day of Liberation. How long, O Lord?

General 'Bor', Commander-in-Chief of the Home Army—always in hiding, always hunted, escaping often with only a few minutes to spare, had still to restrain this impatience. How long could he hold it back—the flaming ardour of his young battalions, eager for action?

CHAPTER XXXVII

STANISLAV was in Italy after his time in Scotland where he had fallen very deeply in love with that Scottish lassie who was intelligent, humorous and kind.

She had allowed him one kiss before he went away when he wanted ten thousand. What a meagre ration for a Polish lover! One kiss when his heart was on fire, when parting from her was tragic, when, as he told her, he might never see her again.

They had had a tussle about that.

"You're as hard-hearted as Mary, Queen of Scots," he told her in his excellent English which he had mostly learnt from her.

She had laughed at that, much amused by his historical error.

"That poor lady had a very passionate heart! Perhaps you're thinking of Bloody Mary who is supposed—quite falsely—to have been a cruel and heartless creature."

"I want to kiss you a thousand times," said Stanislav again.

"Once! she insisted. "And that's a concession. I was born in Scotland. I have Presbyterian relations. I'm not to be carried off my feet by a Polish officer, however beautiful and brave."

But she was carried off her feet, at least ten inches above the ground, when he took advantage of her offer, for one kiss which was long and ardent.

Her face was flushed and her eyes shining when she found her feet on the carpet again.

"Heaven help me!" cried Janet. "I rather liked it! What would John Knox say?"

"I don't know him," said Stanislav. "And anyhow I don't care a curse what he says. Will you marry me if I come back from the war?"

"I shall have to," she confessed, "I shall have to make myself a respectable woman after a kiss like that."

They parted with laughter and yet it was tragic. She was not heartless. He saw the tenderness in her eyes and a look of pity and loving kindness.

"Take care of yourself," said Janet. "Come back to bonny Scotland. I'll be waiting for you."

A queer love affair this, between a Polish officer and a Scottish lassie, but to Stanislav it was more than a flirtation with a pretty girl. She had taken hold of his heart. She dwelt in his mind when he was crawling up a rocky path under German gunfire, when he lay at night under a bit of corrugated iron above two piles of stones with German shells screaming overhead, when one night he saw the stars above Monte Cassino and knew that before the next day darkened it would be victory or death.

'If I get through this,' he thought, 'Janet will be waiting for me.'

Do soldiers think like that on a battlefield? Were these men of the 15th Poznan Lancers—his crowd—thinking of the girls they loved, or of their homes in Poland, or of young sluts they had fondled in Glasgow, as they lay in darkness waiting for the first glimmer of dawn when they would hurl themselves against a powerful enemy in this mountainous country of Italy? Probably they were too exhausted to think much, if at all. Probably they were like the pack-mules which had been prodded up the rocky slopes at night and now lay breathing heavily and stirring convulsively when shells burst near them. Perhaps only a few men like Stanislav, intellectual, sensitive, still capable of thought now and then—the mind getting outside the body, freeing itself of fear, though hating it—could think of any woman in his past life, in a different kind of world, while expecting almost certain death next day.

Before the battle he met his old comrade, Adam Socha, who embraced him warmly and rejoiced to see him. They dined together in Adam's mess with other officers. They drank too much Italian wine and laughed at ridiculous jokes, and talked sentimentally of their families and friends in Poland until suddenly there was a silence among them.

It was when Adam overturned his glass of wine.

"That's lucky!" he said. "And we shall soon need all the luck we can get."

That silence did not last more than a few moments but it was noticeable.

"General Anders is arranging a nice little party for us," said one of the officers. "The Polish Corps will be in the thick of it."

"We're the death-and-glory boys!" said another officer. "It won't be a picnic. We have to show the world how Poles can fight."

"We shall show them," said Adam. "Fill up your glasses, gentlemen."

He rose unsteadily to his feet and raised a glass of wine belonging to another man.

"Poland for ever!" he said solemnly. "To hell with Hitler! We're fighting for our own freedom. God be with us."

There was a banging on the table and a clinking of glasses. In this company there were some who would have to die.

General Anders was in command of the Second Polish Army Corps which he had brought from Poland and the Middle East. They were in the famous Eighth Army, the Desert Rats of North Africa, under the British general, Oliver Leese, and under the supreme command of Alexander, Commander-in-Chief of the Allied Armies in Italy. The Poles would be fighting with British, French and American troops, and they would be the spearhead of attack against Monte Cassino—that formidable stronghold which had been a monastery and was now a German fortress.

The battle was to be one of the most heroic epics of the war. General Anders, that handsome man and fine soldier, *sans peur et sans reproche*, knew that it was to be the supreme test of Polish valour. He knew that his objectives would be taken only by great sacrifice and a dreadful cost in blood. He had no reserves. His Polish battalions sent into battle would have to fight through to a finish.

Sitting in his headquarters he received Orders of the Day from the Allied generals which he distributed to all his units.

Alexander said:

We are going to destroy the German armies in Italy. The fighting will be hard, bitter, and perhaps long, but you are warriors and soldiers of the highest order. . . . So with God's help and blessing we take the field, confident of victory.

In his own Order of the Day to his own troops General Anders addressed the men he loved, those who had served and suffered with him, those who now were facing a deadly and terrible ordeal for Poland's sake.

The task assigned to us will cover with glory the name of the Polish soldier all over the world. At this moment the thoughts and the hearts of our whole nation will be with us. Trusting to the Justice of Divine Providence, we go forward with the sacred slogan in our hearts? God, Honour, Country.

Monte Cassino had held out against many attacks. The rugged hills about it and above were defended by heavy artillery concealed in caves and behind rocks, hidden from observation, not to be blasted out by bombing aircraft or artillery barrage. German guns for a long time in position flung down fire on all tracks under observation from neighbouring peaks. The whole region was stuffed with heavy guns, light guns, machine-guns, observation posts and riflemen.

Monte Cassino was the way into the heart of Italy. The Germans would defend it to the death and their power of defence was terrific.

To General Anders and the Second Polish Corps was given the task of this assault upon positions which the enemy regarded as impregnable.

General Anders had to conserve the strength of his troops as far as possible before the battle but there were hard, perilous, and deadly jobs to do. They had to be done secretly in order to obtain surprise. They had to be done at night because of enemy observation. Tracks had to be broadened by Polish sappers working under bursts of machine-gun fire. Up those tracks had to be carried supplies and ammunition, enormous amounts of ammunition. Part of the way they were taken by lorry, then they had to be packed on mules, then on the shoulders of the men. Automatically the enemy laid down heavy barrage fire at certain points, whatever was happening or not happening. The Poles worked on, losing many men, but never shirking this ghastly business, back-breaking and heart-breaking, except for the bravest hearts which by some miracle of valour they had.

Stanislav was one of those who took turns at this, leading a group of his lancers. Men fell beside him but the others followed him. His heart pounded because of the high climb and the weight of an ammunition box. Several times he had to fight down a kind of animal fear because of shells bursting near him and killing others of his men. Several times he found himself trembling like a man with ague, but had to hide it from his company. No time for thought. No time for dreams. Here it was only a murderous job, with intent on every step ahead, to avoid stumbling over a bit of rock, to halt until a stream of machine-gun bullets had whipped the track, to whisper a few words to the men nearest to him, to keep in touch with them in the darkness and the bewilderment of these infernal boulders.

On the eve of the battle it was quiet until suddenly before midnight there was the thunder of great guns, echoing from peak to peak. The attack was on a wide front. The ultimate objective was Rome itself, still far away. There was a valley running northwest, below the mountains—the Liri Valley, up which the 13th British Army Corps would drive forward. On the right wing of the Polish Corps would be the 10th British Army Corps. The French in the Fifth Army would attack Monte Arunci, and then join the British further up the Liri Valley. The American 2nd Army Corps were to drive along the sea road.

That was the plan, and that was the victory achieved by thousands of men who moved forward in the darkness of that night of May 11th, 1944, following a tempest of gunfire on the enemy positions. But those positions were behind mountain masses and deep in the rocks which made natural fortresses. Their guns were not silenced. Their men fought back fiercely and desperately with German courage.

The chance of victory lay with the Poles.

Until Monte Cassino was taken and passed as far as Piedimonte, the whole operation would be held up. It was the hinge of the door which had to be opened on the way to Rome by blood and sacrifice.

To the right of Monte Cassino was a long crest of a mountainway known as Phantom Ridge and it was from this that the Polish Corps fought through a long and terrible day. The first Carpathian Rifle Brigade stormed many peaks. The Fifth Vilno Brigade captured the ridge under withering fire, and late in the afternoon had fierce hand-to-hand fighting.

"I had often seen pictures of famous battles with the general in command, field glasses to his eyes, watching the progress of his troops and giving orders.

"How different was this from present-day reality when battles for the most part are fought out of sight of the commanding officers."

So afterwards wrote General Anders, remembering with

emotion those fateful hours when he waited for the news of battle.

"At Monte Cassino the darkness of night and smoke prevented anything being seen more than a few steps ahead. Our soldiers, frequently diving to take cover from fire, even had great difficulty in keeping contact with each other. Officer after officer was killed and his place taken by the next in seniority. . . . It is not easy to describe an action made up of the experiences of individual detachments, sections, and even of single soldiers. It was a collection of small epics, many of which can never be told, for their heroes took to their graves the secrets of their exploits. The Polish soldier's dauntless will and his self-sacrifice were the key to a battle in which each man had perforce to play a lonely but heroic part: each minute brought its dreadful experiences, and the sum of them was victory."

Stanislav had been holding a defensive position until the second phase of the battle which captured the monastery of Monte Cassino, while other Polish troops broke through the German lines and drove a spear-head to Piedimonte dominating the position.

Each side was exhausted. General Anders had been right in reckoning that the Germans would be just as exhausted as his own men and that their defence would be weakened. It was only superior will-power, the last leap forward of the spirit, stronger than the body, which overcame the enemy's resistance.

In his own body and soul Stanislav passed through this inferno. Through the darkness he groped and stumbled. Then flashes of light from gunfire and bursting shells stabbed his eyes, revealing the dead and wounded of his own company, his friends and comrades, lighting up the mountain peaks with a terrible and hellish beauty. A young soldier clutched him and he felt the weight of the boy's body sagging before he fell dead. A German soldier lunged at him with a bayonet but was shot through the head before the naked blade reached its mark. Dark figures emerged from caves and rocks. There were single fights ending in a scream. Machine-guns made a devil's tattoo. Stanislav was shouting hoarsely to his men, thinning out around him, but he did not hear his own voice, or know the words that left his lips. He did not know or remember that he had saved one boy's life by shooting a German who had him on the ground and was strangling him with big, convulsive hands. He did not know that his own tall figure, his shouted words, his desperate will-power to struggle forward through this deafening fury of battle rallied up his men when they flung themselves down under this storm of fire. He swore at them, cursed them. He cried out to God on their behalf. He had loved these lads over whose dead bodies he stumbled on. Once he was quite alone. He was alone in the centre of this hell. It was on the last rush to the monastery of Monte Cassino. He was only a short distance ahead, perhaps only a few yards, but he seemed alone for a few terrible moments. He was gasping for breath. He was half-blind and half-deaf. His heart made a noise in his ears. There was a sledge-hammer in his brain. He was stupefied like a dazed and drunken man.

A shell burst close to him. A flying fragment of steel tore into the flesh of his right shoulder but gave him no pain. He was past pain now. The concussion of the shell-burst seemed to blow him to bits and he fell in a heap and knew nothing more until he was in hospital at Anzio. But he was one of those who had fought their way to Monte Cassino, famous now in history as one of the most heroic battles of the war.

For a time he lost his memory. When Adam came to see him he was vague and confused.

"My head is frightful," he said. "I can't remember anything."

Adam tried to cheer him up.

"There are some things best forgotten."

"I knew a girl once," said Stanislav. "I can't remember her name."

"One of our Polish girls?" asked Adam. "One of those who lost their hearts to you?"

Stanislav raised his left hand to his forehead. His right arm and shoulder were in plaster.

"No, not a Polish girl. I met her in Scotland. I fell in love with her. I can't remember her name."

Adam tried him with a few names.

"Mary? . . . Beatrice? . . . Alice? . . . Susan? . . . Those are all I know. Well, one more—Elizabeth?"

"No. . . . Oh, curse it, I can't remember her name!"

It seemed to worry him a lot. Tears came into his eyes. He was feeling very weak and low.

It was in Rome, when his wound had healed, that Stanislav met a friend whom he had known in Warsaw. It was Ferrari who had been in the Italian Embassy. They met outside the Albergo Flora by the Pincio Gardens. Ferrari stared at him, cried "Stanislav! *Amico mio!*" flung his arms round him and kissed him on both cheeks.

Stanislav was pleased to see him but slightly embarrassed. He had no grudge against the Italians, but the Poles had been fighting in Italy and the Allies had been bombing and attacking Italian cities. Ferrari put him at ease on this point.

"This atrocious war!" he cried. "It ought never to have happened. How often I used to say in Warsaw that it must never happen, before the Germans attacked Poland. That monster Hitler, that ridiculous charlatan Mussolini, what blood they have caused to flow! What crimes they have committed. *Madre di Dio!*"

They walked in the Pincio Gardens. Ferrari inquired about the friends he had known in Warsaw.

"How is the beautiful Vanda?"

"She was still alive when last I heard," said Stanislav.

He added a few words with a grin at Ferrari.

"You were very sweet on her, weren't you? I seem to remember."

His memory had returned when he had lain in hospital. One night he had remembered the name of the girl he loved and had called it out loudly, to the surprise of the other wounded men.

Ferrari laughed and clutched his arm.

"More than sweet on her. I was passionately in love with her. I worshipped her. When I had to leave Warsaw I wept bitterly."

"You are still a faithful lover?" asked Stanislav.

It was Ferrari's turn to look slightly embarrassed.

"It was necessary to console myself. Men are men, you understand? I have a charming wife and two delightful children."

Stanislav clapped him on the shoulder.

"I envy you! I should like to have a charming wife and eight delightful children."

They sat on the terrace of the Pincio Gardens overlooking Rome with its domes and palaces. Below them was the Via Colonna and the Piazza del Popolo.

Ferrari talked seriously and in a tragic voice.

"I have suffered intensely during this war. It became known that I was hostile to Mussolini. I was arrested and put in prison for a year. But my own misfortunes were nothing. I suffered mental agony because of the horrors inflicted upon other peoples. My heart bled for Poland which I had come to love very dearly. My happiest days were in Warsaw—those happy days on the Vistula, in summer-time, those excursions and picnics with charming friends, the society of cultured men and women—devoted to art, music, and good books. Terrible news reached me about the martyrdom of Poland.

Stanislav groaned.

"It is still being martyred. Frightful things are happening.

Many of my friends are dead or starve to death in concentration camps. That is why I'm here. We Poles are fighting in Italy as the best way back—as the way of liberation for our own people. Germany is nearing defeat. The Russians are smashing through their lines. The Allies are fighting in France. The Germans know they are doomed."

Ferrari raised both his hands with a tragic gesture as though invoking the help of God.

"I'm afraid of the Russians. They have a Godless creed. They will be worse than the Germans. They will penetrate to the heart of Europe like the hordes of Ghengis Khan. Poland, I greatly fear, my good friend, will exchange one tyranny for another."

Stanislav was silent and stared over the domes and palaces of the Eternal City over which there was a golden haze.

"That's the terrible thought," he admitted, after that moment's silence. "But I put my faith in the Allies, the English and the Americans. They will defend us. They will make a just peace. They will demand the liberation of Poland."

Ferrari shook his head.

"Already they're making great concessions to Russia. They believe in Russia's good intentions! They are ready to sacrifice Poland for fear of displeasing the gentlemen in the Kremlin. I hear whispers and rumours which are very disturbing.

"Don't you believe them!" said Stanislav. "Such things are incredible."

Ferrari rose and said he must return to his wife.

"You must come and dine with us," he said. "We have an apartment near Trinità dei Monti."

"How is Beatrice?" asked Stanislav. It was a question he ought to have asked before. Vanda had been devoted to Beatrice.

Ferrari answered cheerfully.

"She's all right. Happily married to a Polish lieutenant. She never forgets her friendship with Vanda. They were like sisters."

"She was a lovely girl," said Stanislav. "I'm glad she married a Pole. Give them both my best wishes."

They walked together to the Trinità dei Monti and Ferrari embraced Stanislav again before leaving him.

CHAPTER XXXVIII

THERE was an evening gathering in Vanda's home as often happened. Friends came for an hour or two of conversation in this room which seemed to hold something of the elegance and charm—even the peace—of pre-war days. This *salon* in a street of bombed houses still retained its beautiful furniture. There were good pictures on the walls. There was a pleasant pretence of drinking coffee, though now it had to be hot water and burnt sugar. Dr. Mirski was a charming host steeped in classical literature and the history of Poland. He avoided horror-talk and he had a kind of aura of benevolence and sympathy into which still flashed a humorous and cultured mind. The character and spirit of Vanda attracted some of these visitors and Halina was no longer a schoolgirl but developing into the first grace of womanhood and, anyhow, for a little while behind drawn curtains there was the chance of forgetfulness and refreshment.

Father Paul of Warsaw came in, no longer dressed as a priest but in a civilian suit to avoid arrest. No disguise could hide the spirituality of his luminous eyes and fine delicate face. He was *aumonier* of a unit of the Secret Army with officer's rank. He sat talking to Halina who made him laugh several times because of her slang expressions which she had picked up in her student days and her bluntness of speech. Once she startled him by a suggestion which she put to him under cover of the general conversation.

"What we want is another St. Bartholomew massacre. At a given signal everyone kills a German in his bed or in his bathroom."

Father Paul raised his hands and laughed again.

"My dear child! You're talking to a priest. War is one thing—bad enough!—murder is another."

"I don't see the difference," said Halina, but he saw a glint in her eyes which assured him that she was not talking seriously. It was a bit of verbal fireworks.

"Don't let's talk about things like that," said the priest. "I come here for pleasant talk in pleasant company. This room is a survival from the happy past, and your father doesn't like to spoil it by dwelling on the horrors outside."

"Oh, Father's a saint!" said Halina, as though that were a term of reproach.

She left Father Paul to greet a young man who had just arrived. He wore a suit of blue overalls like a mechanic and his hair was deliberately tousled. It was the young man Danek who had tested her out as a 'rush girl' in the liaison service. As one of his unit she saw him a good deal and in an extraordinary way found herself mothering him, though he was a year or so older. He had a nervous temperament. He had to fight against fear. Once he had cried in her presence after a narrow escape from a police patrol. He was losing his nerve and Halina wondered if she ought to report him. He might be a danger to the Cause. If he were caught he might blab. But she was sorry for him and liked him and tried to stiffen him by a little bullying. Now this evening she went over to greet him and laughed when he held her hand longer than necessary. He had fallen in love with her she knew, and found that ridiculous and rather pitiful.

Her uncle the Colonel came in as often as he could from his book shop. He was up to his neck in the Secret Army and one of 'Bor's' advisers and staff officers. It was only now and again that he dared to visit his wife, secretly.

He embraced Vanda after greeting his brother-in-law.

"How's Aunt Krysta?" asked Vanda. "She hasn't been round for some days."

The Colonel laughed good-humouredly.

"Your Aunt is a terrifying woman! She insists on going to the Paviak prison three times a week with food parcels which she gets on the black market at frightful cost. I'm afraid they may take her inside one day."

There was an unexpected visitor and Vanda seeing him come into the room felt a flutter at the heart and a rush of colour to her face. It was Jerzy back again after one of his journeys.

He came over to her and kissed her hand and spoke a few words emotionally.

"How wonderful to be here again! I carry the picture of this room with me."

"An empty room?" asked Vanda, teasing him.

"Always with you in it. Sometimes I seem to be here when I'm a thousand miles away. It's my day dream—extraordinarily vivid."

"Have you seen Stanislav again?" asked Vanda, trying to hide her joy, trying to talk in an ordinary voice—not to give herself away to the others.

"He's in Scotland in a training camp. I didn't see him this time."

He too was trying to hide his gladness at seeing Vanda again and it was a pretty poor effort because of the tenderness in his eyes and his look of devotion.

He greeted Father Paul and Halina and Gena who had come down from the room where her little boy was sleeping.

"A cup of burnt sugar and hot water?" asked Vanda. "We call it coffee. I expect you've been drinking real coffee and wallowing in the fleshpots of London."

"I prefer hot water and burnt sugar in this room," he told her. "May I sit by your side?"

But he was prevented from sitting by her side. Suddenly the windows shook with a violent concussion. Somewhere to the north-west of Warsaw there was the noise of heavy gunfire and the bursting of high explosives.

In the Mirski's *salon* everyone sprang up, listening intently.

"Has it come?" asked Halina, breathlessly. "Is it the Rising?"

"It's over by Povaski," said Vanda, deeply agitated. "Oh, Father, they're firing on the Ghetto. Something terrible is happening."

Father Paul slipped out of the room. Perhaps there was something he might do. Presently the others went, disturbed and frightened by this noise of firing. Jerzy stayed, having been invited by Dr. Mirski to spend the night.

When darkness fell, the windows through the drawn curtains were stabbed by flashes of red light. Over in the north-west suburb the sky throbbed with a scarlet glow. The Ghetto of Warsaw was burning like a furnace with those crowded Jews inside it.

Vanda and Jerzy were staring at this red glare in the sky. Suddenly Vanda turned and put her face down on his shoulder and wept.

"Jerzy! How long must we endure these things? When are they going to end?"

He put his arms round her and kissed her wet eyes and they stayed there a long time in the darkness saying very little, obsessed by thoughts of what was going on in the Ghetto, yet finding some comfort in their love.

That night, very late, there was a knock at the door downstairs and the sound of it was sinister at that hour, and frightening.

"Are your papers all right?" asked Vanda in a whisper, looking at Jerzy anxiously.

"Perfectly good," he told her.

It was Vanda's father who went to the hall door.

He opened it and asked, "Who is there?"

A tall, bearded man stood on the step outside. He was trembling and nearly fell until Mirski clutched him.

"You know me," he said. "I'm Weissmann. I have escaped from the Ghetto. If you would hide me for the night. . . ."

He put both arms across his face as though to blot out a vision of horror.

Weissmann. Jacob Weissmann. Dr. Mirski remembered him. He had been in charge of the *decor* at the Opera House. He was talented with a playful imagination and a rich sense of lighting and colour. He had produced the scenic effects of several ballets before the war. Then he had been a rather elegant fellow, clean-shaven, perfumed, dandyfied. Now there he stood with a straggling beard, haggard, sunken-eyed, in dirty clothes, terror stricken.

"Come in, my poor fellow," said Dr. Mirski. "Tell us what is happening in Povaski. Hold on to me. Steady!"

Mirski managed to get him into the *salon* where he collapsed in a chair, covering his face with his hands while his whole body was shaken.

"Bring some brandy, Halina," said Dr. Mirski. "I've saved a few drops in a medicine bottle. You will find it in my desk—the left-hand top drawer."

"Father!" said Halina in a whisper. "This man is a Jew. If he's found here we shall all be shot."

"Christ was a Jew," said her father. "For His sake. . . ."

"We must hide him," said Vanda. "We can't turn him into the street again. What do you say, Jerzy? You will be in danger, too. We have to ask you."

"What you risk I risk," said Jerzy quietly. "We must take him in, of course."

It was almost an hour before Jacob Weissmann could tell them what was happening and then only in a wild, incoherent way, broken by spasms of grief and horror tearing him by their anguish.

The Jews in the Ghetto had been threatened with wholesale deportation which was a sentence of death. . . . The younger men had called for a rising. . . . They had attacked the German police. . . . A terrible madness had seized everyone. . . . They had gone wild with fury and despair. . . . They were all shouting and screaming and rushing about with what weapons they could find. . . . Young girls had joined the men, even old women and the starving and the half-dead. . . . They had set fire to the music hall and the cafés, to burn out the Germans who were there—the Gestapo and police. . . . Many of the Jews had bribed their way out of the Ghetto. Police had been killed and others fled. . . . Then the place had been surrounded. The police sent up reinforcements and started firing. Artillery was brought up. . . . Weissmann had heard the drone of bombing planes and the roar of high explosives. He had escaped through one of the gates down a street littered with the bodies of men and women and children, all dead in pools of blood. . . . Now the Ghetto was on fire. . . . It was a furnace.

Vanda and the others listened to him in silence. They sat motionless, while he told this frightful story. Several times Vanda shut her eyes to blot out the vision of the Ghetto, which she still saw with closed eyes. She could hardly look at the man who was speaking these dreadful words in a strangled way. His face was contorted with pain. His eyes revealed the agony which shook him. Then suddenly she looked at him intently. Her father had said, "Christ was a Jew". This man was strangely like the figure of Christ on the cross in a Spanish painting she had seen in a public gallery, realistic and harrowing in its study of agony. With his thin, aquiline nose and straggling beard and sharp cheek-bones he looked like that portrait of Christ.

"Father," said Vanda, "Mr. Weissmann must sleep in my room. I'll go to Aunt Krysta's old room."

"Someone must keep awake all night in case of alarm," said her father. "It might be better if Mr. Weissmann slept in the cellar for his own safety and for ours."

"I would rather he slept in my room. Jerzy and I will stay up and keep guard."

They stayed up all night. There was no visit from the Gestapo. They talked in low voices, Vanda sitting on the floor with her head against Jerzy's knees.

Jerzy spoke of what was happening in the war.

"Hitler's Germany is doomed. They can't hold their lines against the Russians. The British and Americans are attacking in the west. The end is in sight."

"That means freedom for us!" said Vanda. "Thank God for that!"

She said something which disturbed him.

"Of course we shall have to fight in the last battles. The Secret Army will rise as one man. Warsaw will be liberated by our own boys."

"I'm afraid of that," said Jerzy. "Any premature rising would be madness."

"We shall have to wait for the Russians," said Vanda. "When they're close. . . ."

"They've betrayed us from the beginning," said Jerzy. "They'll betray us again."

"They're bound to help us," said Vanda. "When they reach the Vistula—'Bor' will know the right time. He will give the signal. Jerzy! All our hopes, all our faith will be like a flame."

"There are flames in the Ghetto tonight," said Jerzy. "The Jews are being slaughtered. It's a warning to us, Vanda—a frightful warning. I tremble at the thought of what may happen."

"God will be with us," said Vanda. "The powers of Evil will be overthrown. Oh, Jerzy, I pray for that day when our boys will come out into the open as soldiers of Christ—and our women and our young girls. We shall all be in it."

She gave a little laugh and drew his head down to her face.

"I wish I had your faith," he told her. "I wish I had a hundredth part of your courage, darling Vanda."

"Courage? Aren't you risking your life every day. When you go away I never know if I shall see you again. I never know if you've been tortured or killed. And you wish you had my courage, Jerzy!"

"It's nothing," he said. "I think only of you. When you talk of the Rising in Warsaw my blood runs cold."

Once during the night she fell asleep with his arms about her.

Upstairs in her room Jacob Weissmann stood staring out of the window at the red, throbbing glow over the Ghetto of Warsaw.

It was not one night only of fire and blood in that ghastly Ghetto. The Jews fought with the heroism of despair—and there were heroes among them—and they killed many Germans, but it was hopeless against artillery and tanks and against poison gas which the Germans used to force the Jews out of the cellars and strongholds. Then, house by house, they burned their way through.

'Bor's' Home Army tried to come to the rescue, but the narrow gaps in the Ghetto walls were covered by German machine-gun fire and there were many casualties.

When it became clear that further resistance was impossible Home Army units tried to rescue the survivors by way of the sewers, but they found the Jewish resistance groups so utterly exhausted that only about 100 were strong enough to make this way of escape.

Once again from the Ghetto there were daily transports of Jews eastwards. They were being driven to their deaths—men, women and children.

CHAPTER XXXIX

HALINA was gathering some flowers in the garden for her mother's grave one afternoon when she saw a man's figure moving behind some bushes. For a moment she felt frightened. It might be one of the Gestapo or some ruffian trying to rob the house. She called out to him sharply.

"Who are you? What do you want?"

It was a tall young man who came out towards her and she was reassured because of his smile and the pleasant look he had in spite of dirty overalls and tousled hair. He was not a Pole but he did not look German though he had fair hair—light brown—and grey-blue eyes.

He spoke to her in English coming forward a little.

"It's all right. Don't be scared. I'm English."

Halina had nothing but schoolgirl English but she understood these last words and stared at him in astonishment.

"English?"

He nodded and laughed and held out his hand, a lean brown, long-fingered hand.

"Glad to meet you," he said. "I should be still more glad if you could give me something to eat. I'm darned hungry. I may say I'm as hungry as a wolf—but as harmless as a lamb, especially when I meet a pretty girl."

She didn't understand a word of that but asked him again.

"You an Englishman? You come here to Warsaw?"

"A perfectly good Englishman," he told her. "I was born in Wimbledon. You know—the place where they play tennis. It's a hell of a long way from Warsaw."

They both laughed for some reason. He looked a very humorous young man though she couldn't understand a word he was saying.

She spoke to him in French.

"*Vous parlez français, peut-être?*"

"*Un peu,*" he answered. "*Où est la plume de ma tante?*"

That was a very extraordinary thing to say—the pen of his aunt? Perhaps it was a secret code or message.

He spoke very terrible French but she could understand him in that language.

"*Prisonier de guerre, vous savez. Echappé.* Did a bunk. Got on a goods train. Hid under some timber. *C'est-à-dire j'avais beaucoup des aventures. Les Polonais sont très bons. Ils ont aidé moi très bien. Vous comprenez, mademoiselle?*"

She understood that the Poles had helped him to escape.

"*Vous êtes un officier Anglais?*"

"*Oui. Officer Anglais. Très sale.* Looking like the very devil, I expect. I apologize for my unfortunate appearance. No credit to the Royal Air Force in which I have the honour to be Squadron Leader. I was shot down over the Polish frontier."

He grinned at her seeing that she didn't understand what he was talking about.

"*Excusez moi, y-a-t-il quelque chose à manger?*"

She understood that. He wanted something to eat. He looked famished. Probably this young man was starving to death.

"Come this way," she said in French. "Come into the kitchen I'll find something for you."

He smiled at the word *cuisine*. He seemed to think it a very good word. Undoubtedly this young girl, as beautiful as the young Madonna—was going to give him something to eat.

She made him sit down in the kitchen and went into the larder and found the remains of a cold chicken which had been brought by one of their peasant friends and some newly baked bread which she put before him on the kitchen table.

He stared at it incredulously and then laughed in a weak kind of way. Cold chicken! Newly baked bread! Very wonderful indeed. But he hesitated to eat it while she stood in front of him watching him. He seemed to find that embarrassing.

"*Prenez une chaise,*" he said in his execrable French. "*Pardonnez moi si je mange ce sacré poulet en face de vous, ma chère mademoiselle.*"

She took a chair in front of him and sat with her arms on the table and her chin cupped in her hands watching him. She was excited. It was amazing to come face to face with an English officer, to have him sitting in her kitchen.

Now and again he spoke to her in English though he was quite aware that it might have been double Dutch as far as she could understand it.

"This is a superb bird, this chicken. It must have come all the way from heaven. I don't want to appear greedy but I'm really hungry, you know. No food for three days. Very, very, trying."

He ate delicately, she noticed. He was certainly a gentleman. He had charming manners.

She made out presently that he was an officer in the British Air Force and that he had been shot down and had landed somewhere by parachute. After questioning him in French she ascertained that his name was Richard Allgrove, a name which she found difficult to pronounce Allgrove . . . Allgrove.

"Just call me Dick," he told her. "What's your name? *Comment vous-appelez-vous, Mademoiselle?*"

"Halina."

He had no difficulty with that.

"Halina. *Un joli nom. Joli comme vous-même, mademoiselle.*"

Halina laughed at him. She felt quite friendly after this brief time of acquaintanceship.

"No compliments," she told him in French. "No insincerities."

"*Je dis la verité,*" he assured her, dealing with another piece of chicken.

Presently he asked a surprising question.

"*Vous vous appellez Halina Mirska?*"

She stared at him with amazement.

"How did you know that?" she asked.

He fumbled in a trouser pocket and drew out a piece of dirty paper which he put down on the table in front of her.

On it was written Vanda Mirska and the address in St. Theresa Street. It was in the handwriting of Stanislav.

"You have met my brother," she asked excitedly in French.

He looked at her with smiling eyes.

"*Mais oui,* as they say. *Je sais vôtre frère. Un bon garçon.* A very nice fellow. *En l'Écosse.* Scotland, you know, where the Highland soldiers wear petticoats which they call kilts. Ladies from Hell they used to call them in World War I. Anyhow that's why I made my way to this house when I crawled out of a train in Warsaw. A young girl came part of the way with me. *Une jeune fille m'a montré cette maison.* Then I hid in the garden, not knowing whether there were Germans inside the house. *J'ai fait une reconnaisance, vous savez.* When I had the luck to meet you in the garden I knew I was on to a good thing. That girl looks like an angel, I thought. *C'etait une rencontre charmante.*"

Presently he regarded the carcass of the chicken with regretful eyes.

"*Vous avez bien mangé?*" asked Halina with a little laugh.

"*Enormément bien.* I feel a different man. I feel on top of the world."

Halina stood up and thought deeply.

"What am I going to do with you?" she asked in Polish which she then translated into French.

"Ay, that's the rub," he answered. "It's a bit of a problem, isn't it? What to do with an escaped prisoner of war in Warsaw? If I'm found here you'll all be shot. If you turn me out I shall be shot. On balance I think it's best if I fade away like a gentleman, like Captain Oates when he walked out into the snow."

Halina had an attack of the giggles. This language difficulty was ridiculous. She began to laugh and Squadron Leader Richard Allgrove saw the humour of it and laughed with her. They were both laughing when Vanda came into the kitchen, astonished by these sounds, more astonished to see Halina laughing with a young man in a boiler suit who was certainly not a Pole and didn't look like a German.

Halina explained the situation to Vanda after recovering her gravity somewhat, and Vanda's English was so much better than hers that she could have a reasonable conversation with this young officer who seemed to have dropped from the skies.

He was introduced to her father and afterwards to Jozef and Aunt Krysta. For some reason they all fell in love with him, partly no doubt because he was English—and by tradition and sentiment they all loved England—but mostly because of his attractive manners, his humorous eyes, his gift of laughter, his youth.

They found a billet for him with the mother of Tereska—that girl who had pulled in Jozef from the street when a *lapanka* was going on. They provided him with a German *Kennkarte* and *Ausweiss*. They gave him a new name which he learnt by heart with considerable difficulty—Bronek Yablonovski. But without a word of Polish he was always in danger lest he should be challenged in the street. There were other British officers in Warsaw. It is a strange and historical fact that quite a number had found their way to this city from prisoner-of-war camps, and Richard Allgrove—Dick as Halina learnt to call him—gradually established contact with some of them. They were all being hidden by Polish families who risked their lives in doing so, and for some time not one of them could speak a word of Polish. How could they find their way about the streets? How could they go into a shop and buy something?

Halina constituted herself their guide. With Vanda's help she learnt English intensively, sitting up late at night over English grammars and story books. Many Polish girls were doing that. Ever since the downfall of France England had been Poland's hope. They put their faith in England. One day the British armies would come to liberate them. It was necessary to learn English. But it was a forbidden language by the Gestapo. Anyone found learning English was liable to be arrested. In any case it was difficult to get text books, dictionaries, teachers. There were a few English girls married to Poles in Warsaw and they were seized upon to give classes. Curiously enough Kipling's 'Barrack Room Ballads' became the most popular reading book, and Vanda had a copy of it which she learnt by heart. Kipling's poem 'If' was a source of inspiration. It was like a hymn of courage to many young people in the Polish Underground.

Halina came to know some of Richard Allgrove's friends and led them through the streets from time to time—three or four at a time. But it had to be done in a way not to arouse suspicion. She spaced them out at some distance apart, leading the way, stopping now and then to look into a shop window so as not to lose these pet lambs in the crowded streets, changing her handbag from one hand to another as a signal that she was going down a side-street on the way to some little restaurant frequented only by Poles, or to a private house where one of them was billeted.

Richard Allgrove gave most trouble to her. She lost him several times because he was interested in a shop window or lagged behind to light a cigarette. Often he walked quickly to overtake her, grinning at her when she turned to see if he was coming.

"Gosh!" he exclaimed on one of these walks, "I thought I had lost you! Let's walk together and talk about pleasant things such as cabbages and kings. I feel in need of intellectual conversation."

"You're very naughty," she told him, but found it impossible to be cross with this humorous young man. "Supposing one of the Gestapo hears us talking English? That would mean a concentration camp for me and a firing squad for you. It's very dangerous Dick. Really!"

"It's all very difficult," he admitted. "I don't want to get you into trouble, but I get the jim-jams if I have to walk all by myself, and I want to see you laugh again. When you laugh I hear fairy bells ringing. You have the merriest laugh of any girl I know."

She laughed then. How was it possible not to laugh at this amusing young Englishman who always had a joke in his eyes.

"Do be sensible," she pleaded. "Drop behind a little. We shall get a chance of talking this evening. Come round and hear Jozef play. You know the way now, don't you?"

"Every stone of it," he told her. "A dog soon learns the way to his next meal—in this case an oasis in the desert of a wicked world."

He came round quite often. He had joined the Polish Underground. He became a friend of the family, and particularly a friend of Halina. They seemed to amuse each other very much. She learnt English quickly in conversation with him. She even learnt such slang words as 'gosh' and 'jim-jams'.

CHAPTER XL

THE spring of 1944 brought Warsaw not only beauty, as each year it did, but a breath of hope, illogical, unreasonable, and pitiful. Vanda was one of those who felt it. Warsaw in spite of many ruins was still lovely, with a cloudless blue sky over its churches and towers and noble buildings. Even the ruins were touched by this atmospheric enchantment, and the Vistula, now patrolled by German police boats, still seemed a river of peace where youth might take its pleasure, except where it was spanned by broken bridges.

In the streets, despite the constant danger of police round-ups, spring seemed to bring a strange hopefulness, visible in people's faces. In the brilliant sunshine children were selling flowers, basketfuls of violets, primroses, and snowdrops done up into little posies. One heard the laughter of children scampering from school. Boys went whistling their way home.

Walking with her father one day, Vanda wondered within herself why she felt this kind of exaltation and hopefulness. It was not only due to the touch of spring and its fresh beauty. The Germans were being defeated. The Russians were smashing through their lines and every day on the wireless from the B.B.C. in London—to which they listened at the risk of death like many people who did this, spreading the news among their friends—there were announcements of new Russian victories and of German retreats. Soon they would be fleeing in panic, and Warsaw would be free from them. The Germans knew that. They were already frightened men. One could see it in their eyes if one cared to look into German eyes. People in touch with them, in factories, and workshops, heard them make these admissions. "Germany is *kaput*. . . . We have lost the war. . . . Hitler has made many mistakes."

"Father," said Vanda, "do you feel happy about the situation? Shall we be liberated from all this terror?"

Dr. Mirski shook his head.

"I shall be glad to see the last of the Germans but I have no illusions about the Russians."

"But, Father," said Vanda, "isn't it possible that they will come as friends and give us our freedom and then withdraw? Victory may sweeten them, don't you think?"

Dr. Mirski laughed and said, "Miracles may happen. Let's hope they will."

They were praying for this miracle of liberation in all the churches of Warsaw. It was the month of May and in Poland, as in all Catholic countries, this month is dedicated to the Virgin Mary. But it was difficult to get to the churches because of German and Russian combats in the air overhead, and the fear of women walking in the streets, so by a kind of common agreement, which seemed to be known without planning or instruction, these May devotions were held at home. Everywhere in the entrance halls of mansions, blocks of flats, and small villas, a picture of Our Lady, as they called her, was hung up, an olive-oil lamp burning beneath it with a little glimmer of light, and fresh flowers placed on a shelf or stool below. In the evening all the inhabitants of the house gathered in the hall and recited the Litany, and sang religious songs, very old and primitive in Polish folk lore and very dear to Polish hearts. From seven o'clock until late at night, from different houses at different times came this sound of singing through the open windows, carried across the town on these fragrant spring evenings, and the German police patrolling the streets were startled and perhaps awestruck by this strange phenomenon of a whole town at prayer. What did it mean? Was it a menace to them? Had these Poles gone mad, or were they conspiring for some desperate act?

Many people were coming into Warsaw as though seeking the refuge of the capital. Eastern Poland had been 'liberated' by the Germans, as they called it, and for some time contact had been re-established between Lvov and Warsaw.

Old friends appeared in the house of Dr. Mirski. Some of them were refugees from Western Poland, who since the beginning of the war were living in hiding, but mostly those from the east, afraid of being caught in the storm of war. Many who could not come were sending their treasures—pictures, tapestries, rare books, old manuscripts, precious things of art—for safe-keeping by their friends in Warsaw. The old folk had had previous experiences of the Russian habit of looting. In 1920 everything had been looted, smashed, and destroyed by the Russian hordes until they were flung back by Pilsudski with the help of General

Weygand. Many of them like Dr. Mirski in his mother-in-law's house in Lvov had had more recent knowledge of this kind of thing.

*   *   *   *   *

Dr. Mirski and his family were living no longer in St. Theresa Street. They were forced to leave their beloved house and garden. It did not come as a surprise. Since the outbreak of the German-Russian war, the Germans among other precautions for their safety, and for other purposes, were making a German district. Polish families had to move out to other parts of Warsaw where only Poles were allowed to live. Any German at any time had the right to requisition the house of a Pole in the Ujazdovska Avenue and its neighbouring streets. This law however was not strictly observed, as the German officials were rather reluctant to move into the exclusively German district, being afraid it might be bombed one day by the Russians. The house in St. Theresa Street was left in peace for a rather long time, and Dr. Mirski hoped it had been forgotten. Then the blow fell and they were ordered to leave at short notice.

They were able to get an apartment on the third floor of a big block of flats at the corner of a green in Obozna Street, facing the University garden, and forming a quadrangle between parallel streets.

They were lucky to get the flat when so many were homeless, but it was of course painful to leave the house and garden with its happy memories of family life before the war. Vanda wept a little at leaving the old house and her father was sad, but accepted it, as he did everything, with quiet resignation.

It also meant parting from the friends they had sheltered there—among them Gena and her child who found a dwelling place with other friends in the suburbs.

Weissmann had already gone. That tragic man had come one morning to say good-bye. He was going into hiding with some of his Jewish friends who had escaped the massacre in the Ghetto.

"I owe my life to you and your family," he said to Vanda, and for a moment his eyes were filled with tears. "Life to me means very little now, but one still clings to it, unreasonably, and whatever one's despair. You risked your own lives to give me shelter and a hiding place, and that was a generosity beyond all words of thanks. But I thank you with the deepest gratitude."

By a special concession they were allowed to take their furniture and pictures. They made the rooms of their new home look as much as possible like the old ones. The apartment on the third floor of the block of flats in Obozna Street became popular among their friends. The unexpected visitors, friends who disappeared after the outbreak of war—old political friends of Dr. Mirski, professors, literary men and artists who had been in Russian prisons, younger friends of Vanda and the family —called almost every day.

It seems unbelievable that at this time of strain and emotional excitement there should have been talks about books and art, a little laughter now and then with unexpected guests, and the silence of music lovers while someone played. It was Jozef who played Chopin to them on one of his rare appearances from the underground printing hall. He was cheerful and inwardly excited because Marta was going to have a baby, and he seemed strangely free from fear, though he was engaged on work which would mean instant death for him if discovered by the Gestapo. One has to get close to the Polish mind and character to understand all this, even to believe it, but it happened in Warsaw in that month in May when the Russians were breaking through the German lines with an overwhelming tide of men and everyone was waiting breathlessly for what was going to happen.

There was quite a party in the *salon* one evening, and Vanda who received the guests had a recurrent thought. 'This may be our last party before things happen.'

She was sitting on the floor when Jozef played. She was thinking of Jerzy. He was due back again from one of his journeys. He would put his arms about her and kiss her closed eyes. He was a faithful lover. . . . Aunt Krysta had come round and was knitting some baby clothes for the new child to be born. Vanda's father was smoking one cigarette after another. Halina was whispering to some of her young friends until Jozef looked across at her and frowned.

Nothing dramatic happened this time—no visit from the Gestapo—when the door opened and a new guest was announced by one of the maids who still served them.

It was Stanislav Vasilevski, the novelist and poet, who had talked to Vanda very charmingly during her visit to Poznan. She hurried across the room to greet him—her father had already clasped his hand—but she was shocked by his appearance. He had been so good-looking, so debonair, so calm with his reassuring courage and cheerful talk. Now there was something queer in his eyes, a dazed look, and his face was curiously expressionless, as though just the mask of a man.

"My dear Mr. Vasilevski," cried Vanda, "how good to see you again!"

He held her hand and seemed to cling to it for a moment.

"You are celebrating something?" he asked, looking round the room at so many guests.

Vanda smiled while he still held her hand.

"It may be our last party. We have a sense that liberation is coming very soon. We're full of hope. The Russians are coming close. The Germans are utterly defeated. They'll soon be out of Warsaw."

"Hope?" he asked. "You're hopeful of that? I've just come from Lvov. I've been under Russian occupation."

He lowered his voice and looked round as though fearing he might be overheard by people who would betray him.

"We're all loyal here," said Vanda's father, cheerfully. "We have no traitors among us, my dear fellow! Sit down and have a hot drink. Halina will bring you one."

Vasilevski took a seat and stared round the room in a stealthy way. His presence had startled the company and seemed to cast a chill upon them. They had been gay and talkative. Now they were silent as though made uneasy by the visit of this man from Lvov.

He seemed aware of this presently and spoke with something of his old charm.

"I'm sorry to be a wet blanket! But this room—this party—this happiness, startles me. I seem to have come back to pre-war days. It's wonderful, but I can't understand it. Forgive me!"

Dr. Mirski laughed at him good-humouredly.

"My dear fellow, in spite of everything we still keep our spirit high in Warsaw, and our young people especially are very hopeful of what is coming. We mustn't discourage them! Hope lives eternal in the human breast. An English poet said that."

"It's amazing," said Vasilevski. "With the Russians advancing upon you?"

Halina sprang up and spoke excitedly.

"It's because the Russians are advancing that we're filled with hope. The Germans will have to retreat from Warsaw. Before the day comes when the Russians are on the Vistula we shall rise to help them. We've been preparing for that day—haven't we?—training for it, panting for it. Warsaw will rise, with everyone of us girls as well as men. God have mercy on the Germans, for we shall have none after all the cruelties they've inflicted on us, after all the horror."

Her face was flushed and there was a fire behind her eyes. Her voice rang out in the room where ten minutes before Jozef had played a melody of Chopin's with its lovely and liquid notes.

"Hush, Halina!" said her father, sternly. "You're talking wildly."

"You had better keep your mouth shut, my child," said Jozef. "We don't cry that kind of thing on the housetops. Haven't you taken the oath of secrecy?"

A young girl spoke. It was one of Halina's friends.

"We're all loyal here, and we're all in it, aren't we? What's the good of pretending? What Halina says is true of everyone of us. We're longing for the day. We're getting impatient for it. We can hardly wait much longer."

"I agree," said a young man, who had been sitting on a rug with his back to the wall and his hands clasped about his knees.

"We're waiting for the call from 'Bor'. Soon it may come."

Other voices spoke in the room.

The day is coming. . . . We're filled with hope."

Dr. Mirski raised his hands with a kind of smiling despair.

"All this spoils the party! You're terrible, you young people. Dangerous talk, my dears! Terribly dangerous!"

Vasilevski stared at all these faces, at the excited light in their eyes, and he spoke again in a low voice.

"In Lvov we didn't dare to speak like this. One couldn't trust one's neighbour or one's friend, or one's servant if one had one. The Russians depraved the minds of the people by their devilish propaganda. They had their spies everywhere. They created an atmosphere of terror and mistrust. They deported our intellectuals, our priests, our younger men. And yet you're ready to welcome them?"

"So long as they help to defeat the Germans," said Halina, fiercely. "That's all we care."

The famous novelist looked over to her and answered gently.

"German cruelties have aroused the heroic spirit of Warsaw. Russian propaganda and Russian espionage demoralize the spirit and debilitate the will-power by a kind of creeping paralysis. And yet you are going to welcome them?"

"Victory may change them," said Vanda. "Isn't that possible?"

Her father looked at her and shook his head as he had done when they were walking together in the street.

The party broke up. Jozef went away with Aunt Krysta.

Others left. Gaiety had been killed by this grim warning about the Russians—but only for an hour or two, or a night or two. The Polish spirit is resilient. There was spring in the streets. There was hope in their hearts. Soon there would be the liberation. The Russians would come as friends. It was an illusion they kept to the very end in spite of all warnings—and secret doubts—and Russian concentration camps and the deportations of Polish citizens—and the betrayal of General Anders and his Army. In spite of the ghosts in the forest of Katyn.

CHAPTER XLI

AUNT KRYSTA was nursing Marta who had had her baby. Dr. Joravski had come round for this event, staying up all night. Jozef had left his printing presses and had smoked innumerable cigarettes to steady his nerves until the news was brought that he was the father of a tiny girl and that Marta was safely delivered of her child.

It was a happy moment for Jozef when he went down on his knees by his wife's bedside and kissed her hands above the coverlet and made them wet with his tears. She put her fingers through his hair and asked, "Why are you crying, Jozef? I'm very happy now."

"It's the pain of happiness which makes me cry," he told her. "But I want to laugh too. It's all so marvellous! I'm the happiest fellow in the world. I must tell the lads downstairs. They all want to be godfathers. They think it's a tremendous joke that I should be a Daddy!"

He laughed excitedly but checked himself because he dared not shake the bed.

Vanda and Halina came round to see the new-born babe and thought her exquisite. Colonel Lopalevski shook hands with Jozef, laughed good-humouredly, and struck him a light blow on the shoulder.

"Fine work!"

Then he spoke thoughtfully.

"One rejoices in a new life whatever the state of the world. Life must go on, eh! in spite of the Gestapo and the German occupation and all this tragedy."

"I don't let it worry me," said Jozef. "Nothing worries me now that Marta has come through all right, and that I'm the father of a charming little lady with dark hair and a big appetite. The fellows downstairs have brought round a bottle of champagne. We're going to have a celebration."

Nothing worried him, but Halina was worried. She told Vanda about it.

"Danek has been missing for three days. It will be frightful if they've caught him. He knows too much—and he's not very brave, poor boy. I'm terribly afraid."

"Maybe he's ill," said Vanda.

Halina shook her head.

"I've asked his people. They're desperately anxious. He hasn't been home."

She gave a little gasp and clutched Vanda's arm.

"Vanda! He knows about the printing hall. One of his cousins works with Jozef. If they force him to tell. . . ."

Vanda looked at her sister gravely. Halina's face was white. She looked frightened and it was not often that Halina showed any sign of fear.

"We daren't think of such a thing," said Vanda. "We must pray to God. . . ."

Aunt Krysta was sitting alone that night after taking some food to Marta. Jozef was underground in the printing hall. The floor-boards under her feet were trembling slightly with the vibration of the printing presses. She could hear the throb of those machines underground. Suddenly there was a heavy knock at the door. Aunt Krysta turned pale and rose from the table at which she had been sitting with her needlework. She was making baby clothes for Marta's child. For a moment she stood motionless. The heavy knock was repeated. Quickly she moved across the room and touched a button in the wall. In a few seconds the throbbing of the printing machines stopped and the vibrations of the floor-boards ceased.

She went downstairs and opened the door. Outside were two men in the uniform of the Gestapo.

One of them spoke in a stern, harsh voice.

"We have orders to search this house. We shall want to see your papers."

He thrust his way past her into the hall and the other man followed, after shutting the front door.

"Come in, gentlemen," said Aunt Krysta, politely, speaking to them in German. "There's nothing to find in this little house."

Her heart was thumping but she kept her voice steady.

"Who is occupying this villa?" asked one of the men.

Aunt Krysta gave a cackle of laughter like a foolish old woman.

"At the moment a young mother and her baby and one old woman who is myself. . . ."

Perhaps because she spoke German so fluently they became less harsh. Perhaps she disarmed their suspicions because of her calm and cheerful manner. They did not hear her thumping heart.

"We have to do our duty," said one of them with a kind of apology. "Your papers, please."

Her papers were in order.

They searched the rooms, turning up the carpets and rugs, stamping their heels on the floor-boards, touching the walls. They strode into the room where Marta was lying in bed with her child and one of them was civil enough to say, *Entschuldigen Sie,* and made a perfunctory examination of the room. Later they bent down and made a search of the floor-boards in the hall, feeling along them, tapping them, but failing to find the trap door down to the printing hall beneath.

"You have no cellar in this house?" asked one of them.

"Cellar?" asked Aunt Krysta, innocently. "None of the houses in this street have cellars."

That was true. They were little two-storey houses without cellars, but with outside sheds for the coal.

The men seemed satisfied and departed, declining a cup of tea offered by Aunt Krysta who played the part of a friendly old mother.

But it had been a shock. When the Colonel came in for a few minutes that night she told him what had happened and was deeply anxious.

"This house is under suspicion, my dear. You mustn't come here any more. I think Jozef ought to go at once. If they discover that printing hall I daren't think what will happen to him and to those other poor boys."

Jozef scoffed at the idea of abandoning his printing presses.

"Anyhow the danger is over," he said. "Those fellows had a good look round and found nothing."

It was two days later when the house was surrounded by police. Marta and the child had been moved to Marta's aunt living in the neighbourhood. The Colonel had gone on a journey to Cracow. Only Aunt Krysta remained to open the door to the knocking, after signalling down to the printing hall where Jozef was working with his friends.

In the street was a lorry-load of police. Five men shoved past her while another gripped her arm and pushed her into the dining-room and stood guard at the door. Outside was the tramp of armed police who had jumped out of the lorry and now came into the hall.

So they knew. Somebody had blabbed. They ripped up the floor-boards and found the trap-door. Aunt Krysta heard the sound of shouting and firing and the noise of a fierce struggle down below.

They fought like tigers in the cellar, the secret cellar which had been dug out below the house. Those boys, stripped to the waist, sold their lives dearly in a half-darkness, but they were overwhelmed by numbers. Jozef defended himself with an iron bar and felled two of the police before he was shot through the head and lay dead by one of his printing presses, with his arms outstretched and the iron bar still grasped by his right hand, that thin, long-fingered hand which had once played Chopin when the Germans were streaming into Warsaw.

Aunt Krysta was taken off to the Paviak prison.

CHAPTER XLII

Colonel Lopalevski had gone to Cracow at the request of 'Bor'. His mission was to get a report upon the situation in Cracow—what support might be expected from the Underground in that city in the event of a Rising in Warsaw and to establish a close liaison with General Piotrovski who had distinguished himself as a military strategist in the Pilsudski campaign.

It was a disappointing interview. The General was an old friend of the Colonel and received him with great cordiality in a small flat belonging to an old lady who had been the governess of his children. Like 'Bor' himself he went under a false name and changed his address very often as a hunted man. He was in shabby clothes but they did not disguise his soldierly bearing nor did a beard hide the unmistakable features and manner of a Polish aristocrat. But very soon there was a sharp clash of opinion between these two old friends. It was when the Colonel spoke of an imminent rising in Warsaw.

"We shall wait until the Russians get to the Vistula. Then we shall come out into the open with a call to arms. 'Bor' has all his plans ready. Every unit is already on the alert, and on tiptoes of anticipation. The day of liberation is at hand, my dear fellow. It will be a glorious day for Poland. I confess that I'm looking forward to it like an excited boy."

General Piotrovski shook his head.

"My dear old friend, it's just madness! The idea fills me with terror."

The Colonel stared at him, incredulously.

"Why do you say that? You of all men—one of our Polish heroes, *sans peur et sans reproche.*"

"Sheer madness," repeated the General. "The Germans are still strong, with formidable reserves. They're not finished yet. They'll fight back like wounded tigers. Any premature rising in Warsaw will be wiped out in blood and fire. Has 'Bor' any heavy artillery, any field guns, any tanks? What about his supplies of ammunition?"

"Plenty of ammunition," said the Colonel. "Plenty of rifles."

"To last how long, this ammunition?" asked the General.

The Colonel laughed and gave an optimistic answer.

"It will be a quick business. Three days will put Warsaw in our hands."

The General raised his hand in protest.

"Supposing it lasts for three weeks?"

"It won't. The Russians will cross the Vistula. The Germans will be caught between two fires. They will be annihilated."

General Piotrovski plucked at his beard and gave a kind of groan.

"Are we sure of those Russians? After all they've done to us in Eastern Poland? Very doubtful customers, aren't they?"

"They're out to defeat the Germans," said the Colonel. "They're bound to cross the Vistula. Their generals know their job. They're not half-wits."

General Piotrovski rose from his chair, paced up and down the small room, and then turned again to the Colonel.

"My old friend, don't think I have cold feet. Don't think that I'm less keen than you or 'Bor' himself to see the end of all this and take a hand in it if possible. Here in Cracow the youngsters are eager to get the call for action, ready to fight and die at any moment. But I should be a murderer if I sent out the call. The Germans have strong garrisons here, and we have nothing—very little—with which to fight them. Doubtless you have greater strength in Warsaw. 'Bor' has been accumulating a certain amount of arms and ammunition. But it's a terrible gamble. Tell 'Bor' from me that I beg of him not to call his lads to arms until he is certain that the Russians will come to his aid—until they're across the bridges, until they're in the outskirts of Warsaw itself."

"Not a very encouraging message!" exclaimed the Colonel. "Nothing very heroic or inspiring about it!"

The General smiled and shrugged his shoulders.

"False heroics are damned dangerous, I believe in commonsense. Never risk your troops in a suicide attack."

The Colonel parted from his old friend coldly. It was not what he had expected, this lack of enthusiasm, this defeatism, as he thought it. One could be over-cautious. It had never been a habit of his as a cavalry officer. These cautious fellows could miss a glorious opportunity for a dash through to victory. That chance, that glorious moment, was coming near to Warsaw. Were they to let it slip, to stay quiet and inactive after all these years of preparation and training in 'Bor's' Secret Army, after all the deadly risks taken by mere boys and girls, after all the shootings and tortures inflicted on those who were caught? They wouldn't stand for it, those youngsters. If there were no call to arms they would rise without it, without direction or command. He would be glad to get back to Warsaw.

In Warsaw he walked to the house in which his wife had been living with young Jozef and Marta. He would be glad to see Krysta for a few minutes. Her courage had never faltered. She had a big heart, filled with love for young people—and for him, thank God. They had seldom exchanged a cross word. They were still lovers in a way.

He stood in front of the house and something made his heart give a lurch, and he turned pale. There was a white slip of paper stuck to the door with a red seal on it. As he knew, it meant that the Germans had arrested the inhabitants and closed the house. He glanced round furtively, entered the garden, ran up the steps and stared through the French window into the hall. The floorboards had been ripped up and there was a gaping hole by the staircase. He could see the little dining-room and every stick of furniture in it had been smashed to bits.

He called out in an agonized voice.

"Krysta! . . . Krysta!"

Then he staggered against one of the walls and stood there trembling and shaken by hard sobs.

So they had found out the printing press. He had always been afraid of that. What had happened to his wife? Where was Jozef and Marta and the child?

Presently he stood up straight, and wiped his face and

orehead with the back of his hand and walked steadily to the
block of flats in Obozna Street.

It was Vanda who told him that Jozef had been killed
and that Aunt Krysta had been taken to the Paviak prison.
She told him, weeping, and held his hand and tried to comfort
him.

"Jozef died like a hero. He died for Poland and Aunt Krysta
has wonderful courage. She knew the risk she was taking. She
was glad to take it."

He patted her hand and spoke calmly.

"I know! I know, my dear! We must all be ready for any kind
of sacrifice. But I'm sorry about young Jozef. As you say, one of
our heroes—a splendid lad—a gay fellow—a fine pianist. I'm
sorry for you, my dear. I'm terribly sorry."

"There are worse things than death," said Vanda. "Sometimes I envy the dead. I envy Jozef who died gloriously for
Poland."

But she wept again.

CHAPTER XLIII

THE two sisters were in the garden behind the block of flats
when they saw a Russian plane circling rather low overhead.
For a few moments they were alarmed. Several times lately the
Russians had made air-raids over Warsaw, bombing in a haphazard way with the object of killing Germans but with the
result of killing Poles or destroying their houses. This one was
not dropping bombs but sheets of white paper which fluttered
down like big snowflakes through the blue sky, falling into
streets and gardens. Halina made a dash for one and grabbed it
as it was being wafted over the hedge.

It was a proclamation to the people of Warsaw in what was
intended to be Polish but was a lamentable and comical effort
by some Russian student of that language.

"Read it out," said Vanda.

Halina read it aloud.

*"Poles! What are you waiting for? Fight the Germans! We are
coming to liberate you. Yours truly, Jozef Stalin."*

In spite of a sense of anguish and great grief which had taken hold of her lately Vanda could not help smiling. It was too ludicrous, that message, in deplorable Polish. "Yours truly, Jozef Stalin." It was laughable, even to those who had no laughter in their hearts.

Vanda was stricken with grief at the death of Jozef. She had tried to comfort herself and her father and others—poor Marta!— by dwelling on the fact that it was a hero's death, but Jozef was gone—the gay, joking, Jozef, the interpreter of Chopin, exquisite in touch, and the beloved brother.

Aunt Krysta had gone. Not a word had come from the Paviak prison.

It seemed likely that she had been taken away to a concentration camp, the brave, cheerful, adorable Aunt Krysta who had been the kindest, and most loving friend of the younger people since they were babies. It was impossible to imagine life without Aunt Krysta. Now she had gone to some living tomb, unless they had killed her.

Vanda herself was having an inward and spiritual struggle unknown to Halina who had no uncertainties about her call to service.

At night Vanda could get little sleep because of the distant firing coming closer, coming closer. Artillery was at work on both sides. Her bedroom shook with the heavy concussions. Beyond the Vistula the night sky, never very dark in this July month, throbbed with the pulsating light of the gun flashes and burning farmsteads.

The streets of Warsaw were crowded again with refugees from the east and with German transport on the way to the railway stations going west. Were the Germans evacuating Warsaw? There were signs that they were packing up, taking away documents, burning some, and sending their wives and children westwards. They knew that defeat was inevitable. They were anxious-eyed and panic-stricken.

Vanda had seen something of this and had heard news and rumours from her friends. She had been disturbed by her father's opinion. Usually so optimistic he was now depressed and nervous. The death of Jozef had been a hard blow to him. One evening he had had a long talk with Vanda.

"I'm deeply anxious," he told her. "It will be sheer madness if there's a rising. I have a terrible conviction that it will end in tragedy.

She argued against him, as once before.

"We shall have the Russians with us, Father. Have you heard their calls to us?"

For several days now following the dropping of these leaflets the Russians had been broadcasting to the people of Warsaw.

Poles! The time of liberation is at hand. Poles, to arms! Every Polish homestead must become a stronghold in the struggle against the invader. . . . There is not a moment to lose.

Over and over again the Russians broadcast these appeals urging the people of Warsaw to rise and fight.

In some cases there were taunts and accusations that the Polish Underground was holding up the fight against the Germans and that the Commander-in-Chief of the Home Army was in collaboration with the enemy. Only the Communist forces were fighting the Germans with any zeal, they said. It was they alone who had harassed the enemy and done heroic sabotage. As there were only a few hundred Communists in Warsaw this was ludicrously untrue but what they lacked in numbers the Communists made up by intensive propaganda, distributing leaflets, putting up posters, proclaiming their own call to arms in support of the Red Army who would advance to meet them with irresistible strength.

Vanda's father was disbelieving.

"How can we trust these people? I have a dreadful presentiment that they will betray us. If the Rising happens and they fail to help us it will mean the death of thousands of our young men."

"Father," said Vanda, "it's because you were in that Russian prison. It colours all your thoughts."

Dr. Mirski shook his head.

"That's not true, my dear. But I remember Katyn. I remember that they prevented our regiments in the east from joining in the first battles of the war."

"It's too late to prevent a Rising," said Vanda. "The Home Army is waiting for the call. If it doesn't come they'll fight without it. I know that. Those boys are burning for the day—all the boys I know."

"Poor lads!" said Dr. Mirski in a low voice. "God be with them. God be with us all."

Vanda suffered a secret agony at this time. She was aware—how could she be unaware?—of the fearful risk of a Rising. In her bedroom she went down on her knees and prayed that those boys might be spared and then said another prayer, tortured by doubts of herself.

"Oh God, help me to be faithful to my oath of service. Give

me courage if the call comes. Kill the coward in my heart, dear God."

She had another cause of anxiety, nagging at her, fraying her nerves. Jerzy was overdue. He had been away longer than usual. Had they caught him at last? Had they killed him—her dear lover?

Then one day he walked into the small garden behind the block of flats. She was sitting there with Halina and Richard Allgrove. The sky was cloudlessly blue above them. The roses were in bloom above unweeded beds and the big chestnut tree in heavy foliage gave welcome shade from the hot sun.

The young Englishman—Dick, as they called him now—was talking seriously for once to Halina.

"It can't be long now. The Russkis are closing in."

As he spoke there was the thudding of heavy guns.

"Will England help us?" asked Halina. "Will the R.A.F. come to our rescue with supplies of food and ammunition?"

"We don't let down our friends," said the young officer. "They'll be here."

"Dick," said Halina presently, "don't be too heroic, will you? I mean don't be more rash than is strictly necessary."

He laughed at her with his eyes.

"I'm no hero! I shall be thoroughly frightened. I can feel the approach of blue funk. I find this strain very trying."

"Is blue funk the same thing as cold feet?" asked Halina.

"Worse," he told her. "I know because I've had them both so many times. I was in the Battle of Britain. Was that a thousand years ago? Anyhow I was a kid then and a very frightened kid."

Halina looked at him with smiling unbelief.

"It's nice to have you with us in Warsaw," she told him. "It's a kind of proof that England is with us."

Richard Allgrove refused to pose as a heroic fellow.

"I wish I were in Wimbledon," he said. "I wish I were watering the flowers in my mother's garden, or mowing the lawn for a good game of tennis. You Polish are far too brave for a timid lad like me."

Halina laughed and said, "You tell very abominable lies. I know you're glad to be here with us."

"For one or two reasons," he admitted, making her blush slightly because of the look he gave her as she sat there on a seat with the sunlight spangling her summer frock.

It was then that Jerzy came to meet them.

Vanda gave a little cry of joy and sprang to meet him and let him take her in his arms.

"How long you have been," she cried. "I thought something terrible might have happened to you."

"They were after me," he told her. "They killed one of our couriers. That way to England is too risky, and now they've discovered our secret route and rounded up all our friends. I had to go into hiding.

She did not question him. She knew that he would not tell her any more than that.

"Jerzy," she said, "I'm sorry as well as glad to see you back. It's not going to be very safe in Warsaw. You know what I mean?"

He knew what she meant. He knew perhaps better than she did. He was carrying secret dispatches from the Polish government in exile addressed to General 'Bor'.

"I wanted to get back in time," he said quietly. "Let's walk on to the Green over there. How peaceful it looks!"

"I wish we couldn't hear the guns," said Vanda.

She gave a little shudder though it was in hot sunshine.

CHAPTER XLIV

In Warsaw there was one small-sized man who had to make a terrific decision involving the lives of thousands of young men and the fate of the capital, and perhaps the destiny of Poland.

It was the man who called himself 'Bor' (which means 'forest') among many other pseudonyms, and who is now known as General Komorowski. He had chosen the word 'Forest' because in Poland it is the symbol of freedom and resistance. In the past when Poland had lost her independence all young men willing to fight for freedom escaped to the vast and ancient forests. It was there they lived in hiding and organized their resistance to the invaders.

He was Commander-in-Chief of the Home Army—the Secret Army—not only in Warsaw but throughout Poland, in its cities, and forests, and farmlands, and factories with all of whom he was in touch by secret wireless, by messages passing to and fro by couriers who risked their lives, by letters in code brought to him in his many lodgings by young girls, ignorant of his name and personality. He was always working far into the night, conferring with men who came to see him stealthily, sending dispatches to London where the Polish government was in exile, receiving answers, orders, news—often disturbing and distressful.

What manner of man was he upon whose shoulders lay such tremendous responsibility, and who now had to make this fateful decision?

A small-sized man, as already said, with a lean face and a high forehead and a little moustache above sensitive lips. Nothing extraordinary about him except very bright, penetrating eyes, very watchful and observant eyes, which often lit up with a smile in spite of all his worries and ceaseless toil. He was not a typical commander of men. Highly strung and sensitive to the sufferings in Poland and all the horrors around him in Warsaw, he was still humorous and human without a touch of arrogance though he could be severe in his condemnation of any traitor—there were a few—within his ranks.

Always in his heart there was the thought of a beautiful woman. It was his dark-eyed wife Renia—Irena Komorowska. Always he thought of her when his mind was not absorbed with those dispatches, messages, orders, which piled up on his desk. Often his thoughts of her were not without the touch of fear and apprehension, for this gay laughing lady was also in hiding and took terrible risks.

What was happening to her? Where was she? When could he see her again?

At the beginning of the war she was in Lvov. There she was arrested by the Russians and evacuated to the east. Somehow she had prevailed on them to let her go—she was a portrait painter and some of them had a soft spot in their hearts for artists—strange as it may seem. She came back to Lvov under Russian occupation and saw its ruthlessness and its policy of breaking the spirit and undermining the faith of the Polish people—with a concentration camp for those who resisted this propaganda. She had met her husband in Cracow. Now here she was in Warsaw, an ardent member of the Underground, sending news to prisoners of war by a secret code.

They could not live under the same roof. They must never be seen together. If he were caught they would track her down. In any case everything must be subordinate to the work he was doing, even his love for his gay, high-spirited wife. They had stolen meetings at friends' houses. Now and then a girl messenger brought a letter from her. She had one baby—little Adam, and was going to have another. If there were to be a Rising in Warsaw—when there would be the Rising—he would be very anxious about Renia. . . .

In June and July there was already fighting in Poland. He had touched off the train for the *Burza* plan, long prepared.

From his government in exile had come the order that Polish partisans behind the Russian lines were to co-operate with the Red Army in attacks upon German positions. *Burza* means Tempest. Operation Tempest. The storm had broken up German armies, already hard pressed. The men in the forests had come out into the open and were fighting with heroic spirit. By radio messages 'Bor' had followed the progress of these battles, proud of victories won by those boys of his. Whole districts had been cleared of the enemy. Volhynia had been liberated. Russian officers and men had cheered the Polish contingents. There had been a camaraderie between them—until orders from Moscow had arrived. Then came the arrest of those Polish commanders in the field, with black ingratitude, with cold treachery.

Nine days after starting Operation Tempest units of the Lublin Home Army had captured seven towns by themselves alone. A marvellous achievement. Aided by Red Army battalions they had captured eleven more, including Lublin itself. They had destroyed a number of heavy German panzers. By incredible valour they had captured important stores of arms and ammunition.

And then 'Bor' had received horrible news. Immediately after these victories the Polish commander, General Tumidajski, who had the pseudonym of 'Marcin', was arrested by the Russian General Kolpachev, commander of the Fourth Soviet Army. He had been given an ultimatum. Either the Home Army would join the so-called People's Army, under Colonel Berling, the Communist Pole attached to the Russian Army, or disband and give up their arms. He chose the second alternative. He was arrested again. He was now on his way to Asiatic Russia.

Where was co-operation? Where was Russian honour?

General Komorowski, as we may now call him, asked himself those questions, terrible and tragic questions bearing down upon the decisions he had to make. What help would he get from the Russians if he gave the order for the Rising in Warsaw?

He thought this out. He discussed it with his staff officers. He had long conferences with Jankovski, the Government Delegate, and with the Council of Ministers. It nagged at him as he walked through the streets, observing, watching.

The Russian Army under Marshal Rokossovsky was on the other side of the Vistula. For strictly military reasons they would be bound to help a Rising. It would open the gate to the west. It would shorten the war. They would be mad not to take this chance. However cynical—however treacherous—what would happen afterwards?—their own military interests dictated their advance across the Vistula to receive a liberated Warsaw from its own inhabitants. Surely that was logical, without wishful thinking?

The Home Army must come into the open and fight for their own freedom. Over and over again there were Russian messages by wireless and leaflets calling upon the people to rise. Could they betray them when they rose? Whether he gave the call or not they would rush to arms now that they saw a retreating German Army passing through the streets at night.

It was fantastic to think that they would remain passive without striking a blow.

Supposing, because of his dread of bloodshed he failed to send out the call? There would be a wild outburst, sporadic fighting, disorderly, without plan, wiped out in blood by the German garrison, still strong in Warsaw and powerfully armed.

He would rather die a thousand deaths than betray these boys. He had recruited them. He was their leader.

There was an urgent reason now for sending out the call. The Germans had ordered 100,000 young men to present themselves for the purpose of digging trenches against the Russians. Not a single man had appeared. But very likely they would be seized and deported. They must take up arms now—or never.

No great stir in the outside world had been made by Operation Tempest. The Russians had taken all the credit. No glory for the Poles! But if Warsaw rose—the capital city itself—if it were liberated by the Home Army, the news would flash around the world. It would be an heroic epic, and an inspiration for generations to come. It *must* happen in spite of pessimists and moments of awful doubt in his own mind—the little devils of doubt which now and then tried to weaken his will-power and pervert his reasoning.

Reports were coming in from his secret agents in the city. All German offices were closing down. Newspapers published by the Germans had ceased. The Gestapo was burning documents—the records of its black crimes—with feverish haste. The German Governor and Mayor had decamped. German civilians and the *Volksdeutsche*—Poles of German origin—were besieging the railway stations. Because of crowded trains, and few of them, sky-high prices were being offered for any kind of horse transport.

To see these things for himself General Komorowski walked through the city. Across the Vistula bridges he saw an endless flow of German transport from the east. Tanks were moving on both sides of the streets, separated and held up by horse-driven carts and marching men, footsore, haggard and dirty, with defeat written on their faces.

His mind was made up on this walk through Warsaw. He had communicated his views in detail to the Polish government in London. On the 25th day of July—that very day—he had received a message sent to him through Jankovski the government delegate in Warsaw by order of Prime Minister Mikolajczyk.

At a session of the Government of the Republic it was unanimously decided to empower you to proclaim the Insurrection at a moment which you will decide as most opportune.

He had decided. The Russians had now reached the suburbs of Warsaw on the right bank of the Vistula. Soviet patrols had reached the outer streets of Praga.

The call to arms would be timed for 5 p.m. on August 1st.

How could he get that message into the hands of 40,000 men still sworn to secrecy? It was the great numbers of young girls, the liaison girls, who took it to every member of the Home Army in the capital, climbing the stairs in blocks of flats, whispering to boys leaving the workshops and factories, pushing envelopes through letter-boxes, telling them to pass the word along to their comrades.

He drafted out his first message to the soldiers of his Home Army.

Soldiers of the Capital,
I have today issued the order which you desire, for open warfare against Poland's age-old enemy, the German invader. After nearly five years of ceaseless and determined struggle, carried on in secret, you stand today openly with arms in your hands, to restore freedom to our country and to mete out fitting punishment to the German criminals for the terror and crimes committed by them on Polish soil.
                                                        Bor.
                                Commander-in-Chief, Home Army.

Five p.m. on August 1st.

General Komorowski left his lodging with his A.D.C. Their revolvers were concealed in a gramophone case. They walked to a building already chosen for headquarters, already fitted up with radio transmitters and receiving instruments—it was the Kammler factory in the Wola district near the ruins of the Ghetto.

Five p.m. on August 1st.

Arms and ammunition had to be smuggled from their hiding places and distributed to all units without attracting suspicion. They were hidden in hand-carts under piles of coal or timber or vegetables. They were concealed in barrels, wheel-barrows, and carried by hand in any innocent-looking package by those girls of Warsaw, by schoolboys with their satchels. Rifles, machine-guns, ammunition. Enough for eight days. The battle must not last more than eight days. Further supplies would have to come from outside or from captured stores within the city. But in eight days they would have Warsaw in their hands.

England would hear of this. Their government had already been informed. For years they had put their faith in England and the British. Now they were advancing in Normandy, breaking through the German lines. They would send their aircraft with food and ammunition. The people of Warsaw would be waiting for them. They had already arranged signals to be seen from the sky.

The R.A.F. would never let them down. Hadn't everyone in Warsaw been learning English?

'Good day. . . . How do you do? . . . Welcome to Warsaw!'

On August 1st General Komorowski waited in his headquarters for the Rising to begin. All day long messages were being brought to him and messages were being sent out. . . .

What was Renia doing with little Adam and her unborn babe?

God save Warsaw! . . . God save Poland!

CHAPTER XLV

IN the first week of July Vanda received an order from the commander of her unit in the Underground to open a canteen in Tamka Street. She knew that this opening of a canteen for soldiers of the Home Army was in preparation of the inevitable Rising which could not be delayed much longer.

The order came from an old lady who went by the pseudonym of 'Granny'. She was the widow of a Polish general and belonged to an aristocratic family with a long tradition as soldiers and statesmen. This spirit had descended to this lady whose courage and patriotism were like a fire in her frail body, thin and delicate and old. Yet there was sweetness as well as steel in her and she was very charming to Vanda and other girls who were under her command.

"I'm afraid you'll find the work hard," she told Vanda. "You will be responsible under me for all the work of the canteen. The other girls will take your orders. The moment of action is at hand. We must be prepared. I have perfect confidence in your courage and devotion, my dear. One has only to look at you. . . ."

Vanda took her hand and raised it to her lips.

"How beautiful you are!" exclaimed the old lady. "You will be an inspiration to us. All our boys will fall in love with you!"

She gave a little silvery laugh and said, "I used to be pretty myself when I was a young girl like you."

Vanda was glad to have this active work with hardly a moment's respite from morning till night. There was no time now for agonizing doubts or tragic apprehension, no more need for forging false passports and identity cards. All that was over.

The Home Army would come out into the open and this was service for those boys who would do the fighting. Her mind became more serene. She was no longer afraid of losing courage. Fear left her. She felt curiously happy and resigned to death itself. Those who were already coming to the canteen would be facing death and they were very cheerful and gay and full of jokes. Why should she shirk what they were ready to risk with such high spirit? Polish girls as well as Polish boys would be ready for any kind of service at whatever cost.

The girls working with her in the canteen showed no sign of fear or doubt. They talked about their brothers and boy friends as though they were all going to a party.

"Tadeusz is longing for the day. . . . Bronek goes about whistling. . . . Jan is getting frightfully excited."

Vanda and her friends were putting up great numbers of small packets which contained emergency rations, with some lumps of sugar, biscuits, cigarettes and adhesive bandages. In the evenings they made white and red armlets for the soldiers who had no military uniforms. All these supplies had been provided in advance but there was a shortage of crockery and Dr. Mirski volunteered to transport this from friends' houses in a hand-cart which would not arouse German suspicions.

"I'm too old to be in the fighting line," he said, "but I'm glad to be of some service."

He seemed to have become reconciled to the Rising now that everybody was called to action. Nobody knew that he fell on his knees at night and prayed that a great bloodshed of youth might be averted.

One afternoon Vanda was in the canteen with the other girls when she saw Jerzy come in. They exchanged smiles and he came towards her and spoke in a low voice.

"Could you spare a few minutes? Could we talk alone somewhere?"

There was a garden outside the block of flats and they walked over to it silently until they were alone there. The sun was very hot and they sat on a seat under one of the trees and Jerzy took her hand.

"It's tomorrow," he said. "I had to come and see you."

She felt ice-cold in spite of the heat of the day.

"It's no secret now," he said. "Everybody knows the Home Army has its orders. General 'Bor' has sent out the call to arms."

She was silent for what seemed like a long time.

"Will you be in the fighting line?" she asked.

"As a private soldier," he told her. "I shan't have officer rank."

He spoke calmly, even cheerfully. She noticed that he had taken off the glove from his left hand. His wound had healed but still showed a scar and two fingers missing. She had wept when he had lain in hospital and told her that he would never play the violin again. Now her eyes swam with tears.

"Don't worry about me," he said. "We're all in it—civilians as well as fighting men, girls as well as boys. I'm deeply anxious about you, my dearest love."

She blinked away her tears, and clasped his hand tighter.

"It makes it easier because we're all in it," she said. "I'm not afraid for myself, Jerzy, and now I see only the splendour of other people's courage—all those boys who are eager to fight for Poland's sake."

"They're pretty wonderful," he said. "I suppose it's because I'm older that I haven't the same sense of exaltation. I haven't warmed up to it!"

He laughed as though he had said something absurd.

"We shan't need any warming up presently. The fires of hell, I'm afraid. I wish I had more courage."

She gave a tragic little laugh.

"That's a foolish wish, Jerzy! Haven't you been risking your life as a courier on those frightful journeys? Haven't you tested your courage to the uttermost?"

"All that was rather passive," he told her lightly.

There were some children playing in the garden and he glanced at them with a smile.

"We needn't mind those little ones. I just want to kiss you once or twice. Do you mind?"

"Why should I mind?"

"If I'm killed," he said simply, "I shall have no complaint about it because of our love and the joy it has given me. And I believe that death isn't the end of all things. I believe that we shall meet again on the other side of the bridge."

"We may go together across the bridge," said Vanda. "I shall be glad of that."

He put his arms round her and drew down her head and kissed her lips with one long, enduring kiss as though their two souls mingled in this physical endearment.

Reluctantly he said, "I must go. I have to join my unit."

"Oh, Jerzy, my darling!" cried Vanda. "May God be with you."

"And with you," he said, gravely.

He took both her hands and held them in his and kissed them. Then, very quickly, not looking at her again he strode out of the garden by another gate.

That night Vanda was sleepless. It would be tomorrow. For a long time she stood by her bedroom window looking up at the night sky, still light in summertime and still with a faint touch of blue. The Russians were over there on the Vistula but their guns were quiet. And the night was quiet. No Russian planes came over dropping bombs on German concentrations as lately they had done on many nights. It was as though the Russian Army had disappeared from the neighbourhood of Warsaw. Down in the street there was the noise of traffic—German transport going by, German guns, German lorries. The light of another dawn was heralding a day of fate for Poland and Polish youth. Before the end of it terrific things would happen. Perhaps it would be the glory of liberation in Warsaw. Was that possible? Would the Germans be caught unawares and demoralized? They had asked for the wrath of God and the vengeance of a people they had oppressed with such cruelty—those boys shot by the firing squads, those deportations to concentration camps, all the horrors of a ruthless occupation. As a Polish girl who had seen these things Vanda could feel no pity for them, but even now hoped that Polish boys would behave with chivalry and without brutality. Somehow during this sleepless night she seemed to see all this in a spiritual way as though she were dead, as though she had already crossed the bridge of which Jerzy had spoken. Why did men make war upon each other? For what purpose and for what good? How could it be that after 1,900 years of Christendom there could be such cruelty as that revealed by the Gestapo and the German S.S.? Such crimes could not go unpunished, but when would man, civilized man, obey the teachings of Christ, the pity, the love, the forgiveness of Christ's teaching and sacrifice?

For a long time Vanda knelt on the floor by her bedside with her arms outstretched and her face buried in the coverlet.

Before leaving home for the canteen that afternoon, after many hours sewing the red and white armlets which were carried to various units by liaison girls, Vanda was startled by the cook asking her to come down to the kitchen which looked on to the street, being a corner house. From the kitchen window they could see into Obozna Street which led up steeply to the Cracow Broadway.

"Our boys are going to the Rising," said Maria, the cook, who was a stout, middle-aged woman. "God bless them, poor lads!"

"How do you know?" asked Vanda, amazed by these words. The cook looked at her with wet eyes.

"Everybody knows. They're our sons and brothers, aren't they?"

Vanda stared out of the window and was overcome by emotion.

In twos and threes at short intervals young men were passing, mere boys, many of them. They were wearing the red and white armbands. Some of them wore big boots up to their knees— 'officers' boots' as they were called by lads who were proud of them as being the nearest they could wear to a soldier's uniform. They were not speaking to each other but walked in silence. They looked as though they were on their way to church or some evening class, rather solemnly.

"Poor children!" cried Maria, the cook, beginning to sob. "Poor young fellows! It breaks my heart to see them."

Vanda's own eyes filled with tears and a great pity and love and pride stirred into her heart. Those boys were front-line soldiers. In less than an hour they would begin the battle—in less than an hour which seemed like a whole day because of the agonizing suspense.

She was in the canteen with the others. The old lady called 'Granny' arrived a few minutes late. There was a bright light in her eyes and she gave a little excited laugh, but her thin delicate hands were trembling with intense emotion.

"The boys are on their way," she said. "There are no Germans about."

She sat down in a chair grasping its arms tightly so that the veins showed in her hands.

There were a few whispered words and then they sat in silence listening. Warsaw was very quiet. It seemed a city of peace. Presently a church clock struck the hour. Five o'clock.

For a little while there was silence again. Then suddenly there was the sound of firing, single rifle shots, the bursting of hand-grenades, the rattle of machine-guns.

"The Day of Liberation!" said the old lady, sitting straight in the armchair. "It has begun. May God be with us."

No other words were spoken for some time. Now and then the firing ceased for a few minutes then broke out again more fiercely.

"It's in the Electric Works," said the old lady. "They're attacking the Power House."

Vanda seemed to have all her soul in her ears. Sitting there, white-faced, she listened intently.

Two battles were going on, those noises told her. One was at the Power House quite close to the Embankment. The other was farther to the west, up town. It was, she was sure, an attack on the University, situated on the hilltop above Cracow Broadway. The University gardens sloped down to Obozna Street, where Vanda was now living, towards the Vistula. The German S.S. had used the University buildings as their headquarters.

Firing broke out in other places, in many directions, some quite close—perhaps along the river bank—others in different parts of Warsaw. There were heavy explosions and always, very close, the deadly rattle of machine-gun fire.

The dusk changed into complete darkness. The hours dragged on. The old lady and the girls sat silently in the big kitchen of the canteen, lit only by the glow of fire in the stoves heating the water which might be wanted for wounded men.

Suddenly Vanda sprang up and cried out.

"I can't stand this any longer. I must go out and see what's happening!"

"We had better go home," said the old lady. "The boys won't come here tonight. They're too busy elsewhere. Anyhow Bronka and Jadviga will stay."

They went out into the street. Spent bullets lay about their feet and overhead came bursts of machine-gun fire. But apart from single shots and that rattle of machine-guns there was no great noise. It was impossible to tell what was happening or what success had been **attained**. The old lady and the young girls stood listening again, staring through the darkness. They were alone in the street.

"We shall know more tomorrow," said the old lady, calmly. "We had better get to bed."

"But not to sleep," said Vanda. "That's impossible."

CHAPTER XLVI

AT four o'clock on the day of the Rising General 'Bor' Komorowski went to the Kammler factory which was to be his headquarters.

It faced two narrow streets with dead ends, adjoining the charred ruins of the Ghetto, surrounded by a blank wall. Down one of the streets was a tobacco factory, held by a German garrison of about thirty men with two machine-guns. Outside were two pill-boxes looking each way.

The factory workers, all of whom belonged to the Home Army, were under the orders of Lieutenant Kammler who owned the factory.

"How are things going?" asked the General.

"Not too good. The Germans increased their garrison to fifty men last night."

"How many men are here with you?"

"Thirty-three, actually on the spot."

"And what arms?"

"Fifteen rifles, maybe forty grenades, and a few *filipinki*."

Filipinki were home-made grenades and had a high explosive power.

The General was not unduly worried—yet. At five o'clock the surrounding sector was to be occupied by the Khedyv Battalion, one of the crack units of the Home Army.

It was then a few minutes past four.

'Bor' went up to the second floor of the factory where his general staff, the government delegate, and the Chairman of the Council of National Unity had already assembled. Some of them were under a high nervous strain but others were calm, or controlled their inevitable anxiety which made them tense during this time of waiting.

Suddenly the General's quick ears heard the approach of a lorry down the street. He went to the window and saw that it carried some German railway police. It passed the factory gate where a Polish sentry had a rifle in his hand. This must have given the alarm to the police. They drove the lorry backwards. There was the sound of shots being fired.

Realizing the danger of giving an alarm before zero hour Lieutenant Kammler rushed out, revolver in hand, with two other soldiers. He shot the lorry driver through the head and killed two other policemen who were standing up. The sound of the shooting had reached the German garrison in the tobacco factory and the pill-boxes. Instantly the street was swept by machine-gun bullets, just as Lieutenant Kammler leapt back to the gate.

An attack was to be expected from the tobacco factory. It came swiftly. The house opposite was occupied by German soldiers, not farther than a grenade's throw away. Fire from the pill-boxes was directed to the high factory window. One burst entered the room in which General Komorowski stood with his friends after he had returned from downstairs where he had watched the street scene. Splintered glass and bullets spattered the walls and ceiling.

There were women in the room and some civilians.

"You must go to the back of the building," said the General.

The women refused. None of them showed a sign of fear.

There was reason for fear. The German police barracks were only 300 to 400 yards away and they sent another lorry-load of their men to attack the Kammler factory. But they were uncertain of the situation and stopped the lorry under the factory windows —a fatal act. From one of the windows a volunteer hurled a hand-grenade which fell straight into the lorry with deadly effect, blowing it to bits and killing the police.

Presently danger came from another point. There were shouts from the attic and from the roof where a spotter had been at his observation post. Germans climbed on to the roof and severely wounded the spotter. They had entered the attic by the time six of the volunteers had rushed upstairs at the sound of the shouting. There was a fierce fight at close quarters in this attic-room until the German police were shot dead.

It was a quarter-past-five. The Battle of Warsaw had begun. From all parts of the city came the sound of firing. The German garrison in the tobacco factory found themselves isolated. But to General Komorowski it seemed doubtful whether the Khedyv battalion would be able to reach him as they were cut off from his factory by streets under heavy fire.

At seven o'clock, to the General's amazement, two men of this battalion arrived very cheerfully.

"How on earth did you get here?" asked the General.

They were an advanced patrol. They had smashed a way through from Okopova Street by blasting through attic walls and climbing over roofs. The others would be arriving soon, they said.

At eight o'clock, or thereabouts, there were more shouts from the attic, but this time they were shouts of exultation. Voices called the General to come up and look over Warsaw.

Up there on the roof by a chimney stack the spotter who had relieved the wounded man shouted excitedly as 'Bor' stood by his side.

"The Flag! The Polish Flag!" he cried, pointing with outstretched arm. "Our Flag—right in the middle of the city!"

"From the roof," wrote General Komorowski in his thrilling book *The Secret Army*, "a wide view of the capital enabled us to see the blaze of the fires. From the tower of the highest building in Warsaw, the sixteen-storey Prudential Building, which dominated the whole centre of the city, flew a large flag. I concentrated my gaze. No, it was not a Nazi flag. Now I could see the white and red. After five years the Polish colours were once more flying defiantly over the city. Looking more closely I saw that similar flags were already flying from the cupola of the Post Office Savings Bank, from the tower of the Town Hall and other buildings. This was the first sign, the first report, on the course of the fighting that I received."

By early the next morning other reports were coming in by liaison girls, runners, wireless. Halina was one of those girls who dodged across bullet-swept streets to deliver a message.

On the whole the news was good. The whole district of Stare Miasto—the Old Town on the left bank of the Vistula—was in their hands. The western district of Vola was being cleared of the enemy. There had been a heavy battle for the General Post Office which was then captured. The Power Station, the gas works, and the Prudential offices had been stormed and taken. Desperate attacks on the Telephone Exchange had so far been repulsed and to the north of the city the Home Army units in Zoliborz had had to withdraw from the advance of German tanks, but were preparing for a counter-attack.

Fighting had flared up at many points in Warsaw. The initiative was in the hands of the Home Army. Every man was fighting with fine spirit and in spite of many casualties their morale was high and heroic. So it was reported to 'Bor' in numerous messages that reached him.

It was unfortunate that some sections of the Home Army had begun the rising two hours before it was timed as the Germans had been given the alarm by their concentrations. This might have upset the whole plan and prevented taking the enemy by surprise everywhere. Fortunately it had not done so. German headquarters pooh-poohed these sporadic outbursts of fire which they thought were trivial. They were actually caught unawares when the Rising became general at the time appointed, and when 40,000 men rushed to the attack.

It was not until 5.15 that the Germans sent out a general alarm to all troops. Groups of tanks and armoured cars had been standing by, and eighteen of their heaviest tanks were seen crossing Lubeliski Square, moving towards the centre of the battle. They were confident, it seemed, that their Panzer units would be sufficient to quell the Rising, but they little knew what would happen to them in the streets of Warsaw where the entire population, civilians as well as soldiers, girls as well as men, rushed out to attack them during the following days of fighting.

There was no front line, no sharp division between Poles and Germans. All over Warsaw the Germans held out in fortified buildings and in strong pockets of resistance while the Home Army captured many areas and enlarged their own fields of manœuvre.

General 'Bor' sat up all night waiting for the reports to come in. He wrote a message to the Government in exile in London, waiting for the news. The whole world ought to be informed.

We began the fight for Warsaw on August 1st at 17.00 hours: Arrange immediately for ammunition and arms to be dropped at the lights (specified) and also in the squares giving on to the city. . . . As the fight to capture Warsaw has begun we ask for Soviet help to be supplied by an immediate attack from outside.

Those were his two anxieties. Ammunition at once. If the battle were protracted they would run out of ammunition. . . . The Soviet Army must come to the aid of the Home Army without delay. When were they coming? They were very quiet over there beyond the Vistula. He had tried to establish contact with them but they had not replied. They failed to reply. . . . Two grave anxieties, yet with very great hope after a magnificent beginning.

He could not send out the message to the world that night of

August 1st. The German attack on the roof had put the transmitter out of action. That was most unfortunate. It was reported to him that the necessary spare parts could be found in an underground stores of signal equipment only 500 yards away. Only 500 yards, but under enemy fire. A volunteer set out on that perilous journey and was killed. Another lad was eager to make the attempt and came back triumphantly with the spare parts, so desperately needed. The transmitter was put into working order again. General Komorowski could send out his messages to the world and to his own Home Army.

In the thick of these stupendous events, under the burden of his terrific responsibility, uplifted by hope, thrusting back anxieties, cheerful in conversation with his staff, quick and alert in brain, there was always somewhere in his mind, deep in his subconscious mind, a little nagging worry.

Where was Renia, his beautiful wife, with little Adam and her unborn child?

Every woman, every child, every babe in Warsaw was in the firing line.

CHAPTER XLVII

THE big block of flats in Obozna Street was being turned into a fortress, or at least a stronghold, in which the inhabitants could be sheltered against machine-gun fire, bombing from the air, and attacks from German sorties.

Vanda and her friends were in the corner house. The front door and the first-floor windows were walled up, only small gaps being left as loopholes. Groups of volunteers worked day and night at this job in strengthening these defences and they broke open a space of about four foot square in the basement walls to give communication between the houses.

All the inhabitants of the six blocks were ordered down to the basements and cellars and lived there as one community. Upstairs the flats were occupied by young soldiers of the Home Army who had already been in action and had had to retire from one of the outposts to this new position.

As the days passed the population in the basements was increased by people who had fled from houses set on fire by the Germans who burned down every house when they had fought their way down a street with tanks and flame-throwers.

That was Vanda's home during the battle for Warsaw. Here was the canteen in which she worked for long hours—all the people had to be fed—with only a few snatches of sleep when her strength was almost spent.

It was a kind of nightmare life, extraordinary and fantastic. There was something dreamlike about it. Sometimes she seemed to be watching a stage play, detached from its grim reality, moving about as one of the characters playing her own part but, now and then, in a queer automatic way, when she was very tired.

Could all this be real? From the floors upstairs came the sound of young soldiers singing. In the basements through which she passed the electric light was on, shaded at night so that people might sleep. Many families were there with a number of young children and babies playing very happily. Here and there on the stone floors were Persian rugs which had been dragged down from the flats above, and sofas and chairs which were 'period' pieces brought down for safety—as though there could be any safety in Warsaw for precious treasures.

She walked among them at night when they were sleeping or trying to sleep, many of them lying on the floors under blankets and eiderdowns. The dimmed electric light touched the faces of young girls deeply asleep after a hard day's work. It revealed the faces of elderly women who had had cultured homes and every comfort in life, and here and there the face of a woman driven from the working-class quarter by the incendiary fires. Some of them stirred in their sleep and were restless or awake. Their eyes followed Vanda as she crept by them. An elderly man raised a hand and smiled. In some of the cellars babies were wailing.

She met her father there. Dr. Mirski was one of the hardest workers in the canteen, serving the food and the hot drinks, refusing to rest when his daughter pleaded with him. He seemed wonderfully cheerful and often she heard him joking and laughing with the children and their mothers whom he served with this food—for which no charge was made, everything being free and shared.

One night he whispered to her.

"Come into the garden, my dear. Let's get a breath of fresh air."

There was a garden to this corner house. It sloped down from a high bank and its wall was a protection from machine-gun fire turned this way from the University building, still held by the German S.S.

He took her hand and they went out into the garden in which there was a scent of flowers and green plants, and sun-baked grass. The night sky was pulsating with the red glow of many fires. In the direction of Stare Miasto—the Old Town—flames licked up through clouds of black smoke. The father and daughter stood in silence watching and listening.

Vanda spoke first in a low voice.

"Father, how is it going?"

Dr. Mirski answered gravely.

"We shall need help before long. I'm very anxious. Our lads are wonderful but unless help comes from outside. . . ."

"They *must* help us," said Vanda. "Where are the English aeroplanes—and the Americans? Why don't they come?"

Dr. Mirski raised his hands.

"God alone knows. Perhaps they're too far away. Perhaps they're too heavily engaged on other battle fronts."

"It will be a betrayal if they don't come," said Vanda, bitterly. "Are we going to be betrayed by all our so-called friends? Where are the Russians? What are they doing?"

Dr. Mirski turned his head towards the east without moving his body. Beyond there, not far away, was the Vistula. On the other side was a Russian Army, a silent army.

"All quiet on the Russian front," said Dr. Mirski with tragic irony.

Presently he spoke again.

"I long for their coming and I dread their coming. How shall we get them out again. We're fighting for the freedom of the soul, but Soviet Russia under those dreadful men in the Kremlin will deny us freedom. They will try to murder the Polish soul. They will try to destroy the faith of our young people. The Germans have been cruel. They have killed the bodies of our young men. But Russian cruelty is worse. Their creed of Communism is an attack upon the human mind and soul. They hate the Church which they know is their greatest enemy. They hate us Poles because we are Catholics. Their victory over Germany will be for us a new and more awful slavery. And yet, having said that, I wait for their coming with an illogical yearning because it would save the lives of our poor boys and prevent the destruction of our beautiful Warsaw with all its palaces and shrines and noble buildings."

"Father," said Vanda, "you're so cheerful in the canteen. You joke and laugh, and yet now you talk in this tragic way and tell me horrible things."

Her father took her hand and pressed it against his left side, nearest to the heart.

"I joke and laugh with the children," he answered, "I have to try to keep them happy and while I'm working I forget the tragedy of it all. But when I'm alone with you, my dear, I feel that I can talk seriously. Hasn't it been like that between us since you were a child?"

"Yes, Father," said Vanda, "and I'm thankful for it."

"You and I can look truth in the face," said Dr. Mirski. "You and I can look death in the face. We're very near to death now, my dear. Keep closer under the wall."

They had moved beyond the shelter of the wall and the earth where they stood was splashed up by machine-gun bullets. Together they stood under the wall again.

"Father," said Vanda, "you know I love Jerzy Boberski?"

"Yes, of course, my dear. It's no secret."

"If he's alive I should like to marry him."

"I shall be very glad," said her father. "I am pleased with your choice. Jerzy certainly is a remarkable young man, and belongs to a family of highly patriotic and noble traditions. His name always makes me think of Lvov and the Boberski's Foundation for youth, the large white building facing the Kilinski Park. You mean to marry after this battle?"

"I mean during the battle, if we have the chance—if we can have that joy for even half an hour."

"I understand, my dear," said Dr. Mirski, who always seemed to understand Vanda.

She spoke a few words about something else.

"I'm getting anxious about Halina. She's been missing for two days."

"I know," said Dr. Mirski. "She's very high-spirited. She's very rash."

They went back to the basement.

Vanda kissed her father and said, "Good night, Father. Try to get some sleep."

One of the extraordinary things about this life in the basement —and in all the districts of Warsaw from which the Germans had been expelled—was the news that came from the outside world, free and uncensored since 1939. The possession of a wireless set had been punishable by death, or at least by a prison sentence. Now in the first days of the Rising thousands of wireless sets appeared. In the basement there were several in the different cellars and they blared out all day long. Music came from the B.B.C. in London—dance music, jazz, classical music, songs from the halls and the concert rooms, while Warsaw was burning and its boys being killed. That in Vanda's mind was part of the reason why all this seemed fantastic and at times unreal.

For the first time since the beginning of the German occupation there was a free uncensored Polish Press. Every morning after the first day of the Rising, a boy or girl dodging the bullet-swept streets, brought round the *Biuletyn Informacyjny*—one of at least ten daily papers, printed in what had been the secret presses like that one to which Jozef had belonged in the underground hall. They were well edited and well written by distinguished writers and experienced journalists. They gave 'front-line news', descriptions of visits to the outposts. They contained poems and even letters from correspondents, announcing that they and the children were alive and well. Children separated from their parents sent their love to their fathers and mothers. Amazing journalism in a city where a battle was raging!

There was a rush for these papers. They were read eagerly by the inhabitants of the blocks of Obozna Street who discussed the news excitedly. It was as though they were miles away from the battle itself, instead of being close to the front line and within reach of machine-gun fire.

For several days they were joyful with hope. "The initiative is in our hands," announced General Komorowski. The enemy had been cleared out of many strongholds. The Central Railway Station had been captured but lost again. Fierce fighting was in progress there. The areas round the Vilno and Eastern stations were occupied by the Home Army. By August 5th Theatre Square, Bank Square, and the Polytechnic had been mastered in spite of the enemy's stronger resistance and heavy counter-attacks.

Wonderful news! Very heartening and hopeful to the basement dwellers and the young soldiers on the upper floors. Their enthusiasm was high. They were singing and shouting and sky-larking.

"Those boys are enjoying themselves!" said an elderly man in the basement. "I wish I were young enough to be with them!"

They knew nothing of the messages being sent out by 'Bor' to the Government in London.

Ammunition is a tormenting anxiety, as our reserves are diminishing from hour to hour, while lack of weapons prevents volunteers, who are reporting in masses, from going into action.

At all costs give us ammunition. . . .

CHAPTER XLVIII

HALINA had been missing for two days.

She had been called away from the canteen to do liaison work for which she had been specially trained. She had said something about returning each night to the basement in the block of flats. She had not returned. She had crawled through the holes knocked into basement walls to get from one street to another. She had groped her way through dark passages by the help of a little glimmer from her torchlight. She had gone through rooms crowded with people but lit only by a candle in streets where the electric light had been cut off by the Germans. She had dodged rifle fire and machine-gun fire in streets where the dead bodies of Polish boys lay unburied. Her fair hair had become tousled. Her frock was torn and dirty with coal dust and filth from the places through which she had crawled, but her blue eyes smiled at the men in the front-line houses to whose commanders she was carrying dispatches from headquarters. They greeted her with jokes, concealing their admiration for this young girl's courage.

"A nice walk this morning? . . . Lovely in the fresh air, no doubt! . . . Must give you a good appetite, getting about like that!"

They were astounded when they heard what a distance she had come in the underground ways or across streets under enemy fire.

In one of the front-line outposts at which she arrived—it was in Napoleon Square—she demanded food.

"I'm starving!" she told them. "Can anybody spare a hunk of bread?"

"You bet! Are biscuits any good?"

A dozen hands held out army biscuits and a tin of sardines and a pot of jam.

They were in a well-furnished room with sandbagged windows. There were chintz-covered chairs and a piano in one corner and some oil paintings on the walls gashed by bullets.

"Good God!" said a voice she knew. "What on earth are you doing here?"

She had come up to this room from the cellar after one of her journeys by underground ways.

It was an English voice. It belonged to her friend Richard Allgrove whom she had learnt to call Dick.

She stared at him incredulously and then laughed.

"You here?" she asked.

He didn't look quite as beautiful as when she had last seen him. He had three days' growth of beard. His face was smudged with dirt. He was in blue overalls torn at the knees with only the armlet to give him a military status—not yet recognized by the Germans or by the Allied orders.

"You look as if you had been down a chimney," he said, answering her laugh. "Still I must say it doesn't make much difference to you. You're still looking marvellous. But what in heaven's name are you doing here?"

"Doing my job," she told him with a flutter of eyelashes because of his admiring gaze. "Is there any chance of a hot drink?"

"Every chance! Tea or coffee, lady? We have all convenience here. I call it the Ritz Hotel. It would be quite all right if it weren't for a lot of lousy Germans fifty yards away. Most unpleasant fellows. They pasted us properly yesterday."

She could not quite understand all he was saying in English but she laughed again as though he had said something very funny.

He spoke a few words in bad Polish to one of the younger men, a boy of eighteen or so, who nodded, grinned and went out of the room.

"That child will bring a nice cup of hot water which we are pleased to call tea," said Dick. "Take a seat, lady. Make yourself at home. It's a cosy little place in hell."

The other young men were much amused by this conversation in English but withdrew a little, delicately, as though not wishing to spoil a *tête-à-tête* between the Englishman and this pretty girl.

They sat at opposite sides of a small table and he spoke to her in a lower voice.

"You ought not to be here. It's a damned dangerous spot. The Germans may attack at any moment. It's madness for you to be here."

"You're here," answered Halina. "And you'll have to stay here while I shall hop off. It's splendid of you, Dick. After all, you're not a Pole."

"Is that an insult or a compliment?" he asked with a quiet laugh.

When the hot drink was brought she looked him in the eyes and spoke seriously.

"I've a grudge against the English—all except you."

"I'm sorry for England," he told her. "What's your complaint?"

"Why don't your aeroplanes come to us with supplies and ammunition? Is the R.A.F. going to let us down?"

Richard Allgrove of the R.A.F. looked embarrassed for a moment.

"I hope not. I hope to God not. Give them time."

"They've had time," said Halina.

He put up a defence.

"It's a hell of a long way. They have to get over Germany and then back again, if they're lucky enough to get through a sky-full of steel."

"Aren't we worth saving whatever the risk?" she asked. "Does England let down her friends?"

He put both arms on the table and laughed again.

"Don't let's talk politics, or world strategy. It's wonderful seeing you here. It's simply miraculous. Do you mind if I kiss you before all the lads?"

"I should mind very much," said Halina, blushing at such an outrageous idea.

"They wouldn't mind. They'd only envy my luck. They're great pals of mine. It may be our last kiss, Halina. This isn't a health resort. It'll be a raging furnace before long. You ought to go. I order you to go."

"Can't you hold out?" she asked. "You seem in a strong position here."

"Not against artillery and tanks and every old thing. They don't like us here. They'll do their damndest to clear us out, and they're massing round us, and our ammunition is running out."

He looked into her eyes again and his own were anxious.

"Halina, it's madness for you to be here. You're so young and lovely. What's the world coming to when young girls have to dodge machine-gun fire and visit front-line outposts about to be wiped off the map?"

"I've turned twenty," said Halina. "Don't look at me as if I were a baby."

"I look at you with adoration," he told her in a low voice. "I think you're wonderful. You're like Joan of Arc."

"Nothing wonderful about me," she answered. "There are dozens of other girls doing the same thing. I only wish I were a soldier, fighting for Poland. Wouldn't English girls be like that if they had been invaded?"

Richard Allgrove did not answer that question.

"You must go," he said. "I can't let you stay here, Halina—for God's sake! The Germans may attack at any moment. I'll come with you as far as the underground passage."

"You don't seem to like my presence," said Halina.

"It's because I love you."

The officer in command of the unit came over to her.

"You must go now," he said, politely but firmly.

She rose at once and the other young men gathered round to say good-bye and several shook hands with her before she went with her English friend down some steps leading to the cellar where the hole had been broken through into the next house down the street. It was dark there in the cellar with only a gleam of light coming through from the street level. A rat scuttled away from them.

"Dick," said Halina, "I want you to do me a favour. I want you to give me something."

"What kind of thing?" he asked. "I've nothing here but these rags I wear and one old pipe without any tobacco—curse it!"

"I want you to give me two *filipinki*."

She could not see the surprise in his eyes—the light was too dim—but she heard it in his voice.

"Two *filipinki*? What on earth for? You're not going out to kill Germans, are you?"

"Self-defence," she told him. "They might be useful."

"Quite impossible," he told her.

"I'll give you a kiss for them," she said.

He hesitated.

"That's very tempting. I'm a weak fellow."

He had a leather case slung at his side and he unfastened it and pulled out two hand-grenades.

"Do you know how to work them? They're dangerous toys, you know."

"Show me."

"You have to pull out this pin. It gives you about three seconds before you throw them. You ought not to have them. On second thoughts I'm not going to give them to you. They're not powder-puffs for pretty girls."

"Then you shan't get a kiss," said Halina. "Good-bye!"

She darted towards the hole in the wall.

He called out after her.

"Halina, darling! Don't run away. You can have them. Only for God's sake, be careful."

She came back and he handed her the *filipinki* and she put them into a small silk bag—a girl's vanity bag—which was fastened to her waistband. She carried her messages in it.

"Many thanks," she said. "Did you say you wanted a kiss?"

"I did!"

She put her face up and he held her in his arms and kissed her.

"I'm terribly fond of you," he said, holding her very tight. "Halina, darling, if only I could take you to Wimbledon one day. That's where they play tennis, you know! Quite a nice place. Wimbledon. I doubt whether I'll ever see it again."

He was talking nonsense—his old kind of comical nonsense—while he held her head with its tousled hair in both hands and pressed his lips to hers.

She struggled away from him.

"I said a kiss—one kiss."

"Don't go!" he pleaded. "It's heaven in this cellar. I had no idea it was such a nice place. Halina, my darling, didn't I say it might be our last kiss? That's a terrible thought."

She gave a little laugh and darted through the hole in the wall.

He called after her again.

"Halina! . . . Dearest Halina!"

But she had gone.

It was on the following day that she came out of a side-street into the Avenue Jerozolimska on her way from Novy Sviat to Marszalkovska Street. The Germans were setting fire to some of the houses at one end and their inhabitants were being cleared out, divided into small groups and led off to unknown destinations. Some of them were weeping. Children were crying. There was a crackling of fire and flame.

Halina watched from some distance. People were going away from the other houses still unburned, fearing that it would be their turn next. They were dragging out bundles and bags. Some of them were packing them into perambulators. Then suddenly they cried out in panic and fled back into the houses. A Tiger tank was coming down the street, very slowly nosing its way over heaps of rubble. Halina stood in a doorway where two or three elderly men were sheltering. One of them spoke to her.

"You had better go inside. They may start firing."

"I'll stay here," said Halina.

Three young men made a dash for the doorway. They were breathing hard and spoke in gasps.

One of them cursed the Germans.

"Swine! . . . To hell with them! Bloody murderers!"

They wore the armlets of the Home Army but were unarmed.

"That tank must be stopped!" said Halina.

One of them stared at her and gave a harsh laugh.

"Are you going to spit at it?"

The tank lurched on. It was nearly opposite the doorway in which Halina and the others were sheltering.

"Get in!" said one of the young men.

Halina did not get in. She undid her vanity bag and pulled something out. Then she ran on to the roadway and flung something at the tank only a yard away. It was one of her *filipinki*. Twice she threw and there were two explosions and two blasts of flame. The tank lurched and stopped. Two of the Germans staggered out with their hands up.

Halina cried out.

"Quick! . . . Let's get it."

The three young men rushed towards her. They leapt on to the tank and dropped into the turret. From other houses men ran out shouting and cheering. The tank moved. It was being driven in reverse. Further down the street the Germans who had been setting fire to houses and dragging out their inhabitants retreated indoors. Rifle bullets ricocheted off the walls.

Halina ran into a side-street. Her *filipinki* had done their job. She had a smile on her lips but suddenly felt faint and stood for a moment clinging on to a lamp-post.

An elderly woman pushing a perambulator with two small children stopped and spoke to her.

"Are you feeling ill, dearie?"

"No, I'm all right."

"I'm scared out of my wits," said the woman. "I don't know where to go with these little ones. We can't stay here. Those devils are coming close. They're burning all our homes. Everybody has fled."

"Come with me," said Halina. "I'll take you to a safer place."

She was not the only girl to put a German tank out of action. There were several cases like it and many tanks were captured and brought into the struggle by young men and civilians of the Home Army who leapt on from behind or attacked them with those deadly *filipinki* in narrow streets where they had to move slowly.

The German Panzer crews were frightened men. They never knew who would attack them. That innocent-looking schoolgirl on the sidewalk might hurl a grenade on them. A bunch of civilians might rush them and clamber on from behind. From any house which looked quiet and deserted there might come a sortie of the Home Army flinging hand-grenades. Fear is the father of cruelty. They tried to safeguard themselves by driving groups of people, mostly women, in front of their tanks and making others walk on both sides so that they could not be fired on from upper windows or high roofs. They protected themselves by the living bodies of these Polish people, by the shield of young girls who scoffed at them and cried out to their friends, "Shoot! Don't mind us."

CHAPTER XLIX

TAMKA and Dobra Streets near the Vistula embankment were dominated by the University which was a German stronghold occupied by S.S. troops. The blocks of flats in which Vanda was now living stood at the cross-roads and they could be swept by machine-gun fire. There was nothing to prevent tanks coming down that way. An order came to build a barricade and at 5 a.m. on the morning of August 2nd many civilians from the flats came out to do this job.

Old men, old women, young girls and boys worked like beavers. Among them was Vanda with the old lady they called 'Granny' and the girls of the canteen. They had delicate hands, unused to rough labourer's work, or the thin vein-lined hands of old age. They had no great physical strength, but they were inspired by a nervous energy which made up for that and under the intensity of emotion there was a queer gaiety among them. Things were going well. The initiative was in the hands of the Home Army. Everywhere the Germans had withdrawn into the fortified buildings at the first signal of attack.

Vanda was uplifted by this emotional exultation. As dawn came with slight rain she saw the Polish flags fluttering on high buildings and she stood staring at them while her eyes filled with tears, and there was joy in her heart. Those Polish flags were symbols of liberation. For nearly five years they had been banned. Now they were fluttering bravely above the city.

"Yes, my dear," said the old lady called 'Granny', "it's a lovely sight! It makes my old heart warm."

In a high silvery voice, standing there with a straight back and upraised face, she cried out, "Long Live Poland! . . . Poland shall be free!"

The other people round her smiled and raised their hands in salute and then bent to their work again. Rough work. Digging

255

up cobble stones, piling them up to build a wall, covering them with earth, higher and stronger. An old lady and gentleman came out of the block of flats staggering under a piece of furniture—a corner cupboard—which younger hands hoisted on top of the barricade. The idea seemed to spread. Chairs, bedsteads, cupboards, book-shelves, were hauled up and heightened the barricade. More earth! more stones! Branches from trees and shrubs to cover the wall, so that it looked like a tall hedge. Below they dug a ditch five feet deep. Vanda borrowed a spade from a tired girl who had let it fall. She dug feverishly. She had never held a spade in her hands before. It gave her a crick in the back. Her arms ached. Moisture trickled down her forehead. It was splendid to be digging like this, she thought. She was digging for freedom. Every spade-full of sandy earth would help in the defence of the city. People would be able to walk down this ditch without being killed by machine-gun, by bullets which during the night had pitted the walls of the houses and lay strewn about the road. She had picked up two or three and put them in a pocket. A souvenir of the Warsaw Rising! She smiled at the thought.

If ever she had children she would show them these things and say, "I was there. I helped to dig the deep ditch across Tamka Street."

She felt a little mad. She was outside herself, as people say. It was a pleasant kind of madness. It had killed all fear in her. She wasn't in the least afraid just then. She felt a kind of communion of spirit with all those boys who were fighting for freedom. There was something wonderful in this comradeship, this fellowship under fire. Under fire now. A burst of machine-gun bullets swept the barricade and spattered against the opposite walls. Nobody flinched, not the old women, nor the young girls around her. They went on digging. 'Granny'—that wonderful old lady—was bending over a pile of loose stones and arranging them in a heap as though building bricks for a small grandchild. Other people were arriving, bringing news. They had made long détours to avoid streets under German fire.

"Everything is going well. . . . It's important to capture the Power Station or we shall be without light and heat. . . . We have cleared many districts. . . . We're up to the Vistula embankment in most places."

Vanda stopped work. She was utterly exhausted and felt breathless and then, suddenly, the spirit with which she had been working dropped to zero and she turned pale.

Some wounded boys were being carried by on stretchers

and with them walked a young priest who was a military chaplain in the Home Army. Their eyes met and he raised a hand.

The stretcher-bearers rested for a moment, putting down their burden.

The priest went down on his knees by one of the wounded men and made the sign of the cross on his forehead.

Vanda went over and said, "Can I help?"

"He's dead," said the priest. "Poor boy!"

Vanda saw the face of the dead soldier. He was hardly more than seventeen. His eyes were open and he seemed to be staring up at the sky with a strange look of surprise as though he saw some vision there. Vanda knew him. It was one of the boys who had played in Aunt Krysta's garden before the war. It was Tadeusz Dyboski, the son of the portrait painter.

Vanda stared at him. She did not weep except in her heart. No one wept. Somebody said, "A hero's death."

The others were lightly wounded. One of them raised himself and said, "Can anybody give me a cigarette?" There was a rush to his stretcher and a packet was put into his hand and one cigarette into his mouth and a girl bent down and lit it for him.

The priest spoke a few words to Vanda.

"The price of freedom!" he said. "God be with us."

Vanda did not answer him. Here was only one dead boy. There would be thousands of others before the battle ended. The price of freedom! It would be terrible. The sense of exultation which had uplifted her had gone. She saw only the tragedy and the price to be paid. All those boys. Where was Jerzy? Was he dead too, already? If so, she would be glad to die. Perhaps the best thing was to be killed quite soon. She was not afraid to die. It would be good to die for Poland. She had laughed with her fellow workers digging the ditch. Now she was grave and thoughtful, but not afraid. She thanked God she was not afraid.

The stretcher-bearers took up their burdens. The priest walked with them by the side of the dead boy while men in the little crowd about them bared their heads.

It was the old lady's idea to go to one of the outposts and a hospital ward in Dobra Street, not far away, but a dangerous way.

"Are you willing to risk it, child?" asked the old lady smiling at Vanda.

"Of course! But do you think *you* ought to go?"

"We might cheer the boys a bit."

She was an astonishing old lady. Nothing would daunt her. She was excited, gay, eager to get closer to the battle like a young soldier before he knows the grim reality of war.

"This is a great day in Polish history," she told Vanda, as they crept along by the barricade they had made that morning. "Freedom! The breath of liberty, my dear! I find it quite rejuvenating."

Vanda clutched her arm and said, "Keep your head down."

Bullets were whistling over them. They could hear the swish of them. S.S. men in the University building were firing continuously in their direction.

"The little birds of death!" said the old lady. "Quite exciting, isn't it? Not frightened, are you?"

"No, I'm not frightened," said Vanda. "But you hold your head too high. Keep close against the wall."

A bullet whistled a few inches above their heads and buried itself in the barricade.

"They're wasting a lot of ammunition," said the old lady. "I expect 'Bor', dear man, would like some of it!"

They reached the outpost in Dobra Street which was in a private flat with one room used as a hospital ward. There were about forty boys there between the ages of seventeen and twenty-three. It was in the late afternoon and they were sitting down to supper. A French window, leading into the garden, was open and a soft breeze came from the Vistula. The young men were in high spirits. They had taken part in the first attacks and had captured German trophies. A few were lightly wounded with bandaged heads and arms but were as cheerful as the others. They were astonished to see the old lady and Vanda and rose to give them places at table. Vanda was put next to one of the nurses.

She looked at all these young faces, gay and high-spirited and for a moment an icy finger seemed to touch her spine, for among them she seemed to see the dead face of young Tadeusz Dyboski. But that was morbid, she said to herself. It was very wrong to have morbid thoughts—or to look miserable—among this little crowd of young men who were talking excitedly with gusts of laughter.

She smiled at a boy by her side who was wounded in the arm.

"Are things going well, do you think?"

His eyes lighted up.

"Magnificently! We hold the best part of Warsaw."

She was searching the faces again. If only Jerzy had been there! But he was not among these boys.

"There's one snag," said the young man at her side. "If we don't capture the Power Station today we shall all be in darkness. No electricity!"

"That would be awful," said Vanda.

After supper the boys sang soldiers' songs in which Vanda's old lady joined in her silvery, quavering voice. She was having a grand time in this outpost among these young soldiers.

Then they all stood up and sang an old hymn written in the eighteenth century by the poet Karpinski, the famous 'Evening Song' sung always in soldiers' camps and bivouacs. This might have been a Boy Scouts' camp in peace time. It was impossible to believe that they were in the front line of a great battle, impossible, except for the sound of gunfire not far away.

It was getting dark. Somebody turned on a switch. Suddenly the room was flooded with light. The electricity was working!

"The Power House!" shouted several voices. "It's in our hands!"

A great cheer rose from forty young throats. The Power House had been captured.

"We must go, my dear," said the old lady. "We've had a wonderful time. Victory is in the air. Victory is in my heart. These boys are splendid. I wish my grandson Janek could be among them."

Vanda walked back with her below the barricade. The night sky was throbbing with scarlet fire. Many houses were burning in Warsaw. They could hear rifle shots not far away.

"A charming evening!" said the old lady, as they arrived at their own block of flats.

CHAPTER L

VANDA's friend Jerzy—her dear lover—had been one of those who captured the Power House containing the electric plant which was necessary for lighting, cooking and working many machines in Warsaw, including broadcasting.

He had worked there in the early days of the occupation as a cover to his activities in the Home Army before becoming a courier to 'Bor'. Now he slipped in among the other workers without attracting the notice of the German garrison.

For months they had turned this place into a fortress with pill-boxes and machine-guns, not only commanding the neighbouring streets but able to direct a withering fire inside the works as though they anticipated an attack by the factory hands and technicians. They must have suspected something, for shortly before the rising they increased their garrison. Trenches and barbed wire entanglements surrounded the building and the men were heavily armed.

Jerzy talked to some of the technicians who spoke in low voices to the hum of the machines. They were highly strung as he could see by their faces. The long wait for action was a heavy strain on their nerves. Several of them kept looking at their wrist-watches. They had concealed their arms below the floors—rifles, hand-grenades, *filipinki*, mines.

Jerzy passed the German soldiers. They were watchful but without more than ordinary suspicion. On one of the upper floors part of the garrison was playing cards. An officer came down into the machine-room and glanced round. Everything was working smoothly. The dynamos were purring. Jerzy was oiling one of them and met the eyes of the German officer and for a moment felt himself go cold. Supposing he was suspected as an unknown man. But the officer turned on his heel and went out.

Jerzy was nervous. This was not his *métier*. He had been a violinist before the war. Then he had made those journeys to England. They had needed a bit of nerve but nothing like this. He was untrained as a soldier and he didn't like what was going to happen. Perhaps he was too thoughtful—a bad thing on the eve of a fight. He was thinking about the imminent chance of death. Death would be a new and strange adventure. He wasn't afraid of it exactly. He had always believed that the spirit went on. But he was certainly afraid—mostly afraid of being afraid. He couldn't let these other fellows down. He couldn't let himself down, or Vanda who believed in his courage. Vanda! . . . The thought of her strengthened him a little. He would have to get through this business for her sake. He would never be able to look into her eyes if he played the coward. Where was the dividing line between courage and cowardice? He felt cold in the hands and feet. Cold feet! The sign of fear. Bad that.

One of the technicians spoke to him.

"Another two hours. Every tick of the clock seems like a minute."

Jerzy nodded.

"It's rather trying," he said, conscious of this ridiculous understatement. Rather trying! It was a hellish strain.

Not to all of them. Some of the younger men were whistling at their work and turned now and then to grin at each other. Jerzy envied them. What courage! What nerves!

The two hours passed like two days. The clocks of Warsaw were striking five. The hour had come.

Before the last stroke had ended there was a tremendous explosion. One of the pill-boxes had been blown up by a mine. It was the signal for action. Twenty men tore up the floor-boards where the weapons had been concealed—tommy-guns and hand-grenades, rifles. There was a rush upstairs. The Germans had come out to the landing. The officer fired his revolver and one of the Polish boys fell dead. The others stormed the staircase, flinging their grenades. Four or five Germans fell. The others retreated, barricading themselves behind a heavy door against which Jerzy's comrades flung themselves. The Germans fired through the door and two young Poles were killed. Then for a few moments there was silence. The enemy had retreated to another room.

Fighting was going on in other parts of the Power House. The Germans took cover behind machinery and furniture and stone pillars. They fought from the cellars and from dark store-rooms. They fought desperately and bravely, selling their lives dearly.

Jerzy was unconscious of himself. It was like a mad nightmare. He was fighting with a kind of frenzied passion. Once he tackled a tall fellow who leapt out at him from a dark recess and fired a revolver at him point-blank. Jerzy ducked, knocked the gun out of his hand and fell on top of him. The man's hands were about his throat. He was being strangled. They were writhing on the stone floor like snakes. The man was stronger than Jerzy, until he gave a convulsive shudder and lay dead. Someone had shot him in the head.

Jerzy was feeling his throat. His neck felt dislocated. He was gasping for breath. Presently he was sick. But he staggered up to join his comrades who had left him alone. He could hear them tramping across a stone floor. Bullets were flying. One of them struck Jerzy in the shoulder, and it was like the kick of a horse. He fell heavily to the stone floor but struggled up again. When he put his hand to his shoulder it became wet with blood.

The battle lasted nineteen hours before German resistance broke down. Some of them surrendered. The Power House was saved.

The dynamos purred softly. Two men were washing away blood from the floor.

One of the technicians spoke to Jerzy. The man's face was dead white but there was a triumphant light in his eyes.

"We've kept the machines working!"

He looked at Jerzy and said, "Are you badly wounded?"

"Bleeding a bit," said Jerzy.

The man with the dead white face gave a harsh laugh.

"You fought like a tiger!"

"I didn't feel like one," said Jerzy. "I didn't know what I was doing. Now I feel—very queer."

His hand slipped from one of the machines on to which he had been holding and he swayed and fell again with a crash to the stone floor.

One of his comrades bent over him.

"He's bleeding to death. Get some bandages. Quick!"

The cost had been heavy in young lives but the lights were up in Warsaw.

CHAPTER LI

VANDA, like her father, tried to keep a brave face and to speak cheerfully among that queer, tragic community crowded into the underground shelters, especially to the children and their mothers. They looked to her for courage. Women seized her hand and clasped it as she passed among them.

"How's it going, dearie? Are we winning?"

She lied to them.

"It's going well. . . . We're expecting the English planes."

But she was getting frightened. She was beginning to despair. Jerzy had told her that the battle must be won in eight days. After that there would be no more ammunition unless dropped from the air. It was the eighth day. More refugees were coming into the basement and cellars. They had fled from houses in the upper part of Obozna Street—their own street—close to the University. At night the S.S. were flinging hand-grenades into the ground-floor windows of houses in neighbouring streets, setting them on fire.

A young officer from 'Bor's' headquarters had come to visit the outpost. Vanda knew him and he gave her news in a low voice out in the garden to which she took him.

"The situation isn't too good," he told her. "The enemy has cleared a way from Volska Street to the Kierbedz bridge. They're pressing us hard in the area of Vola. They've reached Theatre Square and have occupied the Malta Hospital which was used for German wounded."

"Does that mean—defeat?" asked Vanda. "Tell me the truth."

The young lieutenant looked at her searchingly as though to

know whether she could stand the truth. He had danced with her before the war. He had been a friend of Stanislav.

"We may hold out for some time yet. But unless help comes from outside we're lost."

"We must pray for a miracle," said Vanda, but as she spoke her eyes filled with tears and she gave a sob and put her hands to her face.

"Yes we need a miracle," said the lieutenant. "Don't weep, Vanda. Perhaps I ought not to be so pessimistic."

She took her hands from her face, smudging away the tears.

"I'm sorry! Forgive my weakness. I'm all right now. Thanks for telling me."

He raised her hand to his lips before he left her.

For a few minutes she stayed there in the garden alone. It was in the late afternoon with a sky still blue and not yet throbbing with the scarlet of fires. But she could see black smoke rising in the neighbourhood of the University and towards the south-west in the direction of Vola where there was heavy gunfire. As she stood a squadron of German Stukas passed overhead flying very low. It seemed only a second or two before their bombs crashed a few streets away. Three times a day they came like that, carrying death and destruction with them. The ground beneath her feet trembled with the vibration of these explosions. She could hear the twang of flying steel.

This garden where she stood was no safe place. One of those bombs would blot it out with its flowers and plants, and her own body there. She was not afraid of that. Death would be better than life, if defeat came.

For a moment she was tempted to cry out to God to give her death. Then she remembered that many people depended upon her for food and comfort. And she remembered one man who wanted her to live. She had not heard a word from Jerzy, or about him. If he were alive she must go on living. She must try to keep alive for his sake.

'He'll be so disappointed if he finds me dead,' she thought, in a curiously childish way—in a way that people think when they're very close to death and have no fear of it for themselves.

And then, as though someone had answered this thought, she had news of Jerzy. It was brought by Halina who had just come back after her extraordinary adventures. She had heard about Jerzy from the Red Cross men. He was in hospital in Copernicus Street, seriously wounded and very weak. He wanted to send a message to Vanda Mirska.

"He's delirious," said the Red Cross doctor. "He keeps calling out the name of Vanda."

"That's my sister," said Halina. "I'll tell her."

"I must go to him," said Vanda.

This news of Jerzy was like an answer to prayer. It was wonderful to know that he was still alive. Even if he were dying it would be a gift of God to speak to him again, to tell him that it was her love for him which had helped to give her courage, that for his sake she was fighting against despair.

The hospital in Copernicus Street was only ten minutes' walk away. How strange to think that he was lying so near to her—only a few minutes away across a few streets. . . .

She spoke to Halina.

"I must go to him. I must go at once."

Halina looked at her doubtfully.

"It won't be easy to get through to Copernicus Street. The Germans are busy with their machine-guns. You ought not to go really. I'll come with you. I know the best way."

"No, I'll go alone," said Vanda.

"I'm coming with you!" said Halina firmly.

"I must ask 'Granny' for permission," said Vanda.

The old lady gave her permission graciously.

"Of course! But take care. I don't want to lose you. You're a very precious help to me. All the people here cling to you because of your courage and loveliness."

The two sisters went out through the garden entrance in Obozna Street. They had to go along the Green to Tamka Street, then take the third turning right going uphill towards the Copernicus monument facing the Church of the Holy Cross. It was not dark yet and there was a warm, golden light on the walls and trees. There was heavy gun-fire towards the Old Town and away to the south-west of the city. Not far away, along the Vistula embankment, there were spasms of machine-gun fire and scattered rifle shots.

"We're running out of ammunition," said Halina, speaking like a soldier rather than a girl. "It's getting serious."

Vanda clutched her arm.

"Halina, are we losing? Is there no hope?"

"Lots of hope," said Halina. "We've captured fifty of their Tiger tanks."

"But if we have no ammunition?"

"We shall fight them with bayonets and broken bottles. The boys won't give in. Look out! Crouch down!"

She pulled Vanda roughly against a pile of rubble from a

ruined house. Machine-gun bullets were splashing against the broken walls. They stayed there for several minutes, crouching low under the shelter of the rubble.

"Now!" said Halina. "Run for it, Vanda. Keep close to me."

They ran across the street and Halina, holding on to Vanda, took cover in one of the burnt-out houses open to the sky, through the charred beams of its roof.

"We can get out on the other side," she said. "It's a short cut."

There was a smell of smouldering embers and the stench of death. The half-burnt body of a boy lay in their way under a beam which was still smouldering.

Vanda turned her face away and shuddered.

"I'm getting used to dead bodies," said Halina. "It's best not to look at them. That's the soldiers' way."

"You're wonderful," said Vanda. "You have a man's courage. I can't ask you now what you've been doing for two days and nights. I think I'm trembling. It's the horror of it all."

"You'll be all right," said Halina. "Just keep close to me."

She was the younger sister but she was the leader on this dangerous journey. She would have made a gallant officer. Across the next street she put her arm round Vanda's waist and kept on one side of her as though to shield her from machine-gun fire.

Three lads of the Home Army were patrolling the street and came up to them.

"What are you doing here?" asked one of them. "Going for a stroll on a nice summer evening? Quite like old times!"

He stared at the two girls with surprise and amusement.

"We're making for the hospital in Copernicus Street," said Halina.

One of the other lads spoke grimly.

"You mightn't get there. I wouldn't risk it if I were you."

"That's all right," said Halina. "Come on, Vanda."

A shell from a long-range gun crashed into a house further up the street. Vanda felt stunned by the explosion and would have fallen if Halina had not helped her up.

"It's all right," said Halina. "We're not dead yet!"

She gave a queer little laugh, still clutching hold of her sister, and still keeping on one side of her as though to protect Vanda by her own body.

"Only one more street to cross," she said. "Then we can dive through the houses. I know the way. I'm like a Warsaw rat."

"You make me ashamed," said Vanda. "You have such courage and I'm such a coward."

"You have spiritual courage," said Halina. "Mine is just vulgar stuff—a butcher-boy's courage!"

"Oh, my dear," cried Vanda, "shall we ever get there?,"

"We're almost there. Five minutes more. If we can get across the next street. . . ."

The next street was quiet but very sinister. Not a soul stirred in it. The houses looked empty. No light glimmered. The windows were blocked up by mattresses. A dead cat lay in the gutter. From another street there was a sound of crackling and splintering, and a smell of burning.

"We had better run," said Halina. She clutched Vanda's hand again and ran with her across the roadway and then up a flight of steps.

"There are friends of mine here," she said, rather breathlessly. "They've tunnelled through their basement. It's one of our runways."

She rang the bell and then rattled the letter-box. The front door opened cautiously.

"Who's that?" asked a girl's voice.

"It's Halina. Don't be scared."

The door opened a little wider and a white face looked out.

"I thought it might be an S.S. man."

Her voice trembled and she gave a kind of sob.

Five young men wearing the armlets of the Home Army came into the hall and stared at the two sisters.

"Well I'm blessed!" said one of them. "If it isn't Vanda and Halina."

It was a young man named Tomek who had been on the pleasure boat that summer day on the Vistula—before the war began.

"Hullo, Tomek!" said Halina. "We want to use your hole in the basement. We're going to the hospital in Copernicus Street."

"Quite at your service," said the young man. "Mind the rats don't bite your toes!"

He laughed, but then spoke in a tragic voice.

"We haven't a round of ammunition left. It's ghastly. There's nothing we can do. We're sunk."

"Wait till the English planes come," said Halina. "They're expected tomorrow night. They're going to drop ammunition into Napoleon Square."

The young men crowded round her.

"How do you know? Who told you?"

"I hear a few things," said Halina, mysteriously.

"Good God! If that's true!" exclaimed the boy named Tomek.

His eyes were alight with a new hope.

"We must get on," said Vanda. "We mustn't wait and talk."

She was desperate to get to the hospital where Jerzy was lying. It would be terrible if she were not in time.

"Yes," said Halina. "We haven't come for coffee and conversation."

"I'll lead you down," said Tomek. "It's dark down the steps and one of them is broken."

He took a torch and touched its button and showed a light which he guarded with his hand so that it could not be seen from the street through any chink.

He led them downstairs into the basement.

"I know this," said Halina. "I've been here before."

The young man flashed his torch at the hole in the wall.

"We fixed a light part of the way," he said. "I'll switch it on."

Then he turned and smiled at them.

"It's brave of you, but women are as brave as men—perhaps braver. They're wonderful."

He asked a question of Halina.

"It is true about those planes?"

"They're expected," said Halina.

"Thank God for that. Well, good-bye! Good luck!"

They were lighted, as he had said, through part of the tunnel. There was only a short passage of darkness and Halina gave Vanda her hand and guided her along. They came into another basement and Halina found a door which led into the street.

"Copernicus Street," she said. "There's the hospital."

Vanda could feel her heart beating when she stood at the door of a long ward with beds on each side. In one of them was Jerzy. Halina had left her to talk to one of the nurses in another ward.

An elderly man in a white coat came towards her and said, "Vanda, my dear!"

It was an old friend of hers. It was Dr. Joravski whom once—years ago she had asked to give her 'something'—something to put her to sleep for ever.

"I've come to see Jerzy Boberski," she said in a faint voice. "Tell me, Doctor. . . ."

Dr. Joravski saw her distress and he guessed what she wanted to tell her.

"He's still alive. He lost a lot of blood and is very weak of course, but we shall pull him through, I think."

"Thank God for that!" said Vanda in a whisper.

"Dare I see him, Doctor? It won't make him feel worse, will it?"

Dr. Joravski smiled at her.

"It will make him feel better. But you mustn't stay more than a minute or two."

"Where is he?" asked Vanda, looking down the rows of beds.

The doctor took her hand and led her to a bed at the far end of the ward. Two or three lightly wounded men were sitting on the sides of their beds smoking cigarettes. They had bandaged heads and arms but looked cheerful and smiled at Vanda as she passed. Others lay under their blankets breathing heavily. There was a strong smell of disinfectant. A nurse was putting a screen round one bed.

"Here he is," said the doctor in a low voice.

Jerzy was lying with one arm thrown out above his blanket. His face was very pale and his eyes were shut. He was breathing quietly. The hand outside the blanket was as white as his face.

Vanda stooped down over him and said, "Jerzy!" very softly. She was afraid that the tears in her eyes might fall on his face but she kept them back.

He opened his eyes and looked at her. Perhaps he thought he was dreaming because he did not smile or speak to her.

"Jerzy!" said Vanda. "Oh, my dear!"

A look of surprise came into his eyes. Very faintly he smiled and tried to raise his hand and spoke one word in a whisper.

"Vanda!"

She lifted his hand and pressed her lips to it.

He raised his head a little but it fell back on the pillow.

Vanda let his hand go. She stooped low and kissed him on the forehead.

"My dear. . . . My beloved!"

There was a look of joy in his eyes for just a second or two. His lips moved but he could not speak. Then his eyes closed again. She knelt down by his bedside holding his hand again and this time her tears fell upon it but did not disturb him.

She stayed there for three minutes or so, hardly breathing, saying inarticulate prayers in her heart for this lover who lay so still—so still that she thought it might be death.

A hand touched her shoulder. It was Dr. Joravski who whispered to her.

"Don't stay, my dear."

He took her hand again and led her through the ward and spoke to her outside the door.

"He looks bad. It's the loss of blood. But we're not going to let him die, you know. His youth will pull him through."

"Are you telling me the truth?" asked Vanda, who felt faint. She was struggling to keep her tears back. Her heart seemed to be bleeding. She could feel a pain in it.

"I could bear the truth, whatever it is," she said.

Dr. Joravski looked at her reproachfully.

"I'm not lying to you, my dear. One doesn't lie at a time like this with death all round us and eternity very near."

"Thank you," said Vanda. "Forgive me. Jerzy and I love each other so much."

Dr. Joravski took her hand and patted it.

"Good for you! Soon love is all that we shall have left to us. They can't take that from us. They can't kill it. Even if they kill our bodies. Love goes on, doesn't it? I'm certain it goes on in spite of all the atrocities of this frightful battle."

He looked at her with his kindly eyes.

"You look faint, my dear. Come into my room for a few minutes. I'll give you something."

He seemed to remember that evening when she had asked him to give her something.

"Not that 'something' you once asked from me," he said with a smile.

He saw that she was deeply agitated and after giving her a dose he talked quietly and in a way which needed no answers from her.

He spoke of some wounded Germans they had in one of the rooms.

"They're amazed because we care for them just like our own wounded. When they first come in they're in a state of terror, fully believing they're going to be killed. One young fellow screamed when I wanted to give him a shot in the arm. He thought I was going to pump poison into him. They've been told fantastic stories about us, put out, no doubt, as a cover to the cruelties of the S.S."

He told her of a German doctor who had allowed himself to be taken prisoner while he was giving first-aid to some wounded boys of the Home Army.

"He tells me that he loathes the things that are being done to us. He is a pacifist and a Quaker. He asks me to believe that there are still good Germans—millions of them—who would be horrified if they knew what atrocities are being committed in their name, but they're kept in ignorance by the propaganda machine."

Dr. Joravski raised his hands slightly.

"That is hard to believe while our beautiful Warsaw is in flames and civilians are being burnt to death in their houses."

"Yes," said Vanda.

"Anyhow, there's one German whose conscience revolts against these things. I'm glad of that. In the old days I knew many Germans and liked them. How will it be possible for us ever to forgive them?"

He looked at Vanda and saw that a little colour had come back into her face.

"It was brave of you to come here," he said.

"I had to come. Jerzy wanted me."

For a moment he spoke gravely.

"This hospital is too near the front line, and the Germans are coming closer. We're already under shell fire. We shall have to get the wounded away while we have time."

"Oh!" cried Vanda. "What will happen to Jerzy? He's so weak."

"We shall look after him, I hope."

Halina came into the room and said, "We must go, Vanda, I'm afraid."

"Oh no!" exclaimed Vanda. "I can't leave Jerzy. I must stay with him."

The doctor spoke to her.

"It's best for you to go, my dear. If we have to evacuate this hospital the fewer people here the better."

"Besides," said Halina, "Granny will expect you back."

They managed to persuade her that she ought to go.

"Take care of yourselves," said the doctor. "I hate the idea of your crossing the streets again."

He took Vanda's hands and clasped them.

"Don't fret about Jerzy. My heart bleeds for all you young people. I find your courage supernatural."

For a moment his voice broke and tears came into his eyes.

"God have mercy on us all," he said, "in this time of tragedy and sacrifice."

Vanda put her face up and kissed him. She had known him since childhood. She saw that he was in need of comfort. He was wearing himself to death in his devotion to the wounded.

She went back with Halina through those awful passages across the streets again. It was easier this time. There was a respite from the guns. But the sky was throbbing again with the red glow of fire.

CHAPTER LII

FROM his headquarters in the Kammler factory General 'Bor' was sending urgent and desperate messages to the exiled government in London.

I categorically demand help in ammunition and anti-tank weapons forthwith. At all costs give us ammunition for the city to be dropped at three points: the Jewish cemetery, Napoleon Square, and the little Ghetto.

On August 8th he sent out a tragic message.

We have almost completely lost any possibility of aggressive action owing to our remaining ammunition being used up.

Sitting there with his staff, getting constant reports on the progress of the battle he was exasperated by the absence of help from any quarter. No British or American planes came to drop supplies urgently needed. The Russian Army beyond the Vistula was silent and motionless. His mind was filled with bitterness and anger at this betrayal of his hopes and plans, solaced only by the heroic spirit of the young soldiers and of the entire population.

Perhaps tomorrow they would hear the throb of friendly planes. Perhaps tomorrow would see their parachutes dropping new supplies. Perhaps tomorrow there would be an answer to his appeals for Russian aid. Perhaps tomorrow help would arrive in time—but only just in time. The situation was becoming desperate. The enemy was taking the offensive with tanks, flame-throwers, bombing aeroplanes, driving a way through the main highways, isolating the captured positions, preventing communication between them. They were shelling the city from armoured trains on the railway line from the Western Station. They were making encircling attacks on the Old Town and smashing forward through the district of Vola which had been held by the Home Army.

House by house, street by street, they were burning their way through Warsaw, not giving some of the inhabitants time to escape—burning them alive in the cellars and basements. The

Germans were using the Vlasov soldiers for these atrocities. They were Soviet prisoners of war who had been liberated when they volunteered to fight under German orders. They were utterly savage and bestial in their cruelty, cutting the throats of women and children, murdering defenceless civilians, outraging young girls. It was in the year 1944. Had not Europe been civilized for a thousand years? Was there not the tradition of chivalry? Had not Christianity touched the souls of men with mercy and pity and charity? Not Attila and his Huns, nor Ghengis Khan and his hordes, would have been worse than this in Warsaw where the flames rose from burning streets, and the shrieks of women went unheard in the fury of destruction. Yet by some miracle of the spirit the men and women in the quarters which remained in Polish hands—still large sections of the city—refused to despair or even to be down-hearted. Tomorrow would bring them new supplies of ammunition. Tomorrow they would recapture some of the lost ground. Even today without artillery support, with insufficient ammunition, they had counter-attacked and won back some of those positions by hand-to-hand fighting and sudden rushes of reckless youth, shouting and cheering.

On the eighth day of the battle General 'Bor' reported that "The entire population as well as the fighting forces are maintaining their spirit at a high level."

Yet on the ninth day General 'Bor' and his staff knew that without speedy help from outside the battle for Warsaw would be lost.

And on the ninth day there was no sign in the sky, no message from the outside world that rescue was coming.

"We are betrayed," said one of the Staff officers. "The English have betrayed us, the Americans have betrayed us. The Russians have betrayed us."

Over in London in an underground room near Admiralty Arch there was a man with a cigar between his lips, working day and night sending off messages in code, staring at big maps of the whole world war, getting reports from all fronts, dictating dispatches to the commanders of navies and armies. Churchill was a very over-burdened man yet able to feel compassion, and admiration for heroism, with an eagerness to send help where most needed. He knew about this rising in Warsaw. He had read General 'Bor's' urgent calls for help. His heart was moved by the agony of the Polish people in Warsaw. He must send a message to Stalin. It was just possible that Stalin would have some instinct of honour, some care for the reputation of the Soviet Armies.

"Take a code message to Stalin. Give it priority over all others."

It was on August 4th—two days after the news of the Rising in Warsaw had reached London.

It was an urgent appeal to Stalin on behalf of the Polish Underground. It informed him that the R.A.F. were dropping supplies of ammunition into the south-west of Warsaw, subject to weather.

Stalin's answer was to ridicule the strength of the Rising and to say that the Soviet Command had decided to dissociate itself from the 'Warsaw adventure'.

Churchill sent other messages to Stalin one of which, signed also by President Roosevelt, stressed that world opinion would be shocked if the Polish patriots in Warsaw were deserted and abandoned. They urged him to drop immediate supplies and to facilitate this being done by British aircraft.

Stalin refused. He would not allow British or American planes to make use of Russian landing grounds for refuelling and return. He described the Polish patriots as "a group of criminals".

Churchill continued to press for the relief of Warsaw. There was no betrayal of the Poles in his heart or soul. He insisted that the story of this villainy and horror should reach the world. But it was all in vain.

The Polish Prime Minister was in Moscow trying to obtain Stalin's sympathy and help. He was beating his head against iron walls. Stalin had no sympathy for Polish freedom. He was intent upon their enslavement under Communist domination. He preferred their extermination.

That was the tragic and desperate situation which General 'Bor' was facing. With extreme reluctance he had to give orders that ammunition should be strictly economized. Tales of atrocity reached him hourly, frightful cruelties against civilians. He was pressed to take reprisals. To answer cruelty with cruelty, to execute German prisoners of whom there were now more than a thousand. In spite of his anger, his rage, his anguish, he refused any such thing and repeated his orders that all German prisoners should be treated with humanity and with the same care as his own wounded. The Poles had to show the Germans that they were a civilized people inspired by Christian ideals and the tradition of chivalry. Whatever happened they would keep that flag flying above the bodies of the Polish dead. General 'Bor' was a gentleman and a Christian knight.

CHAPTER LIII

HALINA gave herself no rest. This young girl with her slim body and fair hair was endowed with a dauntless spirit beyond that of women—even the women of Warsaw. As a man she would have been one of those young officers who astonish and inspire their men by the recklessness of their courage and ardour in attack. She had none of the doubts and despair that sometimes overwhelmed her sister. She was in this battle of Warsaw with a boy's heart, eager to rush into action, impetuous and unafraid.

She was one of those who volunteered to signal to the aeroplanes—the few aeroplanes—which succeeded in reaching the city to drop supplies of weapons and ammunition. Messages had come by radio that they were on their way.

That night Halina was one of the fifteen young women who went in single file into the centre of Napoleon Square. They carried hurricane lamps but showed no light. All round the square Polish sentries were on guard preventing anyone from entering, except those on this special duty.

Halina spoke in a low voice to the girl ahead of her. It was Barbara who at the beginning of the war had taken shelter in her father's house. Her husband was in one of the outposts.

"We shall soon hear the engines. I find this very thrilling."

"If only they will come!" answered Barbara.

It was nine o'clock. The enemy's fire had quietened down except for intermittent shelling from a tank in some position in the neighbourhood. It was not yet dark. On the roofs nearby shadowy figures moved. They were officers watching for the planes to come. Beyond the square were groups of young soldiers ready to seize any containers that might be dropped beyond the square and near enemy positions.

A signal was given to the girls. They lay down on the ground in the form of a cross.

Halina was nibbling a biscuit and passed one to Barbara. Flat on her back she stared up at the sky in which, as darkness came, many stars were twinkling.

The girls were very quiet. Now and again they spoke in whispers.

"Why don't they come?"

"How frightful it will be if they don't come after all!"

"Of course they'll come," said Halina.

Ten o'clock. Eleven o'clock. Two hours of waiting and then one more. It was cold lying there on the ground in Napoleon Square. It was hard there on the ground.

At midnight there was a shout from one of the roofs.

"Look! . . . They're coming!"

A German searchlight was turned on and its white beam moved like a long finger across the sky. Other searchlights flashed out and the long white beams crossed each other and then converged.

Halina gave a cry of joy.

"They're coming! They're here! I can hear them!"

Distinctly she could hear the drone of aircraft engines with quite a different rhythm from the German Stukas. They were English planes. "The R.A.F.! At last!"

The hurricane lamps were lit. On the ground of Napoleon Square was a large shining cross.

The German anti-aircraft guns were firing. The silence of the night was broken by sharp ear-splitting reports and the rush of shells. The night sky was filled with the lights of their explosions like fireworks on a gala night.

The onlookers could see tracer shells of four colours—red, green, blue and yellow—exploding against the velvet curtain of the night.

Then Halina and the other girls could see, very clearly, a black bat skimming low from the south-west. It was an R.A.F. machine. It came down so low through the flashes of shell-fire that its markings could be seen—the red, white and blue circles— below its wings. The R.A.F., unmistakably, in the dazzling glare of an enemy searchlight which followed it down. It was hardly higher than the roofs. Something was dropping from it. Seven times something dropped and floated slowly to the ground. Containers. Precious supplies, long prayed for. Help at last!

Round the square people had come rushing out of their houses and basements. They were cheering wildly. They were mad with joy.

Halina, lying there with her hurricane lamp, laughed aloud. Her spirit was uplifted beyond her body. She was up there with the stars. Richard Allgrove—her 'Dick' had said they would come. This was the hour of joy. She felt that her heart would burst with joy.

More planes came. One, two, three, four, five, six, seven. They were dropping their loads. One could hear the rush of their wings over the roofs.

Oh God! . . . One was hit. Its engine was on fire. Still it swooped lower. The pilot in the burning plane dropped his loads just beyond the square. It flew on and crossed the Vistula and General 'Bor' himself, watching from the roof of his headquarters, saw 'a vast spurt of flame and smoke rising to the sky'.

No more planes arrived, but the Germans kept on their searchlights and it was like daylight over Warsaw. Small bodies of the Home Army and many civilians searched for the containers. One had fallen on the sports ground called 'Swiss Valley' only fifty yards away from the enemy. Separate attempts were made to get it—repulsed three times by a heavy machine-gun barrage. Regardless of their lives a group of boys crawled towards it and in the morning it was theirs.

General 'Bor' tells the story of how one container was seized. It had landed on the cupola of St. Alexander Church in Three Crosses Square. It was within 300 yards of a German stronghold. Four young men climbed to the cupola to collect it. All of them were killed by a burst of fire. Others then climbed up inside the church holding on to the cornices at great risk. They tore open a hole in the roof of the cupola and the container fell into their hands.

Twice more help was brought by these knights-errant of the air. Each time from ten to fifteen British planes flew low over the city dropping the containers. They had English, South African and Polish crews who fulfilled their task, says 'Bor', "with a courage and skill which filled the onlookers with the deepest admiration."

One crashed to the street within fifty yards of General 'Bor's' headquarters. All the crew were killed but the fire was put out by the inhabitants of this neighbourhood and the rear gunner's heavy machine-guns were saved and used that very night against the enemy.

As reported by General 'Bor' they collected eighty per cent of the containers and the supplies of ammunition, tommy-guns, and other weapons raised the spirit of the soldiers and civilians, and enabled the Home Army to hold some of their positions, and even to attack German outposts with temporary success for another week.

Halina was one of those who joined a group of young people who endeavoured to seize one of the containers lying in a 'No Man's Land' between two outposts—one of them Polish, the other German—not more than 300 yards apart in barricaded houses.

It was at dawn when the last container had been dropped.

"We must get it at all costs," said Halina, who had been one of the signallers again in another square. She spoke to a young soldier who had his head bandaged above a dirt-begrimed face on which was a stubble of beard. He had just emerged from the ruins of a house with the other lads.

"This is no job for girls," he said, sternly. "Keep back, Halina."

She recognized his voice. It was Richard Allgrove whose unit had been ordered to fall back from the position in which she had seen him last.

"Dick!" she cried. "How frightful you look!"

"I feel frightful," he told her. "Get back, Halina, darling, for God's sake. As soon as they see us they'll open fire."

He pushed her, almost roughly, through a hole in a broken wall whose brickwork had been peppered by machine-gun bullets. Some of his comrades were crouching behind this wall. With them was the young officer to whom she had handed her message from 'Bor's' headquarters.

"We had better make a rush for it," he said. "Keep your heads low."

There were about eight or nine of them. One by one they went through the hole in the wall and crouching low ran towards the container which was visible in the half-light of the coming dawn. They were but black shadows running singly and bent almost double. Instantly a machine-gun slashed at them, spurting up gobbets of earth. Two men fell and lay still. Then three more.

The others retreated to the shelter of the wall again.

One of them was Richard Allgrove. He was breathing hard and almost fell on to Halina who was crouching there.

"Bad luck!" she exclaimed. "But we shall have to get it."

"Halina! Sweetheart! Get away from here!"

"Any volunteers?" asked the young officer, who had not gone with the first rush.

"One!" said Halina.

Before any hand could reach out to grab her she dashed through the hole in the wall and ran out into the open towards the container. Again there was a spasm of machine-gun fire.

"Oh, my God!" cried Dick Allgrove.

He too went through the hole in the wall and shouted hoarsely.

"Halina! Come back! Halina!"

She had flung herself down and was crawling towards the container when the young airman reached her. He too flung himself to the ground by her side. Machine-gun bullets were whipping the earth about them.

"You damned little fool!" he shouted, panting for breath. "Do you want to get killed?"

He was in a savage temper with her because he didn't want her to get killed, because he was very much in love with her, because he was horribly distressed.

He heard her give a little laugh. Then she sprang up and ran as far as the container and grabbed it.

"Got it!" she cried. "Give me a hand, Dick."

She stood there utterly careless of the bullets whipping the earth about her. Two other men had dashed forward.

"Hell and damnation!" exclaimed Dick.

He too was standing up now and, regardless of danger, strode towards Halina who was trying to haul the container back.

By some miracle of luck not one of them was killed or wounded though bullets were whistling about them. When they were back behind the wall again with this precious burden Halina laughed again.

"Jolly good, Dick!" she said in English. "Many thanks for your kind help."

He stared at her fiercely.

"You ought to be spanked," he said. "It's a marvel that you're not dead."

"Don't be cross," she pleaded, smiling at him. "It was worth it, wasn't it? Why do you look so angry?"

The anger left his eyes. He began to laugh.

"Gosh!" he cried, "it's a wonder we weren't all killed. You're a terrible young woman. You're a most alarming lady—leading men to their death like that. Disgraceful, I call it!"

"It was worth taking the chance," said Halina. "We've got the goods! Why are you so cross, Dick?"

He told her why he was so cross.

"It's because I love you and think you're the most wonderful girl on earth. If you'd been killed I should have wept tears of blood. Halina, my darling, don't frighten me again like that!"

"I'm glad you love me so much, Dick," she said. "What are we going to do about it?"

"What can we do about it?" he asked.

Halina looked at him with shy eyes and said an extraordinary thing.

"We might get married, Dick, if that would please you at all."

A marriage was arranged between Squadron-Leader Richard

Allgrove and Halina Mirska, while they were taking shelter behind a broken wall spattered now and then by machine-gun bullets.

CHAPTER LIV

HALINA came home that morning to the block of flats in Obozna Street muddy, tousled, sleepless but quietly triumphant. After washing and changing her clothes and sleeping soundly for three hours curled up in an armchair she took Vanda aside and spoke mysteriously.

"Vanda, I must talk to you. Come into the garden."

"What mischief are you up to now?" asked Vanda, smiling at her.

"Something terrific this time," said Halina.

She took Vanda's hand and together they crept out into the little garden where the air was fresh after the crowded basement where many people were still sleeping after a restless night, noisy with gun-fire and heavy bombing.

The garden was untidy and weeds had grown high but flowers were in bloom along the walls and sunflowers were growing tall as grenadiers above clumps of phlox. There was the scent of sweet briar above a wall pitted by machine-gun bullets. The centre of the garden had been planted out with vegetables and the sun was warm on dark beetroot leaves and the delicate plumes of fennel. Bursts of machine-gun fire had slashed through the potatoes, tearing their leaves and ploughing up the earth. But all was quiet now in this little sanctuary, sheltered from shell-fire for that hour at least by the block of flats behind it.

"Halina, darling," said Vanda, "I can only guess what risks you've been taking. Haven't you done enough?"

"I'm taking the biggest risk of all," said Halina, with a queer little laugh. "I'm going to get married. If I'm still alive by tomorrow morning I'm going to marry Dick—if he's still alive."

Vanda was astonished but not amazed. There had been a number of marriages before and during the Rising. Young lovers had decided to marry even if next day they died. It was a kind of sacrament before death and an eternal pledge of love by young girls to the boys who might be killed very soon, as many of them were.

Vanda was deeply moved. She put an arm round her sister's waist and kissed her cheek.

"Oh, my dear, I have nothing to say against it. I'm only envious. I wanted to marry Jerzy but I don't know whether he's alive or dead. I've not heard a word since they had to leave the hospital under heavy fire."

"Poor Vanda!" said Halina. "But life is like that in Warsaw just now. We may be alive one moment and dead the next. I'm getting used to it."

"Are you sure you love your Englishman?" asked Vanda.

"Pretty sure. Anyhow he saved my life so I suppose I have to marry him."

"That's not quite good enough," said Vanda. "Pretty sure isn't enough, my dear!"

Halina turned and smiled at her.

"I've been in love with him since I took him into our kitchen and fed him on cold chicken. He made me laugh and I loved him for it. Now he's fighting for Poland and I love him for it."

"Have you told Father?"

Halina shook her head.

"Do you think he'll object?"

"I don't think so. Father is always on the side of young people and his own heart is full of tenderness."

Later that morning Halina had a talk with Dr. Mirski and he agreed to the marriage without a word of objection. Like Vanda he was much moved by the thought of this marriage in the midst of battle, growing fiercer in intensity, threatening the whole city with destruction.

Once only he raised a doubtful question.

"Wouldn't it be better to wait until the end when we shall know our fate more clearly?"

Halina shook her head.

"Father, we needn't pretend to each other. There's no hope of victory now, though I wouldn't say that to any of the boys. Our fate is already written. We can hold out a bit longer, that's all. Then it will mean surrender or death. Personally I prefer death. It was very near me yesterday and I didn't mind. In a way I'm sorry that Dick dragged me back from it."

Dr. Mirski took her hand and kissed it and then smiled at her.

"And yet you want to marry him, this young Englishman?"

"Well, he must get his reward," she answered. "And anyhow there's something rather lovely in it. I mean it's a kind of spiritual pact which will last beyond the grave. Dick and I will be able to face eternity with a new kind of happiness. Perhaps God will smile at us and bless our love and give us a good honeymoon in heaven."

"You talk like a child," said Dr. Mirski. He held her arm and pressed it to his side and spoke emotionally.

"Good heavens, it seems only yesterday that you were a tiny creature at your mother's breast."

For a moment tears came into his eyes.

"Your mother has gone. Jozef has gone. Our dear Aunt Krysta has gone, and unspeakable horror is around us."

As he spoke there was another air raid over Warsaw and the enemy guns were firing on the Old Town.

Halina went to a convent very close to them in a neighbouring street and made arrangements for her wedding. So far the building had been undamaged and the nuns were looking after wounded and refugees.

The Reverend Mother raised an awkward question.

"Your Englishman—is he a Catholic?"

"Not quite," said Halina.

"Not quite? He must be one thing or the other! Most Englishmen are Protestants."

"Dick is an angel," said Halina. "Doesn't that cover everything?"

The Reverend Mother laughed. She was good enough to admit that if this Englishman were an angel he must have found the grace of God.

"This will have to be adjusted afterwards," she said. "I'm against mixed marriages, but in this case I feel sure that it will work out well. If he loves you he will love your faith."

"Thank you, Reverend Mother," said Halina. "You're a saint!"

The Reverend Mother smiled again.

"Then I'm in good company with your angel of an Englishman!"

Presently she raised her hands, her thin, delicate hands, and spoke in a low, tragic voice.

"Some of the Sisters here ask me why God has abandoned us, why He allows evil to prevail. One can only look at this as one phase in the eternal struggle. Out of this agony may come a new light in the soul of man. Our sacrifice may be needed as a moral lesson to the world."

She looked at Halina and pity was in her eyes.

"My dear child, it's wrong of me to talk to you like this. I wish you great joy in your marriage with a good man, as you tell me he is. Whatever happens you will have that joy to comfort you and sustain you. God bless you. I shall see you tomorrow morning.

Vanda made a few little preparations for this wedding—this wedding beautiful in its way, but also tragic. She thought of what Halina's wedding would have been in the days of peace. Scores of friends would have come. Masses of presents would have arrived. Halina would have been a beautiful bride in her wedding dress with bridesmaids in attendance and page boys holding her train, and the cathedral organ playing the wedding march. Now she would be married in an everyday frock. There would be no presents—except one, except one little gift which Vanda now made for her. It was a tiny sachet less than a square inch in size which she made from a bit of ribbon. In it she put an old Polish coin of gold, a pinch of salt, and a pinch of sugar. It was a very ancient custom in Poland, still observed by many with the belief that a bride should wear it for luck pinned inside her wedding gown. Perhaps the gold coin was for wealth and the sugar for happiness and the salt for wisdom—*salis sapientiae.*

Vanda touched it with her lips before giving it to Halina who pinned it inside her frock and then embraced her sister. For a moment they were clinging to each other, remembering the happiness of pre-war days and their dead mother and their brother Jozef. But Halina quickly recovered and had a look of happiness and courage when they made their way to the convent where 'Dick' would be waiting for her. He had a few hours' leave from his outpost. He would have to part from his bride very quickly.

The wedding was to be at 9 a.m. They had to leave the house early as they had to pass along the barricade in Indian file, first Dr. Mirski, then Halina, then Vanda, then 'Granny' and another girl. There was some shooting in the neighbourhood but they arrived safely.

The white chapel in the convent looked very peaceful, the sun streaming through the windows in which the glass had been shattered by the blast of bombs early in the battle. There were white and red gladioli on the altar gathered by the Sisters from the convent garden, not without risk.

It was a young priest named Father Orski who was going to celebrate the wedding Mass.

Squadron-Leader Richard Allgrove was waiting at the sanctuary steps. He was in his fighting kit of work-a-day clothes but on his chest there was a little row of ribbons which he had won in the Battle of Britain and other combats in the air. By his side was the young lieutenant who had been with him in his outpost and behind the broken wall through which Halina had made a dash.

Dick, this Englishman, turned to smile at Halina as she came into the chapel on her father's arm. It was a smile of tenderness and adoration for this young girl whose courage had amazed him, whose beauty had captured him at their first meeting, and who so often had laughed and joked with him, and teased him because of his bad French and worse Polish. His clean-cut English face, his tall figure and easy pose, gave him a debonair look at the altar steps and Vanda, looking at him, thought he was like an English knight *sans peur et sans reproche*.

Halina was wonderfully calm. There was a little smile about her lips as she knelt by his side. The priest said Mass at the altar and the English airman knelt there like a statue with bowed head until Halina whispered to him and he stood up for the Gospel and then for the marriage service until time for kneeling again.

Vanda watched them with emotion. Halina was helping him through this service like an elder sister coaching a small brother.

An air-raid was going on but no one in the chapel took any notice of it.

Halina made her responses in a firm clear voice, and the young airman spoke them in English when the young priest translated them with some difficulty, but well enough.

"For better or worse . . . till death do us part. . . ." Till death do us part. In Vanda's mind was the tragic thought that death might part them very soon, in a day or two or an hour or two, even while they were making this vow. She could hear the wings of death outside—the rush of a German bomber flying low.

Where was Jerzy? It was terrible not knowing where he was or whether he was alive. She would have been joyful if she could have stood with him at that altar making those vows of undying love.

Father Orski made a very short address and then Halina and her husband came down the chapel, and on Halina's face was that look of joy and a beauty which seemed touched by some supernatural grace.

'She is beautiful,' thought Vanda. 'I have never seen her so beautiful. She looks as though she were in heaven.'

After the service they went back to the block of flats in single file again, Halina and her husband leading the way. There was a wedding feast provided—what a fantastic coincidence—by the enemy. Half a cold pig dropped by a German aircraft and intended for the S.S garrison in the University, who were cut off from food supplies, had fallen into the little garden behind the block of flats. It was cooked and shared by the lads in the outpost with vegetables gathered by one of them who had crawled out to get them under machine-gun fire.

It was all fantastic—this marriage in the midst of a battle.

Dick Allgrove behaved as he might have done in Wimbledon on his wedding day, shy, amusing, embarrassed by being treated as a hero by these young men in the outpost who crowded round to examine his ribbons. Dr. Mirski made a solemn little speech which the young husband answered in such frightful Polish that Halina laughed at him.

Laughter in Warsaw during the Rising! Love in Warsaw with death round the corner.

The time came for him to go. There could be no honeymoon, no privacy. He embraced Halina holding her in his arms.

At this moment they were both very pale. Dr. Mirski had tears in his eyes when he put an arm round the young Englishman's shoulder and kissed him and said, "God bless you."

"Time to go, my dear fellow," said the young lieutenant.

"Take care of yourself, Dick," said Halina.

He released her from his arms.

He was smiling but there was a yearning look in his eyes and he was reluctant to go. He moved towards the door and then turned and looked again at his young wife with devotion and adoration. He raised his hand in salute to these Polish people who had surrounded him.

Then he spoke one word in English.

"Cheerio!"

He went to his post in Stare Miasto.

CHAPTER LV

The struggle for Warsaw by the Polish Home Army is surely one of the most heroic epics in modern history.

On one side was an enemy who after the first surprise brought up every form of modern weapon for destructive power by land and air, with inexhaustible supplies of ammunition. They were able to shell the Polish positions by heavy artillery, mortars, and tank guns. In the air they had complete mastery and their bombing aeroplanes could drop high explosives on any position without challenge. The Russian Air Force remained on the ground.

On the other side were young men whose stock of arms and ammunition would have been exhausted by the eighth day but for the supplies dropped from the air by Allied aircraft which gave them another week of resistance. After that they were dependent mostly on what they could capture from the enemy. Unarmed men used the rifles of dead Germans, attacked enemy positions and captured a few machine-guns. They attacked again and seized enemy stores of light arms and ammunition by hand-to-hand fighting. But even with those successes due to reckless courage they were fearfully short of arms for defence or attack.

Yet they fought on! For several weeks they fought on inflicting severe losses on the enemy, regaining strong points from which they had been forced, actually capturing German strongholds, refusing to be budged from barricades and ruined houses in spite of storms of high explosives hurled at them by day and night. Their losses were terrible. The living stood among the dead. They lay with the dead, their young comrades, behind broken walls and heaped up furniture. They had mastered the Tiger tanks, putting them out of action, seizing and using others—150 of them. But Goliath tanks came into action and the midget tank without any crew, loaded with high explosives blasted their way through the streets of Warsaw.

As late as August 23rd 'Bor' was able to report local successes in spite of increased German pressure in the Old Town and forced retirement from many positions.

The battle for Warsaw is increasing in intensity. Today in Pius Street we took the Telephone Exchange by storm. The action lasted twenty-six hours. The day before the Central Telephone building in Zielna Street was taken. In all some 200 prisoners have been taken in these two operations. Polish losses were not high. Yesterday the Germans opened fire with a mine-thrower in the area south of Jerozolimska Avenue. In two hours they destroyed 22 houses, each of which contained from 20–60 flats.

The fighting for the Old Town with its narrow streets con-tinued with frightful losses until not a house stood intact and most of them were utterly destroyed. It was a densely occupied quarter and its inhabitants were sheltering in the cellars, many of which became graveyards in which hundreds of women and children lay dead beneath the ruins.

The Germans were now directing their main pressure against Powisle, along the Vistula Embankment, in order to hold the bridgeheads against the inevitable Russian advance in days to come, when the people of Warsaw were all dead or when the survivors had surrendered.

Tragic reports came to 'Bor' and his headquarter's staff from district commands and he used them for his own dispatches to the Polish Government in Exile.

August 19th.

In the Old Town from morning until 19.00 hours this was our worst day in regard to air bombing. Only an insignificant number of houses have remained undamaged. There is an enormous number of wounded. Enemy infantry attacks following a fierce barrage have everywhere been repulsed but owing to systematic and mass bombing, shelling, and the use of Goliath tanks, the enemy is infiltrating into our resistance points. In the centre of the city there are desperate struggles at the barricades with intense fire from the heavy mortars.

August 22nd.

We have now been fighting in the capital for 21 days. The most bitter fighting is in the Old Town area where we have suffered the greatest destruction and the greatest losses.

August 25th.

In the Old Town sector there have been further concentrated enemy attacks strongly supported by fire. The enemy is bringing new forces into the struggle. Despite our counter-attacks the enemy is gradually and systematically penetrating our defence system. The situation in this sector is growing more and more serious. Our forces are suffering from great nervous and physical exhaustion

August 26th.

Bloody battles for the State Manufactury of Securities, Old Town. In one counter-attack we captured the western half of the Manufactury. A slow and steady loss of terrain despite the maximum efforts of our own forces.

In attacks on the John the Pious Hospital and the State Manufactury the enemy used grenades with a charge of suffocating gas which incapacitated our holding forces for battle. There is a shortage of bread and to some extent of water. . . . The whole city, especially the Old Town area, is under fire from mortars, grenades, artillery and the air force.

August 28th.

In the Old Town the enemy has begun to cramp our forces by means of tremendous superiority in fire power. The situation in this sector is getting more and more critical. Losses in commanders and in the ranks amount to some seventy per cent of our original force. A counter-attack has thrown the enemy out of St. John's Cathedral.

August 29th.
Old Town. The enemy continues to restrict us and thrust us away from the bridges and the Vistula motor road. Heavy struggles all day for St. John's Cathedral which has changed hands three times. Towards evening the Cathedral was in enemy hands.

August 30th.
Gradual and steady loss of terrain together with the shortage of food, to some extent water and desperate sanitary conditions, is causing a more and more serious situation.

August 31st.
Old Town. Situation critical. Impossible to hold out longer.

September 1st.
The practicability of defending the Old Town is coming to an end. Lack of ammunition, food, medical supplies, and hygienic requisites. Among the soldiers there is determination to fight on, among civilians a breakdown. Regular air attacks carried out by entire squadrons go on all day. Our own losses on August 31st were some 300 dead, seriously wounded, and buried under ruins.

September 3rd.
After nearly four weeks of bloody struggles, and after the exhaustion of all possibilities of defence, our forces abandoned the ruins of the Old Town during the night of September 2nd. About 1,000 armed soldiers with a large group of lightly wounded civilians and others and about 100 prisoners managed to get through to the City Centre. The bulk of the civilian population and some thousands of seriously wounded soldiers and civilians were left behind in the cellars of wrecked and ruined houses. . . . The heroic defence of the Old Town will pass into legend. Its fall means for us the loss of one of the bastions of our defence.

Those dispatches by General Komorowski tell in grim brevity the story of the battle in Warsaw fought by civilians as well as by soldiers, ill-armed and lacking ammunition, against the Regular German Army, with its overwhelming superiority. But those brief messages leave out the human agony, the sacrificial suffering, the terror and torment of those people of Warsaw who had risked everything for freedom with a passionate and heroic spirit which still shone with a supernatural light in many souls even above the stench of blood and death and human excrement. Even now the survivors who reached the City Centre, the new target of destruction, refused to surrender. But towards the end many of the civilian population fled into open country beyond the city, without shelter, without food and without water.

The scenes in the Old Town were hellish. The water supply failed, light was cut off. Food supplies were exhausted. All means of sanitation were destroyed. Down in the cellars women crowded with the children under devastating bombardment. Houses collapsed upon them and buried them dead or alive. Death came as a mercy to wounded soldiers and civilians lying in these ruins in pools of blood. No water for the children or the wounded. No milk. Darkness in those stinking cellars. But hundreds of mere boys, haggard, hungry, with blood-shot eyes for lack of sleep, still held on to ruined buildings or broken walls, until at last the defence of the Old Town was abandoned. No help had come to them from the Russians. Only a few more British aircraft reached the city and what supplies they dropped fell into enemy hands. The people of Warsaw fought their battle alone and no rescue came. 'A heroic legend', said General Komorowski in one of those dispatches, written while the city was under fire. So it is for the Poles, but does the world know even now, the astounding epic of those people, old women and young girls, elderly men and boys, all mixed up together in this desperate fight for freedom which ended in failure? It failed. It was a ghastly tragedy, but the glory of it will live on for ever. It was the crucifixion of a great city, the sacrifice of a nation by the ordeal of flame and slaughter. To what end? Was it all useless? Was it an utter waste of young life, a mad adventure ending in inevitable tragedy? General Komorowski who is still alive, who knows more than any man the full tale of it all, still thinks that it was worth while, and that its failure was also a victory, and that the glory of it is greater than its tragedy. The Crucifixion of Christ seemed to be a failure. The martyrdom of the saints seems to be a failure. All sacrifice seems to be in vain. But above the ashes of martydom and from the cross of sacrifice there rises the spirit of heroic men and women with a call to the human soul to continue the eternal fight of good against evil, of light against darkness, of liberty for faith and conscience against the enslavement of the mind and body. So General Komorowski thinks. So think many who were in the Rising and by a miracle survived it.

CHAPTER LVI

THE Copernicus Street hospital had to be evacuated in a hurry —in too much of a hurry. The enemy's guns had the street under fire and the wounded were in the gravest danger. Dr. Joravski gave orders for their immediate removal with as much hospital equipment as could be taken away in the available transport.

There was feverish activity in the wards but the nurses were wonderfully calm and courageous although they could hear the crash of shell-fire in Copernicus Street itself. Several windows in the wards were shattered by the blast and some of the wounded showed signs of terror.

One of the nurses came to Jerzy Boberski and felt his pulse and put her hand over his heart.

"You'll have to go on a stretcher," she told him. "You're still pretty weak."

"I might walk," he said. "I believe I could walk."

She shook her head.

"Not yet. Quite impossible."

Dr. Joravski had a few words with him.

"We can't find room for you in an ambulance. The stretcher-bearers will look after you."

"I don't want to make trouble," said Jerzy. "I could walk."

The doctor smiled.

"Your mind is stronger than your body. We'll do the best for you. I promised Vanda I would look after you—as far as the enemy will allow me."

The enemy was not agreeable. Copernicus Street was heavily shelled and several houses were on fire. It was at night by the light of those flames that the wounded were put into the few ambulances available, the lightly wounded walked with the nurses and a few, like Jerzy, were carried on stretchers by Red Cross volunteers.

By Dr. Joravski's orders they were not allowed to go in a procession but two or three minutes were given between the start of each ambulance and the walking wounded in twos and threes.

Jerzy was put on a stretcher and two young men carried him carefully with slow strides. Lying there with his face to the sky he could see flames licking through broken roofs. There was a strong smell of burning and he could feel the heat of it. The street was empty. The last ambulance to go had reached a parallel street. He did not know either of his stretcher-bearers but he had had a glimpse of them. One was a young, dark-haired man, the other an elderly man with grey hair who looked like a professor or literary man.

He heard the young man speak.

"First turning to the right, if we can get as far as that."

Why shouldn't he get as far as that?

The answer came immediately. A shell came screaming through the night sky and burst less than fifty yards away into a house already smashed and burning. It was followed by a shell fifty yards or so away on the other side.

"They're bracketing," said the older man. "What shall we do with this poor lad?"

"Better carry him into a house," said the other. "It's his best chance—if there's any. This street is a death trap."

Jerzy felt the swing of his stretcher, jolting him. The two men were running as another shell burst within a yard or two from the spot they had reached a moment before.

They had carried him into the ruin of a house with its roof open to the sky and the first floor gutted, but with walls still standing. Hurriedly and roughly they dumped his stretcher on the floor which was littered with rubble and charred beams. He could hear them breathing noisily.

Presently the elder man spoke.

"We must get back to the hospital. There are two more wounded left behind."

"It's suicidal to go back," said the younger man. "I can't face it. Besides we can't leave this wounded man here."

"We must," said the elder man. "And you'll have to face it, my dear fellow. It's a question of honour."

"I've lost my nerve," said the younger man. "That street is like hell. I just can't go through it again."

"We can't abandon the wounded," said the elder man. "I couldn't face Dr. Joravski with a tale like that. It's our job, isn't it?"

"I can't face it," said the younger man. "Listen!"

There was another crump in the street and the young man shuddered. Jerzy could see his face now, a young, handsome face. but with terror in his eyes.

"I'll give you ten minutes," said the grey-haired man. "You'll feel all right in ten minutes."

Jerzy was filled with pity for the boy who had lost his nerve and spoke to him.

"If I were strong enough I would go in your place."

The boy began to cry with his hands up to his face.

"It's a kind of shell-shock," said the elder man. "He has been all right up to now. Quite brave."

The boy sobbed out some pitiful words.

"I pretended to be brave. I'm a coward. I'm terrified."

Jerzy spoke to him again.

"I'm a coward, too. I've been horribly frightened. It was when I was in the Power House. I fought like a madman because I was so frightened."

The elder man looked down at him.

"Are you one of the heroes of the Power House?"

"I suppose I am," said Jerzy. "But I was very frightened, especially when a giant of a fellow tried to strangle me."

"I expect we're all frightened at times," said the elder man. "Shell fire isn't amusing. Hand-to-hand fighting can't be amusing. But the hero is the fellow who goes on all the same."

Jerzy had confessed to cowardice, as he called it, to comfort the young man and it seemed to do something in that way. He stopped crying and looked down at Jerzy with a queer tragic smile.

"It's kind of you to talk like that," he said in a broken voice. "It helps me a bit."

He sat down on a pile of rubble and took Jerzy's hand and held it tight as though this human contact comforted him.

"I'll say a prayer for you," said Jerzy in a whisper. "It can't do any harm."

"Thanks," said the boy.

They were silent after that. The enemy guns were still firing but the shells were bursting farther away.

The grey-haired man looked at his wrist-watch by the light of a torch guarded by his hand.

"Ten minutes," he said quietly. "Shall we go, my dear lad?"

The boy rose unclasping Jerzy's hand.

"I suppose so."

"You're one of the heroes," said Jerzy.

The two men went out together into Copernicus Street.

He lay in the darkness there for perhaps an hour or two. There was a respite in the gun-fire. It was dark in this ruined house except for the red glow in the sky. Once he felt something moving and touching his body. It gave him a sense of fear for a moment until he raised his head and saw two green eyes looking at him. It was a kitten which snuggled up to him. Its little body was trembling with fear because of the gun-fire. Jerzy stroked it gently and said, "So you're a coward too, my little one!"

Now and again bits of brick and plaster fell to the floor near where he was lying. It was quite likely that he would be buried alive in this ruined house. That thought haunted him for a while and he wondered if he had the strength to get up and walk. He might get as far as Vanda's canteen. It would be a great joy to see Vanda. She was not very far away across Tamka Street. It would be wonderful if he could get as far as Vanda.

He raised his body and found that he could sit up. He was naked from the waist up except for his bandages. Could he stand? He grasped a bit of iron sticking out of the wall and pulled himself up. He was standing. He felt very weak but he was on his feet again, supporting himself by the broken wall.

The shelling had stopped. It was quiet in the street outside. It was a good time to go, before they started again. It was dark in this place of ruin, but he could see the faint light of the night sky above the broken rafters. He stared at the heaps of rubble on the floor. It would never do to stumble and fall over them. He might not be able to get up again. Very carefully he edged his way round them, still groping along one of the broken walls. He was in the doorway now. He was looking into the street. Things were visible by faint moonlight. Dead bodies were lying there, and something which looked like a broken stretcher. Powdered glass glittered like diamonds. An avalanche of rubble was piled up at one end of the street. There was a strong acrid stench of burning, and smoke was creeping out of basement rooms below their ruins.

"I wonder!" said Jerzy aloud.

He wondered if he could walk any way down that street. He felt remarkably weak. There was no strength in his legs.

Suddenly he heard footsteps and saw two figures running towards him. A voice spoke in German.

"Here's one of those swine!"

Jerzy tried to get back into the room but one of the men leapt at him, striking him in the face with the butt-end of a pistol, and he fell with a crash. They must have thought he was dead, or perhaps they thought he would be roasted in the fire they made by flinging hand-grenades into the basement. There was no sign of them when he was able to move again. Perhaps he had lain there unconscious for a time. He was conscious now. He was aware of great heat where he lay. At the end of the room he saw a little flame licking up behind a pile of rubble. His eyes smarted from a thick oily smoke creeping about him. If he stayed here he would be roasted alive.

He put his hand to his face which was aching as though it had been struck by an iron bar. There was a sledge-hammer in his brain. He groaned heavily when he rose and stood up again, supporting himself by the broken wall as he had done before. By a tremendous effort of will-power he staggered to the doorway and stood in the street. It was dawn. The night sky was brightening. There was no more shelling and the street was deserted except for the dead bodies. Jerzy Boberski seemed to be alone in the world.

He walked very slowly, step by step, something like 100 yards which seemed to him like 100 miles. Then he fell and lay gasping, and felt terribly exhausted.

Several times he whispered a name.

"Vanda! . . . Vanda!"

Then he began to crawl like a wounded animal.

He crawled short distances with spells of rest between his efforts to get away from Copernicus Street. Now he was in Tamka Street. He must try walking again. He clutched a lamp-post which was leaning at an angle, having been struck by a bit of shell or blasted sideways. He was on his feet again, but feeling very dizzy—so dizzy that he lost hold of the lamp-post and fell on his face in the roadway.

In the house opposite there were living people. Through broken window panes one of them saw this man, naked to the waist except for the bandages, lying face downwards. Two girls ran out, followed by a middle-aged man.

"Is he dead?" asked one of the girls.

But Jerzy was not dead. When he was aware of things again he found himself on a divan in a well-furnished room. A girl was bending over him, dabbing his face with some liquid which made it smart.

"Am I alive?" he asked, in a bewildered way.

"Among friends," said the girl. "Poor Jerzy!"

Later an ambulance came to fetch him and he was taken to another hospital.

CHAPTER LVII

In the factory near the ruins of the Ghetto and the Jewish cemetery General 'Bor' Komorowski was beginning to find his headquarters untenable. The enemy's aim, after their disorganized fighting in the first days of the Rising, was to drive a line of communication from east to west and the district of Vola in which the factory stood was at the western end of this highway to the Vistula. They attacked it with everything they had in weapons of destruction with storms of incendiary shells, heavy artillery and bombing planes raising fires which quickly spread from one building to another. The Polish outposts had to fall back behind barricades in the ruins until the factory was only 500 yards from the enemy and under fire.

For the General and his Staff the situation was abominable. They were cut off from effective liaison with other sectors. Owing to restricted diet some of the officers were enfeebled by dysentery and 'Bor' himself became ill in this way, but by sheer will-power—he was too busy to be ill, he says—overcame this malady and never stopped working.

His penetrating, watchful eyes, and his quick, human sympathy made him aware of the strain on some of those working with him. Some of his officers showed signs of nervousness which might have been taken for fear if their courage had not been tested to the uttermost in the Underground movement. But his Chief of Staff, General Pelczynski, remained calm and unruffled, and one of the civilian delegates was a humorous fellow who raised a smile even in the darkest moments. But looking back on those days and nights in the Kammler factory 'Bor' gave highest marks to the women for their psychological endurance, superior to that of men. These secretaries and messenger girls never failed in courage and cheerfulness, never showed a sign of fear. They were the heroines of Warsaw.

He decided to move his headquarters to Stare Miasto—the Old Town. That was easier said than done. The enemy had complete observation from a church tower beyond the Ghetto wall. The road outside could be swept by machine-gun fire if any figure moved. By great luck one of the outposts had captured a Tiger tank. It was put into action. It knocked down part of the Ghetto wall and its third shot brought down the church tower. That gave them a chance. They separated into groups, carrying documents and files. 'Bor' led the first group. They had to go in quick short rushes, taking cover behind bits of ruin to avoid machine-gun fire from the Paviak prison. It took them over two hours to reach Karasinki Park.

The new headquarters were established in a school in Barokova Street which the Germans had used as a hospital. From its high roof there was a wide view over the battlefield of Warsaw and it was possible to walk about the narrow streets and alleys through the old archways and below the gabled houses of this mediaeval relic of Warsaw's ancient past.

'Bor' left his headquarters now and then to go through the old streets. They were crowded with refugees who had swarmed in from Vola and other districts. As yet Stare Miasto had not been shelled, and at night when bombing planes came over the refugees went underground to deep crypt-like cellars, and subterranean passages leading from one house to another, built far back in the Middle Ages. There were 170,000 people huddled together in Stare Miasto—twice its normal population.

Inside this old town were strongholds held by the Home Army such as the Treasury Printing Office on the Vistula side, and the Town Hall towards the centre, and the Bank of Poland on the flank of defence.

The young soldiers of the Home Army appeared in fantastic uniforms described afterwards by 'Bor' who passed among them unrecognized.

"The majority were wearing German S.S. uniforms, either taken from captured stores or 'leased' from prisoners: at first sight they looked like the elite German troops except for their white and red arm-bands. Mixed with them were Polish pre-1939 uniforms, carefully preserved as relics, in hiding for five long years. Tin hats varied too: they were German, Polish, French, or Russian some of them from the last war. Others wore firemen's helmets. Finally there were blouses or tunics of every colour and design, made either in the years of occupation or now during the Rising. Another peculiarity was that one-seventh of the force were women. Used chiefly as messengers to maintain liaison with isolated posts and distribute news sheets among soldiers and civilians, they also worked in the medical services and attended to the welfare and feeding of the soldiers."

Soon after his arrival in Stare Miasto 'Bor' was visited by a woman who called herself 'Anka'.

"I have a message from your wife," she said.

She handed him a card which, she said, the Countess Komorowska had thrown across the street to her tied to a bit of string.

It was the first word he had had from his enchanting Renia since the beginning of the Rising. She was living in Foch Street which was under enemy fire, the Poles being at the corner of Theatre Square facing the Germans on the Marshal's Place. She was there with her little boy Adam, aged two, and she was expecting another baby in a month's time. Several times she visited the Polish outpost in order to get news on the radio and crawled through tunnels cut through the basements of the houses. Her neighbours went down to an underground shelter during air-raids, but she had a horror of the place and stayed on the ground floor. There she was one night when an enemy shell cut clean through the flat above her, bringing down plaster and rubble but nothing more. The woman 'Anka' came to her a few days later and urged her to go to another part of the town occupied by Polish troops instead of staying between two fires; but she was in no state to dash across an open street exposed to enemy machine-guns, and she was afraid that little Adam might be killed. She decided to stay where she was whatever might happen.

'Bor' was absorbed in his duties, deeply anxious because of the critical situation, conscious of the terrific responsibility of his position, but this message from his beloved Renia was a joy to him, though it brought renewed anxiety for her safety. She was still alive. Her courage had not failed and never would. He was lucky in getting those words from her. Thousands of his soldiers had no news at all of what was happening to their wives and families.

Stare Miasto—the Old Town—was still a stronghold of defence. Soon it would become the centre of attack and the holocaust of Polish hopes.

CHAPTER LVIII

DURING the last tragic hours of Stare Miasto a terrific decision had to be taken by General 'Bor'. It was to abandon the ruins of the Old Town by withdrawing all men from the last barricades and to make their escape with wounded and civilians. There was only one way of escape and that was threatened. It was by way of the sewers.

The Germans were attacking Krasinski Square with infantry and tanks. They were getting close to the last manhole by which escape might be made. The risk was frightful. After withdrawal from the barricades the enemy could march in and if they discovered that quickly, escape would be cut off for civilians as well as soldiers; or if they became aware of the retreat through the sewers a few grenades down the manholes would block the way and cause a massacre in the tunnels. How could the enemy fail to be aware of what was happening when the manhole was only 200 yards from their own position?

General 'Bor' with the officer commanding the surviving troops decided to take the risk.

The sewers had already been used by units retiring from one position and trying to reach another. Girls called *kanalarki* (*kanal* being the Polish word for sewer) had gone through them with messages and orders. Frightful things had happened in these horrible tunnels. The Germans had opened the manholes in their own occupation and had poured down petrol and set them alight, burning many men to death. Young soldiers emerging from a manhole had fought hand-to-hand with enemy patrols. There had been fights to the death in the filthy slime below. Men brave in attack were horror-stricken in the darkness and stench of these sewers and had gone mad and had had to be gagged or silenced by sacks flung over their heads.

But that was now the only way of escape from Stare Miasto. Fifteen hundred soldiers and civilians would go that way, carrying the wounded on improvised stretchers. Those too badly wounded to make the journey would have to remain behind and one of the heroic priests, Father Thomas, refused to leave them.

'Bor' himself with some of his officers and a brave young woman named Basia, who was his personal typist, went in advance of the others who were to follow later. To get to the manhole they had to go one by one at different intervals, making a dash in the darkness for the sandbags which guarded the entrance. It took an hour to assemble the whole party in the sewer. Ahead were two soldiers with tommy-guns and an experienced guide who led them forward. Then came 'Bor's' A.D.C. and behind him the General himself, followed by the Government delegate. Following him was his secretary Basia. One by one the others came in single file.

They had to go about a mile to reach the City Centre. Sometimes they were thigh deep in water and excrement. The stench was appalling. They walked in silence but suddenly a woman's scream rang out, echoing madly down the tunnel. It came from

Basia who had fallen and was being swept back by the swirling water until grabbed by the Government delegate and held up until she regained her foothold. Now and then they were able to breathe fresh air at an open manhole and at last, after this way of horror, crouching low, ice-cold, half suffocated, they saw a signal lamp which the guide knew was their way of escape. They came up into the City Centre and the air above ground made them feel drunk. For a little while they were safe in streets where houses still stood, unlike the utter ruin of Stare Miasto. They had covered a distance of 1,700 yards and it had taken them many hours of the night.

It was before midnight on September 1st that over 1,000 soldiers withdrew from the barricades. The Old Town was defenceless. One by one the men went down the manhole. One by one 500 civilians, among whom were many girls, followed into this tunnel of darkness and abomination. The wounded were somehow lowered on their stretchers. The sewer was filled by the long column from end to end. When the first arrived others were still waiting at the manhole, knowing that if dawn came before they went down their escape would be cut off. But by some miracle as it seemed, the Germans were unaware of what was happening only 200 yards away from their own line. The Polish units had one stroke of good fortune. The water in the sewer had gone down, leaving only slush and slime.

Father Paul was among the last to leave with a small group of whom he was now in charge, holding officer rank as a military chaplain. He had seen and suffered all the agony of those days and nights in the Old Town. From the beginning he had been with the soldiers and civilians, comforting the wounded, giving the last sacraments to the dying, helping to bury the dead in streets which had become graveyards. He had sat in cellars with burning houses above them. He had walked through heavy shell-fire to the outposts where young men were fighting amidst the dead and wounded. He had recited prayers below ground, giving spiritual comfort to young people who kept their faith in spite of times when they seemed to be abandoned by God and by all human help.

He had had very little sleep and often little food. He worked on his spirit and on his nerves, this tall, thin young man with blue, luminous eyes deep-set in a haggard handsome face. At first he had been able to laugh and smile with the young soldiers wearing the Home Army armlet as their only uniform, recognized before the end of August—late in the day—by the Allies as military combatants, but not recognized as such by the enemy. Under the frightful strain of harrowing scenes, laughter was no longer possible. His big blue eyes were filled with pity and compassion. Many times he had to struggle against a flood of tears which threatened to swamp his eyes. He must not let that happen. These people whom he served looked to him for courage and leadership. Courage? Could there be courage in a cellar with women weeping over dead children, or in an outpost where there were more dead and more wounded, or in a street under fire of heavy artillery with monstrous shells and land mines blasting down the houses? Courage with nerves all frayed, with now and then an animal fear because of these frightful explosions? Yet he was able to subdue that inner torment. They still looked to him for leadership. They still thought he had courage of a supernatural kind. And perhaps he had—only his faith in God could have upheld him at this time. There were moments when he seemed to be touched and uplifted by a divine grace.

His most dreadful hours, dreadful for the others as well as himself, were when he collected a group of young people, women and girls among them, for that escape through the sewers. He knew most of them. Some of them belonged to his own unit. He had known them before the war in pleasant homes and gardens, like Barbara Ziemska, a cousin of Vanda Mirska. Her husband Stefan, the illustrator of many children's books, had been killed in the attack on the University buildings. And here was Nunia Mankovska who had stayed at Dr. Mirski's house at the beginning of the war with her husband Karol, forgetting everything in the joy of a honeymoon. He remembered that Vanda had told him about that. They had come back from Lvov and now Karol had been badly wounded in the fighting for the Telephone Exchange.

Some of the girls were in the liaison service. They were in bad shape with dishevelled hair and filthy frocks. He noticed that one of them had a wild look in her eyes like an animal caught in a trap.

Among them, put into his charge, was the young English airman, Richard Allgrove—Halina's Englishman 'Dick' as she called him. It seemed only a short time since Father Paul had seen him at the house of Dr. Mirski. Now he had been brought from a cellar badly wounded in the thigh but still cheerful and able to walk.

"Good heavens!" exclaimed Father Paul at the sight of him.

Richard Allgrove grinned.

"Those Germans did their best to kill me. I think I must have been saved by Halina's prayers. I hope she is all right. I expect she's doing desperate deeds somewhere."

Suddenly he winced with pain.

"Oh, lordy! This wound of mine!"

Father Paul looked at him anxiously.

"My dear fellow, you're in no fit state to go through the sewers. It won't be a pleasant journey."

Richard Allgrove laughed.

"Better than staying in Stare Miasto. I'll stick it out all right."

Father Paul looked at his watch.

"Our turn to go," he said.

He spoke to his group.

"We must go now. God be with us!"

One by one they went like the others, making a quick dash for the sandbags, scrambling down the iron ladder into the darkness below, into the horror of it and the stench of it, following in the trail of those ahead.

It was a *Via Dolorosa*. The foul air filled lungs and nostrils with an appalling smell. Their feet were deep in excrement and filth. Two of the girls vomited and cried out in horror.

"Silence!" said Father Paul. "Keep quiet, for God's sake."

The English airman was behind him and spoke presently in a low voice.

"My wound is bleeding again. I don't think I can make it."

"Hang on to me," said the priest. "Put your arm round my neck."

"It's frightfully good of you," said Dick. "I didn't know I was so darned feeble."

He put his arm round the priest's shoulder who stumbled and nearly fell under this weight which put him off his balance in the slime and filth.

"We must get a stretcher somehow," he said. "I'll pass the word along."

In the forward part of the column some of the wounded had been carried on stretchers. They may have already reached the City Centre. A stretcher might be sent back if he could get a message through.

It was passed along from one to another—"Stretcher needed!" —but it was more than an hour before one came back over the heads of the long column moving at a snail's pace, feeling their way along the slimy walls, each footstep having to be made cautiously to avoid a fall. During that hour or so Father Paul needed all his physical and spiritual strength to support the young English airman who was perhaps unaware of the strain he was putting on this good friend and leader. Now and again he spoke in a low voice quite cheerily.

"A damned awful place this! . . . Stinks like hell, doesn't it? . . . Those girls are marvellous. . . . Gosh! We very nearly went down that time. . . . Sorry to be such a nuisance, Father. . . . It's very noble of you."

Father Paul did not answer these remarks. He was praying with a kind of desperate urgency.

'Oh God, help us to escape from this darkness. . . . Oh, God, be merciful to us. . . . Oh, God, give those poor girls courage and strength in this place of horror."

When the stretcher arrived at last two of the soldiers crawled back, losing their places ahead, and Dick was put on the stretcher. It was only just in time. He must have been losing blood for the young priest felt him go limp in his arms and he collapsed as the two young soldiers came to the rescue, feeling their way, groping to him in the black tunnel, lifting him up.

Father Paul wiped the sweat off his forehead and gave thanks for this merciful relief. They came to an open manhole and fresh air came down to them, clean and refreshing, like a breath from heaven.

But something was happening ahead, something terrible. One of the girls had gone mad. It was that girl who had had the wild look in her eyes. She gave a scream which came echoing down the tunnel.

"I must go!" she cried. . . . "Let me go!"

Father Paul could not see what was happening. He heard a murmur of voices and some commotion ahead. He heard afterwards that the girl had made a dash for the iron ladder and before they could grab her had climbed up and gone through the manhole. Then she screamed again. She had been caught by a German patrol.

Father Paul did not dare shout to his company to hurry on. He was terrified lest the Germans should throw down hand-grenades as often they had done, but this terror passed when they had got beyond the open manhole. Perhaps it was five minutes later when they heard an explosion down the tunnel. Its echo and concussion reached them, but no one was wounded.

Seventeen hundred yards, and all a long night to go that distance, step by step, through the horrible slime which clung about their feet. Several had fallen and were in a fearful state. The stench was intolerable. The darkness was like a mask of black velvet on their eyes. Some of the girls were weeping and men were cursing in low voices. Only one or two heroic souls—young soldiers—laughed when they stumbled.

Then at last there was the green light and journey's end.

They climbed out of the manhole one by one. It took an incredible time before they were all out. They were out in the City Centre. They were breathing pure air. They had reached a safety zone after the horrors of Stare Miasto. There were helping hands, kind voices, reaching out to them. The first light of dawn was banishing the darkness. They had come out of the black hell of the sewers to an earthly paradise, as then it seemed. Some of them were laughing and shouting with a kind of hysteria. Some fell to the ground having spent the last gasp of physical and moral strength.

Father Paul went towards the stretcher on which Richard Allgrove was lying.

He looked pretty bad there. He looked half dead. But he raised his head slightly and was able to give a feeble laugh.

"Thanks, Father! I owe my miserable life to you. I'm jolly grateful."

Jolly grateful! The English words sounded comical to this young Polish priest.

"I'm jolly glad!" he answered. "Thanks be to God!"

At the exit from the sewers in Varecka Street were some correspondents who were writing reports for those news sheets distributed every day during the Rising. One of them was a young poet named Ubysz. Another was Sophie Kossak, the most eminent writer perhaps in Poland. They stood together silently among the little crowd who had come to render first-aid and any kind of help to those who emerged from the terrible way of escape.

They were overwhelmed by emotion at the sight of those who came up—wet, filthy, exhausted, wounded men on stretchers, or half carried by nurses and comrades, and young girls, drenched and befouled.

Sophie Kossak wept. Could she weep, this woman? Was it possible to weep at the sight of any misery or human suffering after her own experience? She had been arrested and sent to Paviak prison, interrogated day and night. She had been sent to Auschwitz, that terrible concentration camp where she had seen every kind of horror. Then, by some incomprehensible mystery she had been released just before the Rising.

She had a son and daughter, Vitold and Anna, both in the Secret Army, both in outposts from which no word came to her.

The young poet spoke to her.

"I've never seen anything like this. Nothing like it has happened in the world before. What heroism! It's terrible—and yet it's inspiring. It's frightful—but it's magnificent. If only I could tell the world in burning words—Good God! This should be an epic. All the world should weep at the glory of it and the pity of it."

Some such words from the passion and pity of his heart seemed to come scorching to his lips.

But Sophie Kossak did not hear them because of her own tears.

Then something wonderful happened to her. Among those dripping figures who climbed out to the open was a young soldier who cried out to her.

"Mother!"

It was her son Vitold whose whereabouts had been unknown to her and from whom no word had come.

It was as though a miracle had happened, a miracle of joy.

She could only have a few words with this boy and he was taken away to the Adria canteen to be cleansed and to get new clothes and a hot drink.

Sophie Kossak had to remain at her post. She would have to write a description of this scene before the night was out. It had to be translated into English. It was to be sent to England by wireless transmission. If only she could put her own emotion into each word, something of her anguish and something of her joy and pride and pity, so that England might weep as she had done.

Was it possible that a second miracle should happen? Do these things ever happen like that, one after another? It happened to Sophie Kossak, she thought, for among the bedraggled girls, filthy from the sewers, came her daughter Anna. Tall and beautiful she had been, with blue-grey eyes and a laughing spirit, and a love of ski-ing and all sport—now wet and shivering, and gasping for fresh air after the stinking suffocation of the sewers.

So there were two miracles it seemed for Sophie Kossak, who had been behind the bars of the Paviak prison and in the abomination of Auschwitz.

And that night the young poet Ubysz scribbled on a dirty piece of paper a poem on the tragedy of Stare Miasto and its heroic defenders—too difficult perhaps to translate into English, with the rhythm of it and the beauty of it.

CHAPTER LIX

VANDA was exhausted by lack of sleep and intensity of emotion. Halina's wedding had moved her deeply and all the time she was haunted by the thought of Jerzy. A sense of despair took hold of her because of the failure of the Rising which could no longer be doubted. No false hopes were possible. No wishful thinking could alter the grim and terrible fact that the Home Army had lost most of its key positions and that the last desperate stand was being made in isolated outposts.

The certainty of all that was brought to her by her uncle, Colonel Lopalevski. Since the beginning of the battle not a word had come from him. He had been in command of a unit in the City Centre. Now on the day following Halina's wedding he appeared unexpectedly with orders that the outpost of Obozna Street should be withdrawn because of enemy pressure and the impossiblity of holding it any longer. Only a small contingent of young men under their lieutenant would be left to put up a show of resistance until the last possible moment. The others would join him in the City Centre.

It was after giving these orders that he came down to see Dr. Mirski and Vanda. He looked older and his face was grey and he had lost his old cheeriness. He had the look of a man who had been through a tragic ordeal.

He embraced Vanda and then clasped his brother-in-law's hand.

"It's good to find you alive," he said.

He spoke in a broken voice of his wife Krysta.

"I get no news of her. They have probably killed her."

Presently he talked of the battle that was raging—the series of battles in most parts of Warsaw.

"It's hopeless now. The Germans are cutting us to pieces. They've overpowering strength. We're being hemmed in everywhere. It can't last much longer before the end comes."

His voice became harsh and he raised both hands above his head.

"We've been betrayed," he said. "The Russians have betrayed us. Our Allies have betrayed us. Their dishonour will live in history as a shameful thing."

He controlled his anger and became more calm.

"Our young men are magnificent. Nothing will alter that. They're still fighting like heroes. The glory of their courage will live for ever."

Dr. Mirski was silent until presently he spoke a few quiet words.

"Their sacrifice should end now. We ought to save as many lives as possible. Further resistance is in vain."

The Colonel looked at him moodily.

"You mean surrender now?"

"Wouldn't that be best?" asked Dr. Mirski. "Wouldn't it save the further slaughter of precious life?"

"We shall fight to the last," said the Colonel, harshly. "We shall fight until the last cartridge has been spent. Ask any of those lads. They will tell you that. They prefer death to dishonour."

Dr. Mirski gave a long-drawn sigh.

"They have gained honour enough," he said in his quiet voice.

The Colonel's eyes hardened.

"They wouldn't agree with you, their pride is still high. In any case what does life hold for them in the future? Enslavement to the Russians. Concentration camps. Forced labour. The loss of their faith, the demobilization of their souls. Death is preferable. To me it is preferable. I hope I shall die behind the last barricade."

"No, no, my dear fellow," exclaimed Dr. Mirski. "You must go on living for Krysta's sake. She will need you. We all need you."

It was a painful conversation. It deepened Vanda's sense of anguish. She had known her uncle as a gay, cheerful, optimistic man, the perfect type of cavalry officer, a hero to her when she was a child. Now he looked broken. Perhaps he guessed her thoughts because he altered his tone and tried to cast off his gloom.

"The end hasn't come yet and I've been speaking a lot of nonsense—unpardonable in front of Vanda. Tell me about yourselves? What's happening to our pretty Halina who has the spirit of Joan of Arc?"

They told him about the wedding and about her capture of a Tiger tank single-handed.

"Splendid," he exclaimed. "I'm proud to be her uncle. Give her my love and blessings."

He rose and said he had to go. He embraced Vanda again and then straightened himself up and put on a little of his former *panache* of the old cavalry officer which had enchanted Vanda as a child.

But when he had gone she spoke to her father in a low voice. "Father, all is lost. There's no more hope."

Dr. Mirski gave that long-drawn sigh again.

That night Vanda fell asleep though there was a fury of gun-fire over Warsaw. She had been sleeping a few hours when she was awakened by someone shaking her. It was Maria, the cook.

"Wake up, Miss! Something bad is happening. There's water everywhere."

Vanda was sleeping in her clothes and sprang up in alarm.

"Water? What water?"

"It's pouring in," said Maria. "It looks as though we're all going to be drowned."

Vanda ran downstairs and found some of the refugees baling out the water from the basement and cellars.

"Those devils are going to drown us," cried Maria.

"We had better tell the lieutenant," said Vanda. "Come with me."

They had to crawl through holes in the walls to reach the outpost in the corner house. The young lieutenant had already been aroused and looked alarmed.

"The Germans must have closed the sluice on the Vistula," he said. "I don't like the look of it."

He came back with Vanda and Maria, telling some of the boys to follow him.

When they came down into the shelter water was covering the floor and rising rapidly. Everybody was awake and many were frightened. Halina had come back for a brief respite. She had tucked up her skirt and was piling up suitcases and furniture upon which the women and children could take refuge from the flood.

Vanda and Maria with two young men rushed to the ground-floor apartment and carried out the dining-room table upon which they put some chairs. The old lady called 'Granny' was helped to climb up and sat in one of the armchairs with great dignity and calmness though she wanted to give up this place to other and younger women.

"It's a case of all hands to the pump," she cried out. "Tuck up your frocks, my dears, and get busy with some buckets. We're not going to be drowned yet."

When the young men from the outposts arrived they joined the women among whom Halina was the leading spirit. They formed a long queue, each person about two yards from the other. A boy in front filled a bucket and passed it down the line, each one seizing it quickly and handing it to the next. The last boy standing on the top of the stairs on the ground-floor landing emptied the water into the gutter in the street. It was an un interrupted chain of work. Other buckets were brought into use. A rhythm was established with this swinging movement. Vanda felt faint now and then but carried on. There was no time to wipe her forehead or the little drops of sweat running down her neck without breaking the rhythm. The air was hot and close with so many people breathing hard in this low-ceilinged basement. The water-logged carpets gave out a damp stench and in spite of all efforts the water was rising inch by inch. Once Vanda shuddered, not because of the ice-cold water in which she stood with bare feet, but because a big black spider crawled up the white wall near which she stood. She had a horror of spiders. Often she had called out to Halina and others imploring them to remove one of these creatures, very carefully without hurting it, to any place outside the house. Now she was tempted to make the same appeal to Halina but it would seem too absurd. She had walked through gunfire. She had dodged machine-gun bullets. It was too ridiculous to be frightened of a spider, but she kept her eyes on it warily lest it should move nearer.

They worked in silence. There was no sound but the clink of the buckets and the pouring out of water and the hard breathing of the workers. Suddenly one of the boys called out in a clear and cheerful voice.

"Now, who's afraid to die? Hell must be a clean and restful place compared with this!"

That boy's voice, those challenging words in a cheerful tone, eased the nervous tension and everybody had to laugh. Presently they heard shouting. An officer and some men arrived with a motor pump brought from the Electricity Works—the situation was saved. The water went down. They wouldn't die by drowning.

But that night the outpost was to be abandoned except for a small holding force according to Colonel Lopalevski's orders. All the civilians would have to leave this shelter and go elsewhere. A formidable attack with tanks and flame-throwers was expected at dawn.

Lieutenant Miotacz addressed his young men and asked a question.

"Who will volunteer to stay with me? I want twelve of you."

Every one of them volunteered.

He smiled and said, "Well, that makes it difficult. I shall have to choose."

He went down the line and chose every third man.

"I'll stay and cook for you," said Halina.

The lieutenant looked at her and shook his head.

"No, no! I can't accept an offer like that. It's not going to be amusing."

"I don't want to be amused," said Halina. "I want to be of service."

"Halina!" cried Vanda. "You have done enough. You have been too brave. You're now a married woman."

Halina smiled at her.

"Does that make a woman lose her nerve? Of course I shall stay."

On the night of the flood the evacuation began, the old lady called 'Granny', still in command of her unit, discussed the plan of action with Vanda. She had had word from H.Q. that the Germans were preparing an all-out attack on the Vistula Embankment, timed to begin at dawn. The blocks of flats at Obozna would become the front line. The place would be a shambles when daylight came.

"We must go at once," said the old lady. "Tonight we may get as far as Tamka Street where some friends are expecting us. In the dark we shan't be able to get farther than that. Tomorrow some of us must try to get to Novy Sviat where I'm told it's fairly quiet and outside the fighting zone."

"I have friends in Smolna Street," said Vanda. "Professor Laskovski and his wife. It's not far from Novy Sviat. You must come with us."

"Good! Your father and I will come with you and the others must make their own way. We shall have to get up Tamka Street in daylight. It won't be amusing, I dare say—a little dangerous for all of us, no doubt."

She spoke very calmly and cheerfully and Vanda marvelled at the valour of the old lady, so frail and delicate, but with a dauntless spirit beyond the strength of her body. Would she ever be able to get up the long steep rise of Tamka Street almost certain to be under fire from German guns?

"Don't lose your nerve, my dear," said the old lady. "Don't lose heart now when it's very near the end."

So at last she had admitted to herself that the end was in sight.

"Oh, 'Granny'!" cried Vanda. "The end will be terrible. Give me some of your courage. Give me some of your faith."

The old lady clutched her hand and patted it.

"We must accept this cup of sacrifice," she said. "If we have to die—or if we have to live—we shall share some of our Lord's suffering on the cross and earn our reward of eternal bliss. Don't you believe that, my dear?"

"My faith has gone," said Vanda. "I walk in darkness. All this sacrifice seems to me in vain. The horror of it overwhelms me."

The old lady shook her head and looked at Vanda with pity.

"Poor child!" she said. "Many of the saints went through that valley of darkness—the long dark tunnel of doubt and disbelief—but they came through to the light, the glorious light of the divine vision."

Many of the refugees had already left the basement with the young soldiers who had been ordered to withdraw. They were making for the City Centre. Dr. Mirski was waiting with some of the girls and spoke nervously to Vanda.

"It's time we left. My nerves are on edge at this delay."

"I'm ready, Father," said Vanda.

They left the basement and went into the street. It was 4 a.m. Vanda had packed a few things into a small suitcase and carried it in her left hand while with her other hand she held her father's arm. She told him about Halina staying behind and he was deeply distressed.

"Keep together," cried the old lady. "Don't lose yourselves in the darkness."

She stumbled and fell over a heap of rubble.

Vanda left hold of her father and ran to her and helped her up.

"Thank you, my dear," she said. "Very careless of me!"

It was difficult going. The next house had been blasted into ruin and the whole width of the street was piled up with masonry. —broken glass and twisted iron. It seemed like a mountain barring their way in this semi-darkness. Vanda was hampered by her suitcase and after the exertions of the night, baling out the water, she felt weak and tired as she scrambled up, tripping over wires, stumbling over broken woodwork. It was worse going down because it was difficult to get a foothold. Her father did his best for her, helping her up when she fell, guiding her way to avoid holes and jagged bits of iron. He had recovered his nerve and encouraged her by his agility and helpfulness.

"Step here, my dear. Now look out for that iron spike. Hang on to me."

Two young soldiers had taken hold of the old lady and were almost carrying her.

"Now, Grandma," said one of them. "Keep your spirit up."

"It isn't down," she told them. "It's as high as Heaven!"

"You're as light as a feather," said the other boy. "You must have been starving yourself. My Grandma would make ten of you!"

"It's the mind that matters," said the old lady.

It was a strange snatch of conversation in the midst of ruin and in the close neighbourhood of death. They could hear the noise of gunfire. Searchlights were criss-crossing the night sky. Mortars were flinging explosives on to the outskirts of the City Centre.

Tamka Street was Sinister Street.

They fell behind the other refugees and the young soldiers and Granny knocked at the door of a house still standing undamaged except for broken window-panes and pock-marked walls. The door was opened by an elderly man who greeted the old lady with astonishment.

"My dear Countess," he said in a trembling voice. "For God's sake come in and get down to the cellar. This isn't a safe refuge but it's better than the open street."

"My dear Bogdan," said 'Granny', "it's nice of you to have us."

She spoke as though he had invited her to an evening reception with a party of her friends.

In a way it was an evening reception. The cellars of this old house were already crowded with refugees who had come from houses and flats in the neighbourhood. Many of them lay on the floor and were sleeping heavily. Others were standing for lack of space. An armchair was placed for 'Granny' and presently her head nodded and she dozed off.

The man she had called Bogdan—it was Bogdan Dyboski, the Polish novelist—had been a helper in the canteen which had been on the ground floor of this house in Tamka Street and Vanda had been much in contact with him.

He took her on one side and spoke gravely.

"We must all clear out when dawn comes. This place will be a shambles after that."

"Yes," said Vanda. There was nothing she could say. There was nothing she wanted to say. Her mind was numbed. She was dead tired and beyond emotion and beyond fear.

Beyond emotion? Not quite she found. It was when she went into the canteen on the ground floor. It was now an empty and abandoned room full of broken glass and plaster from the walls and ceilings. Not long ago it had been crowded with young soldiers, talking, laughing, smoking cigarettes, singing. Now it was a ghostly place lit dimly by moonlight. She felt the coldness of it creep into her heart. She moved towards one of the windows without panes. She wanted to get a last glimpse of her own house which faced the back of this one across the allotment. Living for the last few nights in the air-raid shelter in the deep basement she had not realized how ruined it was. It had been gashed by shell-fire and bombs and for the first time since the Rising she saw it from the outside. Some of the walls were still standing and through their black gaps a grey-blue smoke was issuing, and little tongues of flame were licking the charred window frames.

Vanda stood staring at this ruin of her home with all its remembered treasures—the family portraits, the grand piano on which Jozef had played—and she herself, lost often in the mystical realm of music—and the old furniture and the cabinets filled with precious porcelain. She would never see those things again. Everything had gone. Warsaw had gone with its palaces and churches and noble buildings and it was one sacrificial pyre. Had it not been too great, that sacrifice, not only of stone and beauty but of young life and blood? Jozef and thousands of those boys were dead. For what purpose had they died—for what purpose were others being killed?

"Oh, God!" cried Vanda. "Why have you abandoned us?"

She stood there at the glassless window unconscious of time, with the moonlight on her face. Jerzy was in her thoughts. 'If he is dead,' she thought, 'his spirit would surely come to me. Somewhere he must be alive.'

She had heard from one of the Red Cross men that the hospital in Copernicus Street had been evacuated and that some of the stretcher cases had been left in empty buildings because of heavy shelling. She might never see him again, never even hear of him. She tried to send him a message and said over and over again in her heart, 'Dear Jerzy, I love you! Dear Jerzy, my spirit is with you!' No sound passed her lips by these words— this cry of love—sent out in search of him.

Presently she collapsed on the floor and fell asleep, perhaps for a few minutes only. Then she was awakened with a start. A faint light was touching her eyelids. It was the dawn of another day. Cold and cramped she stood up and went to the window again and looked out. She could see into the garden. Something was moving there. Figures were creeping stealthily through the bushes. They were soldiers of the *Wehrmacht*.

The sight of them gave her a shock and she became conscious of time and of terror. She rushed down to the basement. Everyone was awake. Some had already gone.

The old lady was giving orders to her own group. She saw Vanda and turned to her with a mild reproach.

"Where have you been, my dear? We thought you were lost."

"Granny," cried Vanda, in a low urgent voice. "There are German soldiers in the allotment. They're only fifty yards away."

The old lady was startled. But without comment she called out to the little group standing around her.

"Forward, my dears! Keep close and obey orders. Dr. Mirski is in command of all of us now. Do what he tells you."

They went out into Tamka Street. Shelling had already begun—heavy shells from big guns which came rushing overhead like express trains through long tunnels and then burst with violent explosions into streets where some houses still stood intact until now. They too were smashed into ruins with the noise of an avalanche—the hideous noise of some big building collapsing like a house of cards.

Dr. Mirski who had once been a soldier looked at his wrist-watch.

"I know those German gunners," he said, calmly. "There'll be five minutes between each shell burst. That will give us time to go ahead in short rushes. When I raise my hand stop and take what cover you can. Lie down flat behind the piles of rubble."

Vanda stared at her father, this gentle father who hated war and had been against the Rising. Something had changed in him. Many lives were in his charge. Upon his leadership and judgement all their lives depended. He had become a soldier again, alert, commanding, fearless.

So he looked and so it happened along Tamka Street which goes uphill steeply to Okolnik Square. At his signal the old lady and the girls and a few young soldiers halted and rushed into doorways and twice into basement rooms. There was only time to get breath again, and then to hurry out again for a two minutes' walk up the steeply rising street. 'Granny' became breathless and nearly fell.

"I can't go any further," she cried, gasping for breath. "Leave me here, my dears. I order you to go on."

Nobody obeyed that order.

"We must take longer rests," said Dr. Mirski. "Let's get down into this basement. We can stay here for a little while if we're lucky."

Down in the basement he whispered to Vanda

"We shall have to carry the old lady. Those boys are sturdy enough."

She refused to be carried, but allowed herself to be supported.

By some miracle of the spirit she reached the steps which went up to Okolnik Square. That was the greatest danger point. They had to cross the street to reach the bottom of the steps, and that side of the street was being shelled. Dead bodies lay in pools of blood. Vanda turned her face away from them and shuddered, but the old lady looked at them with pity and her thin lips muttered a prayer.

Dr. Mirski's signal halted them before they crossed the street and he waited until the next shell burst.

"We have four minutes," he said. "The young people must run for it. The others will follow as quickly as they can."

Vanda looked at the old lady.

"I'll come with you," she said. "Can you do it, 'Granny'?"

"Of course I can do it," she answered. "Needs must when the devil drives and certainly it's the devil that's driving us now."

She seemed to get some supernatural help. Scorning any aid she crossed the street at a quick pace with Vanda by her side and went up the steps with the lightness of a young girl. Then she fell into Vanda's arms, all strength spent.

But they were safe for a time. Okolnik Square was beyond the firing zone. For some unknown reason no shells came that way. The houses beyond, in Smolna Street, were untouched.

CHAPTER LX

PROFESSOR LASKOVSKI and his wife received their visitors with the warmest kindness. After a hot drink the old lady was put to bed by Vanda, looking very frail and weak after the exhaustion of that terrible walk up Tamka Street.

There were beds in this house! Since the beginning of the Rising Vanda had not slept in a bed. She was given a room daintily furnished with little silver pots on the dressing-table, and chintz-covered chairs. Downstairs she sat in Professor Laskovski's study, a pleasant room with hundreds of well-bound books on the shelves, and deep armchairs and Persian rugs on the polished floor.

A neat little maid came into the room and served some herbal tea—there was no real tea now—on little tables with clean doilies.

Could such things be in Warsaw—this undamaged house, this sanctuary of peace, as it seemed, this charming home in the midst of burning houses, mountains of rubble and those dead bodies in pools of blood? The window-panes were unbroken. In the big courtyard outside children were playing and women sitting in the sun.

"This is like a fairy-tale," she told her friend, that elderly man whom she had known since childhood, with his fine, intellectual face, and kind eyes, and witty speech. "You seem to have escaped the war!"

His lips smiled but his eyes looked anxious.

"Not altogether, We had our hours of terror. The Germans attacked from the Museum and flung flame-throwers into the houses opposite and raised hell generally. After that we have been left alone. That may not last much longer."

Vanda watched Mrs. Laskovska with a kind of fascination, as she sat behind a little table serving the so-called tea. It was like being taken back to the days of peace and happiness in Warsaw. It seemed unbelievable.

It was an illusion, this sense of peace. It was not in the minds of these two people.

"We live on the edge of the volcano," said Mrs. Laskovska. "We may be overwhelmed by its fury at any moment."

Professor Laskovski spoke gravely.

"The end is near. The awful truth can't be disguised. Our resistance is broken. Our losses have been terrible."

"What will happen?" asked Vanda.

Her face had gone white. Her voice trembled as she spoke the words.

"We shall have to surrender," said the professor. "We shall all be prisoners. There's only one consolation. The flow of blood will stop."

Vanda was silent. She felt cold to the very heart. She had lived in hope and now there was no hope.

Mrs. Laskovska began to weep and covered her face with her hands.

There was silence in the room until the professor spoke again.

"Perhaps we shan't be prisoners for very long. We have lost, but Germany can't escape defeat. The Allies are marching from the west, the Russians from the east. For Germany also, the end is in sight and they must know they're doomed."

"By that time we shall all be dead in concentration camps," said Mrs. Laskovska, touching her eyes with a tiny handkerchief. She left the room hurriedly as though to hide her despair.

The professor looked at Vanda and gave a slight groan.

"My poor wife!" he said. "She has been so brave until now."

He sat with his long, thin hands clasped between his knees, and spoke a few more words after a long silence.

"We've lost the battle but not our honour. The Rising may have been mad but it has been a glorious madness—an epic of heroism. Our Polish youth. . . ."

He broke off and looked anxiously again at Vanda.

"My dear child, you must go and rest. You're looking ill."

"I feel rather unwell," admitted Vanda. "If you'll excuse me. . . ."

She went to the dainty bedroom but did not lie down. She flung herself on to her knees and put her arms on the bed and her face down on her arms, and her body was shaken by sobs. It was, perhaps, her worst hour.

On the following day the peace in this small corner of Warsaw ended. There was a roar of gun-fire and the sweep of machine-guns. It was the last battle for the barricade in Jerozolimska Avenue, still holding out.

"We must go down to the cellar," said Professor Laskovski. "Vanda, my dear, look after my wife. I'll take care of the old lady."

Below the big block of flats, built in a quadrangle round the central courtyard, there were no air-raid shelters but only the coal cellars where there was no electricity and only a few candles gave a faint flickering light. The cellars were crowded with refugees among whom were many children, white-faced and frightened. All the inhabitants of the flats, numbering hundreds, had taken shelter down there. The cellars were damp and evil-smelling and all these people, with crying babies and small children, huddled together in the semi-darkness, made a tragic picture of misery and terror. Suddenly an explosion of unusual and vast violence shook the earth and a tremor passed through the walls.

"It's the moo-cow!" said a young man of the Home Army standing next to Vanda who had been trying to comfort a young mother weeping over a sick child.

The 'moo-cow' was the name for a big gun which fired a heavy shell and made a monstrous bellowing noise.

Vanda went up to the professor's flat. The atmosphere in the cellars was intolerable. She stepped on broken glass. Every window in the flat had been shattered and there was no more elegance in those rooms which had seemed to her like a fairy-tale. The furniture was smashed, the books were flung across the floor of the study, the little tables lay upturned.

Professor Laskovski stood next to her, having come up from the cellar.

"It was bound to happen," he said quietly. "We couldn't escape for ever."

Vanda helped him to carry down a few of his most precious books. It was extraordinary that he had not done so before.

"How long have we got?" she asked.

He looked her in the eyes as though to see if she could stand the truth.

"Not more than a few hours. Perhaps not so long as that."

He clasped her hand for a moment.

"We shall have to say good-bye in a little while. The men may be separated from the women. God bless you, my dear. It has been a joy knowing you and your family all these years."

Vanda lifted her face and kissed him on the cheek, this friend who had been so kind to her since childhood.

She went into the little bedroom. Everything had been flung into disorder and she trod on broken glass again. She had come for her suitcase. When they were taken prisoner it would be impossible to carry that. She took out her mother's jewels and the diamonds sparkled in the sunlight which came through the broken windows. With a tiny statue of St. Anthony she put them into a handkerchief and covered them with lumps of sugar in a paper bag which she had brought from the flat. Then she put these things into a small handbag with a woolly jacket and some more handkerchiefs, and a silver spoon. It was curious that she should have brought this little silver spoon. It was a souvenir of her home life. In her suitcase she had brought some precious books and family photographs. She burnt the photographs by the flame of a candle but she could not bear to destroy the books. One of them was Kipling's *Songs from the Books* in English. She had learnt some of them by heart and they had given her comfort. She wrapped them up in a cloth, carried them down to the cellar and hid them under a heap of coal.

When she went into the bedroom again somebody was standing by the window. It was her sister.

"Halina!" she cried. "How did you escape?"

"It was quite easy," said Halina. "Just a little bit exciting."

Not then, but afterwards in a prison camp, she told her sister what had happened during the last hours in the outpost. The young lieutenant and the dozen boys were gathered in the entrance hall awaiting the attack. The hall was now a bunker with the windows walled up.

The lieutenant took Halina aside.

"We only have one chance of escape when the time comes," he said. "We must blow up the lift with *filipinki*. When it crashes down it will block up the staircase. Then we shall have to cut and run. We must go through the gap in the wall into the other cellar and then into the garden and along the barricade. With luck we might get away—lots of luck."

"I'll look after the *filipinki*," said Halina.

She collected some of the home-made explosives from a little cellar going out of the basement. When dawn came she made some *kasha* for the hungry lads.

There was a red-haired, freckled boy among them and shyly he passed up his plate and asked whether he might have a second helping.

"Now I'm fit to fight the whole German Army!" he said, grinning at Halina when he had scraped up the last spoonful.

Standing on a chair Halina looked through a slit in the bunker. The next street called Radna Street—300 yards away—was crowded with German soldiers. They were clearing the houses of their inhabitants, dragging out some who resisted. Some of the women were screaming. Halina called out one word and jumped off the chair and put her hands to her head.

"Goliath!"

All the boys crouched down as the midget tank filled with high explosives crashed into the outer barricade with a terrific explosion. Then guns opened on to the block of flats and there was a tramping of feet in the street outside.

"Now!" shouted the lieutenant.

Halina grabbed up two *filipinki* and hurled them at the lift. They exploded with deafening noise and the lift crashed down, blocking the narrow staircase.

"Run!" shouted the lieutenant. "Run for your lives!"

Halina was first to get through the gap in the wall leading to the other flat. The others followed her. Through the garden they reached the last barricade, crouching low as they ran. Alone now, Halina dashed up Tamka Street, with the heat from burning houses almost scorching her. Now here she was with Vanda, but not happy or triumphant.

"If it weren't for Dick I'd kill myself," she said.

She began to weep with a kind of violence.

Vanda put her arms about her and laid her cheek on Halina's wet face.

"Think of Dick," she said. "Think of Dick as I'm thinking of Jerzy. If we can keep alive for their sake. . . ."

"I would rather be dead than a prisoner," cried Halina.

'Granny' came into the room and looked at the two girls and spoke to them.

"Don't let the Germans see you weeping. Hold your heads high. We're still Polish women."

She stood there, a little old lady, white-haired, white-faced, but with bright, defiant eyes.

Some hours passed before the Germans came. In the open courtyard after leaving the cellars people were sending messages to relatives and friends which one day might reach them from a prison camp. Husbands were whispering to their wives, trying to give them courage, trying to hide their own tears. Some of the young soldiers of the Home Army appeared, looking for mothers and sisters. The last hour of liberty had come.

Then the Germans came.

They marched through the gate into the quadrangle. One of them shouted out a command.

"*Alle raus! . . . Hände hoch!*"

Some people had remained behind in the cellars. They were given ten minutes. Halina refused to put her hands up. The German officer looked at her but said nothing. Perhaps the beauty and proud face of this young, fair-haired girl had startled him.

Then a German officer shouted again.

"*Auf! . . .*"

There were now hundreds of people in the courtyard. They were marched out in fours. Vanda was with Halina, 'Granny' and her father. Professor Laskovski and his wife were in another group. In a long, slow trail they walked for an hour through streets so utterly destroyed that Vanda could not recognize her whereabouts. They arrived at a square or open place in this jungle of ruins.

Here they were searched lest they should be carrying weapons and wrist-watches were taken away from them.

"Robbers!" said Halina, quite audibly.

"Hush, my dear!" said 'Granny', clutching her arm.

There were many hundreds of other people gathered in the square, many sitting on the ground—elderly men and women—already exhausted by the long walk. 'Granny' was one of those who sat there.

"I must remember my old bones," she said.

After the check-up they were formed into columns and marched on again, but this time with no *Hände hoch*—hands up. The long column with German guards went down other streets with burnt-out houses and then through the wreckage of private gardens without walls or fences.

Vanda recognized suddenly in the near distance the big buildings of the National Museum, now used as a prison. The gates opened and they went through.

"Here we die," said Halina.

But it wasn't as bad as that. They were herded into the very large courtyard round which the museum was built. It was overcrowded with prisoners and only the long gravel path up which the newcomers had walked was kept free for others to come. People of all ages sat on the pavements, the grass borders, and the terrace steps.

The newcomers were bewildered and uncertain. There seemed to be no place for them. But the others made room, squeezing together.

"Come and sit here. Find a place for yourselves."

Vanda kept close to Halina, the old lady and her father. Soon several hundreds found places where at first sight there seemed no room at all.

In spite of this big crowd there was a strange silence. People spoke to each other in whispers.

"Where do you come from? Was it bad there? Which was your outpost? Did you know my brother? Didn't my sister go to the University with you?"

The weather was beautiful on this day of September. But the blue sky was smudged by dense clouds of black smoke and the smell of it was strong. Somewhere nearby a big fire was burning, and there were sounds of firing not far away. A group of German soldiers stood at one end of the courtyard, taking no notice of the prisoners. One of them had a queer kind of pistol and every time any aircraft appeared overhead he fired it and a rocket went up as a sign that this place was not to be bombed.

After a long wait some more Germans appeared and pointed at one row of people among whom were Vanda and the other three.

"*Vorwärts. . . . Marsch!*"

Halina spoke to Vanda in a low voice.

"Now we're slaves. We have to obey these horrible men."

Vanda felt the same anguish. Liberty had gone. From now onwards they would be ordered about, pushed about, perhaps knocked about.

Presently they were led out of the prison by the back entrance and across some tangled gardens where they had to avoid the shell craters which had ploughed them up. Then they were taken down a steep railway bank and directed towards a tunnel.

Vanda turned pale.

'This is the end,' she thought, 'We're all going to be shot in that tunnel.'

But a young German soldier now in charge of Vanda's group reassured those who held back.

"It's all right. Soon a train will come and take you to a safe place. Don't be frightened."

He was a good-looking young man of the *Wehrmacht* and wanted to be kind to these people. He seemed to be sorry for them and anxious to be helpful. He tried to get into conversation with them but nobody answered him.

A train arrived at last and they crowded in. But it was no long journey and only went as far as the Central Station ten minutes away.

"It's to avoid our last line of resistance," said Halina. "It shows they're still fighting in Jerozolimska Avenue. I wish I were with them!"

Vanda was stirred with admiration for the old lady. It was miraculous, she thought, that 'Granny' could endure the frightful fatigue of this journey. She seemed to have acquired new strength and walked with her head high as she had told the girls to do. Even one or two of the German soldiers looked at her with admiration for her pride and courage. One of them nudged a comrade and said, "*Sehr nette alte Frau!*"

A nice old dame, he thought.

They went on walking . . . and walking. They walked through a ruined street, deep in the soft dust of powdered bricks and plaster. Many stumbled. Some fell and could not walk any longer. They were left there, lying in the blazing sun, while the others were driven on. There was a belief which ran down the column that those who fell would be shot, and this created a panic among some of the walkers, dragging their feet along in utter weariness.

From some rows ahead a woman's voice rang out in anguish.

"My father cannot go any further. Will someone strong help him, for the love of God?"

Two middle-aged civilians went to the old man, put his arms round their shoulders and helped him along.

Vanda was parched with thirst and sweltering under the hot sun. She was wearing, like many other women, a tailor-made coat and skirt under a long fur coat. It was unbearably warm but she had thought of the winter ahead, possibly in a prison camp. Her mouth was full of dust and sand and her tongue was dry and cracked.

Halina, less warmly clad in her uniform frock, as a liaison girl was suffering in the same way, but trudged on in silence. The old lady was supported by Dr. Mirski and one of the girls.

At a turning in the road they came into a street in which the houses were standing and undamaged. It was one of the German sectors. Vanda recognized it. Koshikova Street, near Independence Avenue.

Out of a side-door came a girl of about twelve years of age. She was carrying a bucket of water, very carefully, lest it should spill, and in the other hand a cup.

To Vanda the sight of this water was like coming to an oasis in the desert, but she hardly dared look at it and turned her head away. It must go to 'Granny' first and then to her father and then to Halina.

Suddenly a gun fired very near and the child dropped the bucket, but by good fortune not much water was spilt and the cup was handed round until it came to Vanda's turn. It was like the *elixir vitae*. That explosion which had startled the child seemed to be a signal for an outburst of gun-fire. The shells screamed over the heads of the civilians and burst in a neighbouring zone.

A German officer had halted them until suddenly the firing ceased. Then that shout of *Marsch!* reached them again.

They came into Narutowicz Place, where a convoy of other prisoners was waiting. It was a very large square which once had been surrounded by pleasant and expensive villas. Now it looked as though it had been swept by a tornado, with bits of curtain hanging on the branches of lopped trees and the refuse of ruin scattered over the ground.

Close to where Vanda and the others halted was a young woman, deadly white, lying on a door which had been taken from its hinges. With her was a new born baby with the tiny face of a wax doll.

A young man with his arm in a sling came up to Halina and spoke to her in a whisper.

"That's Jadviga. Do you remember? A fellow student of ours. Her baby was born this morning. We've carried her a long way on that door—six of us at a time."

"With that broken arm?" asked Halina.

"On my good shoulder."

He did not say any more but disappeared quickly through the crowd of prisoners. It would soon be his turn for a prison camp.

Again they trudged on. They were out of town now, following a main road westwards. It was nine o'clock in the evening. The sun was setting with a red glow. Before dusk fell they arrived at the Warsaw West Station. It was a blessing to all of them that they had to wait a long time for another train. They lay down on the platform with aching limbs. A little food was produced from some of the handbags and shared among small groups.

At last the train came and they crowded in. 'Granny' was given a seat because of her age. Halina and Vanda stood with six others.

The train slowed down. Vanda saw the name of the station. Pruszkov. She knew this name. It was the station of the notorious concentration camp in which many Poles had died.

CHAPTER LXI

EVERY preparation had been made in the City Centre for those who escaped through the sewers from Stare Miasto. They could wash and change clothes, held ready for them, and guides led them in small parties as they emerged to the air-raid shelter under the Café Adria which before the war had been a fashionable night club and now had been turned into a canteen. Here hot coffee, bread and jam, were waiting for them, and after the horror of the sewers it truly seemed like a little heaven on earth.

During the fighting in Stare Miasto life here in the City Centre had gone on with a fantastic similarity to normal times, due partly to the light-heartedness of the Polish character which tends to make the best of things, however grim. There were theatrical 'turns' given by the best actors in the numerous canteens. There were musical matinées, given by a symphonic orchestra. Some of the shops still remained open and food and clothing were distributed. Frequent air-raids kept them down in the shelters but there in the underground they had these amusements, listened to good music, watched films of the fighting, read newspapers distributed by the liaison girls, and for some time kept up their spirits by that fair, false mirage, the food of hope.

It was towards the end of all that—but not quite the end— when the long trail emerged from the sewers. The soldiers were given one day's rest and then were sent to the outposts. The wounded, the lightly wounded, who had made the journey were taken to the hospitals.

Among them was Dick Allgrove, three times wounded and very weak but still able to make a joke or two. He lay in a ward next to another Englishman named John Merryfield who had escaped from the Germans and worked in the Polish underground. On the other side of him was Jerzy Boberski who had been moved from another hospital put out of action by bombing.

The ward was crowded with other wounded, mostly young

soldiers from the outposts and civilians injured in air-raids. Now and then a screen was put round one of the beds and the others knew that this was another comrade who was dying or dead.

It was Jerzy who spoke first to Dick Allgrove in fairly good English.

"Aren't you the English airman who made friends with Halina?"

Allgrove turned his head sideways and stared at this young man lying next to him.

"I married her," he said. "Aren't you the fellow who was in love with Vanda?"

"Is Vanda alive?" asked Jerzy. There was a kind of fear in this question. He was afraid of the answer until it came.

"She hasn't been hurt. I saw her when I married Halina."

"You fill me with joy," said Jerzy. "I thank you."

"Badly wounded?" asked young Allgrove.

"No. I ought not to be here. The doctor says I can rejoin my unit in a few days."

Allgrove gave a faint laugh.

"You Poles are terrible fellows! Haven't you had enough?"

"We must go on," said Jerzy. "Until the last cartridge. Isn't that the English way, too? If England had been invaded. . . ."

"I'm not sure," answered Allgrove. "What do you think, Merryfield? Should we have fought like these Poles?"

John Merryfield was a little fellow who looked extraordinarily boyish in his pyjamas. He had been a rear-gunner in a bombing aeroplane. Before then he had been a jockey and spoke with a slight Cockney accent.

"I expect we should have put up a damned good show," he answered. "We should have fought in the last ditches with broken bottles or spades and shovels. Didn't old Winston say so? Didn't they stick out the blitz—the old women and the young girls? But I will say these Poles take a lot of beating. They scare me sometimes. They have a flame inside them. I sometimes think I was a fool to get into this party. A bit too hot for me!"

"I'd rather be in Wimbledon!" said Allgrove, grinning at him.

John Merryfield answered his grin.

"Wimbledon? Gosh! That makes me homesick. I used to live in Barnes. Byfield Villas. With a mother and sister. I expect they think I'm dead. I ought to be really, according to the law of averages."

"Shut up!" said Allgrove. "If you talk like that I shall burst into tears."

These three young men talked to each other in short snatches of conversation between spells of sleep helped by drugs handed to them by friendly nurses.

Jerzy had been suffering mostly from exhaustion and now was restless and anxious to go. He had questioned Allgrove about Halina and Vanda and reached out an arm to shake hands with him, congratulating him on his marriage.

"It is very good to know," he said in his somewhat inadequate English. "Halina is as brave as she is beautiful."

"You're telling me!" said Allgrove with a laugh.

On the third morning Jerzy stood at Allgrove's bedside, fully dressed, and shook hands again.

"I say good-bye. If you see Vanda please give her my dearest love. And to Halina my warm felicitations on her marriage with an Englishman."

"I call that generous," said Allgrove, in his amusing way. "And good luck to you, my dear fellow. Keep your heart up and your head down as they used to say in the trenches, according to my honoured father who was in the First World War."

He watched Jerzy go out of the ward and turned to John Merryfield.

"A nice fellow, but takes life too seriously."

"He doesn't seem to take death very seriously," answered Merryfield. "Anyhow he's going back to the fighting line. I couldn't stick it any more. It was exciting at first, but now it's too dangerous for little Merryfield of Barnes."

The two beds shook with the suppressed laughter of two young Englishmen who by some freak of fate had found themselves in Warsaw, and had joined the Secret Army in return for hospitality, friendship, and the love of women.

The City Centre had enjoyed a certain immunity from attack. Now after Stare Miasto the enemy concentrated their full weight upon this part of Warsaw. It came under the fire of their heaviest artillery. Their Stukas flew low and bombed it unmercifully, destroying street after street of houses, smashing Polish strongholds, and outposts, piling ruin upon tuin, burning and blasting their way by flame and high explosives. If there is any comparison between one hell and another the City Centre became worse in horror and suffering than what had happened in the Old Town.

One man there saw all this agony and knew the full measure of it and walked among the dead and mutilated, but still refused surrender. He had been sending messages out to the world from a transmitting station under the Adria Café—desperate messages, imploring aid which did not come. He was still trying to establish contact with the Russian Red Army without response. He had his own torture beyond actual fighting and destruction. He had to save Poland as well as Warsaw—its independence and freedom from alien rule. Hadn't they been fighting for that? Was all this sacrifice to be in vain because Soviet Russia was deceiving the Allies, who at Yalta had yielded to a partition of Poland—including the ancient city of Lvov—? They had set up a Communist government in Lublin which they pretended to be the representative government of Poland. Mikolajaczyk, the Prime Minister of the exiled government was in Moscow making concessions, yielding, trying to compromise, failing to get any terms which might be accepted by patriotic Poles.

General 'Bor', racked by these anxieties, stricken by the sufferings of the people, sent out messages to London from a basement in the Adria Café after his escape through the sewers, until it became a burning and flaming ruin under a storm of incendiary bombs. Then he sent out other messages from other studios.

"In this crucial moment for Poland's future. . . ."

Once again he demanded that after the appalling sacrifices of the Polish people a solution with Russia should be based on a promise of independence, full sovereignty and the integrity of the Polish Republic.

The future of Poland. . . . Abandonment and betrayal. . . . The last desperate hope that help might come at last.

All that was in the mind of General 'Bor' and the government delegates in Warsaw, and the little group of statesmen, officers, and friends who stayed with him.

But nothing of that was in the minds of women and children crouching in cellars under terrible air-raids. Nothing of that was in the minds of young soldiers holding on to outposts, under slaughtering fire. Nothing of that was in the minds of mothers and children dying of typhus and dysentery, attacked by vermin in cellars without sanitation which presently were plunged into darkness because the electric power stations were destroyed.

General 'Bor' had established his headquarters in the basement of the massive building of the P.K.O. Bank in Jasna Street. A few hundred yards away was the Council of National Unity with whom he kept in close and constant touch. His faithful typist, Basia, who had come with him through the sewers was still working with him. Something went wrong with the ventilating pipe and the rooms were filled with an acrid smoke which made the staff cough and weep, so that from time to time they had to go up to breathe the air.

On September 4th he left the building to go to the National Council. In one of the rooms as he went a young soldier was playing a mandolin. For some reason he had a sense of apprehension extraordinarily strong. He left the meeting early and came back to his headquarters. But the scene had changed during his absence. Whole streets had been annihilated by violent and incessant air-raids. As he approached headquarters there was the scream of a 600 mm. shell, followed by a terrific explosion and a crash of masonry. The whole area was covered with a pall of yellow dust. 'Bor' groped his way through. His headquarters had gone and where the great building had stood was a mountain of rubble. The dome had crashed down and lay in the street— "like a gigantic woman's hat," as he has described. With incredible difficulty he climbed down into the basement room in which he had kept the wireless set and where messenger girls had waited for orders.

"On the floor," he wrote afterwards, "were bodies, among them the soldier with the mandolin still in his hands, partly buried under the middle of the ceiling which had collapsed. The only living person I met was one of my messenger girls. She was carefully packing papers and what remained of our belongings. I learned from her that about thirty people had been killed."

His typist Basia had been badly wounded.

He hurried to the neighbouring hospital where the wounded had been taken.

There too a bomb had fallen right through the whole building penetrating the big cement ceiling of the basement in which the hospital was located and killing many of the patients. Conditions there were infernal.

"Wounded and dying lay close to each other on the floor, in passages and rooms. From all sides came the moaning and choking of the dying."

General 'Bor' stood in the midst of this terrible scene. Some of his best friends were here, his faithful helpers, his brave Basia, who was dying, his Chief of Staff, who had been his right-hand man from the beginning, always calm and brave and humorous.

Among the living was the young Englishman, Richard Allgrove. He had been flung out of his bed and was stunned by the concussion. Near to him lay his friend John Merryfield, the little rear-gunner who had been a jockey. He was one of the dead. He wouldn't be called upon to 'stick it out' any more.

CHAPTER LXII

T was not until October 1st, after the incredible epic of two months' fighting, by men badly armed against an enemy with very modern weapon of destruction, that General 'Bor' Komorowski, Lieutenant General, Commander-in-Chief of the Home Army, decided to capitulate.

Nothing else was possible. Food had given out and his soldiers were starving, the civilian population could endure no more agony and no more death.

For a time during recent days there had been a flicker of hope. The Russians attacked the suburb of Praga on the other side of the Vistula. They had sent over aeroplanes which cleared the sky of German bombers. They had even dropped supplies of ammunition, but without parachutes so that they were damaged and useless when they reached the ground. At last they were coming to the rescue, it seemed—too late to save thousands of lives, but in time, perhaps, to drive the Germans out of Warsaw. Then silence again. Still no answer to 'Bor's' urgent messages, imploring aid, demanding aid.

The Germans had intensified their attacks on the last Polish strongholds along the Vistula. An heroic garrison held out at Zoliborz, beyond Stare Miasto near the Embankment. The enemy concentrated upon this small sector all their available aircraft, artillery and infantry, with two armoured divisions. In spite of their tremendous superiority they suffered heavy losses in tanks and armoured units—heavy losses from this small body of defenders, weak for lack of food, with dead lying around them, with ammunition nearly spent, but with no surrender in their souls. Such courage goes beyond the valour of brave soldiers. It was supernatural in its defiance of abominable things of which death was not the worst. These Polish soldiers, mostly very young, were human targets for heavy shells, ploughing up the ruins about them, for low-flying bombers blasting their positions with hardly a respite, for Tiger tanks firing at short range, for flame-throwers and incendiary shells which raised roaring fires about them. They stumbled over dead comrades, they breathed the stench of death, they were hunger-stricken and lacked water. They had no chance of sleep. Yet they went on fighting, leapt on to enemy tanks and put them out of action. With bloodshot eyes and swollen tongues they held on to this small area knowing that no help could reach them. It was the last heroic stand of the Home Army.

On the last day of September, having received no answer from the Russian General Rokossovski, to whom he had sent his last appeal, 'Bor' gave up all hope of a Soviet reply. Considering that the position of the defenders of Zoliborz was absolutely hopeless, and unable to send them help of any kind, he gave orders that the fighting there was to cease.

The Germans had made several offers for the evacuation of the civilian population and terms were agreed to by the Polish Red Cross. The people of Warsaw would be allowed to leave the city on the first three days of October and would be sent to the camp at Pruszkov.

At the same time 'Bor' entered into negotiations for a cease-fire with the German General von dem Bach, who showed himself extremely anxious to stop the fighting not for any love or pity for the Polish people, but because his army awaited sooner or later the inevitable advance of the Russians. General 'Bor' held out for honourable and humane terms on behalf of the survivors of the Home Army. They were to be assured combatant rights, and treated as prisoners of war according to the rules of the Geneva Convention. Non-combatants, and especially women accompanying the Home Army should also be entitled to the same rights. Soldiers of the Home Army were to be recognized by a white-and-red armband, or pennons, or a Polish eagle.

The German general agreed to those terms which he signed.

It was the end of the Battle of Warsaw. With a heavy heart General 'Bor' Komorowski sent his last order to his troops.

Soldiers of Fighting Warsaw.

Our two months' struggle in Warsaw which has been a chain of heroic actions on the part of the Polish soldiers, is fraught with dread. Yet it is a solemn proof above all of our mighty striving for liberty. Our struggle in the capital under the blows of death and destruction carried on with such tenacity by us is the admiration of the whole world. . . .

Today the technical superiority of the enemy has succeeded in forcing us into the central part of the city, the only district still in our possession. The ruins and rubble are crowded with civilians, co-operating valiantly with the soldiers, but already exhausted beyond measure by the ghastly conditions of existence on the field of battle. There is not sufficient food, even for bare existence, and there is no prospect of a final conquest of the enemy here in the capital. We are now confronted with the complete destruction of the population of Warsaw and the burial of thousands of fighting soldiers and civilians in its ruins.

I have therefore decided to break off the struggle.

I thank all soldiers for their magnificent bearing, which did not succumb even when conditions were at their worst. I pay due tribute to the fallen for their agony. I express the admiration and gratitude of the fighting ranks of the army to the population and declare the army's attachment to them. . . .

You soldiers, my dearest comrades, in these two months of fighting, one and all have been to the very last moment constant in the will to fight on, I ask now to fulfil obediently such orders as arise from the decision to cease fighting.

With faith in ultimate victory of our just cause, with faith in a beloved, great and happy country, we shall all remain soldiers and citizens of an independent Poland, faithful to the standard of the Polish Republic.

Sad and tragic is this last message to his troops by a man who had trained them in his Secret Army, who had called them to arms for the liberation of Warsaw, who had seen and shared their suffering, who had been proud of their heroism, and now had to acknowledge defeat. Throughout that message, written when he was worn out by nervous exhaustion and lack of food and sleep, one word kept recurring. Faith. . . . Faith. . . .

It was the key to this man's character, to his own loyalty and to his own hope. By faith he still believed in the freedom and happiness of his beloved country. Not yet has that hope and faith been fulfilled. Poland is enslaved. There is no freedom. Its religious leaders are persecuted. The soul of Poland is in hiding. There is still a Secret Army of those who cling to the old traditions, the old culture, the old faith. The world should weep for Poland, but has no tears to spare.

One message came to comfort 'Bor' in the hour of anguish. It was brought to him by the woman 'Anka' who had given him news of his wife once before. 'Renia' the Countess Komorowska —was alive with little Adam and a new-born child. That joyful news helped him when the hour came for him to surrender with his men between lines of German S.S. troops and became their prisoner of war.

General von dem Bach received him with honour and expressed his high admiration for the heroism of the Home Army. This admiration had not made him chivalrous during the battle. They had had no mercy on soldiers or civilians who fell into their hands and were shot after capture.

The Countess Komorowska tells the story of what happened to her in a letter to her husband which he prints in his book *The Secret Army*.

As the end of the Rising approached the bombardment came closer to her and she heard its fury from the shelter where she sat with the little boy. Suddenly at 2 a.m. one night, there was the noise of shots, shouts, and people running.

"I heard someone calling 'Escape! Germans in the shelter.' We jumped up but what was the use? There was nowhere to escape. We settled down again to await what would happen. There was a terrible lot of noise, shooting, German commands, every sound magnified by the acoustics of the shelter. A poor old man hobbled by, said he was feeling faint and would probably die. In a corner I found a man sleeping like a log under an umbrella. Later we found out he was an Englishman. I sometimes wonder what happened to him. And so we waited."

At 6 p.m. there was a banging on the door and a German appeared, revolver in hand. "*Was machen Sie hier?*" he shouted. (What are you doing here?) The house was going to be set on fire within ten minutes.

They were driven out into King Albert Street, where a crowd of several hundreds had gathered from neighbouring houses and shelters.

"The Germans were running wild. We heard curses, heavy blows, and from time to time a shot muffled at the barrel end. Quite close to me a German put his rifle against the breast of a man and pulled the trigger: the man groaned and slumped to the ground. He was shot because he had dallied too long in joining the male group, having stayed behind to say farewell to his wife. I sat down on the ground. Little Adam fell asleep on my knees."

At midnight they were rounded up and driven past the Iron Gate, just captured, and down Chlodna Street, over broken barricades and ruins and dead bodies. At the Church of St. Charles Borromeo some of them were stopped and ordered to go in.

The Countess Komorowska sat down with her little one on a piece of ripped-down tapestry. The church was partly ruined. A dead woman covered by a sheet lay at the foot of the altar. All the people there were suffering from intolerable thirst. Around them and close to them was the ceaseless din of gun-fire and shooting. A young S.S. man addressed them harshly. "You are equally responsible for those bandits who are fighting us. It's all the dirty work of the Jews." He ended with the words: "And the worst criminal of the lot is this one"—pointing to the figure of Christ on the ruined altar.

At dawn they had to march again to the Western Railway Station. 'Bor's' wife managed to get a little coffee for the small boy. After that they were put into a train and taken to Prushkov Camp. Here the Countess was not detained long because of the state of her health and the child with her. She was able to get into a little so-called hospital, so ill-equipped that there was not even a midwife available. Her child was born at midnight, an hour and a half before a doctor came. For nearly two months the new-born baby was very ill, but she saved its life and stayed for a time in a tiny thatched cottage near Cracow. She was in the Russian Zone now and hid under an assumed name. The N.K.V.D. was on her trail. The Communists were arresting Polish refugees. Food was difficult to get.

"I felt the noose tightening round my neck," she wrote. "Escape was essential."

By wonderful good luck and some magic in her own personality, she succeeded in escaping from Poland and finally, after many adventures and desperate moments, came to freedom and exile in England, where now, in one of the London suburbs, she is united with her devoted husband—that astonishing man and hero who commanded the Home Army and the Rising in Warsaw.

She is still a laughing lady, very gay and witty in conversation in spite of all the terrible experiences through which she lived, for Polish women, it seems, are like that.

CHAPTER LXII

IT was at night when Vanda and her family reached the concentration camp at Prushkov—a transit camp where they would be sorted out and sent to other places in Germany or in German-occupied Poland.

A multitude of stars were shining and black against the sky stood the watch-towers of the German guards above rows of factory workshops or sheds. One of these was opened for the long trail of the newly arrived civilians, and they were ordered to go inside. It was in complete darkness and hundreds of people swarmed in like frightened sheep being taken to the slaughter-house. Some of them were lost in this darkness and cried out to their relatives and friends. Then they tried to find places where they could sit down or lie down after the exhaustion of the journey.

Vanda's group had been lucky in keeping together—Dr. Mirski, Halina, 'Granny', Maria the cook. They had had no food for twenty-four hours, but just before they entered the camp some children crept through the bushes on the roadside and thrust bread and tomatoes into their hands. Vanda tried to eat a tomato but it made her feel sick. She took off her fur coat and made a cushion for 'Granny' who lay on the stone floor, tired almost to death but still able to murmur a few words of encouragement.

"We must be thankful for small mercies," she said to Vanda. "Try and get some sleep, my dear."

Dr. Mirski was holding Halina's hand and presently spoke to her in an anxious voice.

"Your hand is very hot, Halina."

"I'm hot all over," said Halina. "I think I'm dying, Father."

Her head fell on to his shoulder and her body went limp.

"Dear God!" exclaimed Dr. Mirski. He felt her forehead. It was burning hot.

He spoke to Vanda.

"She's very feverish. What can we do?"

There was nothing to do that night and next morning in this dreadful place, Halina—who had been so active and so brave—lay in her father's arms shivering one moment and hot the next to the great alarm of them all.

In the pale light of dawn which crept through the barred windows the crowd in the big shed looked in a tragic state, dirty, white-faced and worn out. Only Maria and the young women of her class—strong and sturdy—seemed to have lost none of their vitality.

One of Maria's friends came over to her and then bent over Halina and felt her forehead.

"She has the fever, poor child! I have something that will do her good. I'll go and fetch it."

She made her way to her own place where she had been lying with a bundle for her pillow. Then she came back with a small bottle.

"Good stuff!" she said. "Herbal vodka, you know. My mother was a peasant woman and knew all the old cures."

'Granny' had roused herself and a little colour crept into her face which had been dead white.

"That's quite true," she said. "The old cures are the best."

Halina was given a few sips from the bottle and some hours later the fever left her and she sat up and looked at the scene around her, the huddled figures, the sleepers, the white-faced women. Then she began to weep and Vanda went down on her knees beside her and held her in her arms and laid her cheek against her sister's wet face.

"Halina, darling! You've been so brave! You have been the bravest of us all!"

Halina sobbed.

"It's being a prisoner that's so awful. It's worse than death. I wish I had died."

"Death is easy," said 'Granny'. "It needs more courage to live. Don't let your courage fail you now, my dear. You're one of our little heroines. Don't lower your flag in the face of the enemy. Keep on being brave. I'm an old woman, but I refuse to surrender."

The door unlocked, the word was passed that people were lining up for coffee. Hundreds of them were lining up in a long queue for this precious liquid. Vanda joined them desperate to get some for the others and after that for herself. She felt faint and weak and dirty and hopeless, but she kept standing in the long queue which moved slowly towards the canteen.

She saw to her dismay that everyone had to take a cup or jug or some kind of pot to get the coffee and she had nothing.

Inside herself she gave a cry.

"Oh, God, what shall I do?"

A woman like Maria smiled at her with a shy smile in which there was a wonderful sweetness.

"Don't you remember me, Miss Vanda? I used to come to your house to see Maria."

Vanda remembered her and was touched and grateful when this young woman held out a saucepan.

"Take this," she said. "I have another. Cooks always travel with pots and pans, you know!"

The saucepan was full of coffee and Vanda took it after the girl's urgent entreaty. She could not shake hands with Kasia because she was holding it with both hands but she kissed her warmly and spoke her thanks. All class feeling had gone. It had been replaced by a comradeship between all men and women who had been through the Rising.

She went back to the hut and the hot drink seemed to give new life to her father and the faithful Maria, and it brought a little colour again into Halina's white face. But 'Granny' complained of 'pains' and only drank a sip or two.

The day passed painfully. The crowds had to queue up again for soup at midday. There were now thousands in the camp.

Always there was the wailing of hungry babies, some of whom had been born only a few days before their mothers had been rounded up.

There was only one redeeming thing in all this misery. Maria had been moving about the camp and brought the news that it was possible to get a wash. There was a well in the courtyard and people were crowding round the pump.

Vanda made her way to it with a piece of soap from her hand-bag and waited her turn for a long time. When it came she washed her hands and face and felt refreshed when the ice-cold water slipped through her fingers and over her face and forehead. She cupped her hands and drank some of this well-water, but afterwards it made her feel cold and sick again.

Later they had to queue up again, this time for 'screening'. Hand-bags were examined and people separated into groups, the younger and sturdier ones destined for labour camps in Germany. Vanda prayed that she might not be separated from her father and Halina and she was becoming deeply anxious about 'Granny' who looked ill. All the thousands of silent and frightened people, afraid lest they should be separated from their families, moved towards the check points where German officers were examining them not very strictly and without any obvious plan.

Keeping close to her own little group Vanda was interrogated by a young German officer.

"How old are you?"

Vanda was stricken with terror lest she should be parted from the others.

"I feel a hundred years old," she answered.

The German officer glanced at her and then smiled.

"*Nicht so alt, ich glaube.*" (Not so old, I believe).

He pointed to one of the groups in which stood her father and the others.

"You can go with them," he said carelessly. Perhaps he had seen her anxiety to keep with her father and sister. Perhaps her beauty had attracted him. Perhaps—who could tell?—he wanted to be kind.

They were directed to another part of the camp, just like the other one except that the shed into which they were herded was bigger, but even more overcrowded. There seemed no space in which to settle down. But an elderly woman with a young daughter and her baby spoke to Vanda in a friendly way.

"It's difficult to find a place here, but if you like to join us we can squeeze up and make room for you."

It was a place next to a window and near a wall, and Vanda was grateful for both these advantages. She could stand up and lean against the wall. She could even sit on the window sill and breathe the pure air outside and keep watch over 'Granny' and Halina. Lying on the concrete floor there, they both looked very ill and she was terribly scared about them.

She had been glancing through the iron bars. Outside she could see trees and a long, straight road. The sun was warm and shone down upon the white dusty road. Out there was the Polish countryside, beautiful and peaceful-looking as she had known it in the happy days. Now here she was in a prison camp, never perhaps to know freedom again, never to walk in the loveliness of flower-spangled fields or under the shade of spreading trees.

She turned her eyes again to 'Granny' and Halina and all these hundreds of people squatting on the floor, some talking, some whispering, but mostly silent.

Suddenly she felt something touch her shoulder with a gentle kind of push.

She heard a voice speaking to her in a whisper.

"*Schnell!*" (Quickly.)

A loaf was thrust through the iron bars and she grabbed it and turned to see a young German soldier smiling at her. He whispered again.

"*Morgen komm ich wieder.*" (I'll come again tomorrow.)

Vanda was so taken aback that she did not even say "Thank you." She went down from the window sill and showed the loaf to her father and 'Granny'—Halina was sleeping heavily—and told them what had happened.

In spite of feeling ill 'Granny' had not lost her sense of humour.

"Knowing the Germans," she said, "I could more easily believe it was a messenger from heaven, but on second thoughts I don't think an angel would put on a German uniform!"

In spite of her misery Vanda had to laugh.

Dr. Mirski made another kind of comment on this incident.

"I find it a comfort to think that one of our enemies is kind. I dare say there are others who pity us and hate the cruelties they're ordered to do."

'Granny' looked at him and smiled.

"You think that because of your own goodness and your own chivalry."

It was on the next day that this remarkable old lady confessed to feeling very ill indeed. She whispered to Vanda.

"I'm afraid I have dysentery, my dear. I'm afraid I'm going

335

to be a nuisance to you. But don't worry too much about me. If I die say a little prayer for my wicked old soul."

" 'Granny'!" cried Vanda. "My dear, brave 'Granny'! We can't do without you."

"Oh, yes," said the old lady, "I did what I could in the Rising. Now that's finished and I'm no longer of any use to anybody."

Vanda was deeply shocked and distressed. For a long time now she had worked under the command of this old lady and had come to love and revere her, not only for her courage, which was unconquerable, but for her goodness of heart, her spiritual sweetness. Never once had she said an unkind word, or spoken harshly to any one of the girls under her orders. They had obeyed her because they loved her. Vanda ran out into the camp and asked a young woman with a baby if she knew the whereabouts of the camp hospital.

"Over there!" said the young woman, pointing to a building at the far end of the camp. "But it's terribly overcrowded. My baby is only five days old and I'm feeling terribly weak and ill, but they couldn't take me in."

Vanda threaded her way through the crowds who were sitting on the ground or standing in groups, preferring to be out-of-doors rather than in the cheerless sheds. She made her way to the hospital and spoke to one of the nurses—a Polish young woman—who shook her head and said, "There's no more room in the wards."

"It's for 'Granny'," said Vanda. "She's terribly ill."

The nurse stared at her.

"Granny? Do you mean *the* 'Granny'—that heroic old lady?"

"Yes, of course. We mustn't let her die."

The nurse gave her a tragic look.

"Hundreds are dying. . . . But I'll do my best. I'll speak to the doctor. What's the number of your hut?"

She went away and after a time came back to where Vanda waited anxiously.

The doctor knew all about 'Granny' like many people in Warsaw who knew how much she had done for the young soldiers. He promised to send a stretcher for her.

Vanda went back to the shed. 'Granny' was lying on the concrete floor with her eyes shut, but she opened them and smiled when Vanda knelt down by her side. Her beautiful dark eyes were deeply sunk in their sockets and her face was hotly flushed.

"Don't worry about me," she said feebly. "Get some rest, my dear."

She was silent after that for some time and then spoke again.

"We fought for freedom. One has to fight for the freedom of the soul. But war is terrible."

"Yes," said Vanda.

"After this you must work for Peace. The Peace of God."

"Yes," said Vanda, with tears welling into her eyes.

"We have to fight against Evil," said the old lady. "We can't make peace with the Devil, but we must try to live in the spirit of Christ. We must try to forgive our enemies—even the Germans."

She raised her head slightly and gave a little feeble laugh.

"Even the Germans! . . . How hard that will be!"

"Yes," said Vanda.

"I'm sorry for them," said the old lady. "That's funny, isn't it? I'm sorry for them because their punishment will be terrible and the innocent will have to suffer for the guilty. . . . The innocent!"

She gave a faint laugh and after that became delirious and talked incoherently.

Dr. Mirski bent over her.

"She's very bad," he said. "If they don't come soon. . . ."

A stretcher was brought and they lifted her up gently and put her on it. Halina was awake again after her prolonged sleep. She stood up, looking dazed.

"What's the matter with 'Granny'?" she asked.

Maria was weeping.

"She's a featherweight!" said one of the stretcher-bearers.

The old lady opened her eyes when Vanda stooped down and took off her own cardigan and laid it on her and tucked into it a little picture of our Lady of Ostra Brama and then kissed her.

"Good-bye, 'Granny'!" she cried in a broken voice.

The old lady smiled and tried to raise one hand, one thin little hand. Her lips moved but no sound came from them.

CHAPTER LXIV

It was on the third day in the transit camp that Vanda, her father and Halina had a joyful surprise which did much to comfort them in these miserable conditions. Other people were arriving from Warsaw, increasing the overcrowded state of the camp almost to suffocation in the sheds. Vanda watched a group of them, weary, bewildered, in a bad physical state, unwashed and hungry. Suddenly she gave a cry and rushed towards a woman who was carrying one of the babies in her arms for a young mother who could hardly drag her feet along.

"Aunt Krysta! . . . Dear God! . . . Is it possible? . . ."

She could hardly believe her eyes. It was a different Aunt Krysta until she began to speak. She had become an old woman. Her hair had gone white. Her eyes were sunk in their sockets. She was thin and haggard. But when she began to speak it was the same Aunt Krysta.

"It's certainly your old aunt! A bit battered but not quite broken. What a joy to see you again, my dear, even in this frightful place! How many of you are still alive?"

"Father is here and Halina," said Vanda. "Darling aunt! I can't believe it. Is it really you?"

"I'm convinced it is," said Aunt Krysta with a laugh which sounded like her old laugh. "I may have changed a little—people change in Paviak prison—but inside myself I seem to be Krystina Lopalevska and just as wicked as ever I was!"

She had given back the baby to its mother so that she could embrace Vanda.

Halina came rushing up and Dr. Mirski shuffled along, astounded to see his sister, as much astonished as though she had walked out of the grave.

"It's incredible!" he exclaimed several times. "It's a miracle!"

He too found it difficult to believe his eyes. He believed only when he held his sister in his arms and when she spoke in her old cheerful way though her eyes were wet and shining.

"Of course it was a miracle! And may God pardon me all the lies I had to tell. Thousands of lies, day after day, night after night. I knew nothing of those printing presses below the villa. Jozef had never told me. I was just a housekeeper, an innocent old woman, keeping house for refugees."

Later that night, sitting in one of the sheds with hardly room to move she told them how she had escaped being shot. She had laughed at all their questioning. When they threatened to shoot her she laughed again. Speaking German perfectly she made little jokes, which raised a smile even upon the grim faces of those S.S. officers who were questioning her. She was sent to a concentration camp where she nearly starved to death, and it was there perhaps that the miracle happened.

A German soldier arrived to inspect the camp. He had a general's badges. She recognized him from the distant past. She had known him as a girl in Munich, where he had been an art student. He was Karl von Corbach. Once he had been in love with her, the poor boob!

When he came round the camp she went up to him and said, "Good day, Karl. You used to be a nice young man when I knew you first. Do you remember? You used to hate war, and you were a good Catholic. How do you reconcile that with German atrocities in Poland?"

Vanda and Halina listened to this with wide-open eyes. Aunt Krysta's narrative seemed to take their breath away. Other people near them were listening intently.

"It was brave of you to talk like that," said Dr. Mirski. "It was very rash, Krysta. Did he remember you?"

Karl von Corbach remembered her. It was as though he saw her ghost as a young girl. He turned pale, and then in a low voice he said an astonishing thing.

"I still hate war. I deplore what has happened in Poland."

"Liar!" said Halina, fiercely.

Aunt Krysta looked at her and smiled.

"I have an idea that there are still Germans who are fairly civilized, but this is not the time and place to say so. Anyhow, after Karl's visit I was released. One of the guards came to me one morning and said, 'Du bist frei, alte Frau'. Free? I was stunned, my dears. I had made up my mind that I was going to die. It was quite a shock when I found myself outside the concentration camp still alive, after all my resignation and all my prayers for a brave death."

After that she had lived in peasants' cottages. They looked after her as though she had been their own mother. In peasant carts she had reached Warsaw at last in time for the Rising.

"You were there in Warsaw all the time?" asked Vanda, as though stupefied by this news.

"I couldn't get in touch with you," said Aunt Krysta. "I was very bad with pneumonia. Wouldn't it have been silly if I had died of pneumonia after that miracle of release? But I was well looked after in hospital until they dragged me out of the ruins. So here I am, my dears, your old aunt, not quite so merry and bright as in the old days, but with a bit of spirit still left in her."

"Amazing!" exclaimed Dr. Mirski. "God must have watched over you."

Aunt Krysta raised her hands.

"Why should I have been saved when so many others died— young lives more precious than mine? It's all very mysterious, my dears!"

Presently she said something in a low voice.

"My soldier man has been killed, poor darling."

Dr. Mirski and his daughters were silent for a moment.

"How do you know that, Krysta?" asked Dr. Mirski. "I grieve to hear it."

"Don't grieve," she answered. "It was a soldier's death, as he would have wished. He came to me one night. It was when I was ill with pneumonia. It was his spirit. I saw him very clearly. I said, 'Are you dead, my dear?' and he looked at me and smiled. I told the doctor and he said I was delirious. But I know he came to me at the moment of death. One knows."

"Poor aunt!" cried Vanda, taking her hand and kissing it.

"I'm not broken-hearted," said Aunt Krysta. "He died for Poland after a gallant life. I mourn for the young men and for all the women and children."

Dr. Mirski gave a long audible sigh.

"This must never happen again," he said. "Somehow humanity must find the way to peace."

"Father!" exclaimed Halina. "There's no peace. We must go on fighting. We must never surrender."

Dr. Mirski raised trembling hands and spoke in a tragic voice.

"God must weep when he looks down upon this world of war. Was it for this—all this blood and agony—all these frightful weapons of destruction—all this blasting of life's beauty—that He made us in His own image? Surely not. There must be another way."

"Father," protested Halina. "I wish you wouldn't talk like that. It sounds disloyal. Haven't we been fighting for freedom? Haven't we been fighting on the side of God?"

Her father answered her gently but his voice was faint and his words came with difficulty.

"On the other side of the grave—near to us all, my dear—we may look at things differently—with a spiritual vision, with pity for all the children of life. The children of life—blinded with hatred, shedding each other's blood. No. That mustn't go on. . . . Blood! We have had too much. . . . We must get rid of hatred between nations and peoples. Where love is there is God also. Who said that? . . . I forget. . . . We must find another way than war. . . . Another way. . . ."

His voice trailed off and he sank back as though utterly exhausted.

Vanda looked at her father anxiously. Something in his voice, something in his face alarmed her. She took off her fur coat and covered him with it and he fell asleep. She sat up that night, feeling cold and anxious. Halina and the others were asleep. She listened to her father's breathing. He seemed to be breathing hard and with difficulty, until presently it became more even and fainter.

Presently as the pale light of dawn crept into the shed she heard him whisper to her.

"Vanda!"

She bent over him and said, "Yes, Father?"

She held his hand and it was very cold.

"I don't feel very well," he whispered.

"No, Father. Try to sleep again. That terrible journey was too much for you."

"The war is killing me," he said. "I want. . . ."

"What do you want, Father?"

He raised himself into a sitting position as though he had regained strength.

"Peace! The peace of God. No more blood. What did you say, Vanda?"

"What, Father? What do you want me to say?"

"This place is full of light," he said. "I see nothing but light."

There was no light in the shed but the glimmer of the dawn coming through the barred windows.

He spoke the word "Light!" again in a faint whisper. Then he fell back and lay still.

"Father!" cried Vanda in a voice of anguish. She sprang up and cried out again. "Halina! . . . Aunt Krysta! . . ."

They woke up. Other people were awakened by her cry.

"What has happened?" asked Aunt Krysta.

"Father is dead," said Vanda. She fell down on her knees and kissed her father's dead face and made it wet with her tears.

"He'll go straight to heaven," said Aunt Krysta. "His heart was filled with sweetness and love."

Halina was weeping. Other people made more room for this sorrowing family.

The body of Dr. Mirski was taken away for burial—the body of a man who in life had been gentle to all men, who had hated war but had been a good soldier, who believed in love and the beauty of life but had seen the horror and abomination of Poland's martyrdom.

After this terrible shock and an agony of grief Vanda felt a strange sense of relief and almost a gladness that her father had died. He would be spared any further suffering beyond his strength and she had a curious feeling that his spirit was close to her, that he walked beside her, that his love supported her and spoke to her. She and her father had always been near to each other in sympathy and understanding. He had not gone away from her. She felt his presence very near to her amidst the seething crowd of refugees in Prushkov Camp. Now she had to comfort Halina who was weeping her heart out and looked ill and feverish.

CHAPTER LXV

THE next morning at ten o'clock a German soldier came into the shed and told them to get ready for a transport train. They were ordered to form up in two queues, one at each door which were then locked. During that period of waiting they were all talking in low voices. Some were very frightened, believing that they were being taken somewhere to be shot in batches. Others thought they would be transported to concentration camps in Germany. Many of them were ill with dysentery which had become an epidemic in the camp, and they could hardly stand. Halina, who had been so gay and gallant throughout the Rising, looked very unwell and feverish and sorrowful.

"If they send me to a concentration camp I shall kill myself," she said to Vanda.

"Think of Dick," said Vanda. "Think of your English husband who will be waiting for you."

She answered with a little sob.

"It will be the quickest way to meet him."

That was unlike Halina. Something had broken her spirit, or this second touch of fever following her father's death had plunged her into a dark depression.

The crowd in the shed embraced each other many times before the doors were unlocked and they were ordered to come out at each door, four at a time. By a great misfortune Halina was held back when the guards searched all the hand-bags, directing some of the civilians to stand on one side. Maria was one of them—that sturdy and loyal woman who had been their cook and their friend. Vanda, looking back, saw that her sister had been separated from them, and her heart sank. Perhaps she had been held back because she was young and sturdy looking and would be sent to a labour camp in Germany. For one moment their eyes met and Halina raised her hand and then began to sob.

It was with a sense of anguish that Vanda followed her aunt into a train that stood waiting for them beyond the sheds.

It was a coal train with open trucks and the guards counted sixty people for each truck, pushing them in until they were huddled together unable to move. The floors and sides of the trucks were covered with coal dust and the women's frocks became black and filthy.

"We're like sardines in a tin, but not yet beheaded," said Aunt Krysta, whose sense of humour had not been killed even in the Paviak prison.

Another woman was able to make a joke in spite of this miserable ordeal. It was when the train had moved and by jostling and shifting there seemed to be more space.

"It's like a sack of potatoes. When it's well shaken it seems to be less loaded."

Brave words on a journey to the unknown.

Several times the train was shunted into sidings. At one of these halts another train stood on the next lines.

A man's voice shouted out, "Where do you come from?"

A voice answered him.

"From Prushkov Camp—on our way to Germany for forced labour. That means starvation and death."

A woman's voice rang out.

"Don't you worry! The war will soon be over. Then we can come back to Warsaw and build it up again."

At one wayside station they were able to get hot coffee handed up to them from a Red Cross canteen—the first refreshment they had had for twenty-four hours. At six in the morning the train stopped and the German guard shouted out, "*Alle raus. . . . Alle raus!*"

Hundreds of people descended from the trucks, hardly able to stand. Vanda helped out her aunt who had suffered from cramp and looked very tired.

"What happens now?" she asked, after wiping the coal dust off her face with a grimy handkerchief.

A German officer came up and shouted in a loud voice.

"You are free. You can go where you like. Everybody is free!"

Free? A wonderful word. But they were all dazed and bewildered. Where were they? Where should they go? Were they just free to die in this desolate and unknown place? They were on the outskirts of a small town hardly more than a village with rows of little peasant houses mostly deserted as the people had fled. When Vanda and her aunt and many of their fellow travellers walked into the place there was no sign of life. It was

343

a place of silence at this early hour in the morning and they heard only their own footsteps. Then a few inhabitants appeared and told them that there was a Red Cross canteen in which coffee and food was being distributed. It was in the back yard of a farmhouse with stables and pig sties. Here they waited for their turn to be served by some of the Red Cross helpers who were filled with pity for them, but overwhelmed by the numbers who had arrived.

A priest came up and spoke to them.

"I advise you to rest in one of the empty houses for tonight," he said. "But the good peasants round about have arranged to receive you as their guests. They will come and fetch you in their farm carts. They won't take any money. God will reward them."

Vanda heard that there was a little river at the foot of the hill upon which the village stood with its little church. She and Aunt Krysta went down to it after leaving their hand-bags in one of the small houses, no longer deserted but crowded—eight to a room, according to general arrangement.

Down by the river there was a crowd of women washing themselves and washing their children. Vanda and her aunt joined them and down below the steep river bank they washed away the coal dust and the grime, and felt wonderfully refreshed.

Aunt Krysta looked at Vanda with a smile.

"You haven't lost your beauty, my dear," she said. "Do you remember when I took you to the dance in Poznan?"

"That was in another life," said Vanda. "Since then I've grown old in my heart."

"You have your youth," said Aunt Krysta. "One day joy will come back to you and all this misery will seem like a bad dream. Tell me about that young man who loves you. I remember him coming to the house in St. Theresa Street—a little solemn and a little mysterious, but with charming manners."

"I expect he's dead," said Vanda. "With all the others."

She spoke as calmly as if Jerzy's death must be taken as a matter of course, but in her mind she cried out to him.

They were taken away in a farm cart. It was still mild autumn weather and the sun was shining.

The driver was a middle-aged man, friendly in a shy way.

"We think all the world of people who went through the Warsaw fighting," he said. "We're glad to share all we have with them."

Then he laughed, apologetically.

"We don't have much! Just a farmer's cottage. We're simple folk. My name is Jan Jaruga. My wife Bronka is a homely woman, and we have three children."

"How far is it?" asked Vanda.

"About forty kilometres. We're lost in the woods. It ought to be peaceful enough but there are a lot of Germans round about and our partisans fight with them from time to time. They live in the forests like wild men."

The farm cart went slowly with creaking axles and a plodding horse. They went through a valley with hills and dark forests in the background. At last they came to a village called Poremba which means a clearing and that was a good name for it. A small cluster of cottages stood around a clearing among the dense woods on gently sloping ground going down to a river. There were about twenty small houses along the road, and there were still flowers in their gardens—tall hollyhocks and sunflowers growing against white-washed walls and below the thatched roofs.

At the gate of one of the cottages a woman stood waiting for them with a small child clinging to her skirt and two elder ones shy, half in hiding behind her.

"Here we are," said Jan. "There's my wife Bronka."

He helped his passengers down and presented them to his wife who greeted them with smiles and held Vanda's hand and kissed it.

"We're simple folk," she said, "what is ours is yours, my dears. We're glad to welcome you. Dear God, what horrors you must have come through."

It was a welcome into a family of friendly and warm-hearted folk, always thoughtful for their comfort, always ready to do any small service, always apologetic because their food was frugal—'barshch' and potatoes for the main meal—and because their cottage was, they said, a poor, rough place for gentle folk from Warsaw. Vanda fell in love with the children and they with her.

It became their home in the woods. No more gunfire. No more bombs, no more machine-gunning, no more lurid flames above blazing houses. Here was quietude, intensely quiet, in the dark forests about them. Here was human kindness, and a sense of peace—except for torturing thoughts in Vanda's mind—where was Halina? Where was Jerzy? What was happening in Warsaw?

nor the spirit can stand too long a strain, and you have stretched both to the breaking point. We must get some more colour into those cheeks. We must bring back serenity and happiness to your mind. It's going to be my job and Jadviga's. It won't be too difficult with youth on our side. Youth is the best doctor of all."

But it was difficult until three months later Vanda and Aunt Krysta came to the doctor's flat in Nieviadom and brought joy into the eyes of Halina. They had heard of her whereabouts through a young man who was one of the partisans still hiding in the forests and a friend of the farmer in whose hut Vanda and Aunt Krysta had taken refuge. He had been wounded and Dr. Gornicki had attended to him. Casually he had mentioned the two ladies from Warsaw in his friend's cottage.

CHAPTER LXVII

AFTER a brief rest in the City Centre, which seemed like paradise compared with the conditions in the Old Town and the way through the sewers, Father Paul and his unit were ordered to reinforce the Czerniakov outpost on the Vistula Embankment. It was explained to him that it was most important to hold this outpost to the last, as the Vistula Embankment must be kept in Polish hands while there was any chance—the slightest chance— of the Russians advancing across the river to the relief of Warsaw. Meanwhile the Germans were concentrating their attacks along the whole line of the Embankment and had driven in wedges here and there.

The staff officer who communicated this order from 'Bor's' headquarters, looked Father Paul in the eyes and spoke gravely.

"I do not disguise from you that your unit is being asked to defend a very dangerous position."

"I well understand," said Father Paul.

"What about their morale?" asked the staff officer.

"Very high," said the priest. "Supernatural. The women as well as the men."

The officer nodded.

"I know. Unbelievable! That journey through the sewers was a dreadful ordeal."

There were details to arrange. They were to link up with 300 of the 'Berling' boys—young Poles who had been sent over by

Colonel Berling under orders from the Red Army to which he owed allegiance. They had been deported with their families to Russia and had not been released in time to join the army of General Anders. The Russians had formed them into a 'Polish unit' of that army. They would have to make their way through tunnels and basements under streets of ruined houses.

"Not so bad as the sewers," said the staff officer.

"Nothing could be so bad," said the priest, unable to restrain a shudder.

The officer shook his hand warmly before leaving.

"Good luck! God be with you!"

For a few minutes the young priest stood with his head bowed and his hands clasped at his breast. He was in a corner of the café where they had been able to wash and change, where there were easy chairs and writing tables, and every sign of civilization. A gramophone was playing Schubert's *Unfinished Symphony*. In the great lounge were some of those who had been through the sewers with him, reading papers or chatting with each other. Four young soldiers were playing cards. There was the girl Nunia, very pretty in a clean frock. There was Tereska, the girl who had dragged poor Jozef indoors when he was in danger during a *lapanka*. He would have to call upon them for further heroism, perhaps for the last sacrifice. His heart smote him at the thought. He was filled with compassion for these young people who had been working with him in the Underground before the Rising, and had gone through the horrors of the Old Town in its last agony. Their courage, he thought, was greater than his, more wonderful than anything he could have imagined. He was a priest, a dedicated man. He was set aside for leadership and, if necessary, martyrdom. But these young people had no such call. They were sustained by their patriotism and high spirit.

He had no illusions about what they would be called upon to do. He was to be the leader of a forlorn hope. They might help to hold the outpost for a few days more, a week or two at most. They would be advancing into the zone of fire, furious and destroying.

He was not sure of himself.

'My nerve has gone to pieces,' he thought. 'Can I face the next ordeal—perhaps the last ordeal?'

He knew that he would have to do so. He knew that he would do so. He wiped out this thought of self—a moment's temptation of the devil he thought, and now he had only pity and love for those he was called upon to lead.

He was reassured by their response when he told them of the new order. Not one flinched or held back.

"It's an honour for our unit!" said a young soldier. "They must think a lot of us!"

He laughed as though he had been chosen for a football team. Father Paul spoke to the girls in his unit.

"There's no moral compulsion on you to come," he told them.

"Of course we shall come!" exclaimed one of them. It was the girl Tereska who had been one of those to lie down in the square when they made a lighted cross as a signal to the R.A.F. She was a light and graceful little thing, but she had an unconquerable spirit.

"The boys would starve to death without us!" she protested. "Don't we nurse them when they're wounded? Don't we cook for them? Anyhow, I'm a liason girl and how will 'Bor' know what's happening if I don't take back reports? I'm like one of the underground rats."

Even now it seems incredible and to some of us terrible, that these girls should have served in the front line with the fighting men, but that was what happened throughout the battle of Warsaw, as history tells.

So they went some time before midnight. They went through basements and cellars under the streets. They climbed over the débris of rubble and fallen masonry. They crawled through narrow gaps and into dark holes. Rats scuttled wildly when Father Paul flashed his torch. Not all his unit came through for some were lost in underground passages. They had to keep silence except for a whisper now and then. The enemy might be above them. The darkness seemed to press against their eyes. Not even the gleam of a pocket torch could save them from stumbling and bruising themselves.

Father Paul had a map and peered at it to get his whereabouts. They were passing under Wilanovska Street, the Czerniakov outpost was between two parallel streets southward from Obozna Street. It was in a quadrangle formed into a queer coffin-like shape by Solec, Rozbrat and Wilanovska Streets.

Towards journey's end they had to come out into the open because all the houses were burnt to the ground and there was no way underneath. It was where Książeca Street ran steeply down to the Embankment. Here they crawled along the gutter below the stone kerb.

It had been pitch-black below ground. Now in front of them the big buildings along the Vistula Embankment were lit luridly by raging fires, red tongues of flame licking up into the night sky, stabbing through curtains of black smoke. The great blocks of flats along the Embankment were already destroyed leaving only skeletons of steel and masonry, etched blackly against the red sky. Shells crashed into them. They were under the concentrated fire of heavy guns.

Father Paul and his company of soldiers and women stood aghast at the scene in front of them—this flaming hell along the Vistula.

"Our outpost is lost!" said the priest in an agonized voice, but no one heard him because of the fury of the bombardment.

To himself he said, 'We are all lost! This is the end.'

With him were 300 of the 'Berling' boys, thirty young soldiers of his own unit, and sixty girls. He was leading them into the furnace fires. The Berling contingent had moved forward separately at some distance from where he stood. His own young people were all around him.

There was no way back. The German guns had lengthened their range, and the ground over which they had come was being shelled and it was vomiting up earth.

No one spoke. At least he could hear no voice nor any word from the straggling crowd in his charge. No cry of terror came from the girls. The men made no sound. They stood there as though petrified.

An awful thing happened. As they watched they could see people trying to escape from the basements below the blocks of flats. They seemed to rise from the earth and their figures were revealed by the red glare of the fires. They tried to run across the open ground but did not get far. They were slashed by machine-gun fire. They fell in single figures, and in heaps where they had bunched together. They were all civilians with children among them. For the first time above the roar of gun-fire there was the sound of screaming.

Father Paul's blood seemed to freeze in his veins. He stood there trembling like a man with ague. He stared with horror at this massacre of innocent and helpless people.

He felt a hand on his arm. It was the girl Tereska who clung to him. He looked down and saw her face dimly. She spoke to him but he did not hear.

Shells were bursting close to them now. He led a group of them away, beyond the range of fire, towards the river. The others followed. They were in darkness again and concealed by it until a faint glimmer of dawn came into the sky, revealing the faces and figures about him—tragic faces in which there was no light of hope. They were cut off from their own people. They were an isolated crowd—a lost legion. The 300 Berling soldiers were talking among themselves. One man was gesticulating. They looked sullen and panic stricken.

Without formulating his thoughts into any conscious words Father Paul was praying for them all. How could he save them? How could he prevent another massacre? When the Germans saw them as the sky lightened they might turn machine-guns on to them as they had done to the civilians. They were as defenceless as sheep on this open ground beyond the ruins.

Gradually the sky brightened, making more hideous the spectacle of those ruins, grey and horrible now that the flames had died down and only smoke rose from them. After the fury of the night's bombardment there was a strange quietude like the silence of death.

They were all numb with cold. Some of the girls were shivering, and huddled together, and white-faced. Some of the young soldiers were slapping their chests to get some warmth. Others lay down on the damp ground with their arms over their heads as though sleeping and careless of what might happen.

Presently Father Paul saw some German soldiers moving about the ruins. They were only a few hundred yards away from where he stood. One of them looked like an officer. He stood on a pile of rubble and stared towards this crowd of the Polish Home Army, looking like a lot of refugees who had been out all night. That German officer must have been amazed at the sight of these living men and women, but he was too far away for his expression to be seen.

Father Paul walked towards him, slowly, stumbling once or twice. The officer waited for him. He was a young man in the uniform of the *Wehrmacht*. They were close enough to speak.

"*Gott in Himmel!*" said the officer. "*Wer sind Sie? Wovon kommen Sie?*"

Father Paul answered him in German.

"I am a military chaplain and an officer of the Polish Home Army. I am in charge of this unit. I am compelled to surrender in order to save the lives of my company. I ask for combatant rights for all of them as prisoners of war, including the women."

The young German officer still stared at him. For a few moments he seemed speechless. Then he spoke.

"I accept your surrender."

He looked over at the scattered groups of soldiers and girls and raised his voice.

"You Poles! . . . Good God! . . . You're all damned marvellous. What makes you so heroic? . . . You put us to shame. Your women . . . . your young girls. . . . It's incredible!"

"You grant us the rights of combatants?" asked Father Paul. The young officer nodded.

"I do. Take them down to the river. They are prisoners of war. They will be treated accordingly."

He held out his hand as though to confirm his pledge of honour.

He was an officer of the German *Wehrmacht*. There were others like him who were struck with admiration for the heroism of a people to whom they had been ruthless during this battle for Warsaw which now was ending. They had been merciless, but afterwards paid tribute to the valour of their enemy—too late to bring the dead back to life, too late for chivalry, too late for pity.

Father Paul led his unit down to the river. Some of the girls were weeping. Some of his young soldiers had a look of anguish and broken pride. They were prisoners of war. Some of them would rather have been dead.

There was no mercy, no pity, no chivalry among the fighting nations in the Second World War, as the Germans themselves found later on, when all their cities were destroyed as Warsaw was destroyed. Where was mercy when the British and American Air Forces, at the very end, dropped their loads of bombs on to the city of Dresden, crowded with homeless refugees fleeing from the Russian armies, killed in masses with thousands of women and children among those heaps of dead. Where was mercy, where was pity, when the first atom bomb was dropped on Hiroshima, blotting out all human life except the rags and tatters of survivors who had once been human? For what the Germans did in Poland they paid a hundredfold, and among those who paid were those who hated Hitler and the war—the peasants, the civilized, those too young to have had a hand in it. It was they who paid in agony and despair, as always happens now in 'total war'.

CHAPTER LXVIII

For the two sisters and their aunt life at Nieviadom was grim and cheerless. Owing to the doctor's hurried escape from Warsaw and the conditions in the factory town which was occupied by the Germans with an S.S. garrison, his flat was furnished with odd bits and pieces which he had bought in second-hand shops. Food was scarce and hard to get. There was no fuel so that in this winter which had now arrived it was bitterly cold in his rooms and they sat and froze. There were no books to be had so that Vanda, especially, felt deprived of mental relief and a chance of escape from reality by reading imaginative literature which had once been her passion.

It was strange and even painful to have nothing to do after her tireless work in Warsaw and the intense excitement of the Rising, however terrible. Her nervous energy had been at full stretch. Now it was relaxed and she felt emptied of any driving purpose or urge to service, even by the little drugeries of daily life. It was a time of waiting with dark apprehension of what the future might bring. She was waiting for news of Jerzy. If he were a prisoner of war he would be allowed to write, but he would not know her whereabouts and there was no address to which he could send a message. She was waiting for the arrival of the Russians. What would happen then? What new horror? . . .

At least here in Nieviadom there was no more bombardment, no more flame and fury of war, no more hurling of high explosives on to buildings crowded with civilians. The nights were quiet except a few times when Russian planes dropped some incendiary bombs which did little damage. Surely that might have been a blessed balm and anodyne to Vanda's wounded soul. To some extent it was. It was good to look out of a window and see houses with their roofs on and people walking about the streets without the menace of machine-gun fire. Snow fell on those roofs and lay there pure and white, and it covered the factory buildings with ermine mantles and hushed the footsteps of the passers-by as they trudged through this snow which presently turned to slush. She breathed in the cold pure air by an open window, but neither she nor Halina went much out of doors. There was still danger for young women. Even to the last, with a kind of madness of pride, refusing the thought of inevitable defeat, they were still seizing young people and sending them to Labour Camps in Germany.

But she made one expedition into the town for a special purpose. The kind doctor who had taken them in was hard pressed for money with which to buy food for them. He admitted that one evening when there was hardly anything to eat. He confessed it with a laugh.

"I'm desperately sorry that you have to starve under my roof! The fact is that I'm stoney-broke, and food on our miserable Black Market costs a fortune—or at least a fortune when I count the money in my wallet."

His wife Jadviga looked anxious.

"What are we going to do about it, my dear?"

The doctor shrugged his shoulders and laughed again.

"Starvation rations! We shall have to sleep a lot. *Qui dort dine.*"

"It may be good for our health," said Aunt Krysta, who always looked on the best side of things. "Anyhow I'm in training. There wasn't much food in the Paviak prison."

Halina who had recovered her appetite looked at her empty plate and groaned.

"I dream of food," she confessed. "I think of the wonderful meals we had before the war. They haunt me."

It was during the next morning that Vanda went alone through the streets of Nieviadom. In the pocket of her fur coat was one of her mother's gold bracelets, taken from the little bag in which she had put her trinkets and jewels. By wonderful good fortune she had been able to cling to them all the way from Warsaw, even in Prushkov Camp where they might have been taken from her by the German guards.

She went to a chemist's shop, kept by a lady whom she knew because she made up prescriptions for the doctor. Her only son had been killed in the Rising, but she hid her grief and was friendly and helpful. She had contacts with some of the peasants who were her customers and bought from them—lard, eggs, *kasha*, which she brought in great secrecy to the doctor's flat. Food was still strictly rationed in Nieviadom and these fugitives were without ration books and did not dare apply for them lest they should be arrested and deported.

Vanda went into her shop timidly and waited until a woman customer had been served with some soothing medicine for her baby who was teething. Then the chemist looked at her and smiled.

"Good morning, Miss Vanda! What can I do for you? How is the doctor?"

Vanda fumbled in her pocket and drew out the gold bracelet.

"I want to sell this. Can you help me?"

"My word!" said the chemist, cheerily. "That's worth some money if anyone could afford to buy it in these cruel times."

She took the bracelet in her hands and looked at it with a kind of envy.

"Lovely, isn't it? And I dare say it could tell some fine tales if it could speak. I can imagine it on the arm of a lovely lady in the good old days when there were balls and dances in Warsaw."

"It belonged to my mother," said Vanda.

"A shame to sell it!" said the woman. "It's like parting with a precious thing in one's life—when there were beautiful things in life!"

"How much do you think it's worth?" asked Vanda, anxiously. The lady chemist laughed.

"It's not what it's worth—it's what it will fetch."

She promised to do her best. She did her best, having many friends and customers. The next time Vanda went into her shop she waited until three customers had been served—factory workers with coughs and stomach complaints who joked with her in a rough, good-natured way.

"*Volksdeutsche*," she said, making a grimace, when they had left the shop. "Too friendly with the Germans! Not true Poles."

Then she went to a little drawer behind the counter and pulled out some bits of paper, and whispered after looking over her shoulder at the shop door.

"Half what it's worth," she said, "but all I could get."

She handed over some American dollars and said, "Good money anywhere. I was lucky to get it for you."

Vanda thanked her gratefully, stuffed the notes into her handbag and went back with a glow in her heart. Those bits of paper could be converted into food on the Black Market. They could pay something back to the doctor for all his generosity. They need not starve to death. Halina's appetite could be satisfied—to some extent—even if it were only *kasha*.

The doctor accepted some of the money with embarrassment.

"I didn't invite you here as paying guests!" he said. "But we're all in the same boat now, like shipwrecked mariners. We must pool our resources until better times. I'll pay you back one day, God willing."

"We owe you everything," said Vanda. "It's we who can never pay back for all your wonderful kindness."

It was from the lady chemist that they heard of a way of making a little money during this hard winter. If they could knit pullovers she could find a market for them. They would have to spend a bit of money first of course on buying the wool. So in the long winter evenings Aunt Krysta and Halina and Vanda spent the hours in knitting. Part of Vanda's memory of those months in Nieviadom is knitting—knitting—knitting, and now and then dropping stitches when her thoughts went far astray to Jerzy, or to Warsaw from which now and then news came by civilian fugitives.

After the capitulation the Germans had burned down Warsaw methodically and ruthlessly, churches, palaces and mansions which had survived the Rising and the fighting in the early days of the war. The beauty of Warsaw had been destroyed. One of the loveliest cities in Europe had gone up in flames and only the ruins and the ashes remained as a memorial of its magnificence. Very few buildings escaped by some chance, on the banks of the Vistula or on the outskirts of the city.

In Nieviadom the inhabitants were becoming frightened. There were rumours that it would be in the front line of another battle against the Russians by the retreating Germans. They were using forced labour to dig trenches. Peasants were being dragged out of surrounding villages for this work. Factory workers were taken off their jobs for the same toil. The German troops laid mines along the river bank and in the suburbs, putting up notices of *Achtung! Minen!*

Halina went to the Black Market one day and overheard the people talking there. They were filled with terror of what was going to happen.

"We shall all be cleared out of Nieviadom," said a man at one of the stalls. "The Germans say they'll leave nothing but a desert for the Russians."

"They'll kill us all first," said a woman. "One of the *Volk-deutsche* told me that all the people in prison will be executed."

"If there's a battle we shall all be killed anyhow—if not by the Germans then by the Russians."

A woman flung her apron over her head and wept convulsively.

"This life is nothing but misery," said another woman. "Why do we go on living? Two of my sons have been killed. Now I'd be glad to join them."

Halina went back to the flat and described this scene, and a dozen other rumours she had heard about the impending battle.

"Perhaps it will be like Warsaw on a small scale," she said. "I wish I had a few *filipinki*."

Vanda looked at her with a secret fear. Halina had recovered her health and looked beautiful again—too dangerously beautiful. If the Russians came. . . .

The battle was never fought round Nieviadom. Further away the Russians had made a break-through. The Germans were in retreat along the whole line.

It was Jadviga who called to Vanda one morning to come to the window.

"Look!" she cried. "The Germans are retreating through Nieviadom. They're in a fearful state."

Vanda went to the window and looked out, and Halina joined her with Aunt Krysta.

"They're finished," said Halina. "They're getting what they gave us. Their army is just a rabble. If I had a few *filipinki* I'd throw them out of this window."

"Hush!" said Vanda.

For a little while she too had watched this scene of the retreating Germans with a kind of joy that justice was being fulfilled, that this was a righteous punishment for the cruelties inflicted upon the Polish people. The wrath of God was upon them. She understood Halina's bitterness and hatred. For a little while she shared it. Then suddenly, as she looked down upon this army in retreat, pity took hold of her. She saw them not as Germans but as human beings, not as soldiers but as refugees from terror trying to escape from the slaughter-house of war, fleeing before an avenging army.

The house in which the doctor had his flat looked down upon the market place at a corner of the main street leading to the western highway. Through this came a seemingly endless tide of lorries, cars, farm carts, bicycles, and men on the march—young men and boys, foot-sore, haggard, some of them with blood-stained bandages, and cars tried to pass each other. The men behind them stumbled on, dirty, exhausted and dejected. Was this the great German *Wehrmacht*? Now they were in retreat through country which they had oppressed with an iron hand, where every man and woman hated them for senseless cruelty. These men could not shelter behind the plea that all these things had been done by the Gestapo.

Watching this disorderly and panic-stricken flight—probably they were not the fighting battalions, but those on the lines of communication—Vanda's hatred faded away.

'I'm sorry for them,' she thought. 'The innocent suffer for the guilty. Some of them may be like that boy who pushed a loaf through the bars when I was in that filthy shed. They're the gun-fodder of a war which they were powerless to avoid. Anyhow I don't think I hate them any more. I think I pity them. Perhaps pity is better than hatred. My father thought so. He said so when he was dying.'

Those were strange and almost incredible thoughts for a young Polish woman who had gone through the Rising and all the cruel years before. She was startled at her own pity. She was not quite sure whether it was justified or good. She would have to think that out. She dared not tell Halina.

But she was surprised when Halina turned away from the window and said, "I've had enough. One doesn't like to see animals fleeing from a forest fire even if they're wild beasts."

And Aunt Krysta had a few words to say.

"It's their turn now, but in a way I'm sorry for these poor fellows."

The wild surging traffic through the streets went on for forty-eight hours. Then there was silence, strange and ominous. It was broken by the sound of machine-gunning in the direction of the bridge, where a sharp fight went on. Reports came afterwards that the Russian airmen had bombed and machine-gunned the fugitives. The wheel of Fate had turned. Had not German airmen machine-gunned the roads when they were choked with Polish fugitives? Now it was their turn but with different men from those who had been in Poland at the beginning of the war, very young men, the last reserves of the great German Army now being smashed, encircled and slain by the Russian hordes coming in tides from the east.

It was less than eight hours after the last Germans had left that the first Russians came into Nieviadom.

Jadviga, the doctor's wife, called out to Vanda.

"There are Russians in the market place!"

Vanda felt herself turn white. She was more afraid of the Russians even than of the Germans. They were Orientals. She had heard frightful stories of their abuse of women. It was a new horror which awaited Poland.

Aunt Krysta and Halina came to the window again, staring down the street facing their house. The scene was unreal and fantastic, and it was as though they were watching a stage play, except that they knew this was no wild spectacle, but a scene which would envelop their own lives and their own country.

Down the street at a mad speed came hundreds of horse-drawn sleighs with four Russian soldiers in each and a fur-capped driver who flung his long whip over the shaggy horses. Intermingled with them were Studebaker trucks laden with soldiers fully armed. By immense skill the sleigh-drivers manœuvred their way between the motor-driven vehicles but often there was an entanglement of wheels followed by wild shouts and cursings and the crack of whips like pistol shots, and the pounding of horses' hoofs. It was a wild pursuit of the retreating Germans. It was the fury of a conquering and avenging army, savage and barbaric like that of Ghengis Khan or Atilla and his Huns.

Halina gave a cry and went away from the window.

"Oh God! . . . It makes my blood run cold. It fills me with terror."

She had had no terror when crawling through ruined houses

to carry messages in Warsaw, or when she flung her *filipinki* at a Tiger tank.

Aunt Krysta spoke in an awed voice.

"It's as if the waters of a flood were closing over us!"

Jadviga clasped her hands and her head drooped over them, as she spoke in a faint voice.

"They're not civilized—these men. What will they do to us?"

That night came the crashes of heavy explosions. The Germans had placed time-bombs in some of the factories and the food stores—destroying food which was desperately needed by the workers, but denying it to the Russians.

Next day it was quiet with the hush that comes after a heavy fall of snow. Halina had gone out into the garden to make a snowman with a small boy belonging to a family in the ground-floor flat.

Vanda spoke to Aunt Krysta.

"What are we to do? I'm desperately anxious about Halina."

"We can do nothing," said Aunt Krysta, "except stay here and see how these Russians behave—our noble liberators! I know the Russians. When they're drunk they go mad. But when they're sober they can be kind and good-natured. They're like untrained children and they're fond of a joke. If one can make them laugh there's no need to be afraid of them."

Vanda felt slightly reassured. This wonderful aunt of hers was always reassuring, even at the worst moments.

In the afternoon Jadviga came into the room to make a hot 'infusion' which took the place of tea. Suddenly they heard footsteps and men's voices in the yard below. Then heavy footsteps clumped upstairs and there was a bang at the door as though by the butt-end of a rifle.

"I'll go," said Aunt Krysta. "Don't look so frightened, my dear."

She opened the door and two Russian soldiers entered the room, thrusting past Aunt Krysta, without removing their fur caps. One was a typical Slav, a peasant type, square-faced, blue-eyed, broad-chested. The other was of the Mongol race, dark, with high cheek bones and narrow eyes. He was wearing a khaki-quilted jacket.

"*Zdrastwuyties*," said the blue-eyed man.

It was the popular Russian greeting instead of 'good day' or 'good evening'. It means 'Be greeted'.

"*Zdrastwuyties*," answered Aunt Krysta, who spoke Russian.

"We're searching for Germans," said the spokesman. "Maybe some are hiding here."

"There are no Germans here, thank goodness!" said Aunt Krysta. "Would you like to see our identity cards?"

The big fair man shook his head.

"No, no! We're just hunting for Germans."

He spoke in a loud voice as though they were all deaf and when he walked across the room he staggered slightly and there was a whiff of vodka in his breath. He was certainly drunk. It was the first time Vanda had been in a room with a drunken man and it made her frightened. Her aunt had just told her that Russians were beast-like when they were drunk.

He leaned against the door and looked round the room with a kind of amused arrogance. He was not impressed by what he saw. The doctor's furniture, picked up in junk shops, was certainly not impressive. In the centre of the room was a kitchen table, with a sofa pushed alongside because there were no chairs—a rickety sofa with two bricks for its fourth leg which was missing. Along one wall were iron bedsteads, covered by old and discoloured blankets. Near the stove was a cupboard made out of packing cases for the plates, cups and saucers. There was an old-fashioned chest of drawers in one corner, and in another an iron washstand with towels hanging on pegs along the wall. This was not a scene of Western elegance or luxury which afterwards astonished the eyes of Russian soldiers in undamaged cities and country mansions.

"Search the room," commanded the big blonde man to his Mongolian comrade who seemed to obey his orders and made a thorough search of this poorly furnished room. He looked under each bed, felt under the blankets, fumbled under the pillows, where peasant women sometimes hid their money.

Then he went over to the chest of drawers, suspiciously.

"There's nothing inside," said Aunt Krysta. "Certainly no German!"

The big man roared with laughter.

"One never knows with a German!"

The Mongolian pulled out one drawer after another, finding some cakes of soap and a few handkerchiefs and towels which he tossed to one side. The bottom drawer stuck and would not open. The Mongolian pulled at it violently but it would not budge. He grabbed at the handle and wrenched it until it came off in his hand—so that he nearly fell backwards. This seemed to both of them very funny indeed. They shouted with laughter, but the Mongolian meant to have that drawer open, as though it contained rich treasure. He took out a clasp-knife and slashed off a strip of wood, and then tugged the drawer open. There was nothing inside. This seemed another great joke, and the two men laughed heartily in gusts of mirth.

Suddenly the Mongolian asked what time it was. It is likely that this innocent question was to find out if there were any watches to be had—the passion of every Russian soldier.

Guessing it, Aunt Krysta answered him.

"We only have that cheap clock on the wall. We have to take what time it says as we have no other clock or watch."

The man looked disappointed and glared at her. Then the blonde man made an inquiry.

"Which is the housewife?"

For a moment there was silence. Then Jadviga, who had turned very white, answered bravely.

"I am."

The big, blue-eyed Slav lurched towards her and put his arm round her waist and leered at her.

"Now, dearie, we'll behave like lambs if you give us a swig of vodka."

Aunt Krysta, who had pretended to be knitting very calmly, dropped her work and spoke angrily.

"Let that lady alone! We have no vodka. Get out of here."

The good humour of the man left him and he flushed with rage.

"Shut up, old woman!"

Jadviga released herself from the man's grasp and spoke to him in the Ukranian dialect which she knew. She spoke in a friendly way, hiding her fear.

"Tovarish, I am a doctor's wife. We have no vodka, but I can give you a drop of pure alcohol. It's more powerful than vodka. The bottle stands on that shelf in the corner."

Her words worked like magic. The blonde fellow lurched across the room and grabbed the bottle with an expression of anticipated joy, but the Mongolian shouted at him.

"What about me, comrade?"

"You must share it," said Jadviga firmly, "and you must get out of this house like good boys."

"Like pretty little lambs," said the blue-eyed man, whose rage had left him. "We'll get drunk outside, lady. Pure alcohol, did you say? Stronger than vodka, eh?"

He was in a good humour again and clutching his comrade's arm with one hand and waving the bottle of alcohol in the other, left the room. Together they clumped downstairs, laughing and quarrelling.

As soon as they had gone Jadviga's calm deserted her and she broke down in Aunt Krysta's arms sobbing and trembling. Vanda felt as cold as ice. She had been very frightened.

"They were like wild beasts," she said, "and we had no defence against them. It was you who saved us, Jadviga. You were marvellous."

A hard winter had set in with a temperature twenty below zero, and Vanda, less hardy than Halina, suffered intensely from the cold. She had been brought up in comfort before the war, living always in well-warmed rooms, with servants doing the rough work of the house. Now, like most people in Poland she had to wait on herself and others. There was no more class. They were all reduced to the same level—a low level—of social life, in which the daily struggle for a mere existence was the main purpose, the fight against hunger, the way to get a little warmth, the drawing of water from a well in the yard, the washing of clothes with or without soap.

Vanda took turns with Halina in drawing buckets of water from the well. Sometimes she could have cried with pain, and did cry secretly, from sheer physical agony with frozen hands, without gloves, carrying an iron-handled bucket, pumping up the icy water several times a day, quickly exhausted because she was always hungry.

Always hungry. They thought of food, dreamed of food, talked of food, as though they were Arctic explorers or ship-wrecked people. But strangely enough this cold suffering, this hard toil in a frozen world, had a kind of spiritual value for her. When her frozen hands were shooting with pain she thought, 'Peasant women have had to do this for centuries. Now I share their suffering. I am one of them.' When she felt hungry after a scanty meal of cabbage soup she thought, 'Jerzy may be starving in a prisoner-of-war camp. He may be suffering more than this. I'm glad that I have no comfort.'

Such thoughts came to her when her hands were almost frozen to the iron handle of the bucket.

'One ought to be purified by suffering,' she thought. 'One ought to be closer in touch with all fellow-sufferers in this tragic world. It would be unfair to have more than others, to live in comfort when others live in misery. Now we all share alike. It's a new kind of comradeship.'

In the doctor's cheerless and unheated room the women talked over their knitting and the doctor himself joined in their conversation.

"We shall have to adapt ourselves to life under Communism," he said, one evening.

"Never!" exclaimed Halina. "How can we reconcile Communism with Christianity?"

"We must keep our faith," said the doctor, "but adjust ourselves to a Communist way of life. That's really forced on us. We're all reduced to the same level of existence, without property, without belongings, without distinction of class. There is no gulf between rich and poor in Poland now, only an equality of misery. Isn't that a form of Communism?"

Aunt Krysta answered him cheerfully.

"I'm quite ready to share all things in common—if there's anything to share—provided we don't have to share the torture in Russian prisons and the horrors of their concentration camps."

The doctor smiled at her.

"I agree! But we shall have to give these fellows a chance. We shall have to see how they behave in Poland. We must make the best of it and hope for liberation when Germany has surrendered. Then perhaps the Russians will withdraw and Poland will regain its independence. England and America will see to that. Churchill and Roosevelt will know how to talk to Stalin."

He glanced over at Vanda with his friendly smile.

"Don't you agree, Vanda?"

Vanda remembered some of her father's words. Her father had been convinced that Russia would never withdraw to its own frontier after advancing into the heart of Europe.

"It's what we all hope," she answered, "but hasn't hope betrayed us? Haven't we lived too much on hope?"

"Without that we can't live at all," said Halina. "Without that I should kill myself."

Vanda glanced at her. She spoke with a tragic intensity and Vanda's heart bled for her. She was a young wife who had never known the joy of married life. Hardly ever did she speak of Dick Allgrove, but often there was a sad look in her eyes. She too was suffering. She too had a wounded soul. Wasn't Poland crowded with wounded souls? Weren't they all in mourning for the dead and missing?

Thousands of them were going in search of their dead. Through the streets of Nieviadom there was a long trek of people making their way back to Warsaw. They were going to find the graves of their sons or husbands or fathers, buried below little wooden crosses amidst the ruins.

Through Nieviadom also passed an interminable tide of Russians. They stayed only for a night or two, and then went on, followed by thousands more surging westward. There was a battle going on in the district of Poznan. The Germans were still fighting rearguard actions before retreating further.

One day in this January, a young man came to the doctor's flat. Halina had been drawing water at the well again. Vanda was knitting another pullover with Aunt Krysta winding some wool. Jadviga was cooking something at the stove. There was a tap at the door and for a moment there passed through these women a tremor of fear. A knock at the door was still alarming.

It was Aunt Krysta who opened the door.

Outside stood a young man in peasant clothes with a dirty scarf round his neck. He was unshaven and his left arm was in a sling.

"Yes?" asked Aunt Krysta. "What do you want, young man?"

He gave a queer laugh and answered in English.

"I want Halina. Where is she?"

It was Vanda who recognized him. She sprang up with a cry of wonderment and joy.

It was Richard Allgrove. It was Halina's husband.

"Where is she?" he asked. "Is she alive? For God's sake tell me."

"She's here," said Vanda.

Halina came in with the bucket of ice-cold water. She walked towards the stove and put down the bucket.

"What's the matter?" she asked. "Why are you all so silent?"

Then she turned and saw her husband, close to her, moving towards her.

He spoke to her in English. His eyes were shining.

"I've come back. Thank God I've found you. Halina!"

She stared at him with a kind of incredulity. Her face had gone white. Then she rushed at him and put her face down on his breast.

The others were weeping, with an emotion too deep for words or cries of joy.

It was as though he had come back from the dead.

CHAPTER LXIX

DICK ALLGROVE had found out the address of Halina from the chemist's wife, that great-hearted woman who had gone to Warsaw in search of her son's grave. After the capitulation he had not surrendered as a prisoner of war but had put on civilian clothes and gone into hiding in one of the tunnels under the ruins with another English airman named Shuttleworth who had thrown in his lot with the Poles and had fought in the Rising.

They lived like sewer rats for three days and nights until they were forced out of their hiding place for lack of food. The Germans were searching the ruins and the cellars for Polish soldiers who might be in hiding and these two were almost certain to be caught if they stayed in the tunnel. Starvation made them desperate and they decided to go above ground under cover of night and try to establish contact with Polish friends who at least might give them something to eat.

It was Allgrove's idea to find Dr. Joravski whom he had met quite often at Dr. Mirski's house, and he knew that some of his wounded comrades had been taken to a temporary hospital in Milanovek, a small town quite near to Warsaw to which some of the hospitals were evacuated. All the patients knew that this would be their destination.

With Shuttleworth he left the tunnel and emerged into a wilderness of rubble and broken masonry touched by moonlight.

"Curse the moon!" said Shuttleworth. "We're almost certain to be seen by those swine."

But they seemed to be in a dead world. No human being moved amidst these ruins until they left Warsaw and walked a long way and came into the neighbourhood of Milanovek. There, as they crouched behind a broken wall, they heard the heavy footsteps of a police patrol. They remained very still, hardly breathing, until the men had passed speaking to one another in German.

"It's all right, said Allgrove in a whisper. "We must make a dash for it. I know the place, I used to take tea there with a nice family."

"And now we shall be copped there by some nice German policeman," said Shuttleworth. "We haven't the chance of a snowflake in hell."

Allgrove had an uncanny sense of direction and presently they saw lighted windows beyond the darkness in which they stood where the moon cast black shadows from skeleton houses.

"Here we are," said Allgrove. "That doctor is one of the best. He won't give us away."

They went through the doorway, open because the door hung loose on its hinges, after the blast of a land mine which had wrecked the houses around. There was no one in the hall and they went upstairs. In the corridor was a Polish nurse, hurrying along with a bottle of disinfectant. At the sight of these two men, filthy and desperate looking she started back in alarm.

"Who are you?" she asked sharply. "What do you want?"

Shuttleworth spoke Polish fairly well.

"We're English. We've escaped from one of the outposts."

The girl stared at him and then spoke in a whisper.

"You mustn't come here. This place is full of German wounded. Why do you come here of all places?"

"My friend knows Dr. Joravski," said Shuttleworth. "We want to see him. We want food. We're starving. This is our only chance."

"No, no!" exclaimed the nurse. "You must go away. You'll get us all into trouble."

But at that moment Dr. Joravski came out of a door and spoke to the nurse.

"I must have some more dressings."

Allgrove moved a pace forward.

"Doctor," he said, "do you remember me? We used to meet at Dr. Mirski's house. The English airman, you know. I'm Halina's husband."

The doctor looked at him with astonishment, and came nearer and peered into his face by the dim light in the corridor.

"Yes!" he said. "Allgrove, the English airman. I remember. What are you doing here?"

"We're starving," said Allgrove. "We want something to eat."

"Something to eat? This isn't a canteen. This place is choked with German wounded—and our own."

"We're desperate for food," said Allgrove again.

The doctor hesitated. A look of compassion came into his eyes.

"My poor fellow, you look pretty bad," he said.

He turned to the nurse and spoke to her.

"Can you get hold of any food?"

"Only German bread," said the nurse.

"Bread!" exclaimed Allgrove. "That sounds wonderful."

"Look here," said the doctor, "you two fellows had better go down into the cellar. Tomorrow morning we shall be visited by German officers. If you're caught I shall be in grave trouble—and so will you be!"

"Did you say bread?" asked Allgrove, putting a dirty hand across his mouth.

The doctor looked at him curiously.

"Did you say you were Halina's husband? That's news to me."

"We were married," said Allgrove. "My only purpose in life is to find her again."

"I brought that young lady into the world," said the doctor. "For her sake I shall have to take a risk. Nurse, show these young men down to the cellar. Give them some bread. And don't forget the dressings."

He put a hand on Allgrove's shoulder.

"I hope you'll find your wife again," he said. "Our beautiful Halina."

Then he turned and strode a few paces down the corridor and went through one of the doors. As he opened it there came out a waft of disinfectant, chloroform and the stench of gangrene.

Allgrove and Shuttleworth stayed in the cellar for three days, hidden behind piles of packing cases. Bread was brought to them by the young nurse. On the third day the doctor came down.

"You must get away from here," he said. "I've arranged with some friends of mine—brave people—to give you shelter. They're in a neighbouring village. If you have the luck to get there—"

They walked by night and luck was with them. They were hidden in the barn of a small farmhouse by a young farmer and his wife until one morning after Christmas a letter was brought from Dr. Joravski.

"I've found the whereabouts of Halina," he wrote. "She's in a little town called Nieviadom. A woman has just come to see me with a letter from Vanda. She runs the chemist's shop in Nieviadom. She was one of my students in the old days."

"I must go!" said Allgrove, rising as though he were already on his way.

He arrived in Nieviadom in a peasant's cart. Shuttleworth had parted from him on the way, finding refuge in a farmhouse belonging to a brother of the man who drove them. Richard Allgrove was born under a lucky star.

After he had washed himself in ice-cold water at the pump and changed into an old suit belonging to the doctor he looked more like himself when he had first met Halina in the garden of the old house in St. Theresa Street.

At their frugal supper of cheese and boiled potatoes, bought of course on the Black Market, he sat opposite Halina and could hardly take his eyes off her. They exchanged smiles while others did the talking—the doctor, Jadviga and Aunt Krysta. They asked about Warsaw, and in English which they all spoke, or with a bit of broken Polish—he had learnt a lot of soldiers' slang—he gave them a terrible picture of the city after the methodical

368

way in which the Germans had burnt it down, with its churches, palaces, banks and ancient shrines.

They listened sadly and with rage on the part of Halina.

"They must be punished!" she cried. "God must see that they're punished."

"God will," said the doctor. "The end of Germany will be utter destruction."

"I don't crave for another hell on earth," said Aunt Krysta. "I don't lust for vengeance, however justified."

"Aunt!" cried Halina, "you're as bad as the *Volksdeutsche*!"

"I try to be good," answered Aunt Krysta. "It's because I say my prayers and try to be like one of the early Christians— I know I don't look like one!—that I'm on the side of the angels, who can't possibly want more blood and more massacre."

This idea of Aunt Krysta being like one of the early Christians was highly amusing to them and they echoed her laugh.

Vanda sat rather silent. Now and again her lips smiled when she saw the exchange of loving glances between Halina and Dick. It was beautiful to see their joy. Her heart was touched by the sight of Dick's look of adoration across the supper table. Halina was trying to hide the ecstasy which shone in her eyes, but failed to hide it. She looked more beautiful, thought Vanda. She looked as though all care had flown from her and all remembrance of the horrors through which she had passed.

But there was something strange about this young Englishman, thought Vanda, strange with regard to herself. He avoided her glance when she looked over at him. His eyes shifted from hers. He did not speak to her directly. Once when their eyes met for a second or so the smile left his lips and he looked grave, and something more than grave—pitiful.

'I wonder why he shuns me,' thought Vanda. 'I wonder why he doesn't speak to me? Why did he look at me like that?'

It was after supper when the plates and dishes were removed to the cupboard made out of packing cases, that Vanda took advantage of a moment's silence to ask him a question—a question which had been in her heart since he had arrived, back from the dead, as it seemed.

"Do you know anything about my Jerzy?"

Dick Allgrove's face flushed. For a few moments he did not answer. He shifted in his chair uneasily and stared down at the carpetless boards.

Then he looked at Vanda.

"Would you prefer me to tell you when we're alone?" he asked.

Vanda's face had gone white, but she answered quietly.

"No. Tell me now. Is he dead?"

Dick Allgrove nodded.

"Yes. I hate to tell you."

The others were looking at Vanda with immense compassion, with pity beyond words. After a long silence Halina gave a cry.

"Oh, Vanda! Oh, my dear!"

"Do you know how he died?" asked Vanda, in that quiet, calm tone which frightened them.

Dick nodded again and said, "Yes, I was with him."

"Tell me," said Vanda. "Tell the others."

Dick stood up from his chair and moved towards the stove and fingered the handle of a saucepan. His back was to the others. Vanda was watching him intently. When he turned round he spoke to her, as though she were the only person in the room.

"It was two days before the capitulation. I was with a different unit, mine being wiped out. I had joined one of the last outposts near the Vistula Embankment. We were being heavily shelled by every old thing, and bombed from the air. We knew we should be wiped out too. We were on the ground floor of No. 5 Wilanovska—I believe. Yes, that was it. We had very little cover. The sky was open above our heads. While it was still daylight we were astonished to see three young soldiers come into our man trap. They must have got through under heavy fire."

Dick Allgrove stopped and his gaze never left Vanda's face. "Do you want me to go on?" he asked.

"Yes," said Vanda. "Please, Dick."

"I recognized one of the men, which was a bit queer because they were unshaven and looked like scarecrows. Well, not like scarecrows when I'm speaking of Jerzy. He was in the rags of a uniform of course with a blood-stained bandage round his head and blood on his shirt, but there was something in the way he held himself, in his poise—if you know what I mean—rather noble and distinguished-looking—if you know what I mean."

"I know what you mean," said Vanda.

"He didn't seem to care a damn, although the other men were trembling with a kind of shell-shock. I spoke to him. I said, 'Aren't you Jerzy?'"

"He answered, 'Hullo, Dick!'"

"I said, 'What the hell are you here for?'

"'I thought I'd lend a hand,' he told me. 'Do you object?'

"I gave a queer kind of laugh. Of course my nerves were a bit rattled. For the last four hours I had kept saying to myself—'This is death, old boy. You'll never see Halina again. You'll never get back to dear old Wimbledon.' One thinks all kinds of damn silly things when one is in a situation like that, and not one of the heroes—if you know what I mean."

His gaze strayed for the first time to Halina, who was listening intently.

"Go on," she said.

Not one of them moved. Aunt Krysta had clasped her hands and her head drooped above them. The doctor was sitting forward with his hands between his knees and a deep furrow on his forehead. Jadviga was sitting on the floor beside her husband's side and tears filled her eyes and dropped slowly down her face.

Dick Allgrove went on speaking like a man remembering a dream.

"My English friend, Shuttleworth, was with me and he seemed to know Jerzy and said, 'Nice of you to come, but bloody useless. This outpost is lost. Look at those lads. We shall soon be like them.'

"There were about a dozen dead, some of them lying on their backs with their eyes open as though staring at the stars. Jerzy looked down on them and said, 'Now they'll have peace.'

"Our officer was killed. I was in command—in command of the dead and those about to die. I said to Jerzy, 'We shall have to get out of this. It's a death trap.'

"'It's no better outside,' he said.

"Several of our men were struck by falling masonry and killed while we stood there. There was a girl with us—one of those liaison girls—like Halina—apparently quite fearless. She was bandaging one of the wounded who was making a horrible noise. His face was smashed but she went down on her knees and kissed him on the mouth which was dripping with blood. That seemed to quieten him."

He paused and wiped his forehead with the back of his hand.

"I didn't know what to do, being in command. The shelling was very hot all round us. Very difficult to get through it alive.

"Jerzy came up to me and said, 'You know I love Vanda?'

"I nodded and said, 'Yes.'

371

" 'If you get away alive,' he said, 'if you see her again will you give her a message from me?'

" 'Of course,' I told him. 'But you have as much chance as I have, which is not very bright.'

" 'If you see her again,' he said, 'I want you to tell her that I shall be waiting for her on the other side of the bridge.'

" 'What bridge?' I asked stupidly. 'All bridges are in German hands.'

" 'She'll understand,' he answered. 'Don't forget.'

"Presently he looked at me and said, 'You'd better get these lads away. They'll have to take the risk.'

"I suppose I was rattled.

" 'I'm in command here,' I rapped out.

"He gave a faint smile and saluted and said, 'Yes, sir!'

"That knocked me edgewise.

" 'Don't be a damn fool!' I said. 'We're all equal here. High explosives don't acknowledge rank.'

"He gripped my hand and said, 'I don't suppose there's any rank on the other side.'

"Those were the last words I heard him say. I ordered the men to quit the outpost and take what cover they could in the ruins. It was every man for himself now—and every girl—six of them."

Again he stopped and wiped his forehead with the back of his hand.

"How was he killed?" asked Vanda, in her quiet voice.

"I was the last to leave. Jerzy and the girl who had kissed the wounded man on the mouth were just in front of me, running towards a pile of rubble. Suddenly a machine-gun began to chatter. A German must have been behind one of the heaps of ruin. Bullets spattered round Jerzy and the girl. The girl fell and Jerzy flung himself down on her as a shield. Covering her body with his arms outstretched—like a man crucified. His body and arms made a cross. He was killed then."

"Did the girl live?" asked Vanda.

"Yes, she got away as soon as he fell. She wasn't even wounded. Of course Jerzy saved the kid at the price of his own life."

Dick Allgrove moistened his lips with his tongue as though he were parched.

"Thank you," said Vanda. "Thank you for telling me."

She stood up from her chair and walked to the door, and went into the bedroom which she shared with Halina and Aunt Krysta.

Halina was sobbing. Aunt Krysta and Jadviga went down on their knees as though in the presence of death. The doctor gave a deep sigh.

In the bedroom Vanda was alone with her own thoughts and her own grief. When several hours later Halina tiptoed into the room Vanda was asleep.

When Halina stooped and kissed her she stirred and spoke three words as though dreaming or half-awake.

"Across the bridge."

CHAPTER LXX

DICK ALLGROVE and Halina moved into two rooms which they were lucky to find in the house of a factory manager in Nieviadom, previously occupied by S.S. men. Nearly every day they came over to the doctor's house for some kind of meal and brought with them a spirit of happiness and a gift of laughter— they were always laughing these two—which was the best spice for frugal fare.

Dick obtained work in a sugar-beet factory where he learnt to speak Polish with considerable fluency and a working-class accent which was a constant source of amusement to Halina who tried, in vain, to give him a more cultured way of speech and to suppress certain words not used in polite society.

They were happy, that young husband and wife, but all around them was much unhappiness, disillusionment, fear, and the terror of women under this Russian occupation. In their best moods the Russians were good-natured, kindly, jovial men, anxious to make friends with the Polish people. In their worst moods, when they were mad drunk on vodka they were like wild beasts, outraging women, even little girls of thirteen or fourteen, even elderly women with white hair. To the doctor's rooms came weeping mothers and young women with these terrible stories, and Vanda who was helping the doctor, saw the agony in their eyes and their inconsolable despair. Those faces haunt her still and come to her in dreadful dreams.

There was a two-way traffic through Nieviadom—Russians going westwards to a defeated Germany, Russians returning eastwards to their own country, with machinery, cattle, and material of every kind for use in Russia. Herds of cattle were driven through the town in miserable state, just bags of bones—walking skeletons of cows—the Poles called them the 'ghost cows'—mooing lugubriously in a pitiful way. Often the Polish farmers were compelled to give up their own fine beasts in return for those dying creatures.

Lorries drove past with Russians lolling in armchairs, often period pieces from German houses. They were passionate collectors of watches and alarm clocks and any bit of glittering jewellery. So they went roaring through the town, singing and shouting.

On the walls of Nieviadom appeared enormous cardboard effigies of Stalin before which parades were held on Russian days of celebration, with long processions of the Polish townsfolk, ordered under strict penalty to leave their offices, homes, and factories, to join in this march past in honour of the great and glorious Generalissimo Stalin, who had won the war of 'liberation'.

On Victory Day in 1945 there was no rejoicing in the doctor's rooms.

The doctor himself who had been in favour of 'giving these fellows a chance' was now dejected.

He spoke to Dick Allgrove who had come round with Halina.

"I cannot understand your English Prime Minister allowing the Russians to get as far as Berlin. It seems to me a terrible mistake."

Dick laughed and answered carelessly.

"I expect old Roosevelt had something to do with it."

"The conference at Yalta was a calamity for Poland," said the doctor. "We, who fought first—and alone—against Germany, were utterly betrayed. It was another partition of Poland. Surely your great Prime Minister should have set his face against that?"

Dick Allgrove looked slightly embarrassed until Halina came to his rescue.

"Dick had nothing to do with the Yalta conference! He was serving very nobly with our Underground Army."

The doctor smiled at her.

"I apologize! I'm not attacking your husband, my dear."

Dick Allgrove laughed again.

"Good old Winston! I expect he did his best in difficult times. When we were alone too—after the fall of France—he was lion-hearted and called up the old spirit of England, as no other man could have done. Thumbs up! But of course, I don't know a darn thing about the higher strategy. Politics are outside my line. I'm a humble toiler in a beetroot factory somewhere in Poland."

"You're a darling!" said Halina. "For your sake I shall go on loving England—right or wrong."

"England will love you, when I get you there," said Dick.

He did not remain a humble toiler in a beetroot factory. One day a horde of Russian workmen advanced upon the factory, dismantled all the machinery with great good humour, packed it up in lorries, and drove it off to Russia, throwing hundreds of men out of employment.

Perhaps this event led young Allgrove to make a decision which no doubt had long been working in his mind. He announced it one night at the doctor's table, after many talks about it with his wife.

"I'm taking Halina to England. You others must join us when you can. The little house in Wimbledon will be your home."

"No!" cried Halina. "We must all go together. Vanda, darling, and Aunt Krysta you must come with us."

Dick looked doubtful.

"That would make it more difficult. It would be better if you come separately. We shall be waiting for you."

"I agree," said Vanda. "We can't go in a crowd."

After pleading with her for some time Halina looked at Vanda with tears in her eyes.

"Vanda, darling, I hate to leave you!"

Vanda put her ams around her and kissed her.

"You're the wife of an English husband. Of course you must go if Dick thinks he can get you to England. Won't it be very difficult—and very dangerous?"

"How do you propose to get to England, young man?" asked Aunt Krysta, "with all the frontiers closed?"

Dick had worked out a plan. There were Russian lorries going westwards. A little vodka, a wrist-watch or two, a jollying up of a Russian driver, would get places for Halina and himself. They would make for Berlin. Once there they would get into the English sector. The rest would be easy.

"It's taking a big risk," said the doctor. "Halina may be stopped and arrested and sent to a concentration camp in Russia."

"Halina is willing to take the risk," said Dick. "I think we shall get through. I have a hunch that it will be all right. Things are a bit fluid now. People are on the move everywhere. The Russians are like children if one knows how to get on the right side of them. And, after all, I'm an Englishman. That gives me a certain pull, don't you know!"

He was supremely confident and one night came to the doctor's rooms and told them that he and Halina would be off next day. He had fixed it up with a Russian lorry driver and his pals. They were going as far as Poznan. There they would get across the frontier into Germany. Somehow they would get to Berlin.

The next morning very early—at five o'clock—the farewells had to be said. It was painful for Halina and Vanda, and both wept when they embraced. Dick Allgrove wore the clothes of a Polish workman and looked like one. Halina had put on a peasant dress with a scarf round her head. Aunt Krysta had prepared a hamper of food, at least enough to keep them alive for a week or more.

Halina flung her arms round the doctor and his wife, thanking them for their love and kindness. Then she embraced Aunt Krysta who had been a second mother to her.

"We must go!" said Dick. "Those fellows won't wait for us."

So they went on this hazardous adventure, leaving Vanda desolate without them.

That evening Aunt Krysta spoke to her when they were alone together.

"We must think of going too, my dear—perhaps by another route. I should be happy to breathe the air of England where there is still liberty and no cause for fear."

"Stanislav is there," said Vanda wistfully. "Perhaps. . . ."

For some reasons she hated the idea of leaving Poland and going into exile. How could she leave her own people in this time of suffering and misery? Would it not be like desertion? Wouldn't it be braver and more loyal to stay with them and share whatever came?

It was Aunt Krysta who broke down her resistance, by describing the beauty and peace and freedom of England which she had visited as a girl, and by talking of the joy they would have in joining Stanislav and Halina and so many friends.

"England is a Polish sanctuary," she said. "Many of our friends are there already. All those boys who fought under General Anders—thousands of Free Poles. In England we will go on working for Poland. We will join the English people in the spiritual battle against the powers of Darkness."

It was six months later when they travelled to Budapest and by judicious bribery—from the sale of Vanda's jewels, and a few lies—Aunt Krysta asked God to forgive her for those—found seats on a train to Italy.

In Italy Vanda met her former lover Ferrari, now a married man with three children. It was a joy to her when Francesco told her that Beatrice was in England with her husband, a Polish lieutenant. After Poland, after the Germans and the Russians, after all the horrors of Warsaw, Florence seemed like paradise.

In Florence they exchanged telegrams and letters with Halina and her husband who were safe in Wimbledon, after astonishing adventures with many anxious moments, and with Stanislav, who had left the army and was going to be married to a Scottish girl named Janet. He was a portrait painter again and getting some commissions.

Florence. . . . Paris. . . . Calais. . . .

On the boat coming over, Vanda and Aunt Krysta stood on deck amidst a crowd of passengers. It was a fine spring day with a stiff breeze blowing, and white clouds scudding across the sky.

Suddenly Aunt Krysta clutched Vanda's arm and gave a cry.

"Look! The white cliffs of Dover! O, blessed isle! O, land of liberty! England!"

On the quayside of Dover Halina and Dick and Stanislav were waiting to greet them. There were ardent embraces, and Dick kissed Vanda and Aunt Krysta. Stanislav was excited and in a joyous laughing mood. Halina was radiant, though her eyes were wet with tears.

Vanda looked at her and smiled.

"You look very English, Halina!"

"I *am* very English," said Halina. "Dick says I look the wickedest woman in Wimbledon."

"Alliteration's artful aid," said Dick, putting his arm round her.

They were talking nonsense to hide their emotion.

After tragic experience, agonizing memories, this Polish family were together again in the peace of England.

"No Gestapo here!" said Dick, "and no S.S.—not yet!"

"And never will be!" cried Halina, smacking his hand which held one of hers.

Vanda had been rather silent, though she was smiling.

"I wish Jerzy were here," she said presently, and then she added a few words with a mystical look in her eyes.

"Perhaps he is."

She had not forgotten her Polish lover and his spirit seemed very close to her. He was waiting for her, she believed with perfect faith, across the bridge. Neither the Germans nor the Russians had ever captured that one.

THE END